THE LONGINGS OF WOMEN

ALSO BY MARGE PIERCY

Poetry

MARS AND HER CHILDREN

AVAILABLE LIGHT

MY MOTHER'S BODY

STONE, PAPER, KNIFE

CIRCLES ON THE WATER

THE MOON IS ALWAYS FEMALE

THE TWELVE-SPOKED WHEEL FLASHING

LIVING IN THE OPEN

TO BE OF USE

4-TELLING
(with Robert Hershon, Emmett Jarrett, Dick Lourie)

HARD LOVING

BREAKING CAMP

Novels

HE, SHE AND IT

SUMMER PEOPLE

GONE TO SOLDIERS

FLY AWAY HOME

BRAIDED LIVES

VIDA

THE HIGH COST OF LIVING

WOMAN ON THE EDGE OF TIME

SMALL CHANGES

DANCE THE EAGLE TO SLEEP

GOING DOWN FAST

Other

THE LAST WHITE CLASS: A PLAY
(with Ira Wood)

PARTI-COLORED BLOCKS FOR A QUILT: ESSAYS

EARLY RIPENING: AMERICAN WOMEN'S POETRY NOW;
AN ANTHOLOGY

THE EARTH SHINES SECRETLY: A BOOK OF DAYS
(with paintings by Nell Blaine)

THE LONGINGS

OF WOMEN

A NOVEL BY

MARGE PIERCY

FAWCETT COLUMBINE ∽ NEW YORK

A Fawcett Columbine Book

Published by Ballantine Books

 Published in the United States by Ballantine Books, a division of Random House, Inc., New York, and simultaneously in Canada by Random House of Canada Limited, Toronto.

An excerpt, "Becoming a Mouse," was published by *The New England Review*, Fall 1993.

Library of Congress Cataloging-in-Publication Data

Piercy, Marge.
The longings of women : a novel / by Marge Piercy. — 1st ed.
p. cm.
ISBN: 0-449-90907-7
1. Women—Fiction. I. Title.
PS3566.I4L66 1994
813'.54—dc20 93-34125
CIP

TEXT DESIGN BY DEBBY JAY

Manufactured in the United States of America

First Edition: March 1994

10 9 8 7 6 5 4 3 2 1

"The longings of women:
butterflies beating against
ceilings painted blue like sky . . ."

"The Longings of Women," *My Mother's Body*,
MARGE PIERCY

THE LONGINGS OF WOMEN

CHAPTER 1

LEILA

Sitting on a bench outside the courtroom, Leila began looking at her watch at three. She had expected to be called right after lunch as an expert witness on battered women. Now it was almost five and the cross-examination of the doctor who had treated Linda Sue in the emergency room was still continuing. Leila had been scheduled to testify today for the defendant Linda Sue because she had no classes Friday, but she was also supposed to relieve Melanie's mother, Mrs. Peretz, at the hospital. Why did she so often feel as if she should be in three places at the same time, guilty wherever she was because she was not tending to some other problem?

Leila realized with a little surprise that she was bitterly unhappy. She did not want to be sitting in court, where Linda Sue's trial was not going well. Leila hated testifying, hated the rigid protocol of the courts, although she was supposed to be a good witness, the same reason she was in demand as a speaker. She was cool/warm in her public persona, maternal and efficient at once. She thought quickly on her feet. Years of teaching, sounding as if she knew what she was talking about even if she had only read the material for the first time the night before, paid off in voice control, the ability to improvise and to field hostile questions with grace. She would be useful on the stand, if she ever got there, but she was in a bind. She sat by herself on the wooden bench, the victim's sister glaring sideways at her.

Leila's best friend Melanie was dying of breast cancer, after a remission of five years. Leila's son David was off on the West Coast at Cal Tech. Her husband Nick had broken his vow of years and taken a successful local production of *Oedipus Rex* to off-Broadway, recasting in New York. Nick had not returned her last three calls to his answering machine. Her message of last night had been brief but pointed. "Nick, I miss you to distraction. I'm coming to New York this Saturday. I've fixed things so I can stay until Monday morning. I love you. See you Saturday around noon."

Finally she was called, was sworn in and had begun testimony when the judge recessed for the weekend. Great. She had to be here at nine on Monday. She would take a very early shuttle out of LaGuardia. After leaving the courthouse in downtown Boston, she promptly got stuck in rush-hour traffic. It took her twenty minutes just to exit the parking garage and another twenty to reach the end of the block. Leila was listed officially at the hospital as Melanie's sister. When she finally reached the room and Mrs. Peretz could leave for supper, Melanie's mother went out shaking her head and muttering.

This was a bad night. Melanie was conscious but in constant pain. "You still call Mama Mrs. Peretz," she mouthed with a gaunt grin. "You've known her since we were freshmen at Penn. More than half our lives."

"Your mother seemed so old to me then. The age I am now. That must be how I look to my students."

"We were . . . so full of energy. Hope." Melanie tried to squeeze Leila's hand but couldn't. Her hand fell open.

"I haven't given up hope. Don't you."

But Melanie lapsed into unconsciousness. She groaned, tossed, mumbled but did not reopen her eyes. Her glossy black hair had long ago fallen out. Her face was skeletal.

Leila left the hospital feeling despondent. As she drove home to Cambridge, she noticed indifferently that it was finally clearing into the sort of crisp late October night she usually loved. The clouds were ripping visibly as the steely moon shot through. Melanie had her first episode of breast cancer seven years before, and yet her doctor had not caught this in time. Then in March, Melanie's birth month, the tumor had metastasized.

Willowy
Melanie
with the black hair
Leila
is paler
they make quite a pair.

Nonsense rhymes they had made up years before, nonsense rhymes they still wrote for each other every birthday.

Leila is round
and far from the ground
and bites her professors for lunch
Melanie's narrow
eats like a sparrow
and orders up boys by the bunch.

Odd that rhymes they had giggled at twenty-five years ago should ring in her ears tonight: simple exhaustion. She was swamped with her classes, her students, the research project on incest survivors' relationships with their children that was in press now. She was so distant from her own work that it did not even feel interesting. She had to provide support and help not only for Melanie but for Melanie's daughter Shana, who was still in high school, and often for Mrs. Peretz, who had relocated to Boston two months ago.

She did not think, as she pulled into the drive, that she had left so many lights on; on the other hand, a burglar would not turn on every light in the downstairs, and she had been distracted and in a mad rush when she left. She had returned from campus to change for court. She had found an enigmatic call from her son David on the answering machine that suggested problems at Cal Tech; a plaint from a student she had promised to help with research. In her heart Leila knew she loved David more than anyone living, but she was not really sure which one she loved more, Melanie or Nick. Nick was her husband, her mate; but Melanie was her heart's sister, her other self. She was unraveling as Melanie disintegrated. It was just as well that Nick had taken an out-of-town gig this fall, as he often did. She would not be able to be there for him as much as he needed.

The front walk rustled with maple leaves she kicked. The house crowded its lot. It was two-story and wooden with a corner tower that, with lights on in the living room and in the master bedroom above it, looked festive, two wreaths of light through the red and the gold draperies. As soon as she opened the door, she heard Nicolas, and her heart leaped with a sharp pang of startlement and joy. It was all right, it was all right, he had come home to her. He had been too busy to return her calls. Perhaps rehearsals were going poorly. It meant nothing that he had not called her back. He was here to see her, and they were still whole, a family. She flung her coat in the direction of the couch, stopped at the hall mirror and daubed her mouth with lipstick, gave her short thick brown hair a quick punishing brush. She was grinning at herself, her cheeks rosy with the blush of expectation. She ran toward his voice.

He was talking on the phone too loud, as he always did. When they spoke on the phone, she was always turning the volume dial down and then down again, and they were always talking on the phone when he was gone, as he so often was. He projected his voice to the back of the hall, to the balcony. He was a big man with a big presence and a big voice. He got off at once when he heard her—a woman? Don't be silly. He had promised he was done with all that, said he was getting too old for complications with actresses. He merely terminated the call because he wanted to see her. For a year they had had a new marriage, no more out-of-town romances, the two of them working at the relationship wholeheartedly together.

"I didn't know you were coming!" she said, then realized she sounded shrill as an overexcited child. "Why didn't you call the hospital? I had no idea! Oh, I'm so glad to see you. I was worried."

He came striding toward her, gave her a quick kiss and a bear hug. "I tried to call from Penn Station, but you weren't here. I took the train." When he embraced her, he always made her feel petite, anything but the overgrown adolescent who still cowered inside.

She was checking him for signs of trouble. Yet he seemed exuberant, larger than life. He was an imposing man, tall and big-boned and, at forty-eight, not exactly heavyset but solid, almost monumental. "You'll never guess who I ran into yesterday in the lobby of the Brill Building—Al! He was very friendly, remembered me right away. . . ."

Al? Al? She tried to remember somebody they had gone to school with, or someone who had acted in his company at B.U. She ought to know, obviously.

"I told him I'd brought *Oedipus* to New York, and he wished me luck. He looked great. Everyone was scoping me, who he was greeting."

"Nick . . . Al who?"

"Al Pacino. Remember, I met him when I was at the Mark Taper?"

She was still checking him over, like someone who looks over her dog for ticks after he has been in the woods. New York was his bête noir. He was going bald so that his curly grey hair circled the bare spot like a monk's tonsure. His full kinky beard was ash blond, just streaked with grey. His large eyes under jutting brows were as crystalline blue as ever but bloodshot from lack of sleep. She could tell he had been eating and drinking too much. His skin looked ruddy and splotched. His lips were cracked from not drinking enough water. No one else would notice anything wrong, but it was her job to keep him in shape. He was describing the train trip, the man he had sat next to, what had been said, a raconteur's crafting of the ordinary into the memorable, but she had to know his situation. "Is something wrong?"

"They were producing that dry frenzy you sometimes have when you're trying to get an ensemble together. So I gave them the day off. I have to go back in the morning, but I thought I'd just hop a train and check in with you." He put his arm around her and guided her toward the leather couch. "I keep getting your messages too late to call you—after all, you work too, and you're not the most coherent person wakened in the middle of the night."

"I'm a grump, I come apart at both ends," she said apologetically, feeling only a sharp spritzy happiness like the best fruit soda in the world. What fine clear piercing beautiful eyes he had, how strong and yet shapely his hands were, good tools for expression. His nose and chin were finely modeled, his brows thick, his forehead high and broad. He was her love, her treasure. She always forgot how his strong thumbs sprang out toward the end in an arch. She forgot how his eyelids had a natural lavender tint, invisible unless she sat very close, pressed against him as now.

They sat on the couch with a bottle of cabernet sauvignon he selected from the cellar—the area under the stairs she called the wine basement. He put his head in her lap and she rubbed him behind the ears like a great hunting cat who had lain down for a moment and allowed himself to be pleased. "Are you sorry you let them talk you into New York?" He had resisted with every other play that had been a local success. He hated the hold New York had, felt it had almost destroyed theater. Occasionally he lectured on that topic for a fat fee at universities.

"I suppose not to have done it would be dying a virgin. You have to let yourself get really fucked once, right? I didn't want anybody saying that I'm afraid of the challenge. But everything is four times harder and five times more expensive. New York theater is a sewer, a sink of energy."

Her fingers kneaded the tight places in his thick neck. "You're worried."

"I'd be a happy idiot not to worry." He sat bolt upright. "This time it's got to work. I'll show the bastards. I'll ram it down their throat."

"Beloved, I've wanted to get down, but Melanie's very, very bad." They had agreed that, unlike their usual arrangement, this time she would visit occasionally. She had made it to New York exactly once.

"Frankly, I haven't had the time to miss you. It's been fierce. I don't have enough left when I crawl into bed at night to meet the emotional needs of a goldfish." He flopped back down. "It is a stunning piece, I know it."

"But I'm going to come down. Next weekend. How about that?"

"If I could just get the last act sizzling. Faster, hotter."

"Are you satisfied you're ready to open in three weeks?"

"Three and a half. I need every day, every hour." He groaned with vexation. He was too long for the couch. His ankles stuck out into space, rigid, quivering. "Sometimes I want to wring Sheryl's neck. She won't take direction. She nods, she agrees, she wags her tail, and then she does it her way. Yet she has an animal presence that causes audiences to stare at her as if they can't get enough."

Leila had a sixth sense by now. If he wasn't yet involved with Sheryl, he was considering it. She had a moment of total despair. She judged her willing belief that indeed he was finished with affairs as naive, as a weak-kneed desire that it be so. Perhaps she could silently convince him this weekend to hold off. Sheryl: twenty-four and whippet-lean, with a voice like butterscotch. Leila said nothing. What was to say? They had their arrangement, one she had gratefully believed they had outgrown. Only away from home. He wouldn't lie to her. If she asked him about Sheryl, he would tell her, far more than she wanted to know. She didn't ask. She felt a great weariness. After all, she was a forty-five-year-old woman of no great beauty, a hard-working semi-academic who fought a constant daily battle to maintain weight just ten pounds over what she ought to be. In the theater, he dealt with ambitious beauties, willing, young, sometimes very young. Never make him choose. From the beginning he had made clear, only a part of him would be hers—a large part, but only a part. The rest belonged to his work and to his freedom. She would be in the way when he was directing out of town. But there had to be a woman. He was a huge hunger in the shape of a man, not so much for sex but attention, feedback, reassurance. She could not do her work and follow him around; and their household secret was that she was the main breadwinner. Nobody except Melanie knew that. His part-time appointment at B.U. paid less than half what she made as an associate professor at Lesley College not counting her books.

Melanie had always understood her situation with forgiving clarity, understood how lucky Leila felt to have won Nicolas, who had named himself that, born William, Bill Landsman, to a dentist and housewife in Houston, barely Jewish—the handsome one, the genius, the iconoclast. By the time he was Sheryl's age, he had achieved a reasonable success as an actor. At thirty, he had turned to directing. For fifteen years he had been a power in regional theater. When anyone discussed theater in Boston, his name was one of the first that would be mentioned. He taught part of the year at B.U., but mostly he put on plays in a converted movie house near campus, or around the country by invitation at the Guthrie in Minneapolis, at the Actors Theater in Louisville, at the Alley Theater in Houston. He was considered equally adept at staging difficult new plays and at finding startling meanings and unexpected subtexts in classics. He had done a *Changeling* in twenties costumes that shocked and sizzled. Sheryl had been his student and he cast her in the lead. Leila was sure nothing had happened then, but obviously he had remembered Sheryl after she went off to New York to try for a career.

She put on the red silk Victoria's Secret nightgown he had given her for her birthday two years before, rather than the flannel Eileen West she usually wore. But when she climbed into bed he was already asleep. She lay beside him, depressed by Melanie, by having allowed herself to think about the affair that might be going on or about to develop. To any relationship there were costs, there were imposed overt and hidden taxes. She had long ago accepted her role in his life: central but partial. It gave her benefits too. She lay on her side unable for a long time to sleep beside the great mound of his body that put out warmth like a wood stove. He smoldered in his sleep while she pondered that freedom.

Countless women who had married when she did had given up their friends. She could remember when she had felt almost as close to Lisa as to Melanie, Lisa who vanished into her marriage as into a closet. Leila and Melanie had stayed close over the decades, in part because

Nick did not possess her as so many husbands ate up all of their wives' attention. She had enjoyed the time and energy to return to school, to get her doctorate at Brandeis, to take on a career and to go as far as she could. She was able to carry out her research, think through her ideas, write her books. No doubt one reason their marriage had lasted was because she remained interesting to him, and for that she credited her work. She was out in the world too. She had anecdotes, stories, new people, departmental controversies to bring home.

Her friend Jane viewed her marriage as a frightful aberration in an otherwise rational woman. While they'd been friends, Jane had been through tumultuous romances with three very different women who had all similarly broken Jane's frangible heart. "Don't you worry about AIDS?" Jane would demand.

"He doesn't pick up women in the street. He gets involved with one woman at a time whom he knows fairly well—someone connected with a play he's directing." She did not tell Jane what Melanie knew, that ever since she had borne David, she had been less attractive to Nick. From time to time, his desire would surface, like a reprieve of an earlier song. Each time she would talk herself into believing that this time he would once again be as physically smitten with her as she was with him.

She felt her love for him stirring within her. She always loved him, but it was often dormant, a quiet caring. Melanie had several times suggested that one of the strengths of their marriage was that they did lead separate lives and spent part of every year apart. Therefore they were always new to each other. They could never take each other for granted. They were always bringing something, if only a few weeks' experiences, to the other.

Perhaps. But she missed him when he was apart from her, and she loved him most, not in her mind's eye in absentia, but there with her. The house was a hundred-odd years old. They allowed it to be cool, even cold at night. While Nick was away, she slept under a feather quilt her mother Phyllis had given her when she had set up housekeeping. While Nick was with her, she threw the quilt over a chair and slept under a blanket.

She felt herself shifting from one economy, one set of demands to another. Yet he would return tomorrow to New York. This was a flying visit, and they should have made love. In the morning, she would put together a special breakfast to seduce him. She would bring coffee in bed, café au lait with something special. Yes. It had been sweet of him to suddenly want to see her, and she must break from her melancholia and make the time good. She would tear herself away from Melanie and go to New York next weekend.

She woke before him and ran down to make what would not be breakfast exactly—later for that, downstairs—but coffee and something: the something she decided upon, with the freezer blowing in her face, was honey cake Melanie had made at Rosh Hashanah. They often brought their families together for holidays. Leila was the better cook, but Melanie was the better baker. She thawed the honey cake and brought it to him warm on a beautiful Imari plate he had given her. May it sweeten the rest of our years together. The tray looked inviting as she balanced it carefully upstairs, steaming coffee, slices of cake (Nicolas had a sweet tooth the size of his home state of Texas, an accent he had long since discarded except when he wanted it), even a pink chrysanthemum snatched from a bouquet. The Imari plate Nick had brought her one year when he had been at a theater festival in Kyoto.

He woke more slowly than she did, with a widely played drama of yawning and stretching. Bearlike he tossed the covers and flung out his arms. Then he settled back for his coffee, asked about Melanie when the cake was explained to him, clucked sympathetically. Leila learned more from observing Nick than from listening to him. Now she watched him lick his fingers, glance at the clock and then at her body. They would make love. She would know his heaviness on her, his large hands molding her, his mouth tasting of coffee against her tongue, her breasts, her belly, her sex. Her body began to stretch and stir, coming alive from the core as it rarely did these days. Now he was on her and in her, riding far into her as she groaned and her hands scrabbled on his broad back.

By the time he dressed and showered, he had to leave at once—no time for a real breakfast. "I'll get something at the station—or on the train. Not to worry!" He grabbed up the rest of the honey cake from the kitchen table and ran out with only his bulging leather briefcase for luggage.

She watched him off, still in her peignoir, and then wandered disconcerted through the house. As she passed her study, she saw the winking red eye of the answering machine. She still felt guilty she had not managed to get a healthy breakfast into him before he rushed out. She must figure out whether to take the shuttle or the train or to drive to New York next weekend. At least she would be done with the stupid trial.

It was Mrs. Peretz. At the sound of her voice, Leila knew. She knew. "Leila, she died at two A.M. She died last night." Leila sat in her study at the desk covered with student papers. At first she felt nothing. She seemed to have no reaction at all, and she told herself she had done all her grieving in anticipation during the last months.

Then she began to weep spasmodically. She could not seem to stop crying. What she felt most sharply was deserted, abandoned by the woman she had always been able to talk to about anything in her life, in her work, in her mind. Melanie, even Melanie dying, was still her other, better, warmer, gentler half. She had loved Melanie since they had first sat up all night talking instead of studying for a psychology exam. Leila was a commuter and desperately happy to have a friend at school.

She washed her face hard and ran a bath because she did not want to smell of sex. It was a cool gold day under a dark blue ceramic sky. Yellow leaves from the enormous maple in the yard were idling down to the ground paved with gold. She had to get organized. She had to call Mrs. Peretz and Shana. But she needed to be washed and dressed first.

Melanie was someone she could always trust to complain to about Nick or her marriage, because Melanie would—unlike, for instance, Jane—assume that of course Leila had to make it work. Melanie and she had married their college boyfriends, stayed with them, had one child each, ended up in Boston and made careers for themselves a little later than they had at first intended. Their lives had been joined since adolescence. In many ways Melanie was the sister Debbie wasn't, although Debbie was her flesh and blood.

Dressed in white blouse and black suit, she sat down and called Melanie's house. Shana answered, her voice hoarse. "Oh, Leila, I kept thinking Mother was going to come home again. I kept hoping every day. She did it before. Why couldn't she come home?"

"I'll be right over. Is your grandmother there?"

"She's at the hospital, but she'll be back. The funeral will be tomorrow. I already called Rabbi Katz, Grandma told me to. Please come over. I don't know what to do." Shana began sobbing.

By contagion Leila did too, then wiped her face roughly. "There's an enormous amount to do." The busier they were, the better for all of them. Fortunately she was good at doing. "Make yourself a cup of tea and sit down. By the time you drink it, I'll be with you."

In fact there was no one in the world she wanted to be with as much as Shana, because they were equally robbed and bereaved. Melanie had told her seventy times, Watch over Shana, and she would. She had first held Shana right after the home delivery, still stippled with bright birth colors and screaming as if being born were cause for a broken heart. Shana's father had a new family in Amherst. No, Shana had her grandmother and she had Leila, and Leila must make that enough for her. Now she must call David and leave a message for Nick, so that he'd hear it whenever he reached his sublet apartment. It was time to put aside her grief and get moving.

CHAPTER 2

MARY

Mary woke, sleeping on top of Mrs. Douglas's bed. They had canceled her this week because Mr. Douglas was going to a sales conference in Puerto Rico, and Mrs. Douglas was going along to sun herself. That meant Mary was cleaning only four days this week, so she wouldn't be able to put aside her five dollars; but more importantly, it had given her a place to sleep last night and tonight too. They were due back Thursday. She had set their alarm for six so she could take a nice bath this morning. When she had a borrowed house, she took as many baths as she could to make up for the nights she slept at Logan or in a church basement or any other stolen place. Last night she had done her laundry and packed it carefully into her carry-all. She always had her big flowered carry-all and her great old purse, so that she would never give the impression of a bag lady, just a cleaning lady going to work.

Her off-season clothes she shipped every year to her son Jaime in Hawaii. They did not have room in his little apartment for even an extra box, but he stored her things in the back room of his surf shop. Then in spring she would write to him to send her the box, and when it arrived, she would ship her winter stuff off. It would have been easier to send it to her daughter Cindy in Chevy Chase, but Cindy hated storing and shipping Mary's things.

They had four kinds of cereal open: bran flakes, raisin bran, granola and cornflakes. She helped herself to a modest amount of each. She had bought milk and a half pound of hamburger meat the night before and a head of lettuce. The rest of her supper she had put together out of leftovers and items she dared appropriate. When she borrowed her clients' houses—the people whose houses she cleaned or whose animals she fed and walked—she was extremely careful. She was clean, tidy, quiet. She was truly transparent, passing through the lives of the people whose houses she slept in without leaving a trace or residue, except sometimes a sense of puzzlement, minor arguments and accusations. Who ate that lemon yogurt I left in the refrigerator? I could have sworn we had a can of chicken soup.

She had keys to every house. Mostly she brought her own food in, and always she carried her trash out. The movie she had watched on the VCR last night, she had rewound. Any dishes she used, she washed at once. She did not drink or smoke. She slept lightly, a legacy from her time on the street, when she had slept only in snatches. She always had a clear escape route planned. She knew every door and every window. If someone had an alarm system, she made an excuse not to clean for them again. She woke at every sound, bolt upright and ready to flee. She could never let herself fall into a really deep slumber; it reminded her of the way she had spent her nights when her children were infants.

She liked sitting at breakfast with "Good Morning America" on. When she was cleaning, she usually kept a set on so she could follow the talk shows, for company. She had never learned to work stereos, for she was not musical. Her father used to say that she had two clay ears. She loved real coffee. She made it drip right into a mug, for she had a tiny Melitta insert that fit over the cup. The Melitta from a church rummage sale she carried with her along with her fork, spoon and serrated knife, can and bottle opener. Saturday rummage sales were great. She could be there from when they opened until they closed and nobody would look askance. Her good wool skirt came from a sale in Brookline.

Time to leave. She could not wait longer, because the neighbors would be going out to their cars. She was good at slipping in and out of houses and buildings on the sly. She was grey-haired, five feet four, a short stout woman cleanly and respectfully dressed. She was strong, although her feet gave her trouble. Now she had to walk around for an hour and a half until she could go to Mrs. Landsman's at nine. Could she dare arrive fifteen minutes early and say the trains had been quick? She was supposed to be living with her married daughter, who was ashamed of her mother's being a cleaning lady. She had a post office box, she had a checking account with $609 in it, but she could not afford rent deposit, utilities deposit. It had taken her almost five years to save the six hundred. It was a nippy morning and she walked briskly. If she had not been toting her two heavy bags, walking would have been pleasant, but soon, her shoulders and back ached.

She had learned a good pace for residential streets and a faster pace for public streets, with pauses to look into windows and lean against them. To sit down cost money. It was too early for malls. She had spent the night in Arlington, so she would simply walk to Cambridge, use up the time and save the bus fare. After she had walked for forty minutes, her arms were throbbing. Her shoulders felt as if they would pry out of their sockets. She went into a laundrette. She had to use the bathroom, but there was no place to go. She would have to wait till she got to Mrs. Landsman's. She should not have treated herself to that second cup of coffee. A harassed mother trying to get her laundry together before taking her two kids to day care paid her no attention. The woman was using three machines at once.

It felt good to sit, even on a slatted bench. When she had been a girl, Mary remembered that she had adored a comic book character called Invisible Scarlett O'Neill. Scarlett had the ability to press a spot on her wrist and become invisible. Mary had found the idea of escaping from the perennial monitoring of mother, father, older brother, teachers a perfect fantasy. She was a curious child, but whenever she asked about anything, she was told ladies didn't inquire about that or little girls didn't need to know. She had been constantly told that ladies were not nosy. So she had dreamed of being invisible and going where she pleased and learning everything hidden.

Well, at sixty-one, she had succeeded in her wish to become invisible. She walked through walls. She came and went without being seen or heard. Never had she guessed in her years of marriage, childrearing, entertaining for her husband and housekeeping that she would live out that fantasy, often in fear and danger of discovery or violence. Surreptitiously she slipped off her worn shoes. A couple were doing their laundry before work and fighting openly about his mother's demands. Mary sat there as if she were a pile of laundry. They barely registered her presence. She thought that if she were an intelligence agency, she would hire women like herself, because she could go almost anywhere and no one looked at her. Half the time, when she passed a security guard, he thought he knew her. He'd seen dozens like her, and he wouldn't want to look at her anyhow. She was safe in his book, a grandma, an old bag. She didn't count. So they didn't count her.

She was a little alarmed that she had not been able to walk the distance without resting, but the bags were heavy. She had to keep up her strength, her health. Sickness was forbidden. Sickness would be ruin. Years ago, when she was a housewife, she used to have an exercise bicycle. She went horseback riding with her daughter or another housewife in Bethesda, where she lived with her husband Jim. Now she got more exercise than she needed.

She arrived at Mrs. Landsman's just at nine. She was upset to hear Mrs. Landsman on the phone as she walked in. She preferred cleaning when the people were away at work. A client's presence severely limited her scope. Normally she cleaned in a frenzy and then investigated. She played detective. Each time she selected one room to study thoroughly, to learn where everything was kept and to read whatever was legible of their lives and intentions.

She knew a great deal about her clients from their desks, their dressers, their appointment calendars, their wall calendars. She listened to the messages on their answering machines. She could tell their income levels and their major problems, health, business and personal. People did not have many secrets from those who cleaned for them. Mr. Douglas coddled an ulcer and liked dirty movies of women together. Mrs. Douglas had a lover, a married doctor she met every Friday while Mary cleaned her house. Mrs. DeMott had had liposuction. She hid caches of cigarettes all over the house. Mr. DeMott used eight kinds of medicine for constipation. Mr. Anzio was in trouble with the IRS for back taxes. Mrs. Anzio was on tranquilizers. Their daughter was anorexic and wrote fantasies of suicide in her diary. Mr. Landsman was unfaithful to his wife, and she put up with it.

It was important for her to keep track of their habits so that she could fit herself into the interstices of their lives. The class of people she cleaned for traveled a goodly amount, and she must know their times of arrival and departure. During the day, if she had not had a hidey hole the night before where she could catch some sleep, she had to know when it was safe for her to sneak a nap.

But Mary hated to be examined in turn. This was rarely a problem. Some of her clients felt compelled to ask questions, not from any desire to learn about her, but from a misguided sense of courtesy, that they should show some interest. It was easy to disengage. She told them a few truths, that she was of Scotch-Irish lineage, not regular Irish. She let them assume she was an immigrant or that her parents were. She never said that her family had been in this country for one hundred sixty years, that her father had owned his own business, that she grew up in a house as pleasantly furnished and appointed as their own. She implied she was a widow; never that she had married a geologist who, now that he had retired from the Department of Energy, ran a small but lucrative consulting firm while living with his third wife and his second set of offspring. Her class drop would transfix and repel them at once. It would certainly make them uneasy. It was better to seem simpler than she was, a denizen of that class which did for them unobtrusively and faded back into the grey of genteel poverty. Never let them know who you really are, how you live, and that you can observe and think, that was her motto.

They wanted a cleaner to be subservient, busy, with extremely limited horizons. But some were curious. Mrs. Landsman was one of those. She wasn't comfortable with having someone clean her house, but she worked, fortunately, so Mary seldom ran into her. Mary liked the house. Mrs. Landsman was untidy but not dirty, and there were always interesting things to read and look at.

Every so often Mrs. Landsman was around, as this morning. Perhaps it was school vacation? Mr. Landsman seemed to travel a great deal because he directed plays. They both had studies. The walls of his were covered with photos of plays, people in costume. There were two miniature sets in his office, like doll houses for adults. He had won some awards, displayed on a shelf. Mary bet he would rather they had given him money, for the Landsmans always seemed a little short on cash for their lifestyle. She would come across the figures on expenses and the budgets Mrs. L. tried to work out.

Mary had been planning to call into the cleaning agency office, as she liked to do each morning. The secretary took her pet-care messages on the sly. Mary would give her a twenty each month under the table. It meant Mary could use the cleaning service as a phone number. But she didn't like to call in front of her clients. "Mrs. Burke," Mrs. Landsman said, "I've been expecting a phone call from my husband. I have to go to school soon. You'd recognize his voice over the answering machine, wouldn't you?"

"I think so," Mary said dully.

"All you have to do is pick up the phone, and it's like a regular phone call then. Does your daughter have an answering machine?"

Mrs. Landsman seemed compelled to ask her questions. Mary thought that Mrs. L. was some sort of sociologist; certainly she wrote books, usually about women. Mary didn't care for that sort of book, so she'd never done more than glance at the one about women in prison.

"She does, but I don't use it," Mary said. "When I pick up the phone, what do I say to Mr. Landsman?"

"I'm trying to make plans for going to New York, so he has to call me tonight, no matter how late he gets in. . . . Do you ever go to New York?"

"Not in years," Mary said, turning on the vacuum cleaner. A person could have told at once that Mrs. Landsman was used to asking people questions—grilling her, as she experienced it. If Mary ever let herself get sucked into one of those conversations, she could easily give herself away. So she resisted.

"How is your daughter? Does she still feel bad about your cleaning?"

"She's just fine. I haven't asked her lately."

Mary did not like having to work hard at lying; she was raised to tell the truth one hundred percent of the time. Sometimes her family had been unpleasantly outspoken. "Well, Aunt Fran, to tell you the truth, that dress makes you look extremely sallow." "Well, to tell the truth, little Mary, I don't think he loves you." The truth was always sour and harsh, like a powerful emetic. If it didn't hurt, it couldn't really be the truth. Her parents had not been in the least religious, but they acted as if they believed in hell, the slippery slope into sin if they deviated from the straight and narrow one step's width. To this day, when she heard someone say, "To tell you the truth," she drew into herself and waited for the blow in the face.

"What's the weather like outside?"

"Nippy."

"I haven't had a frost yet. Have you, where you live? Was it Dedham?"

"I haven't noticed."

"I haven't used the kitchen much, and David's room just needs dusting. If there's time, do the refrigerator." The woman sighed. "Nothing gets much use this fall."

Mrs. Landsman sat in her office writing checks. In this house, the missus kept the books, paid the bills and balanced the checkbook. Mrs. Landsman was the one who worried about how the oil bill and the property taxes would get paid and whether the old car would make it another year. Now they had college tuition for one son. It cost as much nowadays to send one kid through college as she and Jim had paid for two. Besides, Jaime had had an athletic scholarship. She busied herself upstairs until finally she heard Mrs. Landsman leaving.

Then she switched on the end of "Regis and Kathie Lee." She loved the talk shows. Some of the cleaning women were addicted to the soaps, and when they met, they gossiped about characters as if they were acquaintances. What about Billy? Does he still love Vanessa? She liked a show with some content, some issues, where she felt she was learning something. And it was company. If she did not dare talk with her clients, that did not mean she did not wish for a little conversation.

It was a lonely life, to be honest. Never when she was growing up, when she was having babies, when she was raising her children, did she expect to be alone, ever. She had married right out of college. Two years later, she had borne Cindy. Yet here she was, utterly alone in the world. Even the few people who reached out to her did it in a way she didn't dare respond to. Mrs. Landsman tried to be friendly, but that was only a pit of danger for Mary. She could not let any of her clients find out she was homeless, for she would be out of a job in nothing flat. Nobody would want her in their houses; nobody would trust her. She heard people talking about the homeless, how they were crazy, they were drug addicts, they didn't want to work. How unpleasant it was to be panhandled, how they should be kept off the streets. How pitiful and dirty they were. As if there weren't thousands like her who worked every day without making enough for a deposit and rent.

No wonder she was extraordinarily kind to her clients' animals. With them she did not have to be on guard. The Millers' Airedale Zurich and Mrs. Solano's Siamese Griselda who slept around her head purring were the only beings who ever looked into her eyes and accepted the touch of her hands. She who had lived in her marriage, in a neighborhood of constant socializing with a whole web of friends and family, now had as her only intimates the dogs, the cats, the occasional parrot or ferret she took care of and with whom she shared quarters for a night. That was her new circle of friends.

CHAPTER 3

LEILA

The Monday after Melanie's funeral, Leila went back to work. She had two classes to meet. She did everything with her left hand, lecturing on automatic pilot, dealing with everybody with half a mind. "I'm sorry I couldn't get back to you sooner. A close friend of mine died."

Mourning was a state unsupported by contemporary culture. No one knew what to say, and she ended up feeling she had been unwarrantedly personal, unprofessional, emotional, too female. Yet she could offer little of value to anyone. At odd moments she had the urge to cry, but to do so was simply not an option. It would embarrass everyone around her. A professor doesn't cry in front of students or colleagues. A woman professional can cry only in the bathroom, and then only long enough so that it doesn't show; in the staff women's room, it did not escape comment. "Is something wrong, Leila?" a colleague, Barbara, asked her. "Are things all right with Nicolas?"

That was what they expected to go wrong, all the women around her. She made a brief explanation, scrubbed her face with a paper towel and slathered on makeup. She was beginning to hate herself, this wet gusty creature who could not keep her façade in place.

She taught her classes, met students and sat in on a meeting of her sociology department and voted on two motions without being able to remember, as she picked up her briefcase, what the meeting had been about. She could have voted to abolish her own position, for all she could recall. More phone calls to dispose of. An ex-student wanting a recommendation she must rush out. Her agent. Leila had been with Sally for ten years.

"Hi, Sally. Before you ask, the book is flying along. The revisions they asked for are all getting done."

"Good. When?"

"Last of November. . . ." That was only ten days after the publisher had requested the changes come in. She had learned to be a little late. It seemed to satisfy everyone more fully. If she did things early, they assumed she hadn't really put the work in. Even if she was just on time, they were unimpressed. A little late was perfect. It didn't inconvenience them, and yet they could smell the effort.

"Anyhow, that's not the primary reason I called. Have you been following the Becky Burgess case?"

"Becky Burgess?" Leila's mind was a bowl of gruel.

"The young woman with the much-younger lover who killed her husband. Or so we all suppose."

"In Falmouth, near the bridge onto the Cape . . ." Leila vaguely remembered the TV talking to her at supper. When Nick was home, they ate at eight in the dining room. She and David had always used the kitchen when Nick was away. Now with David at Cal Tech, she ate there with first May Rollins, then Peter Jennings talking to her from a little plastic TV just behind the salt shaker and pepper mill. "She's been tried in the media and convicted of being a bad woman. They'll send her up for that, whether or not she killed her husband."

"There's a lot of interest in this case. I had a call two days ago from your editor. She wants to know if you'd do a book."

"On a murder case? That's hardly my metier."

"Well, Leila, you wrote about women in prison. What's the difference? Burgess sounds like an interesting hussy. I'm just running this by you. The money's good, very good. How does three times your last advance sound?"

"Three times? Do they think it's that big?" That would solve their money problems for a while, pay for David's college.

"It's a hard/soft deal. A quarter on signing. Quarter on completion. Quarter on publication. Quarter when the paperback comes out. I didn't say no, because I figure for this kind of money, you might develop an interest."

"How soon do they want to know?"

"Yesterday. So let's say by ten A.M. tomorrow."

She did think about it walking home. Since daylight saving time had ended, she walked back from Lesley in darkness, but the streets were busy. When she was in a hurry, she drove, because she lived in North Cambridge, about a mile from school. The book on incest survivors was on schedule. She had only to rewrite the introduction. Most of the remaining work, compiling tables, putting the bibliography in order, was up to her assistant. For the first time in fifteen years, Leila had nothing in the pipeline. Melanie's long illness had filled Leila's time and sapped her energy. She did need a project, she needed one badly and at once. But a sensational trial? What was in that for her? She was only marginally respectable academically, although that did not bother her. She made up for any loss of colleagues' respect by the money she made on the speaking circuit. She had been walking a thin and wavering line between the academic and the popular all of her professional life. What did she care if the case was a bit racy? She tried to remember Becky Burgess. A bedroom suburb. A woman in her mid-twenties with a younger man. Some insurance scam.

Mrs. Burke had cleaned today and left her a bill and a note. "Dear Mrs. Landsman, I found the attached letter under your bed. I don't know if you need it, but I did not want to throw it away."

A note? The handwriting belonged to Nick. It was dated the morning they had made love and he returned to New York. He must have left it on her pillow. When she had returned late and exhausted from Melanie's family, she had ripped off the covers, dived in and never noticed the note.

Dearest Leila,

It was a real joy to see you, however briefly, but the brevity got in the way of what I wanted to say to you. It was too late by the time you got home to have a real conversation.

I'm not sure you really want to bolt down to New York next Saturday. We're all absolutely crazed with trying to get the play together, and it might not be entirely comfortable for you.

I've been terribly depressed and worried. You know how New York throws me. I misplace my sense of myself. I lose direction. I really need you, but of course your work means you can't be with me. And you've been spending an awful lot of time with Melanie, who, after all, has her daughter and her mother besides you. What did I have? I was blue and drowning. I couldn't sleep and I forfeited confidence in what I was trying to do. I really just needed somebody, anybody, who'd hold my hand and help me through this brief unhappy mess.

Really, it started with Sheryl just because she simply wouldn't take direction, and I had to get her under control. Jocasta is a critical role, and she was in danger of botching the whole ensemble with her mannerisms.

It's of no importance, and of course she knows we're married and not about to let anything come between us. It's just one of those things I back into when I feel desperate and alone.

The situation with the play is critical. Why not wait until it opens and give me your insight then?

Don't let this awkward little situation with Sheryl upset you. I just need someone to lean on while I'm in New York.

Your loving husband, Nicolas

She heard the crash and saw that she had taken up the Imari plate he had given her three years before and smashed it against the table. The table had a visible scratch and the plate was in fragments at her feet. She had a moment of regret for something beautiful broken; then she was astonished at the rage that burst out of her. She was not a woman who threw objects or scenes. What she had seen in her mind was smashing the plate across his head. She viewed her anger with surprise, as if it were a storm that had suddenly blown in off the ocean, knocking a tree down.

She had truly dared believe he was done with running around. He had told her a long and moving fable about having realized he was really in middle age. He had insisted that his wandering was over. "I've come home to you at last," he said, "really home." It had been touching and for a while their sexual relationship had heated up. It was worse than before, when she had simply accepted his out-of-town affairs as the price of the marriage. She had been overjoyed that he had finally relinquished his long, long adolescence and was settling down with her. She paced through the rooms of their Cambridge house, their gracious house with its comfortable furniture, most of it leather, with its Orientals and paintings by friends and acquaintances, David's attempts at art photography, photos and mementos of Nick's past successes.

She was calling Sally. "Glad I caught you. I'll take that offer. Get me expenses up front. I'll need a lot of transcription for this one."

"This will work only if you can start at once. The trial is set for late January."

"Tomorrow I'll start reading up on the case and trying to see her."

"Oh, they think she'll see you, no problem. She loves to talk."

She realized that Mrs. Burke had probably read the note, and she felt mortified. It was humiliating to have her cleaning lady cognizant of her husband's infidelities. Mrs. Burke was a dour hardworking woman, whom Leila felt to be silently judgmental. Someone whose life had been totally by the book and who thought other choices shameful. She lived with her married daughter in a conventional situation. She was not a friendly woman, although Leila could understand how the situation did not lend itself to intimacy. She was the boss, the one whose dirt was being removed.

She was being ridiculous. Many friends and acquaintances knew. Every so often she would hear someone had seen him with another very young woman in L.A. or Washington. His affairs had begun shortly after David was born. Nick had not particularly wanted a baby. She had not gotten pregnant intentionally, but when she had found herself carrying, she wanted the child. She had seen it as her one chance for a baby from Nick.

She was too upset to eat. But she felt some satisfaction in the idea of doing a book on a woman who had murdered her husband. She knew that if Nick were there he would get round her, but he wasn't. So often he wasn't. She would digest her own anger, she would manage it as she always had. The fear of losing him had constantly forced her to dispose of her negative reactions toward what he did. Her anger toward him caused her the same sense of shame and secretiveness her mother had trained her to feel toward her sanitary napkins, that must not go into the family garbage, that must not be flushed down the toilet lest they clog the pipes, but carried at once outside to the trash.

Her anger had always felt to her too dangerous to let out, a devouring menace. Thus she tried to distance herself from it. But this time that dark energy was propelling her into a new project, something she desperately needed. Her colleagues would be appalled. Good. She had not shocked them in several years. She was becoming dull. It was time to stir up some dust. She would not feel so much a victim; so much a fool. She longed to concern herself with the problems of strangers.

Normally she would have called Melanie. She would pick up the phone with the fury still driving her, and Melanie would take her down. Melanie understood the price of reaction. She had lost her own husband and she would keep Leila from driving Nick away. Melanie had soothed her into acceptance during too many crises to count.

I hope the play fails, she thought, and then felt the hot flush of disloyalty. How could she hope for anything like that? They were a marriage, they were a mutual cooperative society, and what hurt or benefited one must do the same for the other. Oh, but she was bitterly angry with him. It would take a while to wear off. She had allowed herself to hope that his long wandering had finally run its course and a new stage in their marriage had begun. As they moved together through middle age, they would turn toward each other, share more of their lives, and their marriage would grow warmer and more satisfying. Her long patience would receive its lasting payoff. All the friends and acquaintances who had pitied her would admire her persistence and wisdom. At long last, her husband would be entirely hers.

Indeed, New York was an aberration. It was the same as when he had given up smoking and walked into a room full of smokers, he had to have a cigarette. The younger the actresses were, the more quickly he grew bored. Bringing *Oedipus* to New York had caused all his anxieties to flare up. In a situation of high stress, backsliding was not surprising. It was a last fling, brought on by the pressures of an opening in Manhattan.

How could she carry on about his infidelity? It was something she had accepted for two decades. She had known it all from the beginning. Never had Nicolas concealed his nature or his intentions: at twenty-two he had announced to her, I do not believe in fidelity. It's a leash. I don't want to be walked on a leash by any woman. I will always come back to you, I will always love you, but I won't deny my curiosity or my desire. My freedom is as precious as life to me. I won't cut myself to fit.

And he hadn't; but she had.

CHAPTER 4

BECKY

Her mama would never understand it, in fact nobody would, but Becky Souza went to the mall to be alone. In their old two-story house with their last two Chevies in the yard partly cannibalized, her father's fishing gear, a boat he was slowly fixing up for Joey, the oldest boy, two of the local black dogs that were more or less Labs plus some collie and spaniel, her mother's chickens and a portable radio always blasting out some game, while inside everybody tripped over everybody else and baby Sonny, her nephew, bawled, who got privacy—ever? With two bathrooms for twelve of them, no wonder the space between the lilacs and the garage always smelled like a toilet. She shared a bedroom with two sisters, Belle, who was three years older than Becky and studying to be a beautician, and spoiled Laurie, two years younger, who was coming off deciding to be a nun. What did Becky own, besides a cigar box of treasures? Some treasures. A silver dollar from Nevada her Uncle Ray had given her. Her three pairs of clip-on earrings. Her cute black lace bikini panties bought on sale and saved for some guy who would be worth spending her cherry. No calls on that one yet.

Mama shopped their New Bedford neighborhood, where the shopkeepers knew her by name. Half of them spoke Portuguese to Becky, who refused to answer in it. Mama spoke it as well as the French she'd learned at home, but Becky thought it was a mistake to speak anything but English. No, she went to the mall for privacy. She walked from shop to shop, hardly ever with a buck to spend, but pricing everything, looking, studying, seeing what there was to be had when the day came she could have anything in the place. Then she would not waste her money, the way Uncle Ray and Aunt Betty did when they won the lottery—five hundred dollars at once. They had blown it all on a trip to Las Vegas that had ended up costing them more than they won.

A hundred times she had played that game: the game of Becky wins a hundred dollars, Becky wins five hundred dollars, Becky wins a thousand dollars. It wouldn't be fair to play it for more than that, because if she were rich, she wouldn't need to make careful choices, and that was the point of the game.

First, she would get her hair done right. She would have her hair bleached, not like the other kids in eleventh grade, but the right way, so that it looked like hair did in the movies and on TV. Second, she would buy a good blue suit, to bring out the color of her eyes, just the kind her favorite anchorwoman favored. It would be so demure and yet sexy in a quiet, very controlled way. She would buy a real silk blouse. Good shoes from a department store. Then a good wool coat. She had spent all her money. She didn't think she could get the kind of coat she wanted with everything else for five hundred dollars. A coat was the first thing anybody saw, and if you had a cheap sleazy coat, you were out of luck. You were classified before you opened your mouth.

She loved her mama, she really did, but she wouldn't look like Mama if she had to paint herself blue. Mostly she wore the leather jacket that had gotten too tight on her cousin Wanda. It was a bit tough for the image she wanted to project, but it was one hundred percent better than her gross bright green coat with the plaid lining her mother had bought her oldest sister Gracie half a century before. It must be eight years old anyhow. She hated it. She would rather have her teeth chatter like the sound of ice cubes clinking in a glass before she'd wear that stupid green coat where people could look at her. Green was not her color anyhow. Blue was.

A lot of the time in the mall she just drifted past counters piled with sweaters or scarves and she dreamed. If she tried to think about anything at home, Mama would give her a task to do instantly. Go to the store and get two pounds of hamburger for supper. Wash out the tub. If the water's hot, run a load of laundry for Gracie. Help Nana with the baby. Here she could just float along and think and think and think. She could imagine herself as her favorite anchorwoman getting dressed for the evening news. She could imagine herself taking her screen test. She could see herself explaining to Barbara Walters how she had prepared for her difficult, not to say grueling, role as Joan of Arc. Or Marilyn. But she didn't have the cleavage. Well, that's what silicon was for. If she needed big tits, she'd buy them. When she was free and adult, she'd have enough money to buy what she needed. She knew she was smart and fast.

Nobody in her family seemed to know it, but as much as she loved them—and she really did love Mama and Papa and Gracie's kids Sonny and Tina and her sister Belle and her favorite brother Tommy, the closest to her in age and temperament, she loved them and wanted to do for them—she wasn't going to hang around the way everybody else in her family just seemed rooted in the sand of their yard. Nobody ever seemed able to get farther than a neighborhood away. Even Nana was still living in this house that had been hers since 1948.

The mall was clean. Guys swept it every day. Cleaning women made it nice every night. But mostly it was nice because it was full of clean things. Some of them were good things and some of them were sleazy, ugly things she wouldn't wear to drown in, but all of them were new. Not yet broken. Not yet worn, cracked. One of the worst things of never having money was always having to make do with what was second best. She would see something she really wanted, a dress, a kind of shoes, a kind of purse or necklace. But there was never enough money for the real thing, or even for a good imitation of the real thing that nobody could tell apart anyhow. No, she had to make do, if she got anything at all, with the cheapest knockoff that immediately fell apart or began to develop piles like hideous zits or the thin plastic cracked and showed the pasteboard underneath. So that not only didn't she have what she wanted, but the imitation couldn't fool her for five minutes. It was better to have nothing at all. Then she could still dream about the perfect thing. She wanted to be cool and finished, no rough edges, no cracks, nothing raw or unkempt.

She was educating her eye and her hand for the day when she would need to know about clothing and accessories. Fortunately the sales ladies were always being fired or quitting. Therefore few of them gave her dirty looks or tried to make her uncomfortable about trying on skirts she had no money to buy. Sometimes she pretended she was thinking about buying an outfit, but mostly they didn't pay much attention to her, and she could just say it didn't fit.

Sometimes she sat in the mall and studied. It was quieter than at home. There she did her homework sitting in the truck, but Papa and Tommy left really early to go fishing. When it wasn't too cold, she sat in an old car that still had its seats. She had her B-plus average to maintain because, if she failed to get a scholarship, she would not be the first person in her family to go to college. She would not have her exit papers from the fate of her sisters. Already Gracie looked like their mother. Oh, she cut her hair shorter. They both wore polyester pants and overblouses. Their expressions were the same and why not? Their lives were the same, except that Mama had her Church of the Sacred Truth.

Mama had been raised in a family of French-Canadian Catholics who had moved down from Maine to New Bedford, but she had converted to a Pentecostal church that offered talking in tongues, swaying, screaming, confessions in public, nightly excitement. The women had more fun there, Becky could see that. Every so often she went with her mother, just to get out of the house, but it wasn't for her. No exit from the neighborhood there. Just a lot of overweight miserable middle-aged women whose husbands beat them or cheated on them or drank away their earnings or went down in a gale and left them with a houseful of needy noisy kids. Good women, and what did it get them? Goodness had to be its own reward, because they didn't get any other. They could be big shots in the dingy storefront, then they went home to the same dreary mess. Becky knew Mama had been pretty—her wedding picture stood in a forest of snapshots of family—fair like herself and tiny. It was a warning. This could happen to you.

Becky went to Mass sometimes, on the more festive or solemn occasions, but God was a concept she had quietly discarded shortly after her confirmation. She told no one of her loss of faith, because it would have upset Mama, even Papa, no matter that he went to Mass only at Christmas and Easter and when somebody's boat went down. His family was Portuguese and Catholic but only a few of the women took it seriously. The priest was a nice harassed man who did the best he could, but she had stopped telling him anything real even before she lost her faith. How could he help her with being a girl?

Gracie had married her high school sweetheart, and that had lasted long enough to squeeze two babies out of her. Then he'd started knocking her around. One Saturday he went to the corner and never returned. Now Gracie was back, crowded in with the rest of them. There were no role models at home for being a successful modern woman.

Becky had to study it on the TV, paying close attention to details of manner, dress, voice. Those were women who had created themselves, as she would. She read about them in *TV Guide*, in magazines.

Her brothers—except Tommy—teased her about the way she talked, when she remembered to talk correctly, which was most of the time by now. Even the girls at school were nasty about it. She had only one close friend, Sylvie Damato, whose family was Italian and ran a bowling alley and grill. Sylvie did not laugh at her for trying to talk correctly and trying to figure out how to dress. Sylvie had a little pocket money from the grill and she could buy magazines, which they studied together harder than they studied any textbooks unless they had a test coming. They were in the same social studies class. Both did well in school. Sylvie lived in the North End too, but a couple blocks farther north where more trees grew.

Sylvie was just as determined to go to college as she was, but Sylvie had a role model, because her aunt Marie was in real estate and owned her own house in Cohasset. One of their favorite excursions when they could borrow Mr. Damato's car was to visit Aunt Marie, who drove a glossy new Subaru with a sun roof. Aunt Marie had to be at least forty but she did not look old. Her hair was auburn and she worked out at a gym three nights a week. She was the only woman the girls knew who lived on her own (she was divorced) and did not look anything like their mothers or like the whores who worked downtown. Aunt Marie dressed like the women on TV, in smart suits and clean crisp shirts or in silk shirtdresses and her hair always done. She wore little bright earrings and designer scarves. Whenever Becky sat and looked at Aunt Marie, she felt as if she was looking at something she could really, really be. Aunt Marie would give the girls espresso she made in a machine in her beautiful kitchen straight out of a magazine, or even a tiny glass of sherry. The kitchen shone with dark yellow tiles, begonias in the window, bright blue plates all matching.

Becky thought to herself she would give away the next twenty years if she could wake up just like Sylvie's aunt Marie. That was living. Everything else was slow sticky drowning. But Becky was not going to founder. She was going to learn to swim, out of her house that smelled of fishy oil, out of the North End, out of New Bedford, into the world inside the TV where everything was new and nice as a perfect iced layer cake at a wedding.

CHAPTER 5

LEILA

Leila had sworn she would not tell David what was happening with his father, but he could always empty her out. He knew exactly where silences lurked under the conversation, and he would not stop probing them until he found out what she was withholding. Maybe it was his scientist's curiosity. Since kindergarten he had been sensitive to friction between his parents. She held the phone away from her ear and sighed.

"So what news did he have? Of course he didn't come all the way to be charming. He laid something in your lap. Did he tell you not to let me know? Then why are you lying? But sitting on something is lying, Mother. You can't keep family things from me, it concerns all of us." David rarely raised his voice. His manner was gentle, soft-spoken, a new-age wind chime of a late adolescent; but underneath lurked a will like a brass-tipped battering ram.

It was a demanding love, but a very real one. As mother and son, they knew each other unusually well. David had always been available to her as she had been there for him, until he had gone away to college. It was time for him to leave home, to leave her. She knew that but missed him constantly. He had stood in as head of the household for years, dealing with plumbers, electricians, painters. "This is Mr. Landsman," he would say on the phone, lowering his voice. They would assume it was the husband calling. Nick was poor at handling practical problems. He would start out to explain to the contractor that the garage door didn't work and end up drinking with the guy and going to a ball game. The door would never be fixed. He had to charm men as he had to seduce women. Ultimately the contractor liking him was more important than the garage door working. She decided to change the subject. "How's your new girlfriend. Emma?"

"Emma's history. She flunked out."

"That's terrible."

"Not really. She was using up too much time."

"But I thought you liked her." Ease up, Leila. "Anyone new?"

"I went to the movies Sunday with Ikuko."

"Japanese?"

"Only by ancestry. She was born in Santa Clara. She won't flunk out. She's smarter than I am. She's into AI already."

But just before the rambling conversation tapered off and they said good night, he returned to the attack. "Father's a user. You can't let him put you through a shredder. He's having an affair in New York, isn't he? Some ditz near my age. Don't let it get to you."

After she hung up, she felt guilty, self-indulgent. It was too late to undo what years of growing up had produced: a boy who was much closer to his mother than to his father. That did not seem to have hurt him with women. For a straight nerd type, the winner of science fairs and scholarships, he had had his first girlfriend when he was thirteen and never been without since. He was good-looking, certainly, but he seemed completely unaware of his appearance. Always there was something untidy in his dress and wistful in his manner. Every new girlfriend thought she had discovered a sexy soulful unknown beneath the superserious manner and the air of being always a little socially confused and unbuttoned. She tried to like his girlfriends and quietly failed. Her fantasy was to marry him off eventually—at age thirty perhaps—to Shana.

It was three hours earlier in California, and he would have wakened her if she had gone to sleep at her customary hour. Instead she was lying in bed surrounded by photocopies of articles on the murder of Terry Burgess. His distraught widow tried bravely to be helpful to the police. Then some two months later, Becky Burgess and her accomplice Sam Solomon were arrested.

Falmouth, Massachusetts, June 20

Last night, Rebecca Burgess came home from Sound Cable TV company where she works as a secretary to find the body of her husband,

> Terrence Burgess, sprawled in a bed splashed with his blood. Police say he had been beaten to death perhaps two hours before. The bedroom showed signs of a fierce struggle.
>
> According to police sources, the intruder entered the apartment through a sliding glass door from the deck. The TV, the VCR and some gold jewelry were missing, as well as cash.
>
> A neighbor, Mrs. Helen Coreggio, heard thumping from upstairs. She said there had been a robbery in May in the apartment complex. She suggested that the same burglar had returned, but that this time he had encountered Mr. Burgess in bed.

The articles were not helping. The view of Becky Burgess was too abstract. First she was a fragile victim; then she was a murderer. Leila could get no sense of the woman underneath the clippings.

The next day, she called in a favor. She had helped out May Rollins on the evening news when the inmates rioted at Framingham women's prison, and again during the trial of Linda Sue, an abused woman who had killed her husband in her backyard with his own shotgun while he was beating their daughter. Leila had been an instant expert for May. May owed her. And May came through. Leila drove to WBZ at noon to view videotaped footage of Becky. The widow had ceased being Rebecca Burgess to the media by the first week of the case.

There were miles of footage to view and Leila had to skip lunch. Becky had been a willing witness for the news. She had talked and she had talked and she had talked. She was full of helpful theories and suggestions. She couldn't keep her mouth shut.

She was a sharp-faced woman of twenty-five with enormous light blue eyes. Her hair was blond and fleecy, a halo of pale curls around her face giving her a frail ingenue look. At some point she had got rid of her local accent. If Leila shut her eyes, she could not tell May's voice—a tall gorgeous Black woman from Detroit who spoke as if she had gone to Radcliffe—from Becky's. They both sounded brisk, sweet, cultured, perfect ladies but right on the ball. Oh yes. Luncheon voices, tennis voices. Polite, mildly competitive, clean-living ersatz Wasps, but too bright, too edgy finally to pass.

Obviously Becky (Now Leila was doing it; the accused had lost her last name. The Becky case. Did Becky do it?) loved the camera. She flirted with it uncontrollably. She spoke to it earnestly and devotedly. It was the eye of a lover, of God. She was engaged in special pleading with the camera-eye. Look at me, see me, love me. Leila could never stand to watch herself on TV, always asking, Am I really that big? She took up too much space. She was too tall, too busty. Strapping, she had been called since girlhood, a hideous word that suggested that perhaps she should be strapped in or down. But Becky's turning to the camera with a fervid appeal was only another form of wanting to fit in, to be liked, to be accepted. In the shots of Becky's natal home, the Souza family, Leila read the poverty from which Becky was clearly striving and straining upward.

Am I doing it right, Leila felt her asking through all the smiles and bright glances. Am I acceptable? Can you like me? Can I seduce you into approving of me? Becky was small. Her bones seemed as fine as those of a fish. This was the woman supposed to have beaten to death a husband described as six feet tall and an avid skier and golfer and squash player?

Leila could tell how Becky had gotten into trouble. She wanted too desperately to be liked, to be noticed. Becky was always remembering some new tidbit. There had been a man hanging around, sinister, shabby, a big tough-looking man. He kept loitering near the parking lot of the complex. Surely somebody else had run into him and would remember. In fact an old woman insisted she had seen him, but the description she gave was entirely different.

Becky remembered that, just a week before the murder, she had thought she had heard someone outside one evening. More and more details effloresced like plankton in the light of the TV moon. She was like a good student run amok, Leila thought, trying to pass the TV exam, saying whatever she thought would please in order to win notice.

The break in the case occurred when a seventeen-year-old from Barnstable named Gene Wiggins was traced as having sold the VCR and the TV to a pawnshop in New Bedford. His best friend Sam was a high school senior who knew Becky from community theater. Knew her very, very well. The friend's story was that Sam had passed on the stolen property to him. Becky had ordered Sam to sink it in the Sound, but Gene needed the money. He pawned the stuff in New Bedford.

Gene was quickly persuaded to cooperate with the police and offer evidence against Sam and Becky. Sam and Becky had beaten her husband to death. Becky had slipped out of work and met Sam. The juicy details of the Cape theater romance filled the papers and the news programs for a week. A twenty-five-year-old woman and a seventeen-year-old boy. BECKY SEDUCED KID LOVER TO MURDER said the *Boston Herald*.

By the time Leila had finished with the tapes and her clippings, she felt convinced that Becky was being railroaded. She was about to be convicted of having an affair with everybody's son, with breaking the patriarchal rules, with being flagrantly sexual—an affair, Leila thought sourly, no different from fifteen affairs that Nick was guilty of with three times the age gap. Becky denied the affair; she denied the murder. She claimed she had been happily married to the love of her life, and her only regret was that they had not yet had children. She presented herself as a dutiful and loving wife, whom others were slandering from jealousy, from spite. Becky did not doubt that Gene was the sliding-glass door burglar, and she was deeply shocked; she maintained he was trying for a deal by implicating his friend and herself.

The next morning, Leila tried straightforwardly to set up an appointment to see Becky at the Barnstable House of Correction. Her initial attempt met with refusal. Leila would have to find a way in. She was sorry she had taken on the story, but when Leila said she was doing something, she felt obliged to fulfill her promise. She had fought pitched battles with Nicolas about that habit.

People were always asking Nick to come to a party, a dinner, to read a script, to meet an aspiring actress, and he would never say No. He'd say Fine or I'll give it a try, and then forget the promise as if he had never made it. He was sure people would be offended if he refused their requests, preferring simply to forget and assuming the supplicant would do likewise. He would not believe her, when she argued that he got in far more trouble by saying Yes or Very Likely when he meant No, Never, Not on your life; but he was incapable of saying No to anyone except her and his son.

And girlfriends he was tired of. They too suddenly heard No often and firmly. When he was done with a relationship, he was done, and she had twice ended up in the disgusting position of having to deal with tearful ex-lovers who wept on the phone hysterically and begged her for reasons.

She had grown up determined to stand behind her word, whether it was I do or Of course I'll talk to your daughter for you or I'll try to find a home for your kittens. Her mother had scarcely been able to cover for Father, a Jew with a shameful problem. Her father gambled. When he was depressed, he played the horses. When he was happy, he played poker for big stakes. He played the numbers, just in case. He was always being hired in the accounting office of some small company, and then being let go because he would disappear. Once, so did some funds. He paid them back by selling the house. He was always convinced he was about to score big, he was about to hit the jackpot. His debts escalated and he died one night when his car was run off the highway. Leila had been thirteen.

Early Leila had learned she must take over. Phyllis worked as a nurse. Leila must make it all work, whether it was Shabbat or Thanksgiving or Debbie's birthday or supper on the table on a night when her mother came home from the hospital with her feet swollen and her back aching and everything was too much. Leila had to fill in and make things come out right. After her father died, she had assumed full adult responsibility—like David, with Nick off in L.A. or Houston. Leila aimed to be a good woman and a dependable human being. A guilty conscience was as bad as a toothache.

O Negative, Melanie had called her in teasing: O Negative. Can't take from hardly a soul, but the universal donor.

Now she must find a way to judge if what she saw in Becky was really there, a young naive woman who had talked herself into deep trouble. A woman punished for sexual boldness by being accused of violence. Leila consulted May, who advised her, "Talk to the family. Her family. His hates her. Her father's a fisherman in New Bedford." Where the VCR had been pawned—did that mean anything? "They were proud of their daughter, how she got an education, how she lived in a nice apartment. You get in with them and they'll tell Becky to see you. She was the first in her family to go to college."

Shana called her that evening. "I can't stand my father. My father says I have to go and live with him. It's the middle of my junior year!"

"Maybe your grandmother could stay on with you. I'm sure your father doesn't want to uproot you."

"Grandma? She's so old. She sucks on her dentures. My friends are here. I have such good friends, Leila, they really take care of me. Every night one of them comes over. They hold me when I cry about Mother. They understand. They know how special Mother was. The way you do. Daddy left her. How can I go and live with him?"

"Would your grandmother stay?"

"She embarrasses me in front of my friends. She butts in all the time, what she thinks. Aunt Leila, why can't I live with you?"

Her first reaction was panic. Then she realized she was always that way when anyone sprang something on her. Shana had just lost her mother. The divorce had been hard on her. And Melanie's long illness.

"Certainly we have plenty of room for you," she said carefully. "It's a big house. But would Mrs. Peretz and your father agree?"

"I'll make them agree," Shana said darkly.

She must show Shana she still had a home. "You're welcome here. With David away, you'll be wonderful company for me. But your father is the legal guardian, so we can only propose while he disposes."

Shana snorted. "I'm sure he'll be happy to dispose of me. I'd adore living there, I know I would. Nick is so great. He always talks to me as if I'm a real person, not How's school, that awful way adults talk down at you. Whenever he walks into a room, just everybody wants to talk to him."

At ten, Nick called. "Leila, is something wrong? I thought I'd hear from you after you got my note."

"I've been rather busy," she said wearily. She did not feel like talking with him. She was still too full of broken shards of anger, sharp edges and clots of blood. She realized that this was the fourth day since he had left and her whole world had changed. "Melanie died. Her funeral was Sunday. I assume you got my message." And didn't bother to call me until now.

"I was sorry to hear. I know it's been coming for a year, but the two of you were so close. How are you taking it? Are you very depressed?"

"I am. Shana may move in for the remainder of the school year."

"Move in? Where?"

"We have plenty of space. She can use the guest room."

"You asked her without consulting me?"

"You weren't here. Nick, her mother was my best friend. I promised Melanie. Besides, I like having young people around." So did Becky Burgess, a little mischievous voice in the back of Leila's mind spoke up.

"Actually, Shana is a treat and she'll be company for you, with David in California." Nick chuckled. "I'm an idiot. She'll bring some life into the house. I think it's a great idea."

He had switched so abruptly, she was almost dismayed. Instantly she remembered how he flirted with Shana, how Shana flirted with him. He would never lay a finger on Shana, but she shuddered at the image of endless dinners where Nick addressed his charm to the teenager. He did like young women. "Well, nothing's settled yet. It's just an idea."

"But a great one. Youth and energy, that's what we need. The daughter you never had, Leila. Someone for you to hang with when I'm out of town."

"You were calling to make sure I'm not arriving. As you can hear, I'm home and staying."

"Peony, I know you're depressed, but don't take it out on me. If you want to visit, if you want some time in New York, come ahead. I'm always delighted to see you."

Did she really want to quarrel with him, sending him to the arms of his young girlfriend? "Never mind, Nick, let's not quibble. I'll only come to New York if you need me. How are things going?"

He was silent for a moment. When he spoke next, his voice was thick and raw. "I hate New York. Every time you meet somebody, it's prick-measuring time. My success can pee farther than yours, nyah, nyah. I ran into Don Margolis. Remember him?"

"Of course." They'd all lived in the same old factory building cut into illegal and dank lofts. "How's Penny?"

"They split years ago. Anyhow, he's directing at the Public. Bastard held me up for fifteen minutes boasting, practically reading me his reviews."

He was wrought up with fury. He could go on for an hour if she didn't derail his anger. "But the play. How's it going?"

"Like a busted bag of groceries rolling down the steps. That's how it's going—downhill in pieces."

"But you always say before opening that nothing will work."

"This isn't the same thing. They're waiting to piss on me. They're waiting to dance on my grave. All those bastards who think they've made it are waiting for me to prove I don't have it, right in their faces. I've been a fool. I've made myself vulnerable to them. I should have stayed where I belong. Maybe I'm not good enough for the harsh glare of competition."

"What's giving you the most trouble?"

She listened with half an ear. By now she knew that he didn't really want her input into his directing. Her anger calmed as his voice flowed through her like good wine. It might be a false comfort, but she loved his voice.

She must find in Becky something of herself—not what she was in her own life, but a potentiality unexplored. The desire to bash in your husband's head, she thought, every woman can identify with that at least on the odd Monday and bad Friday. Actually why on earth would Becky do that? Why couldn't she just leave? Wouldn't she have got a divorce? Maybe she just couldn't let go of Terry—love/hate. Maybe Sam had committed the murder, and Becky was trying to shield her lover. Maybe the other kid, Gene, really was a burglar. Becky did not look the violent type. That seemed more of the bent of a couple of adolescent boys. Leila could imagine Becky telling any kind of tall tale, pretending to any imaginable skill or ability to garner attention and praise. She read in Becky's face and manner a hunger for visibility, for approval that was familiar to her, another desperately good student who had studied her way out of Strawberry Mansion in Philadelphia.

"I just don't know, Leila, I just don't know. I feel lost here. I feel as if everyone I knew has made it except me."

"But you have a good position in Boston, your own theater, the kind of part-time position that lets you direct anywhere in the country."

"Sometimes it all just feels like shit."

"Come home, then."

"Leila!" His voice changed abruptly, resonant, chiding her. "I've got an opening in two weeks. I'll beat some sense into them. Everybody loved the production in Boston. Hell, I'll be back there soon enough."

"It can't be too soon for me," she said. New York was driving him crazy. Once he was home with her, she could reach him, she could rebuild trust, reweave affection. In the meantime she would try to make fierce progress on the Becky story, so she could clear her desk when he arrived and concentrate on him. There was a lesion, but one that could still be healed.

CHAPTER 6

MARY

Mrs. Landsman's room was an uncommon mess that week, reflecting, Mary was sure, her inner condition. That was some bombshell her husband laid on her. Mary would have had him out the door, but Mrs. L. put up with a lot to stay married. How could Mary judge her harshly, considering what divorce meant to an older woman? Here she was, walking evidence, exhibit number one. Mrs. L. had some kind of job at a college, but this was an expensive house, and surely she didn't pay for it. It cost a fortune to heat, although they tended to keep it chilly. Luckily Mary had her body fat to keep her warm, and when she was cleaning, she was bustling around. In her young days in coal country, her family had kept a warm house. Winters here were hard to get used to, after so many years outside Washington. Even after ten years in Boston, she still thought they kept their houses too cold.

It was easier for her since the son was away. Every so often he would surprise her by appearing during the day, or he would be in his room fiddling with some project instead of being at school, where he belonged. Once when David was supposed to go away with his parents, Mary had planned to stay at the Landsmans'. She went there in mid-evening. The house was dark except for the lights upstairs and down they left on—bathroom and hall lights. Mary was always cautious and circled the house before going in. On a mild Saturday in May, the windows were open. She heard unmistakable signs of lovemaking from upstairs. It was their son, and him still in high school, with some girl in his bed. When Mrs. Landsman was all wound up making plans about him going off to college in California, Mary kept thinking that the girlfriend was going to turn up pregnant, but David was lucky and the roof didn't fall in on him.

Mary was glad when he left for college. He was one spoiled young man. Imagine staying home from a vacation with his family after his grandparents in Texas had been promised he would visit, then having some girl in. Mary doubted that his parents suspected what he was up to, him with his nose in a book or into his computer. He wasn't the sort of boy you'd expect to have a girl in his bed, but then, was Jim, her husband? She had thought she knew him, didn't she? Any man could find a willing woman, provided he kept looking. Every woman, like her daughter Cindy, thought infidelity was some other woman's problem, until one day she might just find it was hers.

David's room had always been hard to dust with a fancy computer he took with him to college, a laser printer, a weird laboratory set up on a library table all along one side of the room. Posters and models of spaceships. Lots of books, but nothing you'd want to read, textbooks of science and mathematics, paperbacks with robots and monsters on the lurid covers. He had pet hamsters for two years, but they died. For all of one summer the first year she cleaned this house, he had a nasty snake in a terrarium. Mary wouldn't go near it. She wouldn't touch anything on that side of the room. Mrs. Landsman tried to tell Mary how it was harmless and all, but Mary didn't see her kissing it either. David kept dirty comics under his bed, but Mary never mentioned them. Her son Jim, Jr., always called Jaime, used to keep girlie magazines in his closet. At least he didn't have girls in his room. He minded his business until he got to college, and then she couldn't keep an eye on him. Cindy she'd kept close watch on. Girls, you had to.

It took Mary the full day to clean. Usually the Landsman house was messy rather than dirty, but this week it was a sight. Mrs. L. was generally neat with her clothes, but the bottom of her closet was a foot deep in a foul mix of dirty laundry and things fallen off of hangers and left lying. There were pieces of paper all over the bedroom. It looked as if she had gone to bed with a pile of newspapers and torn them up for bedding.

No new notes. Mary guessed Mr. Landsman hadn't come back this week. Mrs. L. had been eating salmon out of cans and a frozen casserole she had put by. Mary viewed the state of her ladies' houses as an accurate barometer of what was going on in their lives, and it appeared Mrs. Landsman was a wreck.

It was a blow to Mary too, that tomcatting of Mr. L., and him telling Mrs. L. not to go to New York. Mary had been counting on a nice weekend here. None of Mary's clients were traveling, and no one had asked her to take care of their animals. It looked like a church basement or Logan.

The clippings pertained to that case of a little floozy from the Cape who had a boyfriend ten years younger than her and did in her poor husband. She wondered if Mrs. L. suspected her husband of planning to do away with her, for she wasn't the type to do anything violent. Even when they had a bat dart in and roost in the linen closet, Mrs. L. insisted on handling it without hurting the little flying rat. Mrs. L. carried it outside. Mary doubted Mrs. L. would hurt anyone, let alone her husband. In Mary's opinion, Mrs. L. was crazy about him. In many marriages, one person was the lover and the other the beloved, unless both reached a compromise—the best kind, until the hot wind of lust blew everything inside out. Anyhow, Mrs. L. adored him, and he permitted himself to be adored. Thinking of doing violence to someone who was hurting you could be soothing, in a minor way. She remembered daydreaming about poisoning Jim. Not that she ever would have, but toward the raw end of that marriage, now and then she did derive some relief from contemplating a dash of rat poison in the soup.

She wondered if Mr. Landsman would leave his wife for the actress in New York? Mary never told her ladies about her divorce, even when they were getting divorced themselves. She used to like staying at the Torgersons'. They traveled a great deal, and both sons were away at boarding school. In addition to cleaning their house, she had an agreement with them to walk and feed their poodle Winnie while they were traveling, for which they paid her eight dollars a day. They said Winnie was much better behaved when they got home after Mary had taken care of her. Mary simply lived there and gave Winnie lots of attention. Winnie was fond of Mary and slept with her at night. It was a perfect situation for everyone concerned. Mary walked Winnie twice a day and had her chase her chew-toy. Winnie was happy, the Torgersons were happy (at least about Mary and the dog) and Mary often had a comfortable roost for the night. It was a perfect setup for Mary, who enjoyed Winnie. The dog would put her head on Mary's knee and study her with big black eyes. They watched television together.

However, after the Torgersons divorced, they sold the house and

Winnie died six months later, of a broken heart, Mary thought. Try to explain divorce to children, let alone to animals. Mrs. Torgerson had her clean the house every time someone was scheduled to come and look at it, so she saw a great deal of her; the woman talked incessantly of her divorce. Mary listened sympathetically, and indeed pitied her, but she had a tough and aggressive lawyer. She wasn't the fool Mary had been, and the laws seemed better. Mary didn't think Mrs. T. would be on the streets soon.

Mostly Mary dreaded divorce in her ladies for purely selfish reasons: it disrupted the schedule of where she could stay. Then she had to make do with churches and other cold buildings, sitting in the dark and the chill eating leftovers from a paper bag and never able to bathe or keep herself up the way she must, in order to hold on to her cleaning work and survive.

Whenever she passed that woman who hung around Porter Square with her grocery cart, a woman about her own age, she shuddered. Sometimes Mary made eye contact. If Mary spoke to the woman, she muttered something. Obviously a greeting startled her. She didn't act crazy, just nonplussed, as if she was used to the same level of invisibility Mary relied upon. She didn't beg. She had her stuff in her cart. Mary thought, We have so few possessions that anything we add means subtracting something. I remember how people turned away from me when I had fallen onto the streets. How if they looked, they glared. An affront.

Even in the summer, this bag lady bundled up in layers of clothing, making her look heavy. Her face, though, was thin. Her hair was brown, turning grey. She had a pair of reading glasses she used for newspapers she picked up, but they weren't made for her. Men's glasses? Probably she found them.

Medical problems were what Mary dreaded most, next to being hurt on the streets. When Mary got sick, she had to find a place to hole up. Every so often she rented the cheapest motel room she could find—but often the cheap motels were out past public transportation. From her middle-class life, Mary kept only her MasterCard, which she rarely used but scraped together the money to pay the fee on, and her checking account that still stood at $609, because she hadn't been able to save the last couple of weeks. She held on to those two props of respectability, that meant she was not a bag lady, that she had not yet fallen out of society altogether. Renting a motel room stripped her bare, so that she didn't have food money. Those were the times Mary went hungry or dipped cautiously into the larders of her clients.

That woman who hung around Porter Square and the subway station was about four inches taller than Mary, with a limp on her left-leg side. Maybe her shoes didn't fit. Shoes wore out quickly when you had to walk as much as they both did. Used shoes at rummage sales and thrift shops were half-worn already, and cheap shoes went fast. Mary did not know where the woman slept, but it was somewhere nearby, for when Mary passed in the morning at eight-thirty, she was always about with her rusty cart. Mary could not help but wonder, whenever she saw the woman, if that was her future. That was why she forced herself to look at the woman, to speak to her—out of superstition more than courtesy. To let her know that someone remembered that she was human, that she was still a woman.

Friday evening, Mary blew seven dollars on supper at a Brookline cafeteria. There seemed to be less and less of them. She guessed that people just ate hamburgers and fries at the likes of McDonald's, but cafeterias had tremendous advantages. She could sit nursing a cup of coffee for hours. She could usually scavenge a little extra food. It was possible to make a kind of soup from hot water and condiments to supplement what she bought: mustard, ketchup, relish stirred into hot water or even cold, if necessary. Sugar water was another stratagem to control hunger. She always had several coffees in this place where you could get a free refill.

Cafeterias were for folks without money. She was not conspicuous, not at all. In the other seats were old men and old women just like herself, although probably most had homes. But she would not have been surprised if several turned out to be homeless. There was one woman who lived in her car, for Mary had seen her getting into a Ford Fairlane with bedding and clothes loose in the back. It must be wonderful to have a car, your home at your command. Just park it. It would get cold, and the insurance and gas and upkeep would be hard. But that was her fantasy, the goal of her savings. Then she would be like a snail, with her house always with her. She would never sleep in a garage or under a bush again.

She sat in the warm cafeteria as long as she dared. Then she walked through the cold to the Green Line, heading for Logan Airport. She had no place else to go tonight, and it was the first truly cold night of the year. She needed a heated place. It was too dangerous to risk spending the night in a garage or a car. When she was waiting just inside the doors of the subway station for the airport bus to come, the temperature was fifteen. It was a clear cold night with the stars burning holes in the frozen air, a cold that stung the skin and hurt her nose when she breathed.

Mary found a seat in the women's room of the U.S. Air Terminal, on a worn red plastic couch. She couldn't really lie down, for it wasn't long enough to accommodate even her short body. Mostly she just sat and watched people. She had the day's *Globe* and *Herald* that passengers had discarded, along with copies of *Vogue* and *Sports Illustrated.* The sports magazine was more interesting than the other, for at least it had photos of pleasant athletic young men who reminded her of her son. Sunday the Baers were going to California, if she could just get through tonight and tomorrow. She was exhausted after her day cleaning the Anzios'. It had not been an easy week. She had had only two good squats. She had to get through the weekend until Sunday afternoon, and it seemed interminable. She just wanted to lie down, pull up covers and sleep.

She slid Jaime's picture from her wallet. Precious few photos, worn but carefully kept. Jaime was an all-around athlete. She used to burst with adoration in the stands, and his father was always proud. Oh, she played ladies' tennis at the club courts with other married women, and Jim golfed with his peers every Saturday the weather permitted. But it was more social than athletic. They never understood how they had come to produce between them this tall boy who looked like a statue in a museum or a movie star.

Not that Jaime had a handsome face. He had his pug nose from her and his father's spadelike chin that stuck out a bit, but he had wonderful merry blue eyes and a great warm grin. They spent a fortune on his teeth and it showed in that grin that made her want to eat him up. Just to watch him move in the gym made her feel he could do anything, anything in the world. He could be president or run a company or be a sports star, and her heart would just swell up. He was on the student council too. In college he was in a fraternity, she couldn't remember the name. They all sounded the same to her, but it was a nice brick house.

It was a hard choice for Jaime, what sports to concentrate on, but in the end he went for football and swimming. He was tall like his father, but his father always had a belly and a slouch, and Jaime looked and walked like the all-around superb athlete he was.

She looked at her other photo of him, taken three years before with his second wife and their twins in Waikiki, where he ran a scuba gear and sports fishing shop. Jaime was still trim, for he worked out every day. His wife was darling-looking. Mary couldn't afford to go, and with his child support to pay and his new family to care for and business never as good as he'd like it to be, it was just impossible for him to fly her out. But every year they talked about it. He would get her fare together one of these years when his business took off as it was bound to do, and she would finally see Hawaii and meet his new wife and her grandchildren, the twins.

Then she took a quick peek at the photo of Cindy and her both on their horses from the stables in the park, astride side by side. Cindy was twelve, and the stable boy would pretend to think they were sisters.

Watching all the passengers as they came and went, she noticed a woman emptying her pocketbook on the ledge under the mirror. As she pawed through the contents of her purse, a lipstick rolled away. The woman did not notice. She found the eyeliner she was searching for, stuffed everything back in her purse except the wandering lipstick. As soon as she turned away from the mirror, Mary rose and put her own purse down on the lipstick. When she picked up her purse, she took the lipstick with it.

Makeup was important for her, but she could not afford to buy it. A woman wearing lipstick and foundation and powder was a respectable woman. She could not be homeless. She could not be a vagrant. Whenever Mary went through a department store, she tried out all the makeup samples she could and sprayed perfume on her clothes, so that they would retain the scent for a while. Perfume said *money*. Good perfume. Designer fragrances. But it was hard for her to get makeup regularly.

In the toilet stall, she examined the lipstick. It was only a little used. It would last quite a while. It was a nice ladylike pink shade, and beggars could not be choosers. Women often left combs and brushes in such places. She washed them carefully, then they were hers. But women never lost bottles or tubes of makeup. Sometimes she poured a little from one of her ladies' foundations into a plastic bottle.

When the attendant came to clean the bathroom, just after eleven, she gathered up her things and walked on briskly. She looked at the monitors. The hard time was the middle of the night, when planes seldom took off or landed. Usually she walked through the airport, seeking a delayed flight. A canceled one would do. Otherwise her pretense was that she was on standby and would be taking an early morning flight out. She was careful to read the monitors in every area and be able to say, I was standby on flight 462 to Chicago. Now I'm hoping to take the 6:50 flight.

Fortunately, in the International Terminal, there was a flight that had been delayed for hours. A storm out to sea? At any rate, there were clumps of disconsolate travelers sitting around, and she simply joined them. It was the least comfortable terminal, but she just wanted to get through the night inside. Logan was a potential problem, in that the subway stopped running at midnight, and she had to survive there, in one or another terminal, until morning. She was cut off from other options. This seemed to be a flight to Copenhagen. She had sat down at a table where the remains of a meal had not been cleared. She sat with it as if it were hers.

She noticed a guard watching her. The International Terminal had the most nervous personnel. They were always worried about hijackers or terrorists, although they didn't seem to do much about the threat. Was he really observing her? Cautiously she glanced around, trying to appear nonchalant. Yes, he was looking at her. Why? Had she done something silly? Was her situation showing? Didn't she look middle-class enough? Her heart was pounding and her hands left damp prints on the tabletop. The last thing she wanted was to be questioned by security. Why had he picked her out? Had he noticed her come in and sit? She rose casually and headed for the women's room. When she had waited there for five minutes, she came out, looked at her watch and quickly stepped on the escalator. She would use the next terminal. Her body felt weak from the adrenaline rush and she was troubled not to know why he had zeroed in on her. How had she failed to fit in? Her ability to remain invisible in groups was essential.

In the Delta-TWA Terminal, she slipped into a restroom near the now-quiet luggage carousels. The lights were off, and she left them off. She let herself doze in a chair. This was a long night, and obviously, she was not going to catch any real sleep. Mary had worked hard cleaning and she was exhausted. Now and again she slid into a queasy sleep. The room remained dark. About four-thirty she stirred and began to prepare for the day. She put on the light and began taking a cautious sponge bath with paper towels. She took off her coat, folding it carefully over her things. Then she undid one side of her blouse, washed that area, patted it dry with more towels, and proceeded to the other side. Washing by sectors was tedious and never satisfactory. She loved hot baths, when she could soak her aching body in complete immersion. Now the main thing was to stay clean, not to dirty or wet her clothes. To put herself together so that in spite of sleeping in her clothes, she would not look as if she had. In a toilet stall she changed carefully. She had three blouses, two skirts, a wool dress and a sweater, each rolled and held with rubber bands. She changed her cotton tights and her panties. She must wash clothes soon.

At the Baers', she should be able to do her laundry, soak in a hot bath, get a night's sleep. Today she would spend in a mall. She had a moment of dizziness as she reached for her coat. She was dangerously tired. She needed sleep and she needed rest. It was asking for trouble to get this tired. She might get sick, which could prove fatal. She could make some stupid mistake and ruin everything. She felt like weeping. She felt like lying down on the floor and just giving up. But she must not.

She had always prided herself on her fiber. She had always prided herself on coming through. While she had had a family, she had never failed to cook and clean and provide a good environment for them. She had never slackened attention on them and their friends and what they read and what they watched. She did not miss checking their drawers or under their beds. She did not relax her vigilance so long as they were living under the roof she had thought half hers. She had been a responsible parent, and if life were fair, someone would now take responsibility for helping her. But that was not the way things worked, and there was nothing to do but rest as best she could in the chair until she heard the cleaning people coming. In the meantime, in her bag she had a roll from supper, which she would eat now with water she took from the sink in the plastic cup she always carried with her. She was hungry, but she must watch her spending. If the cold snap lasted, she would have to spend the night in a motel. There was one in Dorchester she could get to by subway and a long hike that had what were considered bottom-end rates. She was going to have to stay warm and sleep inside. Therefore, she could not blow money on breakfast.

A couple of minutes after five-thirty, she left the restroom, turning out the light again behind her. The cleaning women would be coming by soon, and people would begin arriving in the airport for the earliest flights. She could again move around the terminals. She had noticed a 6:10 Delta flight, so she headed for that area. Sometimes she could go through to the gates and sit there. Other times, they were checking tickets at the X-ray machines, and she could not enter. It was always better to sit around near the gates, since in that area, there were almost always people snoozing or passing time, rumpled with traveling and bleary with lack of sleep.

Today they were checking tickets, so she turned away. She walked stiffly. Her carry-all and her bag felt heavy. The bag was not packed well. She had disturbed everything, changing in the restroom. It swung into her side as she walked. She saw an abandoned cart and put her stuff on it. It was a relief to push it for a while instead of carrying her things. Sometimes when she had a bad night and had to keep moving, her shoulders got so sore she felt like moaning aloud.

She could see through the glass doors that it must be bitter cold indeed, for the people rushing for early flights all had their heads tucked into their overcoat lapels and some of them winced against the cold. The exhaust of the buses and taxis beginning to queue outside lay on the street like mounds of dirty cotton batting.

Today must be got through and tonight. Then the Baers' and warmth. The Baers' and hot water. The Baers' and food. No malls really opened before ten, so she simply got on the airport bus and went to the old Eastern Terminal, now Continental, to pass more time. Too much of her life was spent doing nothing in places she did not belong.

CHAPTER 7

BECKY

Becky was majoring in communication arts. She hadn't been sure what it was, exactly, but she knew it had to do with media. Nothing was more exciting and nothing else offered a woman a fast trip out of New Bedj. She couldn't imagine spending eight years to become a doctor—she couldn't wait that long for a payoff, and neither could her family. They could squeeze out minimal support, but paying for college was hurting them. Her being in school meant that her mother couldn't get her teeth fixed, that her father couldn't make repairs on the boat. No, she needed something with a rapid return, where she could find a job, get off their backs and give a little in return. Then she would buy a dishwasher for Mama. Take Nana to a good doctor. Buy Gracie's kids fancy toys. It was up to her to make it, because nobody else would. Then they would fuss over her. She knew how it was in their community when someone made money and brought it back, didn't go off and pretend to be somebody else.

Of course she worked weekends. She tried waiting tables, but she was poor at it. She could not find the right banter to keep the men's hands off her in the grill and yet persuade them they wanted to leave big tips. She was too serious, everybody said, she didn't smile enough, but she didn't find hauling overloaded trays around something to beam about. Finally she got a job at the mall. She worked two evenings and weekends (Saturday ten to nine and Sunday twelve to six) at the Lady Grace lingerie store. She studied undergarments, because she was on commission and had to please the women, who ranged from the barely pubescent dragged in by their mothers for their training bras (a concept she had never heard of—training for what?) to women looking to dazzle and titillate boyfriends and husbands, to women who needed to fit into a too-tight dress. After a rocky beginning, her manager told her the fourth month that, as far as she was concerned, Becky could work full-time. Probably she would during the summer, unless she lined up something better.

So many of the kids she went to school with never seemed to think beyond the next date, but she was always figuring what was going to become of her. Her parents were sweet but hopeless. They'd been had by the bank and the credit companies and the government and the fish packer years and years ago. Everybody had sucked the juices and the strength out of them. Nobody cared what happened to them once you walked past the next house but one. Little people. Even their sweetness had a sour edge, like cream beginning to turn.

One thing she and Sylvie talked about incessantly was how to live, and how to get where they wanted to go. "I love my mama and papa, but I for sure don't want to live like them," Sylvie would say, beginning the discussion that had been going on for five years. "It's a mistake to have your first baby within a year of getting married. Yeah, we're not supposed to use birth control, but Father Corsetti, he doesn't have to get up in the night and change diapers and do a feeding. I think it kills the romance between a man and a woman to have a baby too soon."

Or Becky would say, "I love my parents and my nana, but I'd never have a big family. There's nothing left for the husband, and only rich people who have someone to do all the work can have a life with seven children demanding something every minute. I never got what I wanted, and who did?"

Becky worked hard in her classes. It was easy for her to prepare at school, where she could always find an empty classroom so she could concentrate and study. Since she was super-interested in media, she quickly became one of the top students. Twice she had a teacher who mistrusted her—who seemed to see through the eagerness to the hunger, the calculation underneath—but those were among the few older women. The men responded well to her. She rarely flirted. Mostly she just listened with a passionate, honed attention and gave them whatever they seemed to want. She wanted them to welcome her to what they were and to what they did. They felt her admiration as a stimulant. Most kids sat in class putting in their time.

Several instructors in communication arts taught only part-time, some only one course. One was a journalist who also ran a cable interview show; one worked at the PBS affiliate in Boston; one edited a string of giveaway local papers; one was a disc jockey for a Cape station. She was more attracted to television or cable than to newspapers or radio. She wanted to be seen or to be around people who were looked at. Newspapers were what her father and mother read. She associated them with her father lying on the couch with the seat cover rucked up under him holding the paper out at arm's length over his nose and yelling what the Red Sox had done and what the governor was going to do to them.

Her mother read the astrology column and the advice columns and all the gossip, as if she had ever in her life seen Madonna. Her mother loved newspapers. Becky hated shopping with Mama, because in the checkout line she would stand and read the *National Enquirer* and the *Sun* and cluck out loud over the woman who ate her baby and the television comedian sexually abused by saucer men.

No, she loved the clean tidy space of the evening news. Those people had never seen a roach or a brown rat. Those people had never had ringworm or scabies. Their underwear would be new and crisp as fresh lettuce. They would smell like expensive soap. Their nails would be clean and perfectly symmetrical. They would never belch or fart at the table. They did not drink Rolling Rock beer but champagne or Perrier. If they wanted something, they would not have to remember to say please, and their voices were like heavy silk.

In high school, boys had asked her out and she had gone, but she was tempted by none. Some she liked and some she disliked, but she behaved appropriately in what she and Sylvie called the Good Catholic Girl show. She went out with boys partly for status among her so-called peers, and partly to get out of the house. Sylvie and she double-dated when they could, but that did not always work out, as they had much more to say to each other than to any boy.

They attended Southeastern Massachusetts University together. Sylvie was taking a computer course. Sylvie had a seven-year-old Ford Escort her aunt Marie had given her, so they drove to school and back together. Sylvie subscribed to *Cosmopolitan* and passed on the issues to Becky, so they could discuss the articles that seemed to bear upon their lives and, more importantly, their dreams, their plans. Meeting a man she could really get interested in seemed as remote as being on TV at six every night. "A professional man," Sylvie said. "Suave and gentle. A man you can trust and open up with, the way you can't with these losers."

"A man who could teach you a better way to live. A man who knows how to dress, how to talk to people." Becky's voice softened and she leaned against the door of the Escort as if it were a shoulder offering comfort and support. "A man who could see who you wanted to be and help you become that! A man who respected you."

But in their junior year, Sylvie fell in love with a complete jerk. He was Italian, like Sylvie, and he used to come into the bowling alley and grill. He was four years older than Sylvie and worked in his father's Toyota dealership. His name was Mario and Sylvie kept saying how tall he was, which was true, and how handsome he was, which was ridiculous. He had a nose you could open bottles with. You could see where he had had acne, leaving volcanic craters. Becky could not tell when he was laughing and when he was choking to death. After Sylvie got serious about Mario, she still picked Becky up to drive to school and waited for her afterward, but their wonderful study times and long, long conversations about life and the future and what was truly desirable and tasteful, those precious moments when Becky was not lonely, ended abruptly.

She went out with boys from her classes and she even persuaded herself briefly she was interested in one, Bobby, but he turned out to have a drinking problem after she had already got involved, so she got uninvolved. She had seen too much drinking already. She didn't find guzzling beer the least bit romantic. She seldom found any of these actual or potential boyfriends truly stimulating, except in odd moments, maybe at the beach with the sun setting, sometimes driving down the highway with the roof down in one's convertible or sometimes dancing. Then she would feel herself to be truly alive. With the music turned loud and the roof down and the wind ruffling her hair, she felt like someone in a movie, the way it ought to be. She remembered how once she and Sylvie had been double-dating two lame dudes who had borrowed somebody's four-wheel-drive car for an afternoon's picnic—takeout from McDonald's and a case of beer. They were lurching along a sand road dodging branches. After the first time they stopped and the girls refused to do anything physical with them, the two guys sat in front together, leaving Sylvie and Becky to the narrow bumpy backseat. Sylvie said something then that Becky had always remembered. "You know, if this was a movie and there was a score playing, think how great it would look. I saw a movie once where some woman was shopping in a supermarket and this jazzy music was doing *dum DUM dum DUM DUM* till you felt like she was dancing, but I sat back and said, Whoa, baby, I do that every week and it's no damn fun at all. Music makes it feel like something."

Becky had thought Sylvie's remark an amazingly profound statement. Anything went down better with music. When she had had sex with Bobby, the boy who turned out to have the drinking problem, she had found it went much better if they played something sultry during it, so that it became almost a kind of dance. That made it less tacky.

What she learned quickly from the boys she dated in college was that her parents were as crazy as she thought when they called themselves middle-class. They said, when the issue arose, especially her father, "We're as middle-class as anybody else. We own our own home. We even got the mortgage paid off, which is more than a lot of those yuppies in their new developments can say. I own my boat and I make my payments regular. We always have a car. We always have a truck. We got a TV and a VCR and you're going to college. We done okay for ourselves, and don't you forget it."

She tried to avoid having her dates come to the house to pick her up. She suggested going out from school or meeting them someplace, but inevitably they had to bring her home. She could tell the moment her date saw the family home that she dropped in status several degrees, sinking, sinking, sunk. He became more sexually aggressive, as if because she lived in a sagging wooden house with rusting car hulks in the yard, she had to put out. If a boy didn't treat her with respect, he wasn't going to get a thing off her. That was her rule and she never broke it.

In January, an instructor she had had the fall before began putting himself in her path. He read the local news on a radio station in Providence. She had enjoyed his class, although she was more interested in television news. Nobody was teaching that, however, so she took what she could. Except for the stars who ran talk shows, nobody impressed her more than anchormen. They were the face of the day. They told people in the morning what was to come, and in the evening they explained the world. They were a habit for everybody who watched them, glamorous and familial at once, like Sylvie's aunt Marie.

She had heard Ted Topper's voice many mornings over the car radio. In his class the first day, she had been pleased that, for once, he looked like his voice. So many radio people were really gross when she saw them face to face. He was six feet two, lean and bearded. He stooped a little more than he should have and had an odd shuffling walk, but he dressed conservatively and well. He had an easy honied voice that slid into the ear and made everything seem all right, even if he was describing a six-car pileup on I-95 or a fire that had wiped out a family. His manner in person was soothing too. He seemed relaxed in front of the class, perched on the edge of his desk with his hands in the pockets of his natty blazer, chatting as if to friends of his years in the business. He told funny stories about power failures, hurricanes, snowstorms, celebrity shenanigans, politicians screwing up. She felt invited into the confidence of those who truly knew.

She took his course in the fall, and in the winter, as soon as she was no longer his student, he put himself in her path. He called her into his office and suggested they have a chat about her future in radio. She was too desperate for kind attention from somebody who was almost a celebrity to tell him she had little interest in radio. Better radio than Lady Grace or the grill where Sylvie worked. She realized quickly that he was more interested in her than in her potential as a broadcast journalist. When he asked her out to supper, she was not surprised, but she was mortified about having to ask him for a ride to the mall, sandwiching supper in between classes and the job she did not dare skip out on. Her manager might like her at Lady Grace and she might have a few repeat customers, but she was immediately replaceable.

She was thrilled to go out with Ted, although she had a certain amount of trouble remembering not to call him Mr. Topper. It seemed somehow disrespectful to call him by his first name, since he had been her teacher, but after he kissed her, it felt more natural to say "Ted." It was hard to fit seeing him into her schedule, since he lived twenty minutes the other side of the school, and she was without a car. He seemed very understanding about picking her up somewhere other than her house, and he was tolerant of her ridiculous hours.

The whole tone of the relationship acted on her nerves, waking her sensually. She loved eating in swanky little half-lit restaurants. He especially liked country places where it was quiet and they could really talk. He liked to discuss his work. She knew she had little to offer in return, but she tried hard to respond intelligently to his stories, and that seemed to satisfy him. "Dr. Allen, he does that call-in medical segment. Did you hear him this morning? He had an old lady on who wanted to go on about her hemorrhoids and her bowels. I had to cut them off. I couldn't eat the rest of my doughnut."

"What some people will say in front of thousands of others is really embarrassing. But you were wonderful this morning, Ted," she told him. Of course now when Sylvie drove her to school, they listened religiously in silence, except for making small comments. Sylvie admired him too, loyally. "When you read the headlines, you always make it sound so dignified and yet important too, even when there's hardly any news at all."

"Did you hear my goof this morning? I pronounced the capital of Afghanistan wrong."

"Ted, who knows and who cares? How many people can tell you the capital of New Hampshire, and that's the next state?"

"You really think it slid by?"

"Absolutely. I never noticed it. Will two people even know?"

"But those two people will write in, and the station will think I'm incompetent. There's always guys in the wings waiting to take over."

"Nobody has your voice or your presence. You make people feel good."

When she went back to his apartment with him after the fifth supper, she knew she was going to have sex with him. He was a mature man. She could not pull her Good Catholic Girl act. She had eaten all those expensive meals. At supper she had drunk her share of the wine tonight. She was going to let him do it to her.

But the experience was utterly different. It felt pleasant to lie kissing in his king-sized bed with lovely plaid sheets. Everything was clean and sweet-smelling, including him. He said it was bay rum aftershave. Soft music played. The lights were low and modest. He had a condo in a made-over textile mill. He said it had a water view, of a tidal river, but of course it was dark. He was not in a hurry. She had never been with a man who was leisurely, who touched her as if he knew exactly what he was doing. The second evening they made love in his bed, she had an orgasm. She didn't know at first what was happening. She cried out, then felt embarrassed. When he realized the experience was new to her, he was amused. He teased her, asking her if she liked it well enough to want to do it again, saying that now she would be insatiable.

It was the first affair she had ever had, not counting the aborted mess with Bobby the drunk. Even if they could only see each other

Sunday, Tuesday and Wednesday evenings, he was very understanding and usually they got together twice a week. She could not spend the night at his small but luxurious apartment, but he seemed to accept that also. She was grateful that he did not insist she see him more than she could, and that he accepted the strictures imposed by her living at home—that her family must never guess she was having sex with him. He was far more understanding than the boys her own age she had dated. He seemed determined to watch out for her reputation, and that made her feel he truly cared for her. She felt cherished, as she had always wanted to be; he did not push her, he did not try to make her give what she couldn't. A mature man, a real man, she told herself, had patience those adolescents she had been with before simply could not imagine offering a woman.

She was happier than she had been since she was a very little girl. Maybe since Laurie, the youngest, had been born, replacing her. Her life had truly begun. She had found a man to fit her dreams.

CHAPTER 8

LEILA

Leila had plenty of experience doing interviews. She established her ground rules. Offer only enough of yourself to make the subjects feel you are open. Be sympathetic, always. Appear to be on their side, but make no promises. Never forget what you want to find out, but let them talk about what they want enough of the time so that they don't feel as if you are using them. Take whatever they offer of food or drink, but if nothing is offered, never ask for more than water. Always use the bathroom, even if you don't need to, because much is revealed by a family bathroom.

She drove through New Bedford streets lined flush with three- and four-story frame houses that filled their lots but for a cupcake-sized yard. The stains of industrial-strength air had etched the wood. The Souzas lived in the North End, where the houses were smaller and farther apart, with real backyards and gardens. They had taken over a vacant lot, so there was room for rubbish and old cars in this corner lot, a chicken house in back. Where several of the houses down the block had Virgin Marys in the yard, this one had a small patch of red chrysanthemums still bravely showing blooms withered in the recent cold snap.

The living room of the Souza house was worn and dowdy but bursting with life. Somebody had little children. Snapshots of family members stood on every flat surface. Obviously they did not read much—she did not see a magazine in the house, let alone a book—but toys were everywhere and half-completed projects, somebody's jigsaw puzzle, a coat being hemmed, a chair upended to be reglued. They all looked on the small side, weathered, seamed by life and hard winds blowing untempered to them. They tended to talk at once, the husband, the wife, the teenager they called Laurie, the oldest daughter Gracie who had a little girl. All were fiercely loyal to Becky and all were furious at the newspapers and the TV. They served her homemade brownies and strong coffee.

Mrs. Souza was a square intense woman with slightly popping blue eyes. She kept saying that Becky was a good girl, a loving daughter who had never fooled around but worked hard. *His* family had thought she wasn't good enough, when she was all too good for him. Other Souza family members came in and stood around, generally not sitting but hovering. A swarthy man who resembled the father stood with his arms folded, glowering over his mustache. Tommy, he was introduced. "Tommy has his own boat now." The father was dark, with almost black hair and snapping eyes, skin darkened and roughened by the sea. The mother was fair, and all the children took after one or the other absolutely, as if the genes could not mix. Mrs. Souza said, proudly or defiantly, Leila could not tell, that unlike her husband, she was not Portuguese but French-Canadian.

They all wanted to talk about Becky, stories about how she created a video memorial to a brother who had died at sea. They showed that to her. She extracted little from it, except a sense of how proud they all were that it existed. Mrs. Souza showed her photographs of Becky graduating from grade school, middle school and a local college. Always Becky was smiling a huge white smile, while in each picture her hair was blonder and she was thinner.

"You have to go see where they lived," Gracie said. "At first they lived over a dry cleaner's in Hyannis, but then they bought the condo near the water in Falmouth. Becky fixed it up just lovely. She did that kind of thing."

"It wasn't a house, but it was nice," Mrs. Souza said, shaking her head. "We kept hoping they'd start a family. But then he lost his job, and he never got another one. Never. Months and months went by."

Becky's father made a batting-away motion with his hand. "I offered to bring him in on the boat, but he wasn't interested. He thought he was too good to take to the sea for his living. He'd rather sit on his behind than do an honest day's work he thought beneath him. He believed the sun rose and set on his parents, but they never got him a job."

From the bathroom she learned there were many males in the family who aimed at the toilet and missed, there was still a baby in diapers, and she would use a convenient McDonald's on her way to her next interview instead.

It was Saturday afternoon. Leila headed east on I-195, musing that neither Becky nor she herself came from money. She had grown up in what men she had gone out with in college had freely referred to as a slum, although to her it had just been the neighborhood. Her early childhood had passed in a single family dwelling in Cherry Hill, New Jersey, but by the time she was halfway through grade school, her father had begun the downward slide that carried them all far and fast till they came to rest on what her mother Phyllis's earnings could provide: a two-bedroom apartment in mostly Black Strawberry Mansion in Philly.

How could she compare those streets and alleys, the liveliness and the danger, the gangs and the music that beat always as a background day and night but louder on mild days when the windows were open, to the bleak poverty of New Bedj, as the locals called it? In some ways the Souzas were much more comfortable, with their chickens and garden in the yard, than her family had been, and much safer. But they had less alternatives available, less views outward. She had taken a bus to the museum. She had had the public library with its thousands of volumes to draw her out of her life. Movies, foreign as well as domestic, were just a walk or a bus ride away. She had looked out the windows of their flat not into the dark alley echoing with family quarrels and drunken clashes, but beyond to Paris and Xanadu and London and New York and the eighteenth century and the Attic experience. She had learned early that there were options upon options if she could only escape, if she could only find the road out, which she realized by the tenth grade led through college. Books had been her drug; books had saved her.

She drove to Falmouth, to a shingled two-story condo built around a courtyard, with parking behind the building. It was in an area with many year-round houses and a number of summer cottages. There Becky and Terrence Burgess had lived for the last year and two months of their marriage. It was like a hundred other similar complexes thrown up in the middle and late eighties, vaguely New England in inspiration with imitation miniature cupolas on top.

The condo sat on a hill three-tenths of a mile from a beach, close enough to Buzzards Bay for the air to smell fresh and damp. The condo had been young but not new when the Burgesses moved in, she guessed, time for the drab landscaping of yews and barberries to take root, the little trees to cease looking like green lollipops. Time enough too for the decks to begin to sag, paths to be worn across the skimpy grass, plastic to start cracking and aluminum to warp out of shape, the trim to cry for paint it was not getting.

She found Helen Coreggio, as she had hoped. Mrs. Coreggio was living on social security and a pension, alone in the condo immediately below the one Becky and Terrence had owned. "Oh, it's empty now. It has to stay empty till after the trial. But you know, she didn't do it. I don't believe any of it. Down, Florrie, down! She was always fond of my Florrie. On cold mornings, she'd take Florrie for a walk for me. Becky was truly kind."

Helen Coreggio was a pencil-thin woman who had probably had a stroke, as her face was slightly distorted, the left eye in a permanent half-wink, but she could talk perfectly. She talked fast, showing Leila photos of grandchildren and her husband, who had passed on of a heart attack. A large shaggy fluffy-tailed black and white dog sat beside Mrs. Coreggio's overstuffed chair and punctuated the conversation with a sharp bark from time to time, as if disagreeing. The dog looked even bigger sitting than it had standing. It looked Leila in the eye as she sat on the low listless couch, her knees stuck up before her like a child's drawing of mountains. Great Dane, maybe, mated with something really hairy. It followed the conversation, turning its great head.

Mrs. Coreggio served instant coffee and Sara Lee pound cake. Leila did her best to consume enough of each to pass muster.

"Of course she shouldn't have been having an affair with that boy, if she really did. People will repeat any filth about a good-looking woman, you should know that. Becky is little and too skinny, but she's cute, with those big eyes and that blond hair. She's darling, you'll see. Her husband wasn't good enough for her, I don't care what his family thought. Becky came from nothing, but she made something of herself through hard, hard work, and I respect that. Her husband came from a comfortable home and was content to lie around all day watching the soaps with his TV turned too loud. Now, I don't watch the soaps myself, you understand? Do you watch them? Of course you don't get in the habit when you work, and I worked every day of my life except when the children were little. I worked and my husband worked and my children helped around the house, and never one of them got in a day's trouble. I watch the news every night, and I like the game shows, where they ask questions and you can see what you know. There was this grown lummox watching all that made-up silliness day after day."

When Mrs. Coreggio talked about Terrence Burgess, her mouth pursed. His name was vinegar on her tongue. She spat him out. When she mentioned Becky, she smiled. She smiled and the dog thumped his tail. Becky might be lynched in the media, but she was popular here. "She was a good girl. Whenever she could, she would even run home at noon to make sure he had a hot lunch. What woman acts like that nowadays? She worked all week, on the weekend she did laundry and cleaned, while that useless big sausage lay around watching soaps and sports. I'm sure when she married him, it seemed like a dream. He worked with computers, a job with a future, ho ho. She was crazy about him. But after a while she saw through him, how if it didn't come easy, he wouldn't go after it. He wanted life handed to him like his lunch, that was for sure." Mrs. Coreggio shook her head sadly and heavily. Her good eye held Leila's gaze. "She was trying to make the best of a bad bargain. You wouldn't expect a live wire like her, a young pretty girl, to take any interest in an old woman. Young people nowadays generally detest us. They think we should all die the day after we retire. But not Becky. We were friends."

Leila had trouble disengaging herself from Mrs. Coreggio, but she had the distinct feeling it would not be wise to explain she was due at the older Burgess household. What she did was insist she had to get home to make supper for her husband and her son, and it would be an hour-and-a-half drive.

The Burgess house was in Osterville, only ten miles away. Their house was on a marsh, tawny now in November, on a cul-de-sac after a sprinkling of large modern houses set well back on spacious lots. It was a low long house, a ranch gone sprawling, with well-weathered cedar shingles, enough expanses of decking to hold a large party, the lawn well kept, the foundation plantings trimmed, the little azaleas mulched with pine bark, a holly tree placed symmetrically on either side of the front walk.

She was met at the door and ushered to what must be the formal living room, for the doors of the television were shut and the carpeting was white and spotless. Everything in the room was white or blue. The dried flowers had been purchased dyed blue, although the marshes outside were full of naturally dried grasses. From below came the throb of heavy metal. That was probably the younger brother, Chris, mentioned in the papers.

Mr. Burgess did the talking, while his wife sat upright on a colonial wing chair that matched the couch and wrung her hands. He was a big man, his skin tight on his flesh, as if he had recently gained weight or swelled. "There's nothing to write a book about, nothing to say. That little tramp killed our son. If there was justice, she'd hang for it. As it is, she'll spend the rest of her miserable life in prison, where she belongs."

Mrs. Burgess nodded her head fervently. "Stay calm, Francis, stay calm. Justice will be done."

"But, don't you think it's important that someone objective write about what happened? Wouldn't your son want the real story known? The full human truth never comes out in court. Think of it as a memorial to him."

"We remember him perfectly well. Our family doesn't need a memorial from any outsider. I'm sure you're well intentioned and you want to make a buck, but you can't help us. It won't bring Terry back." Mr. Burgess glared at her.

Mrs. Burgess was watching her husband rather than Leila. "Don't get overwrought, Francis." She turned quickly to Leila. "There's really nothing to be said. Nothing."

"Her defense is bound to present her as sympathetically as possible. I haven't spoken with her. I want to understand your point of view first." Leila rose and admired a studio portrait of Terrence, whose face she recognized from the newspapers. "He was a handsome young man." Actually he was. In spite of Mrs. Coreggio's description of him as a sausage, he appeared tall, lean and good-looking in an unformed way.

Mrs. Burgess came to life. "Wasn't he? He was always the handsome one. He always made friends. Why, the boys in his fraternity in college used to come and see him all the time. When he made a friend, he kept that friend. And he and his brother were close—not like a lot of boys who are at each other's throats. No, they were what brothers are supposed to be, and we were always so proud of them."

But they viewed her with distrust. She had to be careful. She would start out sympathetic to Becky, because the Souzas had been kind and open with her, and down on the victim, because his family was self-righteous and stiffed her. They served nothing. The room was immaculate, with an odor of furniture polish. Even the bathroom gave her little, for when she asked, she was ushered to a guest bathroom nearby. It was small and also blue and white. She wiped her hands gingerly on the tiny embroidered towel, feeling as if she were using someone's scarf. They must not entertain often. Although the room was clean enough to roll about on the tiny floor, if she were so inclined, the guest soaps in the form of blue roses were slightly dusty. Obviously it never occurred to whoever cleaned this superfluous room to dust the soap.

"If you do decide to talk about your son, I'd be glad to return," she said and handed Mrs. Burgess a card.

Mrs. Burgess handed it to her husband, who took out his reading glasses and peered at it suspiciously. LEILA LANDSMAN, Jew and Snake Oil Peddler. Friend of the Corrupt Media. Don't call me, I'll put a tap on you.

She had had enough. She would wait a few days—of necessity, because she must put some genuine effort into her classes and her students and make sure her assistant was finishing the incest bibliography. Then she would attempt once again to see Becky Burgess.

Driving back, she felt a little guilty. She enjoyed interviewing too much. It was a license to tromp through other people's lives. One of the cheap pleasures her parents had when she was little was to visit houses advertised for sale in the Sunday paper. They couldn't afford to buy. It was simply fun for them to see how other people lived. Her father would get ideas for cabinets to build and her mother would decide to redecorate the kitchen. They would gossip about the people, imagining their lives. It was always an intimate evening after the Sunday strolls through opened houses. Her parents would joke a lot and then go to bed early. It was only as an adult she realized they must have made love. Instead she noticed they always turned on the radio in their bedroom Sunday when they retired. She forgot sometimes that there had been a time when they had been loving with each other, when they had seemed happy. Before her father had lost control and thrown their money away.

She too liked to visit other people's scenes. She was endlessly curious. Often she irritated Nick with her chatter about colleagues or neighbors. Oh, Nick liked the results well enough. He did not pay enough attention to what was going on with people. His eye was on his own goal, the work he was creating, the spectacle, the pacing, the style of the performance. He would ask her to explain people to him, he would ask her to tell him why an actor was angry or what Old Simmons, his departmental chair, wanted.

Then she felt valued by him and she worked hard to figure out what he needed to know, bringing all her powers of observation and analysis to bear, wifely Holmes to the detective task. She was a nosy person, one who would never tire of learning about her fellow humans. Women's lives particularly were lived often in a kind of shadow of inattention, and there were hidden dramas to uncover, a perspective that could be shocking or engaging by turns. That was her job perhaps in a sentence: making obvious to people what had been invisible to them before. One of the most interesting discoveries of the day was that probably Helen Coreggio was telling the truth, and there had been a most unlikely friendship between the two women. That made Becky more interesting.

She experienced a sharp drop in energy as she walked into her house, dark except for the hall light she left on. She hung her coat, turned on lights, closed draperies and thermal blinds, turned up the heat to sixty-eight, walked into the kitchen and found herself so depressed she sank in a kitchen chair and sat for half an hour, unmoving. She was not hungry, because of the brownies she had eaten at the Souzas and the Sara Lee pound cake at Helen Coreggio's, but she felt a strong desire for real food, a sit-down dinner face to face with family, companionship. Something warm.

Maybe it would be good to have Shana move in. However, Mrs. Peretz was still living in Melanie's house and, when she had brought up the matter with them, it had been awkward.

It was Saturday night, and where was her life? When Nick was on the road, she would have spent Saturday with Melanie. They would have rented a movie or gone out to one, a play, a concert, supper with other women friends or just the two of them eating Chinese and talking, endlessly talking. That was why she had never felt desolate when Nicolas was off directing a play in San Francisco or Seattle. Moreover, she had also had David.

Cambridge was an easy city in which to stay home or relax with friends. Except for Harvard Square, it did not exactly pulsate with singles life like New York or San Francisco on a Saturday night. The streets did not ask her, where are you going and why aren't you getting laid and don't you want someone to love you right now, or at least someone to pay some attention?

Perhaps she was jolliest when she was focused on some other woman's troubles and decisions, and her own life diplomatically retreated. That made her feel second rate. A human being should not be happiest when thinking about other people, should she? But she felt better after her three interviews—even though the last one had been as total a failure in communication as she had ever undergone—than she had felt since Melanie's death and that bombshell letter from Nick.

She had to forgive him, of course, but she could not quite get around to it yet. She still was too angry, too hurt. What he had done was a great jagged lump that had not shrunk or softened during the past week. She could not even imagine to whom she could pour out her anger. She had said too much to her son already. Jane was too hostile to Nick to fill in for Melanie. No, it was best to try to keep her mind off him and to stay busy with school and with prowling around the life and times of Becky Burgess, the hardworking and apparently quite domestic murderer. Soon Nick would be home, and they would have to renegotiate their marriage, gradually, conversation by conversation. They had come back from separation and his infidelity perhaps fifteen times. They could do it again. They would.

In the meantime she needed some warmth and companionship, and she must buy it. Men bought prostitutes; women got pets. A cat or a dog? She traveled too much for a dog. She hit the lecture circuit often. No, a cat. There would be no problem getting someone to feed it when she traveled. She remembered that her cleaning lady had told her she also ran a pet-feeding service.

Tomorrow she would go out and buy herself companionship. Then when she came home, at least there would be some creature happy to see her.

She nodded her head briskly, glad she had settled something, anything. She opened a can of sardines and threw together a salad from what was left in the crisper. Then she made herself get back in the car and drive to Harvard Square. She would go to one of the big record stores, Tower or HMV, and look at CDs. She should listen to music more. That should take her out of herself. Both stores were open late. After all, Becky Burgess would not be having a jovial and social Saturday evening either. She should be glad for her freedom and her comfort. She had a paid-off house, a good job, a loving son, and an interesting project. Even if she was furious with her husband and he was in New York doing a version of *Oedipus* as South American dictator with Jocasta cum Eva Perón and a rap chorus—a production that had given her a headache—and screwing Jocasta, nevertheless a professional woman with a circle of friends always had other options. If she felt lonely, it must be her own fault. Still, she thought suddenly, a twenty-four-year-old Jocasta rather blew the point of the play, didn't it? Even when producing *Oedipus*, he couldn't imagine a man in love with an older woman.

CHAPTER 9

BECKY

Becky continued seeing Ted all through the winter. The first warm day, a Tuesday in late March, they strolled along a beach near his house, before they went to dinner. He remained patient with her absurd schedule, saying that he understood how working and going to college ate up her time, and that it was very, very important that she stay in school. He never pressed her to spend the night. He too came from a Catholic family. "I can very well imagine the response of your parents. Why should we cause them unnecessary pain? I have to get up fiendishly early anyhow. I'd be gone when you awaken."

She appreciated his understanding. It showed that he cared for her as much as she cared for him. It showed he worried about her well-being, not just what he could get out of her. All that was precious.

He even bought her a beautiful silk scarf and a pair of blue earrings in the form of flowers. He said they were cloisonné, a beautiful word she said over to herself whenever she put them on. His voice moved her far more than his face. He spoke with an exciting precision, his tongue caressing the words, with perfect grammar and crisp inflection. She loved to hear him say her name. She practiced saying words the way he did. She longed to sound educated, so that he would not be ashamed of her. Sylvie teased her about the new words she was using.

She hoped that someday Ted would marry her. When she was standing around the mall waiting for a customer, when she was sitting in a boring lecture, she imagined her life with him once she had her degree and they married. She saw herself laying a beautiful table for him with a perfect rose from the florist beside his plate. She was wearing a fancy long dress and greeting his friends from the station who had come to cocktails, to dinner on the deck. They were rushing off to summer on the Vineyard, where they would spend weekends with his friends who knew everybody there was to know around Providence and even in Boston.

He went to work extremely early, leaving home at five A.M. He took a nap after he got back in the afternoon, or he said, he would not have any evening life at all. She wanted to know everything about him, but she was too polite and too much in awe of him to ask unsuitable questions. She tried to notice everything about him, from the leather bedroom slippers he put on after they made love to the peanut butter (date and peanut, from some health food store) he put on crackers for a snack, not the Jiffy she had grown up with. Everything about him was superior. She listened to his program religiously—in the full meaning of the word. Not only did she listen compulsively and regularly, but she dwelt on every inflection of his rich voice. She studied his pronunciation and intonation. He was her standard of excellence.

"How did you like the little joke I made this morning about all the rain?"

"It's wonderful when you loosen up that way suddenly. It's unexpected and warm. You know how to speak to your listeners." She felt he valued her criticism, her feedback.

She saved up comments from one date to the next. She wanted him to know how much she appreciated him. She thought of all those people listening to him every morning, and she wanted to tell them all that he was her boyfriend. Her fiancé. Boyfriend was such a silly word. He was not a boy, fortunately.

She was happy, terribly happy. Evenings she did not see him, she traveled back to New Bedford with Sylvie, who now wore a large engagement ring. Every weekday morning Sylvie still picked her up. Sylvie was the only person who knew about the affair, but then she was the only one who was aware that Mario and Sylvie were doing it too. They talked at each other about their boyfriends, generously allowing the other equal time.

"He's so solicitous." She said the word carefully. It was a new word she had learned from him, and it sounded sexy to her even as she said it, all those *s*'s, like his dressing gown sliding over his body. "He's always absolutely careful to get me to Lady Grace or home at the time I'm supposed to be there. Never once has he made me late—not once, Sylvie. That's what I call a responsible man."

She would have continued that way through her whole senior year, except that spring vacation came in mid-April. She did not have to go to school and she was working the same hours. She imagined they would have more time to spend together. He said it was a very busy week for him. Very busy. She began to realize painfully that he saw as much of her as he cared to, that their extremely limited schedule suited him fine: why?

After the second argument, she enlisted Sylvie. Sylvie agreed to spend Monday night with her watching his apartment. He did not know Sylvie's car. Sylvie lent her a jacket with a hood to hide her face. They brought a supply of tapes and a pizza and waited. Becky felt like an idiot. Probably he really was busy. He said he did a lot of civic work. However, they had not even waited two hours when he drove up with a woman and they went up to his apartment. They did not come down, although Sylvie and Becky waited as long as they dared. The lights went out up there.

The woman was not young, perhaps thirty, with short brown hair. She wore a trench coat that night, with a flash of black dress under it.

Sunday night, she confronted Ted. She did not say she had spied on him but that a friend of hers had seen him with this other woman several times. She described the woman. At first Ted denied it categorically. "Your friend is crazy. I don't know who he's talking about. I have a lot of friends and acquaintances. Half of them have brown hair. What does that mean?"

Finally he grew annoyed. They were eating in a fish restaurant near Newport. He put his knife and fork down on his plate and frowned. "Did you really expect that you would be the only woman I'd be seeing? A school girl who can only come out for a couple of hours twice a week? That's ridiculous."

"But it's only till I graduate! I thought you loved me. I thought you really cared about me."

"I've enjoyed spending time with you, but we really aren't well matched—surely you realize that. Nadine is a professional woman. She's a successful agent for my condo and dozens of others. I'm still in the process of getting a divorce, but when it's over, probably we'll marry. Who knows? I've enjoyed teaching you about the world. You'd never been in a decent restaurant till I took you to one. I haven't made you any promises, and I find your attitude demanding. I've been kind to you. I've taught you how to behave. I owe you nothing. Now I'll take you home."

She wept all night, silently, lest her sister Laurie hear her. She explained the rupture to her family very simply by saying he began to press her to sleep with him, so she had broken it off. Sylvie she told the full story on the way to school Monday. Sylvie was furious at him, cursed him out. They were both late to class because Becky started crying in the parking lot and they had to wait till she stopped and made up her face.

By the end of the week, Sylvie was tired of hearing about the sins of Ted Topper and told her to forget him. She could not do that. He had lied by omission, as big a crime as lying outright. He had used her to fill in nights when his lady friend was busy, but he had never, never taken her seriously.

She was a dessert on a cart he had pointed at, and it had leapt onto his plate and said, Eat me. Don't think twice. She stopped talking about him, but she thought of him constantly. She considered what to do to him. She thought of going to the authorities at the college, but what could she say? He had not gotten involved with her while she was still his student; he had waited until the next semester. He didn't teach at the college full-time. He was not financially dependent on the school. They probably thought they were lucky to have him teach a course. They would view her only as a nuisance. It would get out that she had had an affair. The rumor might even wind its way back to her parents.

No, she had been discreet and so had he. Even where she worked, he had never walked into the store. Calling him in the middle of the night and waking him was a wonderful idea until she tried it and got his answering machine. Of course. She remembered him pulling the phone from the jack when they had made love—love?—and leaving the machine to deal with any calls.

Mail him a dead rat? He wasn't home during the day. The janitor received packages and would smell something. Besides, what would that really do to him? She imagined running him down in the street, but she didn't have a car, and Sylvie wasn't about to loan hers. She could not count on him standing lamebrained in the middle of the street. His car was parked in the garage under his condo. She could put sugar in the gas tank, if no one saw her, but the chances of being caught were enormous, and how would she ever get there? He would just call his insurance company and rent a car while his was fixed.

Her favorite idea was running him down. She would shout to him, so that he knew who was killing him. She imagined the impact of his body. She imagined putting on her brakes, not screeching, just firmly, then backing over him. With him would die her shame, her foolishness, her sense of being callously and casually used.

She hated feeling as helpless as he assumed she was. She hated feeling like the little innocent simpleton he had written off. His to pick up, put on and discard. She could not endure imagining him dismissing her as easily as he had. I'll take you home. I'll drop you in the trash can. I'll be done with you as quickly as washing my hands. Not so fast, not so easy, she wanted to say. I'm not dead yet.

She had loved him, she had idolized him, and he did not ever think of her. She would show him a thing or two about little diversions from New Bedford who had the nerve to want to make something of themselves.

She called up the number on the front of his condo and thus got the agent's name, Nadine Bavard, and the address of her office. She worked all the next week on a letter, heartfelt and full of remorse, to Nadine, in which she apologized profusely for getting involved with Ted Topper. She had not known about their long-standing affair. He had been her teacher and he had seemed very sincere. She had never been involved with a man before, and she had no idea that this meant nothing to him. When she had gotten pregnant, she had naively expected him to marry her. He had explained then that he was involved with Nadine. She was dreadfully sorry. She had not known. She was having an abortion that weekend and would never see him again, but she wanted Nadine to understand she had not intentionally tried to take away anyone's boyfriend. She felt very guilty about everything and she felt as if her life was over, but she was sure Nadine would understand, as one woman to another, that she had been misled and was more sinned against than sinning.

It was two weeks later in May and approaching finals when Ted Topper caught Becky as she left her class in cable TV production. "I want to talk to you," he said, his voice harsh and rasping.

"Mr. Topper, I don't want to talk with you." She brushed past him.

He grabbed her arm, then looked around and dropped it. "You're a first-class bitch."

"Why do you say that, Mr. Topper? Do you call all the young girls you lie to words like that?"

"You screwed up my relationship with Nadine. I'd like to break your neck."

She smiled as she walked down the steps to meet Sylvie. She did not think of him with pain that week. When she thought of him, she felt a little pulse of delight. It would be a while before he'd take up with one of his ex-students again, she'd bet on that. He'd discovered not every girl was as helpless as he expected. She'd rather have run him down, but this was a reasonable second best. He had hurt her; she had hurt him. The score was one to one, and the game was over.

CHAPTER 10

LEILA

Sunday morning, Leila got a phone call from her sister Debbie, an unusual event. "Red and me are going to be East," she announced. "We're planning to spend Thanksgiving with Mama in Philadelphia. Are you coming?"

It took Leila a moment to remember that Red Rodgers was the current husband. "I can't. Why not come here? David's flying home. Will the kids be with you?"

"Of course. Did you think I'd park them someplace and abandon them? Oh by the way, I'm five months pregnant."

"Yeah, Phyllis told me. Congratulations." Debbie already had three kids by previous husbands or boyfriends. "I'll try to get Phyllis to come up here for Thanksgiving. We'll fit you all in."

"Don't bother," Debbie said. "We can stay in a motel."

"You don't have to do that, Debbie." Leila couldn't remember if this one had any money.

"When I told Red you wouldn't let him smoke in the house, he said we'd stay in a motel."

No doubt Phyllis, who hated to cook anyhow, said, Call your sister. She'll have us up there. "So how come you're flying East?"

"Red had to go to Texas so much this year, with his daddy dying, that he racked up all these frequent flier miles. So we figured we'd come East and let the kids see their grandma before I get tied up with a new baby. A real family Thanksgiving. Last year we went to Red's family in Amarillo."

Debbie was living somewhere near San Diego. Leila had never been there. The last time she had visited Debbie, two years ago when Leila was West for a conference at U.C.L.A., Debbie was living at Pomona, in the Valley, with her then husband, Bruce the therapist. Leila had met the Marlboro Man briefly when she was lecturing in L.A. last April. He was called Red Rodgers, which always gave people a sense of having heard of him until they sorted out they were thinking of Roy Rogers and Red Ryder. Red Rodgers had been a rodeo performer, but now he seemed mainly concerned with real estate scams. He was a gambler too, loved the horses and the poker tables. That was the real reason Leila disliked him. She was crazed about gambling. The idea that Debbie had married a man with their father's vice drove Leila wild. She was sure he would leave Debbie in poverty. Since she was a child, she had felt responsible for Debbie, yet she had never succeeded in taking care of her little sister—only in annoying her. Being judgmental about Debbie's life had never done any good. She must try to be accepting. With Melanie gone, Debbie was more important.

She remembered Robin, the only girl, very well, and Abel, the oldest. She tried to reach Phyllis, but her mother must be at work. She wished her mother had an answering machine. She had bought her one a few years ago, but Phyllis claimed not to be able to use it. Here was a woman who worked in the intensive care unit and ran fourteen different life-support machines, and could not remember how to turn on and off an answering machine. Phyllis wanted to be free of anything complicated when she walked in her front door. Phyllis had had a roommate, another nurse, for the past three years, but she wasn't home either.

Thanksgiving. Leila had not thought about it, beyond sending a ticket to David. She had not even brought up the holiday with Nick. She had been ducking conversation with him, but that avoidance was self-destructive. After all, she loved him, she still loved him passionately, and that was what mattered.

She should start inviting people, make a full table for an opulent spread. That would give her something to plan for. A nice homecoming for Nick. A wonderful feast with people all around the table. She liked to bring Shana and David together. Let him see how pretty she had become. Perhaps that would be a good time to talk to Shana seriously about when she might move in.

Now for the pet. She drove to the Animal Rescue League. The woman on duty took her past the cages of condemned cats in solitary, to the kittens. A strong smell of disinfectant, under it the sharp tang of urine, the smell of fear. "You can think about it," the woman said, as Leila stood confused in front of thirteen assorted kittens tumbling over each other in two spacious cages. "We keep the kittens a couple of weeks."

"What about the cats?"

"The older animals we keep for two or three nights, depending how crowded we are."

She looked at the rows of mature cats, some battered, some looking as if they had homes until some feline catastrophe had sent them on the streets and now to the gas chamber. Execution for homelessness. "I don't want a kitten. I want a mature animal." Like me. Slightly overweight, knowledgeable, having a hard time of it.

She could not bear it as she walked along. Some of the cats had given up and gazed into space, waiting for death. Others pressed against the cage bars. Some stared as if they could with their eyes command her to choose them. Oh, they understood. One cat reached through the bars and laid its paw on her sleeve. No claws showing, just the paw. She turned and looked into its yellow eyes.

"That's an altered male, maybe two years old."

He was a big-boned tabby with thick fur and a nick out of his left ear. He had the slightly jowly look of a male who has been intact past puberty. His eyes were enormous and compelling as he cocked his head and held her with his paw, the claws now very slightly out to keep his grip. "I'll take him."

"We have a few questions first."

A few questions: it was harder to rescue this poor cat who was about to be suffocated than to pry a mortgage out of a bank. She had to specify her intentions, give her history related to animals, explain how her hamsters had died, exactly (as if she knew why hamsters lived or died), promise never to let the cat out of her house or presumably her sight.

She had to buy a carrier from the shelter, since she had not thought to bring anything with her. Of cardboard, it was small for his bulk. He got into it willingly. In the car he howled twice and then was silent, going to whatever fate loomed over him. She could have been an animal experimenter. She could be someone with a pit bull to train on blood. She could be a coke head or a drunk. He had been turned over to her, and he knew only that the unknown was better than the death that every mature cat in that place could smell and taste.

He was hefty, all right. She lugged him gracelessly from the garage to the house and up the steps, thumping in the narrow confines of the box. Finally they were inside. With a big grin, she opened the top of the box. His ears were pinned back against his head and he looked ready to fight. His eyes were yellow slits of menace. In his throat he made a strange guttural sound. She walked away and sat down in the living room. A moment later he jumped from the box, crouched in the hall on the small Oriental there. He examined it like an expert in rugs, every thread. Then he checked out the hall table on which the family mail was usually arrayed. He looked at the stairway but he entered the living room, stiff-legged and half-crouching, stopping when he saw her and then slowly approaching to sniff again.

"It's me, old boy." For the first time she patted him, gingerly. He ducked and then leaned into her hand. Then he began a circuit of the room. She watched him, fascinated by his attention to detail. She had to name him. Let's see, his color was caramel, but that did not seem to suit him. Perhaps she had better wait until he showed more of his personality than a great interest in interior decorating.

When he got to the couch, he disappeared underneath. She tried, "Here, kitty, kitty." Nothing happened. He was playing at being invisible. If you don't see me, nothing bad can happen. This wasn't too amusing. She listened to her messages, returned two calls, including Mrs. Souza's. "I talked to our Becky for you, I told her how you wanted to hear her side. She's had a hard time with the press. But I explained you weren't a reporter but a professor, and she liked that. She agreed to talk to you, okay? You still want to?"

"Oh, yes," Leila said. "I very much want to. When?"

"You'll see what a good girl she is. Now she has to get her lawyer to agree. Okay? You're a good woman, Mrs. Landsman, I know you mean right for our Becky."

"The sooner, the better, Mrs. Souza. I'm eager to hear her side."

She was an idiot. She had gone and gotten a cat and nothing to feed it and nothing to use as a litter box. She was shocked with herself. When Melanie had given her an African violet nine years ago, she had immediately read two books and a Brooklyn Botanical Garden pamphlet. Before David was born, she had read thirty books on child development. The nursery was outfitted by her seventh month. She had never plunged into a book as hastily as into Becky's case; now she had acquired a strange animal on impulse.

She went out at once to Porter Square Star Market, returning in forty-five minutes with a bag of assorted canned cat food and kibble and a big plastic basin she filled with kitty litter and put in the upstairs bathroom. But if she had imagined being greeted, no creature was visible. He was not under the couch. He was not under any of the chairs in the living room. She spent a futile half hour crawling around the living room, the dining room and her downstairs study looking for a cat. He seemed to have evaporated. She opened a can of fishy glop and tried again, calling Kitty Kitty. Nothing.

Her effort to purchase companionship had been a complete bust. Obviously she should have taken one of the kittens. At least the kitten would have accepted her as a mother substitute. Perhaps her yellow-eyed tabby had opened a window and crawled out. He seemed just about hefty enough to raise one by himself. Getting a cat had been a stupid idea.

She walked into her bedroom to dump her purse and there he was, sprawled on her bed at what seemed about twice full-length. He was stretched out with paws extended over his head. When she came in, he opened his enormous yellow eyes and looked at her with studied languor. He did not appear frightened now or apprehensive.

Cautiously she approached him. Sat down on the bed's edge. Reached out tentatively and patted him. This time she was rewarded by a yawn, a loud purr and a paw placed on her arm. I'll take you, I'll keep you, said the cat. You can sit on my bed. You can share my space. I am a great warrior and a great lover, and you are my mistress now. My name is Vronsky. You may call me that and many other things. This strikes me as a satisfactory home.

She called Shana and invited her to Thanksgiving with her grandmother. At one she called David to check that the tickets had come and to tell him about the cat and Thanksgiving. "Is Dad coming home?"

"I haven't had a chance to discuss it with him. I assume so."

David snickered. "Chicken. So I'll see Aunt Debbie and flock. And Jane. You'll have Jane, won't you? Is she still with the weight lifter?"

"She did triathalon. She was a librarian, actually." Her feelings were bruised by her son's calling her a coward. She had been avoiding Nick for many reasons. She did not seek out being hurt. But David was right, she had to confront him.

Vronsky had a loud bone-rattling purr and a body on which there were many old scars and abrasions. His time on the streets had not been long enough to maim or debilitate him, but he had had to fight.

Now he had arrived. He was very well pleased. He was even willing to follow her downstairs and eat a bowl of cat food in forty seconds.

However, when she ran him a bowl of water out of the tap, he gave her a reproachful look and lapped twice only. "You don't like the chlorine?" She poured him a bowl from her water cooler. Everybody in Cambridge who could afford to drank bottled water because the local water not only tasted foul but was reputed to contain fourteen carcinogens. Vronsky drank the cold bottled water quickly. He was thirsty, but he had his standards. Obviously he did not feel it was too soon to begin that vital training that lubricated the loving relationship between the cat and the person he owned.

Jane called to make sure she was planning to attend a faculty meeting that would deal with questions of affirmative choice and tenure. Jane, she realized quickly, was also making sure she was invited to Thanksgiving. Leila might have forgotten the holiday, but nobody else had. She must call Nick. She found herself telling Jane at great length about Vronsky, as if he were a new friend. He was excellent company. He climbed into her lap for the first time. He barely fit, but they both found the contact reassuring and pleasant. She figured out it had required perhaps an hour and a half for him to take over the house. He had already found a table that received afternoon sunlight and butted the magazines from it. He had big strong paws clever and able at opening doors and cabinets and pushing things aside or off surfaces he craved. Alternatively, he could run among her cosmetics with all his bulk and not even tip over a perfume bottle.

"I must call Nick," she said to Vronsky. "He's my husband, but he's with another woman. He won't be at the apartment he's borrowed, but I have to figure out exactly what message to leave. He always says he's at rehearsals, but I bet I have trouble getting him because he's spending nights with *her*—the sugary-voiced Sheryl. Vronsky, what am I going to do?"

Finally she dialed Nick's number. She did get the answering machine, as she'd expected. One hand gripped Vronsky's ruff hard. "Hi, Nick, it's me, Leila. We all need to know when you're coming home for Thanksgiving—when you're arriving. David will be home Wednesday at five. Shana will be here. So will my sister Debbie, her husband and children. Let me know your plans. We'll have a great feast."

Now didn't that sound civilized and inviting? She had kept her voice light. She had often been told she had a pleasant voice; in fact Nicolas used to tell her that. It was a voice in the lower registers for a woman. In glee club in grade school, she had sung alto. In college she had sung in the chorale. She remembered the difficult pleasure of *Carmina Burana* and *Alexander Nevsky.* She and her mother and her sister used to sing while they did household tasks. They joined on pop songs, Beatles songs, songs from her mother's youth. Phyllis was fond of show tunes, Rodgers and Hammerstein. Debbie had a high thin voice. Phyllis had a big voice but scratchy from smoking. Maybe it was a sign of settling into middle age to remember her childhood almost with nostalgia, that poor bumpy overloaded childhood which she felt extremely lucky to have escaped whole and functional.

Now Debbie was coming here. A new man and a new baby for the new man every few years. Red Rodgers had installed her on a sort of mini-ranch in the mountains between San Diego and the desert. He had bought her two horses and a nanny goat. Leila said to Vronsky, who was staring into her face, "What would my sister do with a horse? Like me, the only horses she saw till she was twenty-one were under a cop. Personally I find them intimidating. It's like trying to drive a Mack truck by sitting on the roof."

They had supper together in the kitchen. Vronsky ate on the floor, then sat in the chair on her left, David's place. She had bought swordfish, which she broiled. "See, a real meal." She gave him the skin. He ate it avidly, then counted every bite till she gave him a piece. She was jumping at sounds, waiting for Nick to call her back.

The thought of the holidays coming with all that cooking and eating made her feel clumsy and oversized. Nothing she did or refrained from doing would ever make her slender, but facing the holidays, she was motivated to try to streamline herself, especially with Nick returning soon.

After supper she made sure the draperies were tightly drawn. Then she looked for something to dance to. The classical CDs she and Nick purchased, but David bought the rock. She did not recognize most of the groups. First she put on Bruce Springsteen and went wiggling, lurching, leaping around the living room. Next she found a CD of old Eric Clapton. Many songs were slow, but she danced to three of them before the CD came to "Layla." Suddenly she found herself lying on the couch with Vronsky on her stomach, quietly weeping.

Nineteen-seventy? They had certainly married by then. They were arty hippies. Nick studied at N.Y.U., finding an occasional acting job off-off-Broadway and sometimes even off-Manhattan. She took a secretarial job to pay the rent on a 12th Street walk-up between Avenues

A and B, with a bathtub sink in the kitchen, bars on the windows. They were robbed three times. Fortunately they didn't have time to watch TV, because they never had one after the second burglary. But what made her cry was remembering how Nick had loved her then, how they had danced together in the concave-floored kitchen and then fallen into the jangling bed. She was drunk on love, drunk on his body and his mouth and his hands and his voice, his eyes, his talent. That had been a brief period, after college and before David, when her body had been ripe and glowing. Then she had felt almost pretty, and at parties, men had flocked around her, embarrassing her. She had loved to dance, to use that body that had always been too tall, too big, too in the way, too much. The passion of her new husband for her body made it pleasing even to her. The next year when they lived in a loft building with other would-be theatrical couples, Don Margolis had told her at a party, "You have the body of a primitive queen—proud, sensual. A fertility goddess." She had run away flattered.

She lay listening to the song and it was as if a hot humid wind blew through her reeking of sex and the scent of those days in New York, the odor of young bodies sweating as they danced, of incense and Chinese food, of red wine and spilled beer and ripe peaches, of patchouli and sandalwood, the perfumes she had worn then, cheap, obvious, simple and forever redolent of sexual satisfaction and casual daily joy. Loving had seemed easy and natural, just the way their bodies came together. Then it was gone.

She held Vronsky, who purred and stared into her face with his knowing yellow eyes, and she wept—wept for days and nights gone twenty years, wept long after the CD had finished and she lay on the couch hearing only the sound of an occasional car passing in the street.

Love had been her miracle. That such a man could care for her, the big awkward studious girl from the Philly ghetto, had never ceased to fill her with surprise and quiet anxiety that he would suddenly realize who she really was. But nothing she had given over to him had kept Nick in love with her the way she was still in love with him. All her sacrificing meant was that she was home, paying the bills, and he was off in New York with Sheryl.

CHAPTER 11

MARY

Wednesday morning, Mary arrived to clean the Landsman house. Mrs. L. was off at work, but her new cat Bronskee was overseeing everything. Mary bustled around in a good mood because she had her next week pretty well solved. She had been staying a lot in church basements and, on one mild night, in a gazebo in one of her ladies' yards, and another night, in an unlocked garage. She had a bothersome head cold and her lower back really hurt, from sitting up all night or scrunching up in a seat. But next week was Thanksgiving, and she was set from Sunday night on. Mrs. Landsman had a lot of vitamin C, so she was taking it every two hours with hot peppermint tea. Mrs. L. wasn't a woman who counted her pills. Mary had to get in shape or she'd be in real trouble.

The DeMotts were going to Florida over Thanksgiving, to visit his parents who'd retired to Sanibel Island. About thirty years ago, her husband, her children and Mary spent ten days there. She remembered her two-piece turquoise bathing suit Jim was crazy about. It was a color they used a lot then, in architecture, in furnishings, in clothing. He couldn't keep his hands off her when she wore that suit. She was fair and she had to be careful in the sun. Nobody had heard of sunscreen in those days so she just burned. Seashells. Conch shells. On the terrace was an outdoor shower behind a screen. Once, feeling daring, they had made love in it while the children were at the beach. When a man was so crazy about you, it was hard to imagine that a time would come when he just wanted you out of his way, when he treated you like a piece of cheese that had turned bad. Her sin was to get middle-aged. Time nibbled away at her looks.

It happened so gradually that she simply didn't realize she wasn't a pretty girl any longer. Mary never got fat. Oh, she put on some weight—not as much as he did, but some. She thickened around the middle, in the ankles and upper arms. Since she was a baby she had always been pretty, so she took it for granted. Maybe she should have dyed her hair, but when she asked Jim, he pooh-poohed it, saying he liked her the way she was, he liked her natural. All her ladies dyed their hair. She should have had sense enough just to do it and keep her mouth shut. Most of her women were afraid that their husbands would leave them, the way Mrs. Landsman worried about her husband taking off with one of his bimbos.

Mr. Landsman brought one home once when she was cleaning. He was so shocked when he walked in the door and there she was in the kitchen mopping the floor that he couldn't cover up his astonishment. "Who are you?" he asked. It was true they hardly saw each other, but she'd been cleaning for them for a year. But she wasn't real to him. She wondered if he thought the house cleaned itself every Wednesday. No, because every so often Mrs. Landsman would leave a note, "Mr. Landsman says that he would like the blinds dusted, if you have time this week." Requests were phrased that way. Polite, which Mary appreciated. She despised ladies who spoke to her more rudely than they addressed their dogs.

Anyhow, he walked in with this creature in her early twenties but caked with makeup and wearing what Mary thought was maybe a Halloween costume. They stood flatfooted watching her clean for five minutes. Then he seized his girlfriend by the elbow and they fled.

With the DeMotts gone from Sunday to Sunday, Mary would just move in and stay there, careful as usual. She needed sleep badly. That was one of the worst parts of being homeless, never getting to really sleep. Sometimes Mary could steal an hour and nap at her ladies' houses. Today she cleaned the downstairs frantically. Then she lay down on top of the Landsman king-sized bed, set the alarm and let herself snooze. Fortunately she was a light sleeper. Nobody'd ever caught her sleeping on the job. When she had a real place to stay, she never needed to nap. She was a wee bit run-down, but she mustn't get sick. No, with a nice quiet week at the DeMotts, she'd get herself together and come out of it fit and rested. Her life was always about to tip over like a precarious pile of crockery she must keep balanced.

Mrs. Landsman had picked up an alley cat and now he was lord of all he surveyed. Mrs. L. left Mary notes about not letting him out the door, as if he were stupid enough to walk out on a good deal. He looked Mary over and told her where he wanted to be rubbed and scratched, but he pretty much stayed out of her way. He wasn't spooked by the vacuum cleaner. He just climbed on top of the bookcase. When she took a nap, he lay down next to her. "Oh, now I'm good enough to cuddle up to." She thanked the Lord that cats couldn't talk, or she could just imagine what an earful her ladies would get, because most pets were bored and they watched every step she took. They practically counted the silverware. She'd be fired on the spot, if Bronskee could speak English.

The house was different. She could tell the husband or the son was coming home. She thought it was the son for sure, because Mrs. L. had left instructions she was to clean his room, which Mrs. L. hadn't bothered with since Labor Day. She told Mary if she got done early, she could leave early. Mrs. L. didn't understand: she had no place to go.

Until she could squat for the night, whether in a basement or a garage or someone's momentarily vacated house, she had hours to kill. She rode public transportation out to the end of the line and back. She walked around. Malls were for sitting. She always looked respectable enough not to be bothered, so long as she didn't become familiar. Once again, her invisibility helped. Malls were full of old people killing time, retirees, people on fixed incomes in tiny rooms. We're all superfluous and we go to the mall the way in the past we might have sat in the sun in the village center watching the world go by.

She knew all the malls she could reach by public transportation. She went today to Chestnut Hill, where there were comfortable seats and greenery and even music to listen to. If they had live music, she could safely sit for a long time. She used to go to the Museum of Fine Arts on their free days, but now they had none. Didn't want the homeless sitting among the paintings feeling good.

Sometimes she went to the Lechmere Mall. It hadn't enough benches. Strip malls were no good, like Fresh Pond. No place to rest her bones. She could shuffle from store to store, but there was no proper inside. Arsenal Mall was useful. Harvard Square, Porter Square and Downtown Crossing had buildings made over with shops inside, good for bathrooms and getting out of the cold, but not as good for sitting around all evening. In nice weather, Downtown Crossing was okay, but she had to watch her bags. Faneuil Hall was great, but there was a lot of security, so she had to be cautious. She bought something, ate it slowly and kept the wrappers so that she could appear to be having a snack.

The trick was not to sit in one place too long, to move in and out of the shops regularly. As long as she appeared to be shopping, and she always had a shopping bag, then she was fine. She was careful to change her bag regularly so that it was not shabby. In sunny weather, there were joggers and mimes and lovers holding hands. Lots of kids didn't finish their lunches before they started asking for dessert.

The way to manage in stores was to look intently at the merchandise but be very careful not to want it. She had developed a mindset where she viewed everything as if she were in a museum. She wouldn't walk into the MFA and start wanting that Rembrandt. If a salesgirl became persistent, she said she needed a gift for her daughter, and she'd know it when she saw it, as her daughter was very particular. Then she would move on.

The clothing they sold was often an imitation of older clothing. Therefore it *was* like a museum, wandering around Filene's or Lord & Taylor. There was a dress cut just like one she had in 1964. There was a jacket like one her mother used to wear. There was a pin she'd been given in high school, and there was a blue cashmere sweater from her college days. Of course the major difference was that nothing was made as well. It was all shoddy, even the clothes that cost so much she wanted to laugh out loud before she got angry, that people spent on a stupid designer blouse that looked like forty others enough for her to live on for a month in comfort and safety.

Her ladies would have been shocked to learn she had not only gone to college but gotten her degree. They would have been uncomfortable or even frightened. She had been a nice middle-class girl and she had taken a teaching course. The month she graduated, she married Jim, got her Mrs., as they called it.

Her husband was a year older, as they thought appropriate then. He had graduated and taken a job with the state of Illinois. He had been afraid of losing her to other boys after he graduated and bought her a ring he insisted she wear. She had sold it long ago for hardly anything. She went to college in Normal, Illinois. She used to say to people, to make them smile, I'm just a normal girl from Normal, Illinois. Actually she came from Centralia.

When she was sixteen and saw her life unfolding, just beginning to go out on dates to the movies or for sodas and so innocent she believed kissing was only if you really cared for a boy, she assumed she would be married by the time she was twenty-one. To her loving faceless husband, she would bear two children, a boy and a girl, and live in a nice house where she would cook good meals for her family and care for them. Until she turned forty-five, her life was just that way, although the crowd they moved in was more sophisticated and affluent than she would have guessed at sixteen. Still her life was the one she had been bred and trained to lead: by the rules.

Anyhow, Mrs. Landsman's house was a mess. Cat toys everyplace. She was spoiling this cat the way she spoiled her son. Mary shook her head. Why did she call this Mrs. Landsman's house? Probably Mrs. L. thought it was hers, the way Mary had thought her house was hers, but it must be his, like the car and the money and the stock and everything else.

Mary had thought she was exempt from the adultery she knew had rotted many suburban marriages around them. Those scandals were the problems of other women, who had failed in their marriages. She thought, because she knew how to shop and how to run a house and how to make conversation with a judge or an undersecretary's wife or a urologist, that she knew all about life. She imagined, because her husband wanted her passionately into her thirties, that he would always want her.

A housewife didn't give much weight to boredom, because whether she was waiting for a husband to come home or a baby to be born or a load of clothes to dry or a roast to cook, she spent a lot of time exercising her patience. From one little crisis to the next pressing job, the days unwound. She was worrying about Jaime's grades in algebra or whether Cindy was going to fit into her prom dress, and she was thinking about how they said a new diet would take off weight or help the heart, and whether she could get her family to eat that way. She was thinking that Jaime didn't want to go to the Maryland shore this year and where should they take a vacation that would satisfy everybody—not including herself, because she took for granted that if they were satisfied, so was she. She was thinking, the driveway cement is cracking and the dog has to go to the vet for his shots and is it Ed Vickers or Ed Simmons that Dr. Caldwell can't stand at the dinner table with him? Yes, she had been swimming in a big pink aquarium, and she never thought that somebody would come along with a hammer and break it until she was gasping for her life and everything she had taken for granted, for permanent, was gone.

So no wonder Mrs. L. was sprucing the place up. She was cooking again. She was doing that trick of making a meal, eating it once and freezing the rest. The empty freezer was filling up with neatly labeled cartons; CHICKEN SOUP 11/14; SPAGHETTI SAUCE 11/16. The leaves were finally raked and the yard and the walk looked neat. The old newspapers kicking around had been burned in the fireplace. The master must be about to put in an appearance. Why didn't he take off? Maybe it was just too convenient. Mrs. L. didn't seem to throw scenes or issue ultimatums. She just endured.

If Mary were back in Bethesda, age forty-five, and she discovered all over again that her husband had been getting it on with his secretary for the past two years, what would she do? Would she swallow her pride? Would she be able to act as if she didn't know? Would she be able to string him along? But he didn't marry the secretary. He married the ex-wife of one of his best friends, which always made her wonder what had been going on there. They were getting a divorce while she was getting a divorce. Then four years later Jim left that wife also.

Mary had far more pride than Mrs. Landsman, because she wouldn't take his crap, which was not a nice expression, but accurate. She had been a good wife and a good mother, and she was entitled to a good husband. Sometimes she still went over and over it, trying to understand what she did wrong. Did she pick the wrong man? But they had seemed happy for twenty years. Should she have pretended she didn't know? Should she have said, Whatever you want, dear, as Mrs. Landsman did, and just hoped he wouldn't bring home some disease or get his mistress pregnant?

What had Mary done wrong? As she cleaned other women's houses, she tried to figure out where she had gone astray and how her life had derailed, but she couldn't comprehend it. Watching her ladies' lives fall apart didn't teach her much. The only one of them playing around was Mrs. Douglas, and her marriage didn't seem in danger. Every other woman, she thought, lived in ignorance or in fear.

CHAPTER 12

BECKY

One Saturday morning, as Becky was waiting for the bathroom so she could go off to work, Becky's mom caught her own mother throwing up blood. Everybody was scared and started fighting about how serious it was. Nana held the house together. If Becky's mother was swamped, she cooked. She cleaned up what got missed in the confusion. She did the extra laundry. She wiped up what the baby spilled while Gracie was putting him to bed. She made up brews of herbs and weeds for ailments and heartaches. She made a piece of beef or fish go further. She could cook soup out of anything edible, and she fermented wine in the basement from blueberries, cherries or strawberries.

Becky's graduation was no big deal, because by the time commencement dragged around, Nana was diagnosed with advanced stomach cancer. She chose to die at home, but still the bills were like a wasting disease, another cancer that sickened the family. The house smelled of decay and bedpans and medicine. Money, money, every morning muttered. Becky's mother went around turning off lights while people were trying to dress or read the paper. They lived off whatever fish were running, and an occasional leathery chicken from Mama's flock that had stopped laying, or trash fish bartered for backyard rabbits from a neighbor. Nana's garden was choked in weeds. Nobody had the energy to harvest the poor lettuces under the lamb's-quarters, even though they had to go to the store and buy lettuce. The garden too smelled like death. But Tommy, her favorite brother, took off from fishing to go to her commencement, and he bought an almost-new VCR someplace to celebrate the event.

Mama was arguing with the phone company, with the electric company, wait, wait. They offered to take Becky on full-time at Lady Grace, and she pretended to be thinking about it, but she had not spent four years and all that effort and money for a job she could have had all this time.

The week of graduation, she took on three more evenings at the mall and started job-hunting during the day with a dogged insistence. She did not mind working the extra evenings. She had not dated anyone since Ted Topper had fooled her. She felt charred around the edges. She covered all the towns halfway to Boston. She wanted desperately to look in Boston, but there the competition was fierce for media jobs, and she could not afford to live away from home. She had to help her parents now. She had to have a job right away. She used the facilities at school to create a hundred resumés, and she carried them around, mailed them in, dropped them off, did everything but stand on a street corner downtown and hand them to passersby. Her cousin Wanda gave her an old sick car that Tommy worked on till it ran. It made a funny noise and missed, but it got her from job interview to job interview.

She looked over the other applicants carefully, observed women in the offices. She got her sister Belle—who worked in a beauty salon—to cut her hair the way she wanted it and slip her in for a permanent. The results impressed even her. That style she had seen on the girl who got the job at Quali-Cable was right for her. Her face looked much softer surrounded by a cloud of curls. Her hair looked fuller and her eyes looked bigger. As for clothing, blue seemed to be the safest color, with grey next, for a nice job-hunting girl. No black, no red, no yellow until you had the job. Small earrings.

She went for a job at Sound Cable, even though it was across the Canal in Falmouth, a forty-minute commute even in light traffic. It would be murderous crossing the bridge on busy mornings. Cape Cod, full of Yankees and yuppies and tourists, was another world from immigrant New Bedj. Only the fishermen were the same. She was hoping to host the community show, but they wanted a guy. They offered her a job as receptionist. Theirs was pregnant. "Can't have a bulging receptionist," said the egg-shaped man who was ready to hire her.

It was a foot in the door. She took it on the spot. It was better pay and a regular nine-to-five job with benefits. She had laid her resumé everyplace, and if something better came up, she would quit this in a finger snap. In the meantime, she had to dress decently, but it was mostly sizing folks up as to who was likely to matter and who didn't, learning everybody's rank and schedule. A lot of the on-camera people just came in one day a week to do a particular show. The management and the technical people were the daily faces. She made a point of learning their names at once and always, always smiling at them. She practiced smiling in the mirror. Her real personal expression was one of intense grim observation. That would not do. A man's face in repose was supposed to be serious; a woman's face in repose was supposed to be smiling.

She kept on at Lady Grace evenings and weekends for two weeks until she was sure she really had the other job. When she finished in the late evening, she was too exhausted for anything but sleep. Often she was not even hungry. Then she gave her notice. They seemed to like her at Sound Cable, and the work was easier. She was able to pay off the electric company. New England Telephone she nickled and dimed, sending five dollars, ten dollars, another seven. She was determined to keep the phone connected, in case one of those job possibilities in media came through.

She was coasting on the clothes she had, because she really wanted to get the family current before she started spending. At least she had enough fancy underwear to last for years. Sylvie was getting married at the end of June. Becky had bought Sylvie a negligee and nightie while she still had the discount. Sylvie asked Becky to be a bridesmaid, but she didn't know if she could afford the bridesmaid outfit.

Aunt Marie stepped in. Becky had been seeing her independently of Sylvie, who was too involved with Mario to bother with her aunt. The first time, Becky drove to Cohasset and parked in a mall, trying to get up the nerve. Finally she called Marie and told her she was just passing by. Marie invited her over.

Marie treated Becky like her own niece. She knew Becky didn't have the money for the bridesmaid's dress. When Marie offered, Becky did not play coy or pretend to refuse. The wedding was going to be all peach. Except for Sylvie in white, Sylvie's sister, her cousin and Becky would wear peach and so would Mrs. Damato. The reception would be at a big restaurant with platters of Italian food and pastries. There would be a band. Becky and Sylvie danced together, practicing, because they had not gone to many dances. They took turns leading. It made them giggle like the old days. Becky loved having her weekends back. She felt like a lady of leisure, working just five days.

As she said to Sylvie, "I really envy you. It's like a movie, and you're the heroine. Mario is just a prop. There's nothing like it again. You're the star and all of us just back you up."

"Just as well it's only this once." Sylvie laughed. "I've never been so worried I'll get a zit or sunburned or what else awful can you think of? Gain ten pounds. I could, with all the parties. I keep telling Mama if she doesn't lay off, they won't be able to get me into The Dress without the help of a cheese slicer." She mimicked cutting off slices from her hips.

Becky felt as if nothing was settled in her own life. She could not get away from home, because her parents needed her. She wasn't making the kind of money where she could live in a nice place like Ted Topper's, anyhow. She knew what she wanted, but had not come a step closer to getting it. The more clearly she understood what she wanted, the farther away those precious things seemed.

She had a college degree. She had learned how to speak correctly and how to dress like one of them, attractive girls born to the right suburbs, and she had learned to use makeup, by watching, by reading magazines, by imitating, and how to wear her hair in a flattering fashion up-to-date but not extreme. She had given herself those advantages, and here she was, a receptionist at a cable TV office, which was better than the mall and better than New Bedj but not even halfway where she wanted to go.

She could not see any way to climb the glass mountain. She could see no route, no toeholds, no place her carefully kept not overly long but always polished nails could grasp. They had her on a shelf. She had to find someone to pick her off that shelf.

The first way was to crawl up the cable company ladder. She smiled and she smiled and she smiled. She had taken typing in high school. She began to practice again. She got Sylvie to teach her about computers. She made herself available to everybody to run errands. The secretaries were always being told to pick up something on their lunch hours. She brought her lunch and ate it in the women's john, quickly. She would gladly drive to the next town and buy flowers. She would gladly pick up the soundman's dry cleaning. She would wait for the package supposed to come.

When she did a little job for one of the secretaries, she tried to make sure that the particular boss or beneficiary knew it was her. She couched it in terms of, I hope this is what you wanted? Mr. White's secretary, Rosemary, said to her, "Look, as far as I'm concerned, when I leave, you can have my job. Not before. We're trying to have a baby. I know what you're pushing for. Just don't try to push through me. Understood?"

Becky could see no reason to pretend to be stupid when her bluff was called. She nodded, and when Rosemary went on fixing her with a hard stare, said, "I'm just trying to position myself to make a little more money. My family needs it, frankly."

"Who doesn't?"

Most of the people who worked here didn't, not like she did. She priced their coats when they walked in. She saw their cars in the lot. Some of them had tape decks and two had cellular phones. But she smiled and ran errands and flattered them and waited for someone to slip, so she could move up.

One cameraman was leaning on her desk whenever he could, but he was married. She smiled and played the old Nice Catholic Girl game. She pretended she didn't understand sexual allusions. No payoff in being some married cameraman's bimbo, really. They must think she was even more desperate than she was. She said nothing about herself at work except that she had enjoyed college, that she loved cable TV as a business, and that she lived at home with her family. Then she would immediately ask them questions, and the need to lie would disappear. People liked to talk about themselves.

Most of the girls in the office were married, but Gwen was divorced and one was single, only two years older than her. They asked her out with them on Friday, once to pizza and once when they were going for Chinese food and then to a movie. She went for the pizza, but everything they did cost money. They didn't just hang out as she always had with Sylvie. The way things were at home, she could not waste money. She said she had a date.

Sylvie and Mario were married on the Saturday just before the Fourth of July. The weather was hot and sultry. It had rained the day before, and Sylvie had burst into tears. There was a low lid of clouds, but the rain had stopped. It was ninety-three and the air felt like hot glue. Becky could scarcely walk in the voluminous dress, and she felt ready to pass out. Discipline, she told herself, discipline. She imagined she was being taken to her own wedding. She was marrying . . . no, not an old man like Ted Topper, the lying lecher. Someone just three years older, a successful lawyer in a high-rise in Boston who drove a Mercedes like the sales manager Mr. Corman, who had wavy blond hair. She would marry her lawyer and move into a beautiful house in Cohasset, like Aunt Marie. Except when she was watching TV, she seldom saw a life she wanted, a situation, even a place in which she could imagine inserting herself. When she was daydreaming, sometimes she borrowed the sets from her favorite shows, but she could never control what the family watched, and their set was old. The picture had dandruff.

Aunt Marie winked at her. "You look gorgeous, kid." But never did she say things like, you'll be the next bride. No, Marie told her, take your time. The world is full of men. They all want one thing, so be sure that's what you want. Marie did not know about Ted Topper. Marie was the only person she sometimes thought of telling, now that they were friends, but she did not want Marie to think less of her. Better that Marie should think of her as sensible: she had learned to be. She might daydream, but she did not let any man come close, for she was watching for someone worthy. Daydreams were cheap. Sylvie asked her once if she ever touched herself. She had trouble understanding what Sylvie meant. Then she said, "I share a bed with Laurie. How could I?"

The only time she had ever really known sexual feelings was with Ted Topper, the user. One night she watched an old movie on TV, gladiators and Romans in armor. It was a bad night for Nana, and Becky was sitting up with her. Nana lay on the couch moaning. Becky imagined that she was a Roman aristocrat watching Ted Topper fight a lion. She was supposed to think the women watching the men fight were evil, but she could imagine getting a lot of pleasure out of seeing Ted Topper hacked up. She had shown him a little trouble, but as long as he lived she would feel he had a piece of her she couldn't get back.

She stood in the vestry of Sancti Antonii with the other members of the wedding imagining the slow death of Ted Topper, but then it was time to march. She held her head high and tried to sweep gracefully down the aisle in her tons of peach taffeta. She felt like a one-woman float, but every bridesmaid was similarly overladen, broad as barges. Sylvie was a huge white satin sailboat wide in the beam with yards of tulle sail unfurled. Becky could smell mock orange. The air was dense and sticky. Mario was pale as Dracula and seven feet tall. There was a stirring in the room of women fanning themselves.

The food was glorious and they were allowed to change out of their dresses so they could dance. She wore a little blue dress. She had had it for three years, bought at the mall marked way down, but it still looked good. It was on the bare side. She ate and she danced with every guy who asked her, even people's daddies. One chance, she thought, give me one decent chance, as she tried to keep Mario's older brother from dancing too close. There were men from Sylvie's family, from Mario's, and there was the third in command of what her own Papa always called The Guys. Some of the boats made a lot of money. Scalloping was good money, but drugs made more, and the fishing industry offered a great way to launder cash. If someone was in with The Guys, they did all right. Her Papa was too honest and patriotic besides. He stayed clear, but twice he had been beaten, just so he wouldn't think he was too good. Things happened on the docks. A car was fire-bombed. A rival packing business had a mysterious fire. Somebody who didn't play along had his refrigeration sabotaged so he lost thousands of dollars.

She knew The Guys, everybody did, but while they were rich, she wanted no part of them. She didn't need some man who, if she pulled what she had pulled on Ted Topper, would put out a contract on her or beat her toothless. She wasn't the long-suffering type like those wives who sat out the dances gossiping. She wanted a man who would be faithful to her, not some wise guy who ran around getting diseases and dumping his money on other girls. Besides, they played around outside, but they married their own. Her eyes passed over the men in the room, one by one scanning them for a reasonable hope. Some were cute and a few were handsome, but none of them would take her up and out.

CHAPTER 13

LEILA

"He sits on the monitor while I work at the computer. When I take a bath, he lies on the rim of the tub and dips his tail in the water."

Jane shook her red bob in exasperation. "You sound just like me when I fall in love, do you know that? But I fall in love with women, not some tomcat."

"He's a perfect companion. And when I talk, at least he listens."

"You've been in a bad marriage so long, a cat seems like a lover to you."

"Oh, Jane, I'm just enjoying having a pet. I haven't had one in years. I never imagined I'd be crazy about a cat, but you mustn't talk on as if I'm an aging spinster with twenty-two cats—"

"I have nothing against spinsters, my dear. Some of the greatest women who ever lived were spinsters. For the last two thousand years, spinsters were far more apt to get something done, including spinning, than married women." Jane put her feet in their gorgeously tooled leather boots up on her desk, grinning slyly. Jane was almost always in some costume; today she was Western. Her students adored her. She was slim, out, quick-witted and sexy.

"You have a prejudice against marriage. Marriage is like the weather, always changing in its own cycles. If I had married six times instead of only once, each marriage would be a strange house, one Victorian, one a studio apartment, one neoclassical—"

"From the outside, most look depressingly similar. But I admit yours is unique. He doesn't cheat on you. He just has carte blanche and you smile and bear it and hope he doesn't give you AIDS into the bargain."

"Jane, he doesn't pick up prostitutes in Times Square. Sheryl went to B.U. He's the careful type. We have an agreement. Never at home. What he does when he has a play in Minneapolis or Los Angeles, I don't want to know about. Didn't Shaw say that a woman would rather have a part of a good man than all of a boring one?"

"I noticed he didn't say a man would rather have a good woman one day a week and share her with six other men, than have a stupid wife every day and night. I am sure he insisted on fidelity from Mrs. Shaw. You're boringly faithful, except for this affair with your cat."

"I don't much like men. Not as a group. I'm hardly ever tempted. And, no, I'm not drawn to women. I'm the wife-type. When he's with me, which is, after all, seventy percent of the time, he's really with me."

"You're the Patient Griselda type." Jane put her feet down and planted her elbows on the desk, clearing a place among student exams. That was her signal that the social hour was over, and it was time to get to faculty business before the meeting at four. "Okay, what are we going to do about the dean's new regulations on copying?"

Becky's lawyer forbade her to talk to Leila. Leila decided to start on the boyfriend, family first. Always best to have advocates. His mother was widowed and Sam had lived with her. Mrs. Solomon would be glad to see Mrs. Landsman on Sunday afternoon. Saturday, Nick's play was opening.

In Boston, at least she was part of the activities. When he had an opening away from her, she could only wait. It would have felt disloyal to go out to a movie or over to a friend's. She listened to Bach, read the *Globe*, a professional journal, played with Vronsky. Then she straightened her drawer of pantyhose, placing blacks with blacks and reds with reds. It momentarily soothed her. She sewed a button on her black silk blazer. She mended the pocket of her raincoat. She put her earrings together by pairs. She tried to read student papers. When she finished one, she realized she could not remember what it was about. Not fair. She put it back in the unread pile.

She paced. She examined the phone to make sure it was actually working. She took the answering machine off-line. She picked up the receiver again to make sure she had a dial tone. Then she hung up quickly, so that when Nicolas called, he would not get a false busy signal.

She poured herself a small glass of cognac. Then it was empty. She had no desire to get drunk. She wanted to talk to someone. Actually she wanted to talk to Melanie. Melanie had spent these evenings with her, so that Leila would not implode with tension. After all these years in the theater, Nick remained vulnerable to reviews. No amount of success seemed to harden him to the terror of someone suddenly calling his bluff. He always thought he was somehow putting something over on everybody, underneath all the confidence and the honors and the experience. He still expected to be laughed at. He feared mockery more than death. The good reviews he would nod at, accept as if they were his due, but the bad reviews pierced him. He seemed to memorize them as he read them through rapidly and tossed them away. Phrases would return to him in the middle of the night, at supper the next day. Two years later he would suddenly remember an insult from a review. She was sure he had perfect recall of the first hostile comment he had ever received.

Sometimes her books got good reviews, sometimes bad. Except for a few people in her field, she did not greatly care. She was always working on the next project when a book came out, and that helped shield her from the opinions of others. A book made its way or it didn't, and the notices of those who read hastily and badly, who had a cause to fight or push, could never worm their way into her psyche as reviews did into Nicolas.

It was past time for the play to have ended. She expected him to call and tell her how the audience had reacted. Her stomach hurt and for a moment she wondered if something had been wrong with the soup she had eaten; but it was only anxiety. She wished she could care less. She wished she could simply dismiss him from her mind as he seemed to do when he was away from her. Sometimes when he was off in another city, she could talk to him and mention some problem of David's or Melanie's illness, and there would be a moment when she would know that Nicolas had drawn a mental blank. Then he would shift gears and dredge from his memory what was concerning her, and they could talk again.

She looked into Vronsky's calm and skeptical yellow eyes, feeling as if he measured her tension and judged it foolish. Finally at midnight, the phone rang. Nick sounded as if he was calling from a party, the most likely case. "It seems to have gone well enough. Not a huge success, but not a failure. I expect we'll have a decent run."

"You always think it will be a matter of extremes."

"I do, don't I? I can never imagine a mixed reaction." He chuckled. "You see right through me. I expect doom or bliss."

"But you're all right with it? You can come home for Thanksgiving?"

"Of course. I'll see how it goes the next couple of days. I may have to dash back to make sure things are staying on target. It still needs speed in the second act. Be home Wednesday—the train again. More relaxing."

That night she dreamed that Vronsky was having sex with her. He was large and amazingly gentle. When she awoke, she was deeply embarrassed. Who had ever been so shameless as to dream about making love with their altered cat? Or an unaltered cat, for that matter? Vronsky lay at his most extended, washing himself with grave satisfaction as if after exactly such an act. She felt as if she should avoid going out into the world, lest anyone could read what sick and silly dreams she was subjected to by her subconscious. It was Jane's fault, for saying she was talking about Vronsky like a lover. That had triggered the dream. She was glad she need not see Jane today at school.

That noon she drove down to Sandwich, to the Solomons'. The house was off 6A, the most picturesque of the Cape roads, down a narrow blacktop and then along a sand road past two houses, shuttered for the season. The house, when she came to it, was chaste and handsome, probably older than the other houses and far more permanent-looking. It was a full cape painted pale yellow now chipping, with modern decking on the side that faced a tidal stream. A rickety dock stuck into the river. In the yard a dinghy sat under a plastic tarp for the winter.

The garden had grown over and the fence was sagging to the ground. A five- or six-year-old Buick, its finish pitted by salt, stood at the end of the road in the middle of the casual yard. The road did not so much end as give up. Someone at the window had been watching for her. She parked beside the old green Buick and walked briskly toward the door. The screen door was still on it, in November, but the glass storm door was sitting against the house as if putting it on had been at least contemplated recently.

Like many Cape houses, it faced its view, and the door she was let in was the kitchen door. A slender man with dense curly hair and an even denser beard opened it, frowning. His glasses enlarged his green eyes. Reading glasses. He took them off, polished them carelessly and stuffed them in his shirt pocket. It was denim but well tailored, a dressy shirt disguised as a work shirt.

She introduced herself politely, adding, "And you are?"

"I'm Zak Solomon." He would not smile. He was not welcoming.

"You're Sam's older brother?"

"I'm his uncle."

Of course. He was in his forties. Her age.

A woman came dashing in. "Zak, why didn't you tell me she'd come? I was on the telephone and I didn't even hear you knock. I'm so sorry."

"If you're on the phone, I can wait."

"No, it was just a friend. I'll call him back later. Please, let's go in the living room. Zak, where's your hospitality?"

She was a little older than Zak, with hair that was probably at her age kept blond, pulled back in a ponytail. She wore large parrot earrings, balsa wood painted brightly, an oversized sweater printed with marching poodles, and well-washed jeans. Her voice was breathy and she spoke quickly, smiling placatingly at Leila.

Leila smiled broadly back, trying to put the woman at ease. "You're Cathy Solomon?"

"With a *C*. That's me. Come, sit down. Would you like tea? Some tonic?" She plumped down in the middle of the Danish sofa. The room was well furnished, but like the car outside, a little the worse for wear. Studded about the room were truly ghastly pieces of pottery, most in the shapes of vegetables and flowers. "Or would you like coffee? It's instant. I can't drink the stuff myself, it gives me heartburn, but my husband used to drink it by the gallon."

"There's real coffee. I brought some. I found a Chemex in the top of the cupboard." Zak was standing in the doorway, frowning again. "It's on the stove." He seemed to want Cathy to get it, although he was obviously at home in the kitchen and closer to it. Were they involved? He seemed controlling. He did not want Cathy talking too much.

As soon as Cathy went through the doorway, he sat down facing Leila, who wished he would let her look around at the room. Instead he fixed her with a stare. "My brother, Cathy's husband, died four years ago. That was a shock for her and for my nephew."

"How did he die?"

"The family heart. He dropped dead one morning as he was raking the lawn. By the time Cathy went outside to bring him in to lunch, the body was almost cold. It was a great shock, understand. He was only forty-two. He'd never had a heart attack. But it runs in the family. Sudden death."

This lugubrious tale was delivered with a brisk sententiousness while he watched her. She was taking an instant dislike to him. Theatrical, manipulative. What was he doing here? "Do you live here?" She asked gently.

"I live in Truro, about an hour from here. I try to help out."

Cathy swept back with the coffee. "I really am so glad you want to hear Sam's story. I mean, we thought she had just taken him under her wing. Her wing! Ha. Becky Burgess doesn't have wings, does she, Zak? I heard you asking about Zak. He's tried hard to be supportive. When my husband died, Zak was living in L.A." She nodded at him, smiling as if forgivingly. "But since he came back here, he's been good to us, really." Cathy Solomon had large dark blue eyes that she kept widening as she talked. Once it had probably been flirtatious, but now it was a tic.

"What is it you're trying to find out?" he asked, folding his arms.

"Basically I want to understand the case and explain it. There's a great deal of interest. Most of what's getting into print is just daily journalism, the obvious response. I think everyone involved has a story to tell."

"You have a contract?"

She hesitated. "Yes."

"Who with? Who's your agent? What other books have you published?"

She answered his questions, but she was growing increasingly restive. "You seem to know a fair amount about the book business," she said dryly. She wished she could get him out of the room, for she was sure Cathy Solomon was dying to talk.

"I've done a book or two on animal behavior," he said coldly. "I'd like to see something of yours, to judge what kind of treatment you give."

"I'm sure at least one of them must be in your local library."

"Zak's a vet. Everybody swears by him." Cathy trotted to a shelf and pulled down three books in a similar format: *Living with Dogs, Living with Cats, Living with Parrots and Other Exotic Birds.* On each cover, there was Zak looking a great deal more pleasant, beaming and stroking, in an armchair surrounded by the animal in question. Parrots to the right of him, parakeets on his shoulders, a crow on his left: that was her favorite.

"I just got a cat," she offered.

He groaned. "Please don't ask me about what to do. I can't go to a party, I can't go to the supermarket, without somebody backing me into a corner and describing their dog's incontinence."

"I'd be happy to send you a copy of *Mothers Barred*, Mrs. Solomon. I teach at Lesley, but while the study is serious, I don't think you'll find it too academic to read." Rattle my credentials.

"Call me Cathy. I don't get a chance to read much. I teach pottery in my studio and I do production work, and with all these legal fees. . . . Zak is helping us out, but still, it isn't easy, believe me. So you're a professor?"

"Just call me Leila." If that skinny glaring man would clear out, she knew she could get Cathy talking. She was a chatty woman and her seams were loose. Cathy would be a fine informant if Leila could get one-on-one with her. "Could I see Sam's room? That would make him more real to me."

"Sure." Cathy bounced off the couch to lead the way upstairs. It was an old-enough house to have one of those steep straight-up narrow stairways the eighteenth-century Cape houses had lying in wait for the careless, the dim-sighted and drunken, the unwary tourist. Leila, who had once rented such a house for August, climbed cautiously. She no longer thought that Cathy and Zak might be lovers. Cathy acted too nervous around him.

His room reminded her a little of her own son's. They both had computers obviously well used. Both had shelves of science fiction, but David's shelves also contained hard science books, math, physics, while Sam's ran to mysteries and how-to books. There were many pop psych books on gaining confidence, dealing successfully with women, making people respect and admire you. He had perhaps twenty-five such manuals on the shelf above his single bed. The other prominent objects in the room were a rowing machine in the middle of the floor and some sort of apparatus of pulleys and weights on the wall. On the bulletin board were photos of what must have been his father with his mother and himself at perhaps twelve, his uncle somewhat younger with a stunning redhead in a sort of abbreviated white romper, and several pictures of what appeared to be the cast of a play, including what she could recognize now as Sam and what she knew from newspaper photos and video was Becky Burgess. There was also a snapshot of Becky alone standing under a pine tree and smiling wistfully at the camera.

Leila took a seat in the desk chair, swinging it around. "It must be very hard on you, worrying about your son."

Cathy perched on the bed, sighing deeply. "I'm awfully worried about him, but Zak found him a good lawyer, I hope, anyhow. That woman put him up to everything. She had a hypnotic influence over him." Cathy stared at her to see if she agreed.

"I haven't even met her yet. I understand how upset you must be. Is Sam your only child?"

"I have a daughter, but she's already married." Cathy sighed. "Too young, if you ask me, but of course she didn't. Do you have children?"

Leila answered her with a description of her son aimed at maximizing similarities. She must have succeeded, for Cathy said softly, "It must frighten you, learning about Sam, because you know, they sound like they could be brothers. Not that brothers are always the same. I mean, my husband Mike and Zak were nothing alike, except in their eyes and their hair. Mike was much . . . stronger. He sold real estate, and he was great at it, you know? He could sell an empty bag. He was real ambitious. If he hadn't invested some of the money he made, we wouldn't have anything today. Not a thing!"

"Don't be melodramatic, Cathy." Zak had crept up the stairs and now he spoke from the doorway. "You make some money from your students, and I can always help you. You mustn't give Mrs. Landsman the impression that Sam got into trouble because he needed money. He was just under the influence of an older woman who mesmerized him."

Hypnotize, mesmerize, they had a line going. She decided to give up for the day and see Cathy another time, without the overseer. She took down the information on Cathy's studio. She would phone her there, tomorrow.

She walked into her house, calling loudly. She was distinctly better pleased to be home than a week ago. She talked to Vronsky in the kitchen while she cooked. He ate his cat food and then sampled her cuisine, taking a faint superior interest in the news from his habitual perch on David's old chair.

Anytime she shut a door in his face, she heard a plaintive mew, then a louder noise, then a louder cry until he was bellowing. "Who did you live with? Why did they discard you? What happened? Did your person die? Move away?" She had trouble imagining anyone voluntarily releasing such a loving creature, but people threw away their lovers and their wives and husbands and friends every day. She did not. She persisted. She cherished. She held on.

Every morning after breakfast, rain or sun, he asked to go out. When she refused, he turned from the door and forgot. He liked looking out the windows, especially when birds or squirrels were about. On her lunch hour, she visited a pet store and bought him toys—balls that tinkled, feathered snippets on fishing poles, catnip mice. He found the jingle balls puerile. He batted them once or twice, politely, and then knocked them under the couch and forgot them, hoping she would also. However, anything that moved under her power he would chase, whether it was an elaborate feathered creature on a fishing pole or a piece of string from a bakery box of rugalach.

In the first days she stepped on his tail and his paws often, until they choreographed their movements in the kitchen. She found him large-hearted and forgiving. When she came home from Lesley, there he was, as she had imagined, looking out the window. She remembered to leave a note for Mrs. Burke not to let him out. When she got home, there was a note in return. "In any pet supply store, buy a fine-toothed comb. Comb for fleas. Dip the comb in very hot water and dry on a paper towel. You will have the fleas under control in two weeks, Mary Burke. P.S. I make house calls to feed and spend time with cats when their owners travel. Please make arrangements well in advance if possible."

She had not seen any fleas, but Vronsky did scratch from time to time. She was not surprised Mrs. Burke knew about fleas, for she knew how to take tannin stains from teapots and how to fix a sticky drawer. Phyllis had not passed on household lore, as their apartment had been cleaned sporadically by whichever of them could no longer stand the dirt. Supper was slapped together by whoever was hungriest. When they had enough money, they got takeout. She grew up on a great many tuna noodle casseroles and macaroni and cheese dishes. Debbie's general method of cooking was to open a can of creamed soup—mushroom was her favorite—and pour it over the chicken or fish or hamburger.

Nicolas had converted her to good food and gourmet specifications. His mother was still an excellent cook, switching between three styles with ease: general Texas, best displayed in chili or barbecue; Mexican; German Jewish, especially when dealing with chicken or noodles or cabbage. The first time Leila had made supper for him, he had been appalled. After they married, he presented her with Julia Child Volumes One and Two.

He was a man for whom the quality of things mattered, whether it was the wine he drank with supper or the vodka he consumed just before. He was just as fussy about his clothes, although many people would not have guessed so, since his taste did not run to American or Italian designers. He liked cashmere or merino black turtlenecks worn with one of three Harris tweed jackets. For pants he liked chinos or cords that coordinated with the jackets. The most expensive item on his body was usually his shoes or boots. He had wide feet. She used to tease him that his feet were square. They were hard to fit and he was extremely sensitive to the kind of leather and cut. Usually she was the one who replaced whatever wore out, but it had taken him years to train her in exactly what he would wear and what he would never, never be seen in.

Christmas. She had forgotten it. She had not grown up observing it, but in his Texas home, they had made a great deal about it. She had learned to oblige. She was fitted to him. She simply knew thoroughly his likes and dislikes, what it took to please and comfort him, what amused him, what disturbed him. Such knowledge was even more specialized than Mary Burke's lore of how to remove stains from baseboards and how to identify the spore of mice. He was coming home for Thanksgiving. She had permitted herself to become extremely annoyed about an unimportant affair such as he had had fifteen times before. That relationship would be ending this very week. The play was open. It was a brief unpleasant incident she must put behind her. He needed a woman when he was out of town with a play, and he always found one, young, insecure, hopeful.

When the play was set to run, the relationship was over. She did not like it, but it was nothing that would affect either of them a week after he returned. It was ending, whether Sheryl knew that or not. She thought of that young woman, twenty-four and probably lonely and desperate in New York. Soon Sheryl would be alone again. It was not fair, but getting involved with a very married man was not smart. She could pity the young woman, abstractly. But Sheryl had not asked her for advice or input, had she? Leila was about to pull her own life back together.

CHAPTER 14

BECKY

Becky heard the first report at work. Sound Cable had a local news show at 12:30, after the regular channels did their noon news. They figured they picked up people who were mad for yet more news, or who hadn't got to sit down in front of the TV before they missed the headlines. Roger, who read the news as well as doing the interview show and "Dining Out," was recently divorced, but he wasn't interested in her. He went for private school graduates with family money. She could not help disliking him because he reminded her of Ted Topper. Besides, she didn't like being obviously written off by one of the few possibilities at the office.

Therefore she wasn't really listening to the live news as it was pumped throughout the office. She had finished her sandwich and black coffee, scanned the want ads quickly, making sure nobody saw what she was doing, tore out the one possibility and stuffed it in her wallet. Then a name penetrated her consciousness. The *Mary Helena* out of New Bedford. Distress call received by the Coast Guard.

She called home. The phone rang and rang. Finally little Tina picked it up. After a frustrating conversation with the four-year-old, Becky got Tina to fetch Nana. It was hard on Nana to come to the phone, but Becky had to know. The *Mary Helena* was Uncle Ray's boat, the one her brother Joey worked on. Tommy worked with Papa, but Ray had only daughters. Everybody had gone down to the docks, except for Nana whom Gracie had left with the kids.

Becky got an immediate tension headache fitting over her skull. A distress call but the Coast Guard helicopter couldn't find them. Radio silence now. It was a stormy day, the wind lashing curtains of water scudding across the parking lot, the pines swaying and the oaks swishing their heavy leaves. Why had they gone out, with a storm predicted? Because half the time there wasn't a storm when the radio said so, and it was money. Ray was sending his girls through college. Joey wanted to marry his girlfriend. Ray had been fishing for thirty-five years. He boasted, "I know the sea better than any yuppie in a blue suit who stands in front of a weather map."

The fleet was made up of old boats they kept repairing. The prices were better than they used to be, but there were less fish and they had to go farther and stay out longer. Scallops were the meal ticket. But the rake was dangerous and hard to manage in heavy seas.

She had never been as close to her brothers Joey or Rennie as to Tommy, her favorite, but she loved Joey. He was not as bright as Tommy but sweeter tempered. Laurie had gone through a period of being extra holy, of wanting to be a nun, and Joey, Tommy and Becky had caught the brunt of her piety. She was always telling on them. That had made them pull together against her. Laurie and Becky never got along. They were always fighting over the same space, the same things. Laurie was only two years younger, but Becky never felt they looked like sisters. Laurie was plain and taller, with long brown hair that was her best feature, pouring like silk down her back. She was studying to be a dental technician. She was always doing something to her teeth. For six months she had worn a chlorine mouthpiece to bed to bleach her teeth white. Now she had alarmingly white teeth that looked like so many well-scrubbed washbasins. When she opened her mouth, they seemed to leap out of her sallow narrow face.

Joey was the plainest of the boys, as if what looks the family enjoyed had been lavished on Tommy and Grace, when she was younger, that is, and, Becky felt, had fallen on her and certainly on Grace's kids. Belle was plain, but she made herself up and did her hair in the latest style. Joey was of middle height with a red birthmark on his cheek that looked like a burn. He was soft-spoken with a raspy cigarette voice, for he had smoked compulsively from the year he turned thirteen. He smoked Camels and his fingers had a yellow tinge. He was lean, hard-muscled like all the boys. The dogs were more his than anybody's. He went hunting all fall but he never caught anything but an occasional skinny rabbit. He just liked to take the dogs into the marshes. They all came back stinking from the muck, exhausted and happy.

He'd barely scraped through high school, still had the same girl. Becky was scared for Joey, in a cold sweat. She ground her teeth from nervousness, clutched herself, paced the office.

She called her uncle Ray's house, got his wife, who fell on the phone as if parked right over it. "The Coast Guard won't go out again. They say it's too rough. They won't send up a helicopter. I'm sick. What's the use of them? We should ask them to go out when it's eighty and the Sound is flat as a parking lot? Now's when we need them, and they say it's too rough. I hate them! Ray's such a good man, and they won't go out."

Becky went back hesitantly from her desk to the studio. When Roger got off the air, she asked him, "If something comes in about the *Mary Helena*, would you let me know? Please. If you hear anything."

"How come?" Roger stared at her. "A fishing boat?"

"My brother's one of the crew," she mumbled. She was embarrassed. Nice middle-class girls did not have brothers on fishing boats.

But she guessed wrong about their reaction. One by one her superiors and the other secretaries and the cameramen and even the manager came and spoke to her. It was as if, by having a brother on the news, she had gained status. With her, they too became part of the news. Nobody suggested she go home early, which is what she would have liked most and what she did not dare ask for, but they all wanted to chat her up sympathetically.

"We could do a little memorial on it. Boost our ratings in New Bedford," she heard the manager saying to Roger. "Community service. Get on it."

She wanted to tell them that they couldn't bury her brother yet. Boats often disappeared and then showed up again. They could be blown off course by the storm. Their radio could be dead. They could be drifting. Nobody had found wreckage. She was angry, but she could not let her anger show. It was bad luck as well as meanness to write off somebody's life like that.

The wreckage showed up two days later, when the seas had subsided. Ray and Joey did not wash up. The memorial Mass was held without a body. They had nobody to bury in the family plot. Joey was gone as if he had dissolved. Everyone in the family was grieved, but in a strange subdued prolonged way. Belle had nightmares and kept waking Becky, who wasn't sleeping too well to begin with. He had vanished from his place. Not that there was anyplace really his in the tiny overcrowded house.

Sound Cable did put on a memorial program, with local big shots from the co-op and the packers. They put her on too and her brother Tommy in the navy suit he had graduated high school in, tight but serviceable, and Papa and Uncle Ray's wife, two of the daughters, Joey's girlfriend.

Becky did not like the way she looked in black. Lisa, one of the secretaries, lent her a grey suit, which she wore with her own best blue blouse for taping. Roger wrote out a speech for her, which was dopey but she did not fight. She stood looking into the camera. Out of the corner of her eye she could see herself on the monitor. They promised her a tape afterward.

She was the only person besides Roger, who was narrating, to be on twice. She got to talk about Joey first, and then about the family's feelings for the sea, one of the speeches Roger had written. She spoke right to the camera and kept her gaze on its big eye with the red light overhead.

Afterward Roger said, "You came across very well. Good presence."

"I studied media in college. It was my major," she said, to remind him that she had gone to college and that she had been trained. She passionately hoped that the bosses had felt that way too. Maybe they would use her in front of the camera again. They had to see that she was not just a receptionist.

The next week, her family had another requiem Mass to attend, but this time there was a body and a real funeral. Nana woke them screaming and then groaning, but by the time they got her to the hospital, she was unconscious. The next day she was dead.

Mama said after the funeral, "It's a pity they don't make a video for every time somebody dies, and then you'd have something to hold on to. With your poor brother, we don't have a grave, but at least we have that video, and you look so pretty. It makes me feel better that they did that." Mama patted Becky's shoulder gently. She was not a woman for a lot of hugging, she was too tired most of the time. But lately she had been touching all of them, as if to make sure they were really still there. "I wish we had one of Nana, from before she got cancer."

Belle nodded her high do fervently. "That video was something special. And if you didn't know them personal, they wouldn't have done that for us, let's not fool ourselves. Boats go down every summer and winter, and they don't ever make a video for the family."

Within a couple of weeks, they all seemed to breathe easier. Becky missed Nana, but her long slow dying had drained energy that none of them had. Maybe the reason people like her parents had big families wasn't the Church nattering at them, but so that if somebody died, the house was still full of people. Middle-class people hardly ever had seven kids. In future, she might edit her family down to a more acceptable size. I am one of four children. Three would be better, but she felt that was too much of a reach.

At Sound Cable, nobody suggested she go on camera again, although she kept hoping. She knew she had done a good job. Even Roger had said so. However, one married secretary would be leaving in October and moving to Hartford. Becky was told she would take over that job, and she should improve her typing skills. She did.

It was hard to get time alone in the house, but sometimes at night when everybody else had gone to bed or was out late, she would play the tape. She turned the sound way down or muted it, but seeing herself framed in the TV gave her patience. At least she had that video. In the borrowed dark grey suit and the perfect blue blouse, she looked right. She appeared as if she belonged there, in the eye of the camera. Perched on a stool in front of the set, Becky was moved by herself, her obvious sincerity, her candor, her presence. Why hadn't the others at Sound Cable noticed how natural she was on camera? She did not know how to break through to be noticed.

If people did not look at you, did not listen to you, it did not matter who or what you were. The myth was that if you were pretty and smart, you would get what you wanted, but she could stare at herself on the video and see that she was pretty. Her face was as pretty as half the women on the TV every night. She was blond, she was young, she was thin. She was the smartest person in her family, and she had more brains than anybody else at Sound Cable.

So why, when she spoke, did no one listen? Why didn't they notice how effective she was on camera? Why didn't anyone pay attention? It took something she didn't have yet, but she did not know what. Luck, certainly, but you couldn't earn that or buy it at the mall. Those girls that Roger went out with, they were not as pretty as she was, but they got good jobs. Money made people pay attention. Money made them turn and notice you, and then they saw how pretty you were, and then they said how smart you were. Good clothes made a woman visible. Now they all looked right through her. She sat in that office useful and unnoticed as a computer terminal.

CHAPTER 15

LEILA

David arrived back before Nicolas. Leila chattered with David nonstop from the time David got into the car at Logan, even though they had talked two or three times a week since he'd left for California. He was tanned and had grown another inch. He would end up as tall as Nicolas but smaller boned. He had a slightly hunched look, a starchless way of standing as if to contrast with his father's massive presence.

He had new glasses, she noticed, dark brown frames, better looking on him. She drank him in in sideways glances as she drove. In him she had always been able to see herself and Nick, as well as her own father and mother. His hands were most like her father's, shapely hands with long tapering fingers that looked more fragile than they were. In reaction, perhaps, to his father's booming projection, he spoke softly. Often people had to lean a little forward to hear him. He could sound shy, but it was restraint, rather, a control. He did not like his temper or his voice to get away from him.

She adored her son, she admitted it freely to herself. She attempted to open her hands and her mind and let him go into the world, but she had always been an anxious and an interfering mother. She fought herself, but she knew she was only partly successful at controlling her fierce love.

"Did you get the new glasses because your eyes changed? Or just for cosmetic reasons?"

"My eyes changed."

"In what way?"

"I'm a little more myopic."

"Are you reading with good light in your dorm room?"

"Mother, myopia is hereditary."

"If it's hereditary, why don't your father or I have it?"

"He *is* nearsighted. He just won't wear glasses unless he's driving."

She wanted to know if his bed was hard enough for his back. She wanted to know if he had the right rain gear. She wanted to know if he was getting enough sleep, for he had a tendency to read late in bed. She wanted to know exactly what he ate for breakfast. She wanted to know about his new girlfriend Ikuko. She wanted to know how his roommates treated him, and whether he was tempted to settle in California after graduation (so far, far away from her). She controlled herself. He would be home until Sunday. She could gradually ask questions, she could proceed gently and slowly. She had him for almost five days now. She must keep from clutching.

She had done her shopping, picking up a fresh organic turkey from Bread and Circus, two fat buff butternut squashes, a pie pumpkin, salad greens including a pretty bouquet of radicchio that cost as much as gold per ounce, leeks to be braised, cranberries for sauce. She had bought a good fresh pumpernickel from Brookline and the hard rolls Nick loved in the morning.

"How's Shana doing? Is her grandmother still there?"

"She may move in with me, as I told you. Have you thought about how you feel?"

He shrugged. "Shana's okay. She's like a pesky little sister. I figure you have to take her in if that's what she wants."

"Don't you think Melanie would have tried to do for you? She certainly would have made Thanksgiving dinner for you."

"Mother! Gross! Have you arranged for someone to sew the buttons back on my shirts should you be run over by a large truck?"

Vronsky was waiting just inside the big front door swishing his tail impatiently. When he saw David, he frowned, she thought. But David was an animal person. He had Vronsky circling him and purring in five minutes, rubbing against this new body servant who scratched under his chin correctly and behind his ears, slightly tufted as if he were a little lynx.

There was a message on her answering machine from Debbie, saying they were at the Westin, near the Prudential Center in Boston. She called back.

"Yeah, where were you? I called an hour ago."

"At the airport picking up David. I'm hardly ever home before five. Would you like to come over?" Should she offer to go get them?

"Red wants to eat at this famous place he heard of. Red, honey, what's the name of that restaurant? Durbin Park."

"Durgin," Leila corrected automatically. "I'm still waiting for Nick to arrive from New York, and I have cooking to do tonight. I don't know what time Nick will be home. Could you maybe come over here?"

"Well, you sound a bit put out. Besides, Red has been looking forward to this place. He read about it in an airplane magazine."

"Why don't you go ahead? If Nick comes soon and he's up for it, we'll find you there." Fat chance. That was not the sort of restaurant Nick enjoyed and she did not feel like running around town with him before they'd had a chance for some sort of communication.

"Whatever. We'll see you tomorrow. What time do you want us?"

"Around five for dinner, but why don't we get together earlier?"

"We promised the kids something nice—"

David spoke up. "I'll meet you at the hotel at ten and we'll figure something out. Most good things for kids are shut, but I promise to look at the papers." At some point he'd picked up the extension and been listening.

"Ten's too early, we're on California time," Debbie said. Leila excused herself, leaving them to negotiate. She was still expecting Phyllis.

She made her maple Bavarian cream for tomorrow while David was unpacking his suitcase stuffed with dirty laundry. Then he lay on the couch with Vronsky on his chest telling her his adventures at school while she trotted in circles straightening, fluffing pillows, waiting for the cream to set enough to add Madeira. She put the cranberries on to cook in kosher wine, threw in a handful of orange peel, rushed back to David. His eyes were a lighter brown than hers, the color of wet sand. Her own eyes were strong coffee. "Ikuko has eyes as dark as yours," he told her.

Nick had called three times during the day: once to say he was leaving New York at eleven; once from New Haven where he had got off the train to see a friend in the drama department; once more from the train station after David was home to say he was boarding the train but that it looked to be very crowded and he would probably have to stand all the way. She wondered if she were supposed to say, Oh, how terrible, why don't you stay where you are? She did not. She said she would meet the train out at Route 128, because downtown would be a mess. He said he'd take the train to South Station and a cab home, not to worry. He'd be there by eight at the latest and they could all dine.

It was actually nine-fifteen before she served Nick supper. David and she had eaten a pickup meal of spaghetti with wild mushrooms and a little chopped meat and lots of basil. She heated it for Nick, who ate with enjoyment but obviously not with real hunger. He had been taken out to a great lunch in New Haven to discuss collaborating on Ibsen's *Master Builder.* Nick saw in it a great and lasting parable of male and female relationships.

Nick was intrigued by her own new project, although he lost interest when she confessed she had not yet met Becky. "They sound like a boring bunch of suburban losers," he said. "Speaking of losers, critics are a sorry lot these days. Even the ones who liked my *Oedipus* missed the point. Critics are getting younger and stupider. What isn't based on comic books or the TV they grew up on, is beyond them. They have no knowledge of culture beyond the last ten years."

"What we find, Dad, is that you people thought of culture as Greece and Rome and some Victorians. We have to be multicultural—that dirty word—because the world we live in isn't white and European any longer. I meet guys who couldn't tell you who Oedipus was, but they know all about Japanese sword fighting and anime. There are dozens and dozens of 'cultures.' "

"Anyone want dessert? I have two kinds of cookies, some rugalach I got in Brookline this morning—"

"Rugalach always reminds me how when I was little, you used to make pies. Apple, rhubarb, blueberry. And you'd make extra dough and roll it out and bake it sprinkled with cinnamon and sugar for me. . . ." Sometimes when David was remembering his childhood, his voice would take on a slow, hypnotic coloration.

"I brought you a present." Nick rummaged in his briefcase. "Peterson's *Field Guide To Western Birds.* I figured you've been doing some hiking."

"Let me see. That's great. Ikuko and I spent a weekend in Joshua Tree. It's really gorgeous."

"What does she look like? Got a photo?" Nick asked.

"Actually, yeah." Grimacing, David dug out his wallet. He looked torn between embarrassment and pride. "That's her leaning against the rock."

Nick smiled. "She's lovely. Classic Japanese features."

"She's really bright," David said with mild defensiveness, lest he be thought to have selected his girl for her looks.

Phyllis called. "I'm out on 128 in a Sheraton. Where's Debbie?"

"At the Westin. Mother, how come you're out there? You were going to stay with me."

"My roommate Joan decided to come. She didn't have anything special to do, and we usually have Thanksgiving together. So, we'll see you tomorrow."

Maybe Phyllis hadn't wanted to do all the driving herself. She had insisted on driving rather than taking a plane. It was eight hours, and Leila was willing to bet that when Phyllis had contemplated all that driving, she had drafted her roommate. She had been sharing her apartment in the Mt. Airy neighborhood of Philadelphia with another nurse for three years. They were both in their early sixties—about the age of Leila's cleaning lady.

"Well, we ended up with seven less people in the house than we might have had," Leila said as she finally faced Nick alone. "Maybe we can talk."

"Not tonight, light of my eyes. I'm half drunk, half hungover and all bushed. You won't get more than mumbling and a hug out of me tonight."

"Nevertheless, Nick, we're going to have to talk. Tomorrow might be really crazy, but Friday then. We have a lot to work out."

He groaned and mumbled something, his eyes already closed. Vronsky got into her side of the bed and tried to get her to move over to the middle, where she usually slept. She must let go of her anger, she must. She would ruin her life if she did not. Tomorrow was a holiday, and it was the duty of a hostess to put aside her small problems to make nice. After all, Becky would not be enjoying Thanksgiving dinner with her family. Cathy Solomon might have her prickly brother-in-law Zak for dinner, but she would not have her only son. Terry's parents would never see him again. Melanie's daughter had to come to Leila. Of all the families she had begun to study over the past couple of weeks, only hers was intact. She must make herself rejoice and she must create a warm holiday that would reconfirm the three of them as a family unit. It was her job to rebuild and conserve. And how often did she manage to see her mother? She saw Debbie every two years at most. This was a holiday in which everyone was coming together, and she had to forget her disappointments and her moodiness and make it work.

About noon, Jane called. "What do you want us to bring?"

"Oh, some wine."

"Emily doesn't drink wine."

"Then bring what she does drink," Leila said patiently. She had met Emily a couple of times, but she tended to get her confused with the one before, the librarian who did triathlon. Emily was tall too but she was an ear, nose and throat doctor. Jane had recited to her once some statistic on how few women were that kind of doctor.

"You remember that she has two boys."

"Boys?" Leila did not remember. Jane went on about her lovers and it was hard to keep them separate. "How old?"

"Eight and ten."

Leila started to say, I wish you'd told me, but of course Jane must have. "If they need anything special to eat, bring that if you don't mind. But you know there's always lots of food." It was a tenet of Leila's that at Passover and at Thanksgiving, there should be way too much food: product of a childhood of haphazard meals and half-empty refrigerators with nothing more substantial than open jars of pickles and maraschino cherries and ketchup to satisfy the hunger of an oversized and rapidly growing girl child. "Anyhow, they won't be the only children. We'll have my sister Debbie's kids. Bring a lot of wine anyhow. We're going to be, let me see, if I count Shana and David as adults, we'll be at least eleven adults and five children."

There was a little silence. "Are we holding this in the Harvard gym? What you're really going to need is some chairs. Got enough dishes?"

"You know me. I have dishes and dishes. But chairs, yes, that's a great idea. Avoids me having to sit on a footstool and three phone books."

She had cooked no feasts, no real dinners in the last month. She wondered why a day of cooking made her feel like a good woman. Her own mother had been inept in the kitchen. Perhaps she was living out a myth of the ideal mother. Phyllis was quite real and lumpy and nothing like the mothers of the sitcoms that issued into her brain from the grainy black-and-white TV of her childhood.

Phyllis would clump home from the hospital and put her feet in a tub of hot water with piney soak in it in the kitchen with the TV on, smoking and reading women's magazines, regaling them with the latest tidbits. "Do you know if you wash your hands in coconut milk, you'll look years younger?" Neither Debbie nor Leila wanted to look years younger. They could not wait to grow up. "Ha. They ask fifty men what they look at first, and they say a woman's face. Barefaced liars! You talk to fifty men, and forty-nine of them talk to your tits.'' Phyllis had a great raucous laugh.

It was early afternoon when Leila heard that laugh exploding in the front hall. Apparently Nick had let her in. ''Yeah, this is my mate Joan. So, how have they been treating you? Looks like my daughter hasn't stopped feeding you too much and too often, hey, Nick?''

Leila tossed her apron on a chair, rushing in. Phyllis gave her a peck on the cheek. She wasn't one for a fuss. Then Leila shook hands with Joan, a woman who could have passed for Phyllis's twin. They were both five feet six, solidly built women neither thin nor fat, with broad faces and grey hair chopped short, both wearing loose pants and tunics with earrings to show they were dressed up. Phyllis's were gold hoops inlaid with her birthstone, garnet, Leila had given her; Joan's were plastic turkeys in honor of the day.

''So did Debbie really fly out here?'' Phyllis bellowed. ''She never comes East. She hates the East. She likes those wide open spaces. She's even got horses now. I can't imagine a horse for a pet. Joan and I have a poodle.''

''Maybe I'll get one of those Shetland ponies,'' Joan said. ''If people can keep little pigs for pets, why not little horses? Course we'd have to yank out the wall-to-wall and put in straw.''

''The way we keep that apartment, who ever sees the floor?''

Both women laughed and let Nick bring them a couple of beers. Phyllis always had her cronies, nurses she had been close to for twenty years, thirty years, women in whose lives men came and went like colds that arrived suddenly and hung on a while, or else guys who couldn't marry them because, like Phyllis's last boyfriend, they had a wife somewhere. If one of this circle of tough hardworking loud and foul-mouthed women married, it was generally to a husband who turned out to be a compulsive drinker or gambler or something worse, and pretty soon all the other women were saying, Louise, you got to dump him, Louise, you got to show him the door. And Louise did. In childhood Leila had told herself, I will pick a bright healthy worthwhile man and I will make a lifelong marriage with him, I will.

Both Phyllis and Joan made perfunctory gestures at helping, but Leila knew better than to let her mother near her kitchen. Phyllis, Joan and Nick sat watching football, none of them real fans but all willing to pass the time and make lewd comments. Nick offered to bet on the outcome of the game, but Phyllis refused adamantly. She would not bet on anything. She would not even play penny-ante poker. "Gambling stole my husband's life. Gambling took the roof off our heads. Flush your money down the toilet instead. Or just give it to me. I know how to use it."

Joan chuckled. "She won't let me play the lottery, even."

"Everybody in theater is a gambler," Nick said. "Who needs the thrill of a horse race when you're betting your career on an idiot play?"

Leila liked the ritual feel of preparing a feast. Some items on the long menu were new, clipped from the paper or found in a cookbook read in bed the week before, but some were old favorites David would have been furious if she forgot, like the two desserts, the cold maple Bavarian cream and the hot rum pumpkin pie. It was her folly, partly designed to please her family but partly designed to please herself. Beyond that, she aimed to impress some archaic deity, a goddess who would reward her for being a good woman by allowing her to keep what she had. Soon she would add a daughter, Shana, to the household. The family still held and even grew.

CHAPTER 16

LEILA

Debbie, Red, Robin and the littlest, Ben, arrived at four-thirty. As David had advised her, Abel, the fourteen-year-old, had stayed in California with his best friend. Watching Debbie and Phyllis greet each other, Leila thought that, while she always felt the odd one out, everyone in her family was awkward in affection. Phyllis, however, was at ease with her grandchildren, getting down on the floor and making faces at Ben, who clutched his mother's leg and glowered. Within five minutes, Phyllis had him giggling helplessly. Robin was the fey dark one, the only girl, and Phyllis was able to kiss her as she could not her own daughters. But Phyllis looked up at the six-foot-two, potbellied frame of Red Rodgers, and she had nothing to say except Hi there. Finally they bonded around smoking, standing together in exile on the porch puffing at the street.

Joan said, "She's promised to quit, and she's supposed to get one of those patches installed as a Christmas present for me. I'm not Jewish. She won't let me give her a Christmas present, but that's hers to me."

"It's a present for all of us," Leila said. "I've been trying to get her to stop for the last twenty years."

"If you had more children, Leila, you wouldn't fuss so much. Mother's an adult—she's a nurse, for heaven's sake." Debbie shook her head pityingly. Three children and a fourth on the way and she was still thin. Her belly was growing, but the rest of her remained childlike. Standing near Debbie made Leila feel oversized, baggy, sagging, bursting with flesh. Debbie was petite. She herself was the economy size. Debbie's hair was lighter than Leila's and finer, and her features more delicate. They had early been assigned their roles: Leila was the smart one; Debbie, the pretty one. Leila was responsible; Debbie, sensitive. They were still fighting for Mama's attention, and Mama was still overtaxed and wanting them both to cool it and shut up.

Nick and Red went to work on the problem of the table: it would accept enough leaves (with some help from a screwdriver and an oil can and a lot of heaving and cursing) to seat twelve comfortably, but they were fifteen. A card table had to be stuck on the end, either straight or as an L. Then Debbie realized Ben had disappeared. After a frantic half hour, he was located under Leila's bed, nose to nose with Vronsky like two cats having a Mexican standoff. Robin was happy at David's computer playing some space game.

Joan and Debbie took over the setting of the table, getting into an intense and technical conversation on massage techniques. Joan was a nurse; Debbie was a massage therapist. Leila, whose meal was under control and on schedule, basted the turkey and prepared the pie. Now Phyllis was regaling everyone with hospital horror stories, while they hauled every available chair to the L-shaped table hidden under two solid-color cloths and one Guatemalan print.

In the living room, Red began to entice Nick with real estate. "Just thirty down and you have hold of property worth two hundred big ones in today's marketplace. You can't pass this up. It's a sure thing."

At four-thirty Shana and Mrs. Peretz came in carrying a covered dish. Shana was all in black, with heavy eye makeup. She had cut off her hair, which intensified her starved hollow-cheeked look over her black turtleneck. She flung herself in a chair in the living room and looked around. "Where's David?" Nick sat down next to her and tried to chat her up. Mrs. Peretz had brought a sweet-potato dish which had to be heated, an almost impossible task that required repacking both ovens. Joan took that over, while Leila ran upstairs to fetch David to talk to Shana. Shana was talking to Nick about death.

Shana bowed her head when she saw David, but the effect was spoiled when she burst out, "Guess what, David. My dad's arranged for me to attend Westborn–Mt. Stephens! I can enter next week, in mid-semester, and I can ride. They have horses!"

"Where is Westborn–Mt. Stephens?" Leila asked, confused.

"Just ten miles from Dad. I saw the school and it's great! It looks like a little village, with two horse barns and a paddock and miles of trails. I can't wait!"

Leila went slowly out to the kitchen. She didn't know whether to be disappointed or relieved, but she felt like a fool. Only she seemed to have taken seriously Shana's request to live with her. David appeared a moment later. "Well, so much for that. I'm ecstatic her father bribed her to move. She loves to be the center of a drama, doesn't she?"

"Look, she underwent a great strain and a great loss. Whatever makes her feel better."

David surveyed the stove top, the countertops, peered into both ovens. "There's too much food."

"There's supposed to be too much food at Thanksgiving. That's the point of it," she said patiently.

Nick appeared in the doorway. "Leila, you've forgotten to change. Time to get dressed."

She looked down. She was still wearing the pants she had been baking and cooking in all day. "Oh well. Nobody comes to look at me."

"Come on," Nick said severely. "David will take over while you're upstairs." Taking her arm, he led her off. On her bed she saw that he had laid out three dresses. Nick had the same critical eye for women's clothes he did for men's. He had made over her style years ago. She had tended to wear layers and layers, under the impression it concealed the body that had always felt too big. He had trained her to dress to emphasize her stature and figure.

"I doubt I can wear the blue one. I have to be at my less chubby range."

"You look to me as if you've lost weight. Try it. . . . There, see? Now, wear navy tights with it, navy pumps and let me see your earrings. Something big and dangling."

Nick was the only straight man she had ever known who could dress a woman head to toe attractively and efficiently. He had an eye. He was putting together a costume for her. He had her dressed in twelve minutes. The dress did fit. She had not weighed herself all fall. She was grateful to him for thinking of how she looked. Maybe he was beginning a cycle of finding her attractive again. Shyly she glanced at herself in the mirror, and for once, she rather liked what she saw. She would never look petite or svelte, but she did look rather elegant, almost handsome.

Nick gave her a quick but feeling pat on the rump as they left the bedroom. "That's my big beautiful doll. Strut your stuff."

It was five-thirty when Leila passed the hall clock, and Jane and company were nowhere to be seen. Everybody had been invited long before she intended to serve, just to avoid this kind of fretting. She called Jane's house. Jane answered.

"Where are you? This is Leila."

"We're getting ready. Why, what time are you going to serve?"

"Right now," Leila said. "Please just come as you are."

Debbie and Shana had formed an alliance, Leila noted. Shana had abandoned the attempt to impress David and was looking at photos of Debbie's horses. "Two of them all your own!" Shana crooned. "How happy you must be."

A little later Leila heard Debbie saying, "Oh, so she was trying to get you to move in with her. She tries to take over."

"Oh no!" Shana said. "It was my fantasy. I didn't think my dad wanted me, and I was leery of his new family."

Finally at five after six Jane sauntered in. Jane was the style of lesbian that men usually liked, because she was elegant and attractive to just about everybody. She wore her auburn hair as a sleek cap. Her blouse was creamy silk under a cashmere blazer. Her pants were draped black silk. She wore large square-cut earrings of amethyst. Jane was never without a partner for longer than a month. She had incorporated elements of style usually labelled masculine or feminine into her range of costumes. Today she was the young Katharine Hepburn, Leila guessed.

Her newish partner, Emily, was tall. She was also big-boned, on the heavy side and wearing shit-kicker boots. She was all in various levels and layers of tweed. Her hair was flyaway pale brown. She wore no jewelry except for a gold watch. She looked uncomfortable and sullen, dragging along two boys who looked much like her, except for being half her height. One, Tim, was working on the girth. The older, Chuck, went straight for the TV and the football game.

Nonetheless, Leila herded them all toward the improvised table. Every chair she could muster and four from Jane. She had Nick at one end, herself at the other. She was flanked by Mrs. Peretz on her left, who looked terrified and had withdrawn into a crouch in her seat, and Phyllis on the other—so she might monopolize her mother's attention. Joan was next to Phyllis, so she would be near someone she knew. Then came Emily. Maybe they could talk medicine? Then Emily's two boys. Jane was on one side of Nick and Shana on the other. That should improve his spirits. He always flirted with Jane, who flirted back. Next to Shana she had put David. Then Robin, who related to David with enthusiasm. Then Debbie between her two children. Then Red next to Mrs. Peretz, and back to herself. She would be up and down half the meal anyhow. Her chair was nearest to the kitchen door, and that was convenient.

"What is this stuff? It looks like Wheatena," Chuck said.

"Cream of chestnut soup." She reflected fondly, glancing at her son's fine profile, that David had been a willing eater. After a finicky period around seven, he would try anything. "Catfish and rattlesnake, wow."

"The Boston Lyric Opera approached me about staging *Don Juan* next winter. I'm considering it. An intriguing figure," Nick said. "The great lover."

"I never saw Don Juan as anything but a notch collector," Jane replied. "A seducer if the woman succumbed on schedule, otherwise a rapist. A lover? He never loved anything but his prick."

Chuck giggled. Emily threw Jane a look of cold fury. "We should watch our language at table," she said in a throaty voice, beautiful and rich.

"Do you sing?" Leila asked on impulse. David was clearing and she was carrying out the turkey and its accompaniments.

"Contralto. I'm in the chorus of the Handel Society. Do you sing?"

"I used to."

"She has a fine voice but she hardly ever raises it," Nick said. "An admirable thing in a woman." He made the mistake of trying to fill Emily's glass as he poured out a chardonnay around the table.

"I think there's a great deal too much of that at Thanksgiving," Emily said. "Perhaps that causes some people to forget there are children at the table."

"That's one thing we've never had a problem with," Mrs. Peretz said. She was looking over Jane and Emily carefully. "Drinking. Jews drink wine, but we don't get drunk. I think people who grow up drinking wine don't have so much trouble with alcohol. It's just a food you take in moderation."

"Wine has the same effect as any other form of alcohol," Emily said. "Wine is not food."

Nick said expansively, "We're in a time when people more and more define themselves by what they consume and do not consume—

vegetarians, vegans, smokers, nonsmokers, macrobiotic, low-fat, no-sugar. It becomes a full-time occupation keeping track of what each person eats or drinks, so that a dinner party like this almost needs to be run through a computer first. Europeans find us ridiculous in the moral importance we attach to our habits of consumption." He was trying to defuse Emily's reaction by making the topic more general. Down the length of the table, he gave Leila a rueful look. She felt the old connection with him. They were in tune.

"Several European countries have much higher rates of alcoholism than we do," Emily said firmly, putting her fork down.

Even Mrs. Peretz began to eat much more slowly. Leila cast about for a riff, any riff, to move the conversation to cheerier grounds. "Turkey is a funny name, isn't it, for a native American bird?"

David understood her ploy. "Maybe they thought that's what the birds were saying: *'Turk-kah-turk-kah-turk,'* " he gobbled by way of illustration.

Robin and Tim found that hilarious. For the next twenty minutes, they kept repeating, *"Turk-kah-turk-kah-turk."* Emily beamed. Leila at once understood that Emily was her kind of mother, overprotective, anxious, reining herself in but always on the prowl for trouble.

The tempo of the eating picked up again and everybody seemed determined to be jolly. Jane said conversationally to Joan and Phyllis, "How long have you two been together? As a couple."

Phyllis grinned. "Are we that obvious? Actually we meant to be. It's been three years. It's the best damned marriage I ever had."

David gave a low whistle. Red scratched his head and made a face at Debbie, who looked at Phyllis with her finger against her lips and then at her children, who were still gobbling, in both senses. Leila was too stunned to say anything at all. Nick came to the rescue. "I propose a toast to the new couple—new to us. You seem well suited." He raised his glass.

Emily did not allow herself to be provoked this time. "To Phyllis and Joan. It's never too late to get your life together."

Leila found her voice. "I only wish you'd told me sooner. All that time wasted worrying about your being lonely. Mazel tov."

Then the phone rang. The answering machine was usually on, but someone had turned it off. "Let it go," Leila suggested. "They can call back."

But Nick was already on his way. He answered it in the kitchen and then raced up to his study to talk. "I won't be long," he said.

Everyone had seconds and some had thirds. Leila kept wondering why she hadn't guessed about her mother. But who attributed any sexuality to their own mother? She'd stuffed Joan into the category of nurse-friend. David helped her clear. The phone was still off the hook in the kitchen. David put his finger to his lips and moved toward the phone. She shook her head wildly NO and he shook his head vehemently YES. He wrote on her grocery pad, *Scared? We need info.*

Silently they leaned over the phone where it dangled. Nick spoke loudly, as he always did. "Honey, babe, but you're with your friends. I set up a cast party. I'm sorry I can't be there with you—"

"It's so depressing without you," a soft voice said. Their foreheads touched as they bent to hear. "Everything's empty when you're gone from me. My morning sickness came back again."

The room whirled around Leila. She leaned on the table, suddenly nauseous, dizzy.

"Now don't use that as an excuse for doing anything foolish, Sherri. You know I'm crazy about you, and I'll be back Sunday. Maybe sooner if I can get away. I have obligations here."

Leila grimaced. Here she was, a big fat forty-five-year-old obligation.

"Don't you think you have obligations to me as well? But I don't care about obligations. I care about seeing you, holding you, being with you. . . ."

"Do you need help?" Debbie asked dubiously.

Her face burning, Leila leaped in front of David to block the phone from view, but she was sure Debbie had seen something. Behind her she heard David hang up the phone, none too quietly. "David's just loading the dishwasher. Why don't you and I put the Bavarian cream and the pie on the table?"

Leila was shaking when she sat down. When Nick finally reappeared, nineteen minutes later, everybody else was eating dessert.

"I'm a sorry excuse for a host, but that was a call from my cast. In New York, where we just opened," he explained to the table at large. "They're partying together and put in a group call."

Leila was deeply involved in a conversation with her mother about how she had met Joan and how they had got together. Phyllis seemed embarrassed but also relieved. All those stupid conversations, Leila thought, about her situation. It seemed to her a marvelous and sensible choice. Here they were, two old women considered by society to be on the shelf, who had managed to find each other attractive and lovable. She kept her gaze on Phyllis, who was beaming. She could not look at Nick: she was in equal parts ashamed and angry. He wanted to leave early? Great, she wanted him gone. Let him charm Shana. Let him charm Jane, who could never resist flirting with him, while Emily glared. Leila was on Emily's side, plain big Emily with the two kids who obviously was crazy about flashy Jane. Emily seemed to sense her sympathy and warmed to her. All four kids, including the toddler Ben, left the table to watch TV. Emily turned toward Phyllis and Leila.

"My mother was a nurse too. But she quit a few years after she married my dad. The nurse's dream. She married a doctor. Then she gave birth to two doctors." Emily grinned. "I want my kids to be auto mechanics or whatever. But I never, never, never will urge them into medicine."

"It's not such a bad job, being a nurse. And you meet some great women. Besides, three more years and I retire. We're going to buy ourselves a Winnebago and hit the road." Phyllis smiled at all of them and took Joan's hand.

Emily was looking at Jane. Love shone in her eyes, making them luminous in her long face. Leila felt a pang of envy. She wanted to be looked at that way. Nick was giving her occasional glances of apprehension. Perhaps he remembered he had not hung up the phone in the kitchen. Perhaps he had left the phone off, hoping she would overhear and he would not have to tell her. Perhaps he was merely worrying about how to get away. Emily looked at Jane with the glow of love, and Nick looked at her as one might view a car door that would not shut properly. This Thanksgiving was doing nothing to bring them together, but rather she felt the disquieting rift widening between them. If Sheryl was pregnant, she would never forgive Nick: never.

"You got some crazy family," Red was saying to Debbie just behind her in the kitchen. "We should have gone to Texas."

"But your mother doesn't like me."

"Your mother's a dyke," he said. "I can't believe it. We're getting out of here tomorrow. I don't want the kids exposed to this kind of thing."

"Red, they're just old ladies, what do you want? The kids don't understand."

"We're getting out," Red said. "We'll go to New York."

Bon voyage, Leila thought, but I must keep Phyllis from figuring it out. She won't get mad at Debbie, she'll just assign me to straighten her out. I don't have the energy to clear up anyone else's confusion. I'm suffocating in my own. What is going to happen to me? What can I do? Debbie will call me to commiserate and be furious when I tell the truth, that Phyllis has the best marriage in our family.

CHAPTER 17

MARY

Mary had Thanksgiving nailed down. Thanksgiving wasn't much of a holiday if you weren't married, she thought. Fortunately at least one of her clients went away every year: if not one of her cleaning clients, then one of her pet service clients. Mrs. Carten said to her, "My Boots really takes to you. He never seemed to like the pet sitter I had before."

"He can tell I'm fond of him," she said vehemently. The truth was, of course they liked her. She didn't bop in, throw some kibble in a bowl and rush out. They were allowed to sleep with her. Naturally they perked up when they saw her, impressing their owners. The Rogers had a parrot she managed to befriend, so it greeted her. She had this ridiculous fear the parrot would somehow tell on her, but it could only repeat phrases. Good morning, Good morning, it would say any time of day or night. Luckily, she did genuinely like animals, because she thought they could see through people who put on a show. They remembered who was kind and who was mean to them. In her old age sometimes she liked animals better than people. Certainly no dog or cat left you because your hair turned grey or you got thick around the waist.

When the DeMotts flew to Sanibel Island, she was at their house within an hour, having looked at the tickets in his top bureau drawer, where he kept cash and tickets to the Celtics and Red Sox and planes.

She wouldn't have minded if the DeMotts had a doggie or a cat, for the company. She cleaned elsewhere every day but Thanksgiving itself, but she had a home to come to right from work. It was dark by four-thirty, so she just unlocked the back door and made herself at home. Thanksgiving she spent a long time in the tub, cleaned it thoroughly, watched TV for a while but mostly just stayed in bed, shaking a cold that had been plaguing her. She tanked up on vitamin C.

By Friday morning, she was fit again. It was those church basements that got her, and hanging around the streets till she could sneak in someplace. Summers had their own problems—she couldn't close up the houses as tight so that the light wouldn't show (although in her observation, most people left lights on nowadays), and the sun set so late that she had to wait till eight-thirty to slip into her chosen shelter. But if she got caught short, she could sleep in a garage for a night. It was dirty and it didn't feel safe, but it was better than the streets. Twice she spent the night in a gazebo of a fancy house on Brattle Street.

Winter was a different story. Night came down early, but sleeping outside would kill her. Hadn't she almost died, back when she was new to life on the streets? It was always dangerous from the weather and from the men who would hurt any woman they could.

Saturday she had a cleaning job at the Mafekings. The kitchen was an incredible mess from Thanksgiving, burnt fat all over the oven, run-over sauce on the stove, a mess of dirty pans in the sink. They had an old dishwasher that couldn't handle pans. She resented having to scrub pans from two days before, but she didn't say anything. It would be too easy for them to complain.

The Mafekings had her only occasionally, when the house had got out of control, and they were always there. If she dared, she would have refused the job. One of their kids was visiting with a baby, so the house was full. She had to clean around them.

They gave her some leftovers. She was sure they were sick of the turkey—they'd made one the size of a rhinoceros, and about as tough—but she was pleased. She took the offered turkey and cranberry sauce in an old ice cream carton. "I imagine your daughter makes turkey too," Mrs. Mafeking said. She was a sly sort always trying to pry, always alluding to Mary's daughter.

"No, ma'am, my daughter roasts a goose. I prefer turkey, so I do dearly appreciate your sharing a piece of yours."

"A goose!"

She just nodded, and Mrs. Mafeking went away looking impressed. Mary had no idea where these ideas came from, but they were convincing. She never knew she had it in her to be a champion liar.

Home at the DeMotts, she spread out a sheet of newspaper and ate her turkey and cranberry sauce at the kitchen table with a nice chutney from the refrigerator. Then she toasted a slice of the DeMotts' bread and ate two sticks of celery. Nobody counted their celery sticks. She finished with an apple. She put her garbage neatly into a plastic bag in her shopping bag. She was always prepared. She carried her own knife, fork, spoon and plastic bowl; anything of theirs she used, she washed at once: compulsive, but part of her daily discipline. She had always been a mad housekeeper who never left dishes in the sink or beds unmade or dust under the couch. Besides, she owed it to the people whose houses she borrowed to return them at least as clean as she found them. Third, she had a policy, leave no traces.

She was stretched out on the couch in the living room, just taking it easy and enjoying the warmth and the soft living. She was lying in the dark, too lazy to get up and turn on the TV, thinking that maybe her daughter Cindy would invite her for Christmas. Twice Mary had saved money for the bus. One year Cindy sent air tickets, and Mary flew out of Logan to Washington and her own granddaughter Marissa picked her up at the gate and took her to their home in Chevy Chase. Cindy wasn't much at writing, and of course, they couldn't talk often on the phone. One year Mary had a client with a WATS line at home that included Washington, but his boss didn't get reelected, and the family moved to New York. That was the year she had really stayed in touch.

Cindy couldn't have Mary often, because Cindy was thick with her dad. She was always his favorite, his Cinderella girl—not that she ever sat in the ashes. They had tried to give her whatever her friends had that she really wanted. She was the best behaved of all their friends' girls, never in trouble, never boy crazy. If she went out with a boy, it wasn't because he had a convertible or a lot of money to spend or a bad reputation, which attracted some females like flies to a pile of dog do. No, if she went out with a boy, it was for sound reasons. He was a good risk. He was steady, reliable, an asset. Cindy married well and was still married, with two adolescent children. She had a little business on the side, a boutique where she sold dresses to oversized women, named the Goddess Shop.

Cindy's dad lived in a suburb near Norfolk. They were still close.

So the only time Cindy could invite her mother was when Jim was away with wife number three on a cruise or something. Cindy made sure he didn't forget her. Mary couldn't be judgmental, for her daughter was a woman who always noticed, while the slice was still falling, which side it was going to land on. She looked out for her children first and foremost, it was only natural. Cindy must have figured out from watching Mary that, if a woman wasn't shrewd for herself, nobody else would guard her. Cindy had no idea how Mary lived. Nobody in the family did. How could she tell them? She would be too ashamed.

A couple of times she had to ask Cindy for help. When she was losing her apartment, Cindy sent a check for five hundred. Another time, she sent three hundred, when Mary had to have dental work done. Cindy also gave her a long list of things her kids needed and the house needed and her husband needed, and made very, very clear that giving her money could not be a regular event. Mary figured if she was in terrible trouble, for instance if she broke a leg, she could ask Cindy; otherwise, she had better not.

She would call Cindy from Logan tomorrow night when she was waiting around. She knew a place there was still phone booths where she could sit and shut the door. She could stay a long time pretending to be making calls, and she would actually call Cindy. Sometimes there was a machine that would take MasterCard, her precious plastic proof she was real. She had never missed a payment. For two or three months at a time, she didn't use it. But she had to buy Christmas presents for all her grandchildren. That was the hardest time financially. People went away a lot, which meant she could stay in their houses, but she got very low on cash. Shopping for all of the grandchildren was fun but expensive. It was easy with Jaime's kids—they were young, and a toy was just fine, although toys too were dear beyond comprehension. Cindy's daughter Marissa and her son Cole always wanted specific expensive things she could not afford, so she had to find some compromise.

Mary was lying in the dark imagining Christmas at Cindy's when the headlights pulled into the drive and shone right into the living room and then the car passed. She was off that couch fast and fumbling in the dark for her boots, shoving her feet in, getting them on wrong but stumbling across the floor. She grabbed her coat and bags and raced to peep out the back. Only one of them in the car, Mr. DeMott. She ran out the front door without putting on her coat. Then she bolted, still with the boots on the wrong feet, down the steps and dived around the corner of the house, where the big porch would protect her from his sight. Then she crawled under their front porch and huddled there. She could hear the back door opening, slamming. He was going to be surprised it was warm in the house. She had turned up the heat from fifty-five to sixty-five. She hoped he'd think it was their mistake. She cowered there while the lights went on in the house.

She was afraid to move. All the outside floodlights turned on at once from master switches just inside the front and the back doors. If she attempted to leave, she would be clearly visible. She could imagine no explanation for why she would be crouching in his yard. She wriggled around, putting her boots on the correct feet and buttoning her coat, pulling on her knit hat. Cindy had given that to her seven years ago Christmas. It was royal blue, and she adored it. It had saved her health and her poor ears many a time. She felt cold and rattled. Suppose she had fallen asleep. He would have caught her dead to rights on his couch. She was shaking with a nervous reaction and chilled from running out without her coat on.

Once the Millers had come home early and caught her in the house, but she had told them that Zurich had been throwing up and she had been waiting to see if he was truly ill. She had been afraid to leave him alone and figured that in the morning, if he was still sick, she would take him to the vet's in a taxi. The Millers had been impressed by her devotion to Zurich.

Why had Mr. DeMott come home suddenly? Why did he turn on the outside lights? She was terrified that perhaps one of the neighbors had noticed something and called them in Sanibel Island. She was wary of neighbors and tried to remain invisible. But had she slipped? She heard the door open in back of the house again. She would have liked to make a run for it, but she was too scared of being seen in all that light. She huddled in the dirt under the porch. This night, it was not fiercely cold, perhaps twenty-eight or thirty, but it was damp and she was tired. Her poor hams were aching from the chill.

She heard him shut the garage with the automatic box. Still he left the outdoor lights on. She had to squat beside the porch, clutching herself and growing colder, crawling way under the porch to pee from the cold, until finally the downstairs went dark and then at last he shut off the lights outside. Now she was free to go, but where?

Here she was on the street at eleven twenty-two, and what the hell was she going to do? It was too late to wander around. An old lady invisible in daylight was all too obvious now. Saturday night was a poor time to hang out at Logan. Sunday night would be fine, because there would be Thanksgiving traffic. The subway in Boston stopped running just after midnight, so she had little time to make up her mind. She couldn't even go find one of her church basements this late. The trick was entering while things were unlocked, or when someone circling a church caused no suspicion. This late she would risk notice by a policeman or a watchman.

She was really in trouble. She huddled there under the porch trying to come up with a solution. Clearly she would get no sleep. What she needed was someplace she wouldn't freeze. She waited until the light had gone out in his room upstairs. Except for the bathroom light upstairs, always on, the house was dark. She gave him another half hour. She was leaning against the wood of the house by now, her legs drawn up under her coat, shivering. She did not dare fall asleep under the porch.

Then she crept round the back. She knew the garage opened and closed by an electronic device, but old garages in Cambridge often had a side door, usually unlocked or held with a lock a sixth grader could open. However, their garage had no side door. There was a window, nailed shut.

It was twelve-ten now and she was sunk. There was absolutely no place to go this late at night in the winter. Very quietly she went to the back door and moving so slowly her hands ached, unlocked it with her key. Their back door was what she had grown up calling a grade door, in between the basement and the kitchen. The kitchen door was closed. With infinite slowness she let herself down into the dark basement. She sat on the bottom stair. It was dank but a lot warmer than out of doors. Then she took out her tiny flashlight and made her way to the furnace room. It was warm with a little space next to the burner, even if it reeked of oil. She folded her coat and sat on it. She did not dare sleep. She dozed from time to time. Her back ached. Finally she let herself curl on her coat on the cement floor. It was not cold because the furnace radiated heat to the cement, but it was hard.

Every time she heard a sound, her heart started trying to break out of the wall of her chest. She was scared. She could be arrested for this. Her life would be over. She would be on the streets like that woman she passed in Porter Square. She could not see why he would come down into the basement first thing in the morning, and she planned to get up long before he did.

She dozed off now and again, but her head lolling forward would wake her or she'd jump with anxiety, her sleeping mind conjuring up footsteps, doors opening. It was a grim night. She found herself remembering the basement of her parental home. They had a coal furnace. After all, it was coal-mining country. Everybody burned soft coal. The fire would always go out during the night, so that when they wakened, her father's first task would be to tramp downstairs and get the furnace going. Her older brother Donald, rest his soul, used to send her fifty a month after her divorce. Anyhow, Donald had the task of hauling out the ashes and the clinkers. She remembered the harsh dank smell of the coal bin. She remembered the roar the day the coal was delivered through a window chute. The whole house shook.

When she was in high school, they got an automatic stoker. Then the furnace would run all night. It was a big machine that stood in front of the furnace and blocked the passage that, when she was little, she used to ride her tricycle through, round and round on rainy days. By the time they got the stoker, of course, she no longer rode a bike in the basement. Round and round, past the wringer washing machine, past the wash tubs, past the workbench where her father did home repairs and Donald built model airplanes, past the fruit cellar and the pantry where canned goods were stored, past the coal cellar and around again. It was soothing to remember being that little girl with the barrettes shaped like ducks or butterflies, with the blond shining hair and the crisp pinafores. How did this ever happen to her? How?

She had been a good wife and mother. She didn't drink secretly, like other women in the neighborhood, or spend all her husband's money, or gamble even at bingo, or have affairs with her dentist or her husband's best friend. She didn't abuse her children or beat them or try to make them feel bad. Sometimes on "Oprah" there were these women or men saying, My mother locked me in the closet for five years, My mother beat me with a tire chain, My father made me wear girls' clothes at home. She rarely saw her children. Why? She was too proud to beg them to take her in, but would they, even if she begged? What was going to happen to her? She tried not to think about it. What good did it do? She tried as hard as she could to save money to buy an old car. Then she would have her own shelter.

As dawn was breaking she let herself out. It was still dark enough for her to slip around to the front of the house—stiffly limp, was more like it. She had the day to kill. She never worked Sundays. The service didn't give out jobs, and nobody had ever asked her to work off the books on Sunday. The best thing that had happened recently was that the malls opened at twelve. In the meantime, she would slip into a church—any church. She had a little bread in her carry-all and an apple. She shuffled along, eating her apple as slowly as she could. She had counted on breakfast at the DeMotts. What she wouldn't give for a cup of coffee. She might even have to buy one, to warm herself, before she could slip into the first church she saw open.

Her whole body ached for a warm bath and a warm bed. Her eyes kept shutting as she lumbered along on her sore feet. Tonight it was Logan again. She might have to break down and spend a day-and-a-half's wages on a motel for a night tomorrow or Tuesday, but then she would save nothing at all, not for her fantasy car, not for presents. She knew the Rogerses were skiing next weekend, and she was set to feed their parrot and stay over, but she had Monday through Thursday to solve. It looked like a week of church basements for her. She remembered when she used to enjoy winter.

CHAPTER 18

BECKY

Becky's wages disappeared into the family need like bath salts dissolving. They were still paying off Nana's illness and death. Rennie—Lorenzo—joined the army, so they had one less at home. Almost a year had passed since Becky had got the receptionist job at Sound Cable. Now she was secretary to Danny White, the business manager. She had her own cubicle before the entrance to the offices of Mr. White and the bookkeeper, Mrs. O'Neill, a thin silent woman of forty-five, whom Becky had never seen eat or go to the bathroom. Mrs. O'Neill had an immovable will. She wanted a new computer system for billing and running the station, and they were getting one.

A year and Becky was making more, but standing still otherwise. She could only move up from this job to be the station manager's secretary, another buck-fifty an hour, the same benefits and twice as much work. Lani did not get out of the station before seven some nights. Becky at least got out at five, except when there was a bad crunch.

Becky loved to hang out Saturday afternoons at Sylvie's when Mario was off playing tennis or on somebody's boat. It was a condo in a three-story building that still smelled oaky and clean with an aroma of polished wood. Sylvie's apartment was a blend of big ornate furniture-store pieces her parents had given her, showing wear but still, as they said, as good as they'd ever been. Becky agreed. They were as good as they'd ever been. There was nothing in her family home half as respectable, but still, lamps with fringe? Tufted sofas. Tables with odd knobs and flourishes. Becky was a furniture snob. She never gave up studying How Things Should Be, in case she ever had a crack at making something nice in her life.

The bedroom had furniture Sylvie had selected. It was a sunny room with a king-sized brass bed and everything else Shaker. It was elegant, all light blue and lighter grey. Becky adored it. When Mario was out and she came visiting, she and Sylvie always sat in matching rockers there, facing the windows or else outside on wicker chairs on the little deck. Sylvie told her that her parents thought the room dreary.

Yes, Sylvie was married and had her apartment, but she was pregnant. Becky knew that was an accident, but once Sylvie found out, she had decided she was actually pleased. Becky was disappointed in her friend. Sylvie should have had the strength of character to wait to have babies, to put off a family until they were well established financially.

What hurt the most, though, as they sat on the spidery rockers sipping diet soft drinks and leafing through *Cosmopolitan* and *Better Homes and Gardens*, was that Becky could tell that Sylvie felt sorry for her. Sylvie considered her a basket case socially. Sylvie was always trying to introduce her to some dude Mario was tight with. Thanks, but no thanks. Sylvie really thought that Becky couldn't meet men. Becky met men every damned day of every stupid week, but they weren't what she wanted. She couldn't make Sylvie understand. A man was a potential future.

"You're too fussy. Once you get to know a man, you forget all that stuff you thought you wanted or needed. You have to get real."

"Why is it real to take what I don't want?"

"A man isn't like a chair you buy because it looks good in your room."

"It isn't looking good I care about."

At least Sylvie could understand her frustration at work. Lately Danny White had been calling her into his office, shutting the door, and finding excuses to lean over her shoulder. He touched her too much. She pretended she didn't notice. He was a decent business manager, but he was married and had two boys. She wasn't having anything to do with him off the job, and he'd better realize that. She worked hard, she did all the errands he sent her on, she stayed late without complaining when she had to. But she made her body rigid under his hand when he grasped her shoulder or her arm, and she would not meet his gaze when he put his big face into hers.

If she thought he would do her any good, she supposed she would go to a motel with him, lie down and do it. But she knew better. One of the other girls had an affair with the special programming director. As soon as the affair ended, she was let go. They didn't give you anything but a hard time when you gave in.

The other girls did not particularly like her. They didn't gang up on her the way they had on the woman having the affair, but they would not go out of their way to cover for her either. They didn't like her not going out after work with them, and she was not about to explain to them that her family was taking just about every cent she earned. The girls bowled together on Thursdays and ate out, even the married ones and the ones with boyfriends.

She heard Vicki telling Lani she was cold. She did not know how to make the kind of fuss they did with each other. Oh, Lani, that's the most gorgeous dress, that is just the perfect color for you! Where did you ever find it? What a steal!

Lani, Mrs. Ledbetter, didn't gush, but she was a plump motherly woman and she was considered warm and maternal without having to work at it. Nobody thought that Becky was warm and maternal. She did not honestly know what they wanted from her. She covered for them. She thought she was damned nice to all of them. When they made a pool to buy a gift for someone's shower or whatever, she always put in as much as she had to. It reminded her of school where girls in her classes had signed each other's yearbooks with cute sayings (Yours till Mrs. Snow melts), and she could only think to write, Best Wishes, Becky Souza.

The next week was hell. They were replacing the computers and the systems all at once. Everything had to be done on the stupid typewriter, and she had to redo a letter four times to get it right. Everybody was cross. Only Mrs. O'Neill was in a good mood, but she was still as a stone. She liked getting her way—like every other living being, Becky thought. She would have liked to get her way too; she would have liked to drown Danny White and take the week off until these people were done playing with the new system.

Tuesday the techie from the computer company came into her cubicle to install her work station. She pulled her chair out of the way and watched. She could hardly work with him all over her office. "Do you mind if I sit here?" she asked, to make conversation.

"Long as you don't ask questions," he said, glancing at her. Then he looked back a second time and grinned.

He was a moderately tall man, with wispy blond hair and very white teeth. His eyes were almost too pale, grey-blue, and he blinked frequently, like someone trying to accustom himself to contact lenses; but he wore glasses. When he was bending over the circuit boards, he kept pushing the glasses back on his head. When he smiled, his face seemed twice as attractive. She found herself staring at him.

"I'm Becky Souza," she said.

"You don't look Portuguese."

"Portuguese look all kinds of ways," she said defensively. "But my mother's family is French." She had learned that French-Canadian seemed to Wasps as suspicious as Portuguese. She wasn't about to say, Oh, I was born with brown hair, but I bleach it. "Do you have a name? Or is it Mr. A-B-C Business Systems?"

"You can just call me A-there. Terry. Terry Burgess." Mockingly he extended his hand and they shook. "Such a little hand," he said, giving it a gentle squeeze and then quickly dropping it. He looked at her guardedly to see if she was annoyed.

She decided not to be. He wasn't wearing a ring. That didn't mean too much, but she would find out. She smiled. "It must feel good to walk into an office and solve people's problems."

"Oh, come on. Am I solving your problems? You probably didn't want a new system you have to learn. Your boss decided on it, right?" He glanced at the closed door.

"He's not there. They're all in a meeting, killing time while the system's down," she said conspiratorially. He really was nice-looking. And he spoke well. He had no local accent. He was clean, well dressed in a slightly nerdy way. The chinos were too baggy, for instance, and the shirt seemed to belong to another outfit. "Since I'm just sitting here watching you, can I help in any way? Hand you things? Maybe you'd like a cup of our terrible coffee. I could make it fresh, which helps."

He looked surprised. He must not have a bunny assistant to fetch and carry for him, the way all the men here did. "I'd like that a lot."

She did make fresh coffee. After all, charming T. Burgess was a way to pass the morning. Terry was actually a nice name. He had neat buns, bending over the connecting cables. "I went to college with a woman who married a Burgess. Crystal. I thought he was in computers too. Crystal isn't your wife, is she? I've lost track of her since commencement." Thus letting him know she had gone all the way through college and also trying to find out the Big Question.

"I'm not married," he said with an even bigger grin. "And I was planning to ask you out."

She gave him a warm smile back, drawing her eyes very wide and tilting her head. "And I was planning to say yes. How nice we agree."

"Where do you live?"

"I don't need to go home first, unless you do. I live way the other side of the bridge."

"I figured you'd want to change. We'll eat out, take in a movie."

She couldn't think of any way out. She was silent for a couple of minutes, trying to figure some excuse for meeting him.

"You don't want me to pick you up. What gives? Do you live with a guy?"

With this one she decided on total honesty, or some fraction thereof. He seemed to like frontal assaults. "I'm the first person in my family to go to college." She looked him right in the eyes, rising to her feet. She did not smile. "My father is a poor fisherman. I find that whenever I go out with men who come from different, more affluent backgrounds, they have a tendency to look down on me when they see where I come from."

He flushed. He actually reddened. She watched carefully to see if her tactic had been successful. "I wouldn't judge you because of that," he said quickly. "I can see what an unusual girl you are. I'm not such a crazy yuppie as to think everybody's as good as the labels on their clothes. I want to pick you up at your parents'. I admire people who overcome obstacles."

She couldn't wait to tell Sylvie. She crouched in the rocker, knees drawn up to her chin in one of her favorite positions since babyhood. "He's tall . . ." She never cared about height, but other women always mentioned it, so she did. "He's blond and good-looking and he has a terrific job. He's a programmer and he installs computer systems at companies. They have a system especially for cable TV companies. He wears sport jackets and nice sport shirts and expensive sneakers. He looks like money, Sylvie, he really does."

"How did the date go?" Sylvie was as excited as she was. "Are you going to see him again?"

"Friday. We're going into Boston. He has tickets to a Red Sox night game. I've never been to a real ball game."

"What do you know about baseball?"

"Nothing, but I asked Tommy. He promised to fill me in at supper. You know Tommy, I can level with him. He doesn't make fun of me the way Rennie or Laurie do. He understands wanting to make something of yourself. . . . I don't want to act like a fool in front of Terry."

"Do you think you're really interested in him? I mean, for real, like you were with Ted Topper?"

"I'm crazy about him," Becky said, but she knew she was lying. He was the best thing she'd ever had a chance at. He had a real professional-type job. He drove a Subaru with a fancy tape deck and four speakers. The sound could have blown her through the roof when he turned it on. Everything about him was superior. He did not smell of sweat or beer or tobacco, but discreetly of lemony aftershave. He wore tassel loafers shiny enough to slide on or good sneakers. His hands were always clean and his fingernails trimmed evenly across. She could have eaten him up one finger at a time, but she was cool, very cool.

She got him talking about his job and tried to memorize key phrases. She knew girls who asked men the right questions, then spaced out on the boring answers. When she wanted someone, no answer was boring that gave her information she could use. His conversation was like a set of instructions to his world, his ideas, his habits. He was a course she was taking, and she planned to ace it.

Sunday morning, she and Sylvie drove past his house. His parents' house, where he lived, was at the end of a road, on what Sylvie said was called a cul-de-sac. It was a huge house that went along on ground level, occasionally putting out wide decks. The marsh was just beyond it. She could not wait until he invited her home so that she could see the inside. It was a much bigger house than Sylvie's aunt Marie lived in. She began to revise her notion of the good life. There was room between this house and the next for a whole row of houses like her parents'. She smiled sourly. He must really have been taken aback. Lucky she had given it to him right in his face first.

He asked her about herself. She gave him little facts, with a slightly pathetic air she noticed went over with him. He was becoming protective, which she encouraged. He saw her as brave but fragile. That was a persona she could live with. She gave him a few carefully chosen facts or equally carefully constructed anecdotes, and then she quickly nudged the conversation back to his interests. He was far more interested in her than Ted Topper had been. Nobody had ever looked at her like that. Oh, guys had wanted to get into her pants, sure, and they had come on like a truck out of control down a mountain road; but it was not her they were staring at, just body parts.

Here was someone beginning to fixate on her in the right romantic way. She was not going to screw up. She was not going to do anything with him she didn't study first and work out with all the intelligence she could muster. She knew she was bright, and while she was less well educated than he was (he had gone to better schools, including Babson), she suspected she was sharper. She certainly had a much clearer idea what she wanted, and that was Terrence Burgess to be her lawful wedded husband. She wasn't going to do any better than this. She had to capture him without raising his suspicions that she was engaged in a campaign. She had a big reputation with him already for being blunt and honest. She didn't care about Danny White at work any longer, although she planned to confess to Terry that evening how her boss had been harassing her. She had been right to wait and watch and be careful. Terry Burgess was her prize. She had only to collect him.

CHAPTER 19

LEILA

On Saturday morning, Leila graded papers. David was visiting a friend from high school. Nick had gone out. She had managed to keep from having an intimate conversation with him; she suspected that he was also avoiding her. However, just before noon, she heard the door bang open and his resonant voice filled the hall with her name. "In here," she called, but like a good wife, got up to see what he needed.

He bowed and presented her with a large bouquet of red roses and white carnations. "Flowers to my peony."

An old love name. She put her hands on her hips, not yet taking the bouquet. "If you want to go back to New York early, you don't have to bury me under forty dollars' worth of flowers."

"I don't *want* to go back early, but I have unfinished business. The cast hasn't completely settled into their roles. I'm not quite ready to let go."

"Of them or obviously of Sheryl. I'm sure she wants you back."

He sighed. "It's an unfortunate situation."

"You can say that from my heart." She wondered if he was going to tell her the truth. "Exactly what sort of situation is it?" she pressed.

"But I don't see why it need affect us. It'll be over soon."

"Are you sure?" She decided to push the envelope. "What if she should happen to get pregnant? When you have an affair with a woman, you choose the possibility she may bear you a child."

He looked at her warily. The silence stretched taut and hummed like a live wire. Finally he said, "Why discuss something hypothetical? I'll be home soon. We can iron all this out then."

"That will take some doing," she said dryly. Then she began to feel guilty—not toward him, but toward the flowers. They must go into water. She knew it was ridiculous to feel a sense of obligation toward cut flowers, but she was what she was. She took down two vases, dividing the flowers between the table and the living room. "They do look inviting."

Vronsky, who had been watching all this, walked up to the vase, sniffed and then bit a rose experimentally. It proved disappointing and he backed off, shaking his head with bared teeth of disgust.

"I wish you'd be a little more inviting, yourself." Nick sat in the middle of the couch with his arms extended in both directions. "I'd like half the tender looks you give that cat."

"Vronsky sleeps with me, and only with me. That creates a bond." She sat stiffly on the edge of an adjacent chair. "He lives here."

"We never felt we had to be together seven days a week fifty-two weeks a year to prove our affection." He sat forward, letting his hand close on her knee. "I may travel around, but I come back. I always come back to you."

"But I don't stay in the same place. I'm not exactly the same river you step in," she said, not moving her knee away but holding rigid. "Perhaps because I'm growing older or because David has left—I feel the aloneness more acutely. This affair with Sheryl—it seems different and far more serious."

"Maybe it is a good idea to have Shana move in. When will that happen?"

"Didn't you hear her say she's moving to a school near Amherst?"

"She's a sweet kid. I like to look at her, but she runs off at the mouth. Too bad for you. It was an appealing idea."

"Perhaps," Leila said noncommittally. Her period of intense loneliness had diffused. Vronsky was company, as she had hoped. She was frantically busy. She had begun to enjoy setting her own hours and eating when and if she chose, letting her stuff lie about, having music when she wanted music and silence when she craved the air to be still.

She could let herself go after work, loll about in a bathrobe and put her feet up. Maybe this was the pleasant side of middle age. She realized, looking at Nick, that she wasn't desperate for him to return. He would surely come home well before Christmas. His classes resumed after the New Year. He liked to teach, and he enjoyed his position at B.U. Why did she feel at most a sense of acquiescence? If Sheryl were really pregnant, why hadn't he taken the opportunity she had thrust at him to tell her?

"I can't get over your mother, coming out at her age. It's kind of cute, although your sister didn't see it that way."

"Debbie's all over the road, but she takes sex roles religiously. We each set out to be a WOMAN, all caps, but we made up different models. I think it's a great choice for my mother. She's not the recluse type."

"Do you think if something happened to me, to us, you'd be a lesbian?"

"I doubt it. I'm too invested in the mama-daddy-child family."

"But you don't really like most men."

"Well, failing polyandry, I only need to like one."

"I have to confess, I find it flattering that you are such a one-man woman. In the theater, that's scarcer than genius."

He was frowning at some private thought or recollection, still holding her knee in his hand. His hands were large, strong and always warmer than hers. She often felt a wave of sexual feeling when she looked at his hands on the steering wheel or even picking up a book or a bowl.

"One of the jack-hole critics said that the second act was paced too slowly in the first half. I can fix it. I have to work with them, but I know I can pick up the pace. On the train I marked a few cuts, and perhaps there's too much business—people physically dancing around each other. I may have overdone it. I can fix it, I know I can. Then it's time to work on the Wendy Wasserstein I'll be casting here. Because of the *Don Juan* offer, I've been thinking about Shaw's *Man and Superman*. We need a whole new way of staging Shaw."

Maybe an abortion was planned and he simply did not intend ever to mention what he considered a non-event. It was pure accident she had found out. And had she really heard what she thought Sheryl said? Was she making up a whole drama out of a misunderstood allusion overheard on a bad phone connection? She began to feel foolish. Had she misinterpreted Sheryl's comments?

"I always wanted to play John Tanner, and now I'm past it. Never will I play Hamlet, and never will I play half the roles I imagined. I wonder if I gave up acting prematurely. But I'm not one of those whizzes who can act and direct at once. It fucks up my head. I have to see the cast in my mind all the time, as well as on the stage, and if I'm acting, I can't do it. I need to stand back and watch them all and feel the choreography of the scene, and watch the larger movement of the play."

"I can understand that," she said, half-reluctantly drawn into discourse. "Even nonfiction books of the sort I write have structure, and I have to keep that structure in mind. Everything from a class to a lecture has pacing. Even a dinner has its proper rhythm." It occurred to her to remark that in sex, too, pacing was important, but she felt inhibited with him. Talking about sex always seemed a form of flirtation among verbal people.

"It's been praised and attacked. I brought all the reviews for you."

She hated reading his reviews, but he liked her to. When he had an opening in Boston, she was the one who scanned them and simply reported to him, good, bad, mixed. He would read them all eventually, but it put off the inevitable bad scene for a while, his obsessive vulnerability to criticism. Experimentally she asked, "Do you want me to see the play before you leave New York?" Sometimes he liked her to come in toward the end of a run. She always felt it had something to do with detaching from the cast, from whoever he had become involved with. She was summoned to signal his retreat.

"I'm conflicted about it," he said, grabbing hold of her and pulling her onto the couch beside him. "I'd like you to see it, for sure. Who else can compare it with the production here? How do you feel about coming down?"

"I'm not sure," she said honestly. She would have to weigh the possible pain and discomfort—and the loss of time she didn't have to spare—against her own curiosity, the sense that not to know what she was up against was foolish. "I'll let you know."

"Fine," he said with obvious relief. "You decide and let me know."

Why was he leaving it up to her? If she did come, he could honestly tell Sheryl and company that she had been determined to see the play in New York. Nick and she were in agreement: she preferred to make her own decision. Another woman might rush to confront Sheryl, but she could see no purpose in such a scene. Nick was her problem, not Sheryl.

His arm around her, he was talking about Shaw. "When I first read him, I was smitten by the prefaces. It wasn't till I saw an excellent production of *Major Barbara* that I began to realize that the plays were rich. If Shaw were only the polemicist of his essays, we wouldn't keep putting on his plays. It's because they're full of marvelous roles, especially for actresses. Kinky juicy people marching around the stage being witty and perverse but seething inside. His characters have a great deal of inner *stuff*."

She was drawn irresistibly into conversation. The sexiest thing about him was the way he talked. She could not help but be flattered that, after all these years, he was still interested in communicating with her. She was one of his favorite sounding boards. Reluctantly she found herself warming toward him.

She could read his body language clearly: he was trying to be open and close. Only spite could armor her against his appeal, and what use was spite? It felt good for a moment to reject him, but the damage could be long-lasting. What she most desired was for the two of them to be a couple again. Love was not a constant, she had learned that years before. It swelled and shrank, it grew weak and recovered into vigor. Vronsky sat on the small Oriental staring at the two of them, as if at a puzzle he was attempting to figure out. His eyes were fixed and very yellow. He was a question in the form of a furry tabby.

The answer to the question, she told him silently, was a tentative but optimistic *yes*. Yes, I will try to love Nick. Yes, I will let you try to love me, Nick. She let herself lean into him. At once his hand clasped her shoulder more firmly and his thigh pressed against hers.

In bed she enjoyed herself more than she had thought she would, but she felt oddly detached, as if she were studying each gesture, each kiss, each embrace, familiar and yet slightly distant, as if she were watching them from above, from the perspective of absence. There was something elegiac about the lovemaking. It might be that this time, something was broken beyond mending between them. She had worked hard at the relationship for years, and perhaps she simply lacked the energy to continue that labor. She felt some deep fierce grasping in herself slowly beginning to relax. It was not over, but neither was it as it had been.

She rose from their bed and ran the bath water, listening to make sure David had not come home in the meantime. She went from Nick loose and easy from her orgasm, yet thoughtful and detached. She had used to wonder how he could go from her bed to another woman in another city, but now she could almost mimic his ability to be intensely with her, then quite gone and forgetful.

She had much to consider. She had much to decide, alone.

CHAPTER 20

MARY

Mary spent an unquiet night in an ex-client's apartment. Mrs. McNamara no longer used the cleaning service—she was saving money and had moved into a three-room apartment near Washington Street in Brookline—but she still needed her schnauzer Serena fed and walked whenever she went to New York to see her son. Mary didn't sleep well, because she was far more nervous in an apartment than in a house. She'd have no warning at all if Mrs. McNamara suddenly returned. Neighbors' voices, their TV laughing, water running in the tub, the whir of a blender or the whine of a vacuum, made her wonder if, no matter how quiet she tried to be, they couldn't equally well hear her. She kept her carryall by the back door, to retreat quickly if need be down to the service door.

As she rode up out of the Porter Square subway station the next morning, she knew something was wrong. Five policemen milled around the parking lot of the shopping center across the street. They were going through the contents of a large Dumpster. Last night it had snowed. Crossing to pass near the police, curious, wary, she saw that the snow near the Dumpster was maroon. Blood?

She wondered if someone had been run down in the parking lot. Sometimes local kids used the lot as a shortcut and drove through as if the checkered flag was down at Indianapolis. Her ex-husband had harbored a weakness for races. He saw himself as a racing car driver, *vroom, vroom*, taking the corners at Monte Carlo in his Ferrari. He drove a Lincoln, too fast and too aggressively. Only after she and the children had been in two minor but terrifying accidents was she able to persuade him to drive more reasonably when the children were in the car. But he resented her interference. He sulked for months. "Okay, you do all the driving" was his response if she criticized.

She was a serviceable chauffeur for children needing to be taken to ballet lessons, basketball practice: she was a capable delivery boy bringing suits to the dry cleaner's and bags of groceries home. But trucks made her nervous, fearful they were going to drive right over her car. Enormous and male, they made her car feel small and feminine and in danger. She had a moment of longing for her last car, a green Datsun station wagon. It had been part of her.

She realized she was standing there flatfooted beside the parking lot staring at a white car and paying no attention to how she appeared. She glanced around quickly, but many passersby had stopped to watch the police. She was early this morning, because of being anxious in the apartment and because she had slept poorly. Well, at least she had been warm and safe. Two inches of snow had fallen during the night. Now the sky was a spongy grey, just below freezing, but nothing more was coming down. Tonight she could count on another anxious night at Mrs. McNamara's; then tomorrow early, she must get out.

Two people were asking a third what had happened. She edged close to hear. A hale elderly man in a tweed overcoat was holding forth loudly. "It was only a bag lady. Happened late last night apparently in the doorway of the video shop." He was one of those self-important types who like to be in the know, so he was in his element, people pressing to hear him.

She clutched herself. She could not keep from asking, "What happened? Is that the lady who always hangs around here with a shopping cart?"

"I don't know her personally," the speaker said loftily. "I wouldn't know. She was sexually assaulted. Isn't that unbelievable?" He shook his head with a grimace of disgust.

"Is she alive?" she asked.

"She was beaten, stabbed, then pushed into the Dumpster. A security guard noticed the blood. She was taken away in an ambulance. . . . I couldn't tell if she was alive—I really wouldn't know."

She was going to have to take a chance and make herself talk to the police, no matter how fearful of calling attention to herself she always was. "Sir," she approached the youngest. She made it a policy to be super polite. She prided herself on keeping the manners of a lady. Anyone hearing her voice could tell she had a good upbringing. "I work near here and I used to see that woman who was attacked. I wonder, is she all right?"

The policeman grimaced. "She got stabbed and beaten up pretty badly. She was unconscious when we got here."

"You wouldn't happen to know where the ambulance took her?"

"Cambridge City Hospital. When was the last time you saw her?"

"Last week, Wednesday. I'd just see her near the subway. I never even knew her name," she said truthfully and backed away. She hastened across the street, afraid the policeman would decide to question her further. She didn't slow down until she'd turned off Massachusetts Avenue. She had three routes between the subway and Mrs. Landsman's house. Today her priority was getting out of sight before the policeman decided she might have valuable information.

The house had not returned to its abandoned air. Mrs. Landsman seemed to be eating regularly and keeping things in reasonable order, although untidy. She tended to read the paper all over the living room and kitchen and leave open books on half the surfaces, as if she was reading seven books at once.

Mrs. Landsman didn't expect her to take out Bronskee's litter box, which she appreciated, although she had to do it for other clients. Mrs. Landsman had a frozen pint of homemade spaghetti sauce and a quarter pound of lean ground beef defrosting on the drainboard of the sink. She had been stocking the refrigerator with juice, skim milk, lots of fruit and vegetables and bakery bread. Maybe the husband was coming home soon.

Mrs. L. was reading about murder lately. Mostly she read academic books and journals downstairs, but her bedroom reading was usually recipe books and autobiographies of women. Most people had going-to-bed rituals. Some of her couples slept together and some slept separately. It did not seem related to whether they made love. Mrs. Stone used to have her change her sheets when she came in Mondays, and her bed always smelled as if they'd spent the whole weekend in it; but Mr. Stone had his own room. Some people kept the wand for the TV right on the bedside table, so Mary knew they dozed off to "The Tonight Show" or David Letterman. Others, she saw a movie in the VCR partway played. Some like Mrs. Landsman read. Romance novels, mysteries seemed most popular for putting her ladies to sleep. Mrs. DeMott had a white-noise machine.

She used to favor steamed milk with nutmeg. She slept poorly when the babies were little. After that, she had an off-switch in her head, and once that was thrown, it was good-bye for eight hours. Now she must remain alert. She never slept soundly. There was no unbroken peaceful rest for those without their own safe place in the world. Even mice had their nests in the walls and squirrels in the trees.

She rushed through the cleaning so that she could call the hospital. She had been putting it off, out of embarrassment. She did not even know the woman's name. Her concern was superstitious; she cared about the woman lest she become like her. Mary had slept on the street and barely survived, wouldn't have but for the kindness of other women who had shown her how to manage.

At twelve, she did call. The desk was suspicious of her. She had to give them her name and a phone number, so she gave them Mrs. Landsman's number. Yes, the victim was admitted. They would not give out her name, although they seemed to know it now. The victim was still unconscious.

She reflected as she cleaned how odd it was as a job. She was paid the same for cleaning the house after Thanksgiving, when mobs of people seemed to have been camping there and every room was overused, as she was for the weeks it was just Mrs. Landsman and her cat. Today she took some time out to shower. She always had her towel and wash cloth along in her carry-all. Fortunately no one seemed to find it odd for a cleaning lady to tote the equivalent of a suitcase with her. Mary had not dared bathe at the apartment, for fear the neighbors would overhear.

She could not get that woman out of her mind. She kept telling herself it was no business of hers. The victim, as they called her, was probably crazy and weird—weird the way she was during those months she lived on the streets with people looking through her as if she was a hydrant. Mary couldn't stop seeing the woman's prematurely lined face, her soft brown eyes, hunched over the shopping cart to make herself smaller, to take up less space. She could not stop imagining some brutal hoodlum forcing himself on her, into her, her trying to fight but scared to make too much noise, because wherever she was, she wasn't supposed to be there.

Her mind would not obey her and forget. That was how it happened that she was on the downstairs phone when Mrs. Landsman rushed in.

She was home early. She almost never got there before Mary left. They communicated through notes. She seemed surprised to see Mary on the phone, and Mary was mortified. She had a policy of not letting her ladies catch her using anything but the vacuum cleaner. "Go right ahead," Mrs. L. said. "Is something wrong, Mrs. Burke?"

She decided to try the truth. After all, she was allowed to be concerned, even if she could hardly explain why she was fixed on that poor woman.

Mrs. Landsman was indignant. "That's savage. And he stuffed her in a Dumpster? How is she?"

"They won't tell me," Mary said. "I don't even know her name. I pass her whenever I come to clean. I used to say hello. I felt sorry for her."

"Of course. I've seen her near the subway." She took off her coat and sat at the phone, frowning. "I've done a lot of favors for people around here over the years. When I was researching rape victims, I ran sessions for the police—now there are psychologists who specialize, but then it was too new. Make yourself a cup of tea and sit down for a while."

Mrs. Landsman turned into somebody else. She was calling and chatting up people and insisting. She talked to someone at the precinct, she talked to a reporter on the *Globe*, she talked to a doctor at the hospital. She was galvanized, talking fast. Mary was bemused. She drank her tea and waited. She was terrific at waiting silently and almost invisibly.

Finally Mrs. L. put down the phone and handed Mary a note. "Your woman's name is Beverly Bozeman. She was admitted under Jane Doe, but when they went through her coat, she had an expired driver's license sewn in the lining. She's suffering from concussion, a broken arm and two stab wounds, exposure, shock and loss of blood. She's not conscious, and she's listed as critical. You should be able to get news of her now when you call. Here's the extension for her ward."

Mary left a bit dazed, with that note tucked carefully in her wallet. The way Mrs. Landsman went at it took her aback. People in authority did not impress Mrs. L., and she had no trouble asking for what she wanted. Mrs. L. must have two personalities, one in the family and one in the outer world. Mary had always thought of her as a long-suffering woman. It seemed stranger than ever what she put up with, but Mrs. L. must be crazy about her husband. Probably Mrs. L. figured the way things are that she wouldn't find another. But Mary was impressed.

She appreciated Mrs. L. taking the time to find out the facts, and she was grateful that her client didn't think Mary was foolish.

Beverly Bozeman. The poor creature had a name. Tonight from Mrs. McNamara's apartment, she would put a blanket over her head to make a tent that would muffle her voice, and she would call the hospital again. Let the hospital know that somebody cared about the torn body of Beverly.

CHAPTER 21

LEILA

Leila was sitting at Cathy's kitchen table drinking spearmint tea out of a heavy and strangely squashed mug of spotted maroon. She did not ask for coffee, as she remembered that Zak had been required to produce that, and she finally had Cathy to herself. The table was glass on wrought-iron legs. The chairs had wrought-iron backs in the shape of hearts. Leila found them painful, but Cathy seemed comfortable. She was wearing jeans and a sweater with a blue background and large white and orange daisies knitted in. Her hair hung straight, no longer in a ponytail.

"Sam's lawyer told me to get it cut," she explained. "He said I couldn't go into court with a ponytail. I don't see why. I don't think hookers wear ponytails, do they? I've worn my hair that way since college."

"Lawyers have some kind of science of what you should wear in court to influence juries. I always think, how do they know? But then maybe they pick out people who fit the profile that likes the kind of clothes they tell you to wear, so it's a self-enclosed system. When I've had to testify, I've been told to wear a navy or grey suit with a white blouse, small earrings."

Cathy giggled. "Yeah, he told me I have to wear a flowered dress. I don't own a flowered dress. So he said, Go buy one. Up to the neck, with a white lace collar. I don't have money to waste on clothes I'll never wear again. But Zak said I have to do it for Sam, and he's going to give me the money. He said, go to Talbots in Centerville and you can pick out something Waspy. I am a Wasp, I said, and so what I wear is Waspy enough!'' Cathy's habit of widening her eyes as she spoke was disconcerting. Perhaps years ago, she had been told she had beautiful eyes, and that widening them made them more prominent, but Leila doubted she had any notion how often and how automatically she did it.

''I thought . . .'' Actually she realized she had known Cathy was not Jewish. It was the dead husband, brother of the annoying Zak, who had been Jewish.

''Because of the name. My husband was brought up Jewish. I am not much of anything, but my family were Congregationalists. We had the prettiest church in town. Like a postcard. Mostly we went to hear the choir and the organ.''

''What was Sam brought up?''

''He was bar mitzvahed—my husband insisted. He said it would shock his family not to. Then a year later, he was dead. I felt like my life had stopped. I couldn't function. If Zak hadn't taken over, our lives would have disintegrated. I just couldn't cope!''

''I understand. . . . Zak doesn't have a family of his own, obviously.''

''He was married. He had a kid. You have to understand, his family has the worst luck in the world. They're always dying. His wife and his baby daughter were killed in a fire. She was a musician. She was gorgeous and all that, but they lived out in L.A. and we only saw them maybe four times. They seemed very glamorous to me, I can remember.'' She shook her head at the idea of Zak being glamorous. ''Even Mike was a little jealous of his younger brother. Once I got to know Zak, that made me laugh. He's a dear soul but antisocial. He tries to be a part-time daddy. And he's helped us.''

''Helped you out with money?''

''That and dealing with the bank and doctors and lawyers. I just get lost in what they tell me. My boyfriend helps me too. I'm not supposed to mention him in court, but I can't see why. He's in construction. He was married to a first-class bitch, but he's been divorced for years—''

''Does Sam feel close to his uncle?''

''Sam changed. He *was* very close to Zak. But I think that Becky took him over body and soul. He got weird. He started lying a lot.'' Cathy sighed, leaning her elbows on the table top. ''I'm easy to fool.

I never think somebody's lying to me unless it hits me right between the eyes."

"What did he start lying about?"

"Where he was, what he was doing. He met her at a local theater company. His high school English teacher encouraged him to get interested in community theater, and so did I. We thought it would be good for him. Ha!"

"Theater companies seem to spawn romance," Leila said sourly. "It comes with the territory, I guess." She did not bother saying that her husband was in theater. Cathy distracted too easily.

Cathy snorted. "I can remember how happy I was when he joined. He was making new friends. First he was painting scenery and fetching and carrying. Then he started acting. He gained so much confidence, I had no idea it wasn't coming from doing Agatha Christie in the old Masonic Hall."

"When did you become aware they were involved?"

"I was suspicious a couple of times something was going on. It would seem to me he was out a lot at odd hours. But rehearsals drag on, and who could tell when they finished at ten and he pretended ten-thirty or eleven? I guess I'm the trusting type." Cathy fluttered her lashes. Leila realized there was nothing personal involved. It was a mannerism she attached to that statement. It was part of Cathy's image of herself. "But Sam's always been a good conscientious boy."

"Did he talk about Becky?"

"He kept saying how she was good to him, how she was teaching him so much. I thought he had a crush on her, but I never dreamed they were having an affair. After all, he was in high school and she was a married woman! I'd have as soon suspected . . . you."

"But she wasn't that much older. Not old enough to be his mother."

"She's eight years older. At his age, that's a huge difference. When I married Mike, he was four years older than me, and believe me, I was a kid compared to him. I was fresh from college and he had been out in the world."

"So they met in a community theater?"

"The Canal Players. In the winter, we go because it's something to do, and in the summer, the tourists go." Cathy bounced up and looked at her bulletin board. "They're putting on *The Glass Menagerie* now. You could see it."

Leila fervently hoped she would not have to. She was not overly fond of Tennessee Williams even in the productions Nick mounted, although one of his early successes in summer stock had been playing the Marlon Brando role in *Streetcar.* "If you were me, which of the regulars would you talk to?"

Cathy frowned, raising one shoulder. "Well . . . Mr. Berg, Sam's English teacher—Sam confided in him some. He's the one who suggested that Sam might enjoy theater. I don't blame him. He thought it would help Sam overcome his tendency to be shy. It did give him confidence, but I guess it was the wrong kind. Really, how was I to know?"

"You naturally encouraged him. It must have seemed like a nice hobby for a boy his age, much better than hanging around getting into trouble."

"That's it exactly—you understand, because you're the mother of a teenage boy too. Right, you worry they're going to get into drugs. I know there are drugs in the high school."

She remembered how she had worried herself, and then felt hypocritical, because Nick and she and all their friends had smoked dope when they were scarcely older than David. It had been part of the national underground youth culture, as common as the current fad of baseball caps.

"I fretted about drinking. Every couple of years some of them wreck up a car and kill each other. I worried that when he didn't go out with girls, maybe he was gay. Then I worried when he started seeing a girl, that he would have sex with her and make her pregnant. I was always worrying. I was actually looking forward to Sam going away to college. Then *bang*! the police."

It made Leila nod. "It starts when you're pregnant, doesn't it? You're scared the baby will be born with two heads or webbed feet. Then you're afraid he won't start walking on time, he won't start talking. Is he smart enough? Can he read early enough? Developmental obsession."

"The way it is, my boyfriend can't stay over. I just wouldn't feel right about it with a teenage boy in the house. It's asking for him to get into trouble. So what with worrying and trying to make ends meet and not having enough hours in the day, I admit I was looking forward to having some time to myself I haven't had since my daughter Miri was born." She grimaced, fluffing her hair. "It feels funny without the ponytail. I miss it."

"But it looks nice this way too," Leila said diplomatically. "It costs so much to send a kid to college, I still can't believe it."

"Tell me about it. He got a scholarship. Zak was going to pay the rest. Now I suppose they'll take the scholarship away from him even if he gets off." Cathy's face screwed up and she looked as if she were going to cry.

"It's a sad situation." Leila took her hand.

Two large drops ran down Cathy's face, blurring her eye makeup. "I don't see how it can ever work out again! It's all a mess, no matter what happens! Zak's raising bail, so we'll have him home soon. I don't know how that's going to be, frankly."

"He's young," Leila said. "And so really are you. You have your home. You have your friends. I hope the lawyer is good."

"I just don't know what's going to become of Sam. When he wasn't wanting to be a vet like Zak, he wanted to be an astronomer. He even had a telescope Zak gave him. He showed me the rings of Saturn. Now he's going to be on trial for murder. I feel so ashamed, and I'm scared sick for him!"

As Leila drove back to Cambridge, she thought that she had never had a book to work on where the circles just kept widening. She supposed that from one murder she could interview people the rest of her life. She could interview all the people who'd ever known Terry, Becky, Sam, Sam's friend—what was his name? She had forgotten to ask about him. All the families. Those who had worked with them, gone to school with them. She had imagined murderers as solitary beings. These people trailed nets of connection. She felt overwhelmed and also intrigued. Ordinary lives, but how often did a project give her a license to prowl through other people's families and social webs?

She was not sorry to have the house to herself. She had enjoyed David's visit and, during the last day, Nick's company; but while they were present, she was aligned toward them, meeting their needs, paying attention, making nice. Her gaze came to rest on the pile of clippings on the coffee table. She had promised Nick she would read them. That meant turn them into something acceptable to him. She suddenly remembered she had also promised to make up her mind whether to go to New York. She must decide if she wanted to look over the competition or wait for his return. Sheryl had sounded demanding on the phone; that would alienate Nick quickly. Nick had had enough of her energy for a while. She had been neglecting her students. Besides legitimate needs, some students wanted her in the mentor or the mommy role, both of which she filled comfortably. Everyone needed attention. Perhaps even herself. But Melanie was dead.

She sank into the couch. Vronsky climbed into her lap and stared into her face, putting his paws on her shoulders. What's wrong? she imagined him asking. Nothing, really. Nothing that mattered.

Saturday morning about eleven as she was going over the notes from her interviews, the doorbell rang. Jehovah's Witnesses? She had not seen a door-to-door salesman in ten years. Express Mail? What could possibly be delivered on Saturday? Someone soliciting for something, political or charitable? Her friends called before appearing; they were trained. Some over-eager, over-pushy student who had wormed her address out of a secretary?

Slowly she stalked over, sure whoever was at the door had little right to be there. She looked out through the narrow window that flanked it. It took her a moment to recognize the man, in bulky parka because it was snowing and quite cold. His collar was turned up and a furry trooper hat was yanked over his ears. His hair was unmistakable around the base of the hat, as was his thick curly beard. It was the brother-in-law—Zak.

She groaned and thought of pretending to be away, but she was looking at him through the window and he was looking at her. He had a great deal of influence over Cathy; she seemed dependent upon him for money and for doing tasks she considered beyond herself.

Reluctantly she opened the door. "Hello . . . Zak Solomon." She emphasized stumbling over his name. "I remember you from Sandwich. Cathy's brother-in-law, isn't it? It's a good idea to call first, since I'm frequently away, and you had quite a drive."

"I was in town," he said shortly. "May I come in?"

"Of course," she said politely. "May I take your coat?" She intentionally did not hang it up, as she did not want to encourage him to stay long. She simply folded it over the back of a rocking chair.

When she turned he was busy examining the items on the coffee table. "Your husband is in theater?" He wore a dark green turtleneck and chinos. His hands were shoved in his pockets as he canted forward, peering.

Sometimes people knew who Nick was, sometimes not. Fame was a specialized commodity, not exportable past the natural barriers of different interests. She couldn't name a famous golfer or soccer player. However, she could produce a bibliography on violence against women dictated without notes. She knew which U.C.L.A. sociologist had just left his colleague-wife for a graduate student of twenty-three, and which Russian sociologist had just been unmasked for faking statistics on urban crime, which colleague had almost won a Pulitzer for his study of Asian gangs.

She contented herself with saying, "A director. He has a play in New York that just opened, but usually he works in regional theater. He's mounted plays at the Los Angeles Theater Center and the Mark Taper Forum—I believe you lived in L.A.?"

He sat in the chair she usually took, refusing her offer of coffee or tea. "May I ask why you're interested in this case? You must turn down book offers. Why did you take this one?"

"The timing seemed right," she said almost truthfully.

"You mean you expect the trial to attract as much attention as the case has. Reasonable assumption."

"I thought you'd understand how long it takes to write a book. By the time my book is out, any interest in the outcome will have gone the way of last year's fads."

Vronsky had come in and was staring at Zak. Then he approached stiff-legged and sniffed at his trouser legs. Zak started scratching behind the cat's ears and Vronsky suddenly jumped into his lap. Traitor!

"Oh, but if the material is juicy enough, or can be made to seem so—"

"Mr. Solomon, I sent Cathy one of my books. I thought you might look at it before allowing your suspicions to run riot. I don't deal in the sensational—"

"Women in prison, sexually abused women, women who abuse their children—sounds like material for 'Oprah,' any afternoon."

"Sodomy, father-daughter incest, fratricide, mass murder—all Torah. We're a bloody lot, human beings. Everything depends on what you do with material. Even dealing with animals, you must run into sex and violence—no?"

"I'm treating companion animals. Unfortunately, you're attempting to deal with my nephew, my sister-in-law, people I care about."

"Mr. Solomon, I am not responsible for your nephew's involvement in a murder case. I'm not responsible for the publicity this case is getting or how the media is handling it." She stood and paced toward the windows, launching into a defense she had perfected over the years, with variations. "I'm responsible for a serious and in-depth study of the meaning of the case. If I don't do it, someone else will. I have a son close in age to Sam and with similarities, so I'm programmed to be more sympathetic. Plus I'm Jewish, and I'm not a self-hating Jew who turns on other Jews out of unresolved identity problems. I'm as good as you're likely to get, from Sam's point of view." Teaching was great training in speaking and arguing, one reason the local TV station liked to use her as an expert witness. She was not photogenic, but she came across as knowledgeable, kind, articulate. Now she moved closer and took a seat on the arm of a chair about ten feet from him. Closer, not too close. Change of voice. Pitched lower, more intimate. "Why be hostile? What advantage is that? If you persuade Cathy and Sam not to talk to me, it won't stop Becky's family and Terry's family from serving as informants. Only the final product will be biased toward them, because they will have shared their experiences with me—and if you're successful, Sam won't have." Her concentration was slightly spoiled by Vronsky, who was sitting in her enemy's lap and watching her as if she were entertainment for both of them.

Zak leaned back in the chair and grinned. It was the first time she had seen any expression but hostility or anxiety on his face. "I take it you're saying that I can't stop this case from being written about, so it's ultimately better for Cathy and Sam if I con you instead of fighting you."

"You can try." She smiled back, thinly. "You don't have to like me. Just don't try to keep me from talking to Cathy and Sam and others in their circle. You won't keep me from writing the book, no matter what you do."

"I understand. Some people pick up the garbage, some people write about other people's misfortunes."

"Perhaps you feel it is only correct to apply one's intelligence to cocker spaniels and cockatoos, but sometimes people like to try to understand each other—whether it's war, panic in crowds, the behavior of street gangs or murder cases that people are curious about because they strike some nerve. I believe I've had a small influence in legislation concerning the rights of women in prison vis-à-vis their children in three states. I've been able to make audiences understand something about the experience of incest in childhood and what happens to abused women when they are dealing with their own children. I think I've been able to give victims more sense of dignity." She folded her arms.

"It's hard for me to imagine, looking at you in your own setting, how you could drum up much real empathy for women who are poor, disorganized, confused, impulsive—for people with sloppy lives."

"It's hard to judge someone's life experiences by their living room, Mr. Solomon. I wouldn't try, myself."

He stood. "I suspect you're a lot more judgmental than you let on. I'll clear out. I'm sure I'm using up time you don't have, in your busy and well-organized day." He took his coat from the rocking chair and shrugged it on. "Do you know when your cat had that hematoma?"

"I got him from the Animal Rescue League about a month ago."

"He's three, I'd say, was intact for at least two years, had several serious fights. Well fed as a kitten but had a period of malnutrition."

"Thank you." She walked him to the door, mostly to make sure he was actually leaving. Then she raced up the stairs to look over the hedge. He had a loping stride. He drove a Toyota pickup, dark blue, high up off the road with four-wheel drive. He stopped at the stop sign at the end of the block, drove off neither too fast nor too slow, deliberately. She plumped down in her desk chair with a deep sigh.

Cathy wanted to talk to her, and she was simply going to proceed. Why was he so proprietary? If this were a neat who-done-it, he would be the real murderer, and she would clear Sam and Becky. He was going to be a nuisance. She'd run into men before who resented a woman professional researching in their backyard. She had simply detoured them.

She was disconcerted by his appearance at her home. This was the first time anyone from her researches had invaded her life. It made her feel vulnerable. No matter how she examined him, Zak represented trouble.

CHAPTER 22

BECKY

"I'm in love," she told her mother in the kitchen. By getting up very early she caught Mama alone except for the baby in the high chair.

Mama looked wrung out. Joey's death had taken something vital out of her. "With this boy? This strange boy?"

"He has a good job. He's not a kid."

"Becky my rose, he's not our kind. He'll look down on you. He thinks there's nothing to learn from people with less money. We're just losers to him."

Becky wanted to say that, in many ways, Terry understood her far better than her mother did, but she could not bear to hurt Mama. Mama simply could not see past the great walls of the rut where she labored daily, trying to hold her family together, trying to pay off the bills, trying to survive. "He cares for me. Maybe that's more important."

"It's important that he knows who you are, what it is he thinks he likes so much."

"Haven't you noticed how he looks at me? Like I'm something precious."

"You're precious to me. I see how he looks around the house. Like he doesn't want to touch it, dirt and trouble might come off on his fingers."

"He's never said a word of criticism. Never."

"That's good," Mama said, relenting a trifle. "He's a polite boy, his mama raised him right. He always speaks to us nicely. He always asks how I am. He is a good boy, Becky, I know. But so different."

She could not say that what she loved in Terry was that difference. He was the perfect walking embodiment of all she longed for. He was educated, he was clean, he was golden and soft-spoken. He worked with clean intelligent things, computers. He drank a little beer or white wine. He did not touch drugs. He played tennis and golf and sailed his family's boat. He did all the right things in the right way, and her heart would shimmer with electricity sometimes just to watch the way he hefted the tautly strung racquet. His wrists melted her. His bones were elegant. He moved like a diffident prince. The silky blond hair would tumble over his forehead, and with a gesture at once lordly and casual, he would flip it back. She loved to lay her cheek against his hair. Baby hair. It was perfect too.

She had never in her life wanted anything the way she wanted Terry. She wanted to hold him, she wanted to be him. She played cool as long as she could, then she collapsed utterly into him. "No one has ever loved me the way you do," he said in wonder, again and again. "I always imagined that someday a girl would love me like this. But most of them are too selfish. I want to pick you up and carry you off with me and have you at my side, always at my side."

She wanted more than that: she wanted to melt into his side, the rib given back. She wanted to become one with him. Man and wife, one flesh. It was mystical. She could hardly say that to Mama. She wanted to confide, but the words would not work. She could not confess passion to her mother. She could only say weakly, I care for him. It sounded like an ad for health insurance.

Mama peered nearsightedly into her face, as if trying to read what Becky really meant. Then she sighed. "It's hopeless. The Lord knows, I try to raise you all right. But there's no good end. We just can't figure out the way to live."

She must keep her mother from starting to cry. Mama was always halfway toward tears these days. Sometimes Becky would see her slicing carrots or scaling a fish, with tears running unheeded down her face. Sometimes Mama would be eating and the tears would leak from her eyes. Becky longed to make her mother relax and laugh again. "It's not a catastrophe, Mama. He's a good man, hardworking, educated. He's what I want. He'll be good to me."

"I hope so," Mama whispered. "I pray for you every night."

It depressed Becky to imagine her mother praying for her. "Mama, pray for yourself. Pray for Papa on the sea. Pray for Gracie and Tommy and the little ones. I've got an okay job, and I found a good man to care about. I'm twenty-three and I'm doing all right, Mama."

"Of course you are." Mama's hands washed each other in her lap.

Terry had been talking for weeks about bringing her to meet his family. They saw each other every night except Monday and Wednesday. Monday nights she helped with the household laundry, still going on when she got home. Wednesday nights he played squash with his younger brother. It was a habit since they were both in high school, and Becky learned to treat it as a sacred obligation. She imagined a soft squishy ball they tossed slowly to and fro. Some things she was eager to ask about; but others she felt she could just let go by. She could not be asking him for a translation of everything he said.

He had told her that tonight he would pick her up at work and take her directly to his parents' house. She wore her navy suit that Aunt Marie had gone with her to pick out. On sale it had still cost more than she could afford, but she had to have it. She kept it wrapped in plastic and took it out only for special occasions, like today, when she was meeting what she hoped would be her future in-laws. She had gotten up extra early to wash her hair while she could get in the bathroom and while there was still hot water. Only Mama was up. "All dressed up today. Something special?"

She could not bring herself to tell Mama she was wearing her best for Terry's parents; it seemed disrespectful, when Mama seldom saw her so dressy unless somebody died or got married. "A going-away luncheon for one of the girls."

"How nice they are where you work. Try not to get anything on your suit." Mama picked at the lapel. She loved the suit too.

She could not pack a lunch with Mama watching. She usually did not eat the doughnuts, but that day, she ate all she dared, for it was her only food. Terry's family dined late, at eight on Fridays. He was a half an hour tardy picking her up. She was getting edgy, wondering if he had changed his mind, if his parents had canceled the visit.

"Had to finish up a job. You look just fine. They'll love you."

If he was so sure they'd love her, why had he waited four months to introduce her? Never mind. He was finally doing so. She was glad he seemed pleased at how she had dressed for the evening. She needed confirmation that she had made the right choice, although she had no idea what she might have worn instead. That party dress Gracie had remodeled from her bridesmaid outfit seemed a poor choice. Mostly she wore skirts and blouses to work, or her blue shirtdress.

She didn't let on she'd driven by the house before with Sylvie. As soon as they were introduced and she was ushered to a seat on a large blue sofa, she studied the room. It was like a stage setting. It made her stare for a moment, almost stunned, for it was all white and blue, everything perfect, everything placed carefully. There wasn't a broken or spoiled or soiled object. Every little lamp with its tutu shade, every vase of dried flowers that were blue and white too, every cushion was artfully placed in a scene of domestic beauty intentionally created. She had seen such rooms in magazines, but never in life.

"Mrs. Burgess, what a beautiful room. I love the color scheme."

Mrs. Burgess smiled thinly, the first movement of her face since Becky had come in the door. "I did it myself. People always think, when they see this room, that I hired some interior decorator. Never. I had the idea and I picked everything out." She was as slender as Becky, wearing a green silk gown with a high neck, pearls over it. They looked real. Becky wondered what a real pearl felt like. That was the only jewelry Mrs. Burgess wore except for her wedding and engagement rings. Becky wanted to freeze-frame Mrs. Burgess to go over every inch of her. She was obviously a lady, a pattern Becky must understand. It must be important that rooms be put together like an outfit of clothing; Becky could remember when she had learned about outfits. It had been Sylvie who had taught her, in middle school. Sylvie would love this room.

From his wing chair, Mr. Burgess, who had so far addressed not a word to her but only a grunt, said proudly, "Mrs. Burgess studied it all out of magazines. She's a quick woman."

Terry looked at Becky, rolling his eyes upward. "Where's Chris?"

"We're waiting for him," Mr. Burgess said sourly. "Some client he's sweetening."

"Sometimes I believe I should have gone into interior decorating myself. What do you think?" Mrs. Burgess looked sharply at Becky.

"I think you'd be wonderful at it. This room is perfect."

"Nothing's perfect," Mrs. Burgess said decisively. "And I'd have to deal with all sorts if I went into business. I like to pick and choose my friends and my acquaintances. I think that's so important."

Becky felt a little shiver. She had the feeling Mrs. Burgess was pushing her away. She decided her best strategy was to ignore any digs and act resolutely pleasant.

Mrs. Burgess had light brown hair, very close to the shade Becky's had been before she started working on it. Becky could not tell what color her eyes were behind her glasses. Her face was long and pointy. She sat extremely still, not moving a muscle, except for her mouth and occasionally her head.

Mr. Burgess was as tall as Terry but much heavier. He was ruddy, with a receding forehead and glasses, a face that seemed oversized, overblown, as if it occupied too much of his head. Becky knew he was an engineer with a small company that installed air-conditioning and heating systems. He wore a thick gold band on his wedding finger and a gold digital watch with his grey suit. She knew nothing about men's suits, so she had to assume it was a good one. Men's clothing remained mysterious. She knew it radiated class and background to those who could decipher it. Terry had firm opinions on what was correct to wear. He sounded more shocked when someone turned up wearing the wrong socks with the wrong shoes than when he reported someone in his company had been fired for using cocaine. Mr. Burgess gave her little to work with. She could see a few resemblances to Terry—his father's hair was equally fine, although there was less of it. They were tall and had noses that marched rather far from the face before stopping, high commanding foreheads, big hands and feet. But Terry seemed to her a miracle next to his ungainly father.

She could see more of his mother in him. Mrs. Burgess rose to pass the nuts and the canapés, like miniature sandwiches. Her movements were economical and not ungraceful. In her slenderness, her elegance, Becky could see Terry. Yes, she decided, he took after his mother. Becky was very hungry and had to resist the desire to fall on the canapés and the salted nuts and consume them in handfuls; however her anxiety made it easier to control her appetite. She had to chew and chew each mouthful, in order not to choke from nerves. She nursed her little glass of dry sherry, for she was terrified of being even slightly giddy. She could all too easily see herself beginning to giggle and tell inappropriate stories—stories about her real life. She almost expected them to be teetotalers, there was something pinched and tight about them, but Mrs. Burgess had put away a glass of sherry and was working on her second, while Terry and his father both had Scotch. Terry did not drink liquor normally, so she assumed he had Scotch with his father because that was the older man's choice and Terry was being agreeable. His father was on his second since she had come in. Terry, like her, was still loitering cautiously over his nearly full glass.

"I'm looking forward to seeing Chris again," she gushed, for she had actually met Chris when they had all gone to a Red Sox game. He sold insurance. He was simpler, noisier than Terry. He seemed to her far more ordinary, in appearance, in tastes, in quality of mind. But she had flattered him that afternoon, and he had gobbled it down like the hot dogs he bolted.

"We're waiting for him." Mrs. Burgess sounded annoyed. "I can't imagine why he scheduled an appointment so late on Friday afternoon."

"If you're selling something, Mom, the client picks the time," Terry said. "He's still trying to establish himself. It's a cutthroat business."

"A salesman," said Mrs. Burgess bitterly. "Really."

Becky was not quite sure what was wrong with that. Papa had contempt for salesmen too, because he said they had soft hands and they only lived off other people's work, but she had the feeling that was not the basis of Mrs. Burgess's disapproval. Her mother always added softly, At least they're safe.

She tried to imagine Gracie or the twins or Tommy sitting around the living room, and it simply would not work. But Mama. She seated Mama on the other sofa, the white one, where Mama could put her feet up on the white leather hassock. Mama would love the room. It would feel better than church, clean and uplifting and nothing to do in it, nothing to straighten or scrub or dust. She could see Mama perched on the white sofa with her skirt spread out around her the way she did sometimes when she was dressed up and able to sit for a moment, so that Becky would catch a quick glimpse in Mama's lined face of a young girl waiting in barely suppressed joy for something that surely would happen. Something nice for once.

In spite of her dainty eating, she and Terry had gone through the tiny sandwiches and finished the nuts. Finally at twenty past eight, Chris arrived. He was the same height as Terry, almost as big as their father. "Hey, I told you I was going to be on the late side. Forget it. I ate with my client."

"How could you, Chris?" His father frowned. "You knew your mother would wait dinner for you."

"The client wanted to, what does it matter? I'll sit down with you and watch you eat."

"After the trouble I went to prepare it just the way you like. . . ."

Mrs. Burgess had worked hard to make everything nice, and Chris just took all that effort for granted. Becky would show Mrs. Burgess she knew how to appreciate someone who tried to create domestic order, who tried to make things pretty and right. Terry said his mother was a good cook.

Dinner began with half grapefruits with a deadly red maraschino cherry in the bull's-eye center. Then came some kind of white fish in a cheese sauce. Fisherman's daughter that she was, she still could not identify the species. Whatever it was, it had been dead awhile. White rice, white fish, pale sauce, white bread, she almost expected cauliflower, but the peas were bright green. The food tasted as if it were made of magazine pages.

With the meal they had a white California wine. Ted Topper would have shown her the bottle and given her a lecture, but she had already learned that Terry drank wine without thinking about it, ordering mostly by price (something about a third of the way up the price list) or saying, not too sweet, okay, to the waitress. They didn't display the bottle so she could read the label, so she assumed she wasn't to comment on the wine. Just give me half a chance, she prayed to Mrs. Burgess's face, which scarcely moved a muscle even while chewing, and I'll show you how fast I can learn. I'll be the daughter-in-law of your dreams, if you only let me see what you want. Whatever it is, I can do it for you. Terry winked at her as he helped himself to more of everything. Under the table he put his hand on her knee. Later, said the hand. Later.

CHAPTER 23

LEILA

Becky's sister Belle called Leila, very excited. "I discussed the situation with Mr. Green—he's Becky's lawyer—and he's going to talk to you. I persuaded him." Belle sounded proud and Leila praised her warmly. Belle had been trying to win Leila's attention and admiration. She worked in a local beauty salon; every time Leila, who stayed in close touch with the Souza family, saw Belle, her hair was some new concoction of curls or rolls or sharp boxy angles, in varying shades of blond. But Belle, as she told Leila, had loved English in high school and she longed to write a book. Now Belle opened for her another anteroom to storm: Becky's lawyer. Belle had said that Tommy had hired him and that her parents had mortgaged their house to pay his fees.

Robert Green's office was in downtown New Bedford, where the streets had been restored to cobblestone and old brick buildings had been renovated for offices. His business was obviously not going downhill. May, her expert on the case, said Green was considered one of the two best criminal lawyers in New Bedford. He perhaps had mob ties, or perhaps not, but he had a good track record with drug offenders. Robert Green was a partner in his firm. He had a corner office in which everything seemed of a piece, nicely finished wood of interesting textures—affluence and taste, custom-made—but something odd. Then she realized: Green was an abnormally tall man, towering over her when he shook her hand: Perhaps six six. Everything in the office was scaled to his size. The desk was high. The chairs were high. Even a large woman like herself, five eight, felt as if she were a child sitting in adult furniture. Her feet just reached the floor. She wondered if he derived a psychological advantage from the oversizing. Or was it that he could simply afford to make his microworld to his scale?

He was going bald, like Nick, but he had hair transplants spotting his head, looking like dunes in the seashore when they set out dune grass to hold the sand in little holes all over denuded slopes. In spite of that oddity, he was a pleasant-looking man about her own age, with the frame of an athlete and a carrying voice, but a smile that was tentative, thin eyebrows that rose in perpetual surprise beneath a forehead prematurely lined. She showed him her book on women in prison; sometimes lawyers had heard about it, although of course they had not bothered to read it. He examined it meticulously, as if it were an exhibit of the state. "You wrote this?" he asked at length as if unconvinced.

"It's my most recent book, my fourth. My fifth is in production. It's about childrearing practices and experiences of incest survivors." She rattled off her academic credentials, deciding that was a better route than talking about the audience for her books.

"That's some difference from the reporters that have been coming around . . . Do you mind if I keep this?" He waved the book.

Of course she minded. She got only eight complimentary copies of her book, and by the time the immediate relatives were given the books they expected, she had four left. She had not intended to give him a book, merely to show him what she did. But she needed to see Becky, and he was the guardian of that door. She mustered graciousness. "If you'd really like to have it, certainly. But I'm not expecting you to read it. I was simply showing it to you."

"Sign it." He pushed the book across his desk. "I like to have little mementos. It helps me remember cases long after they're decided."

Obediently she reached for the book, toying with the idea of grabbing it and running. But she would sacrifice the book to her desire to see Becky. "It's very important for me to meet with your client as soon as possible."

"It's my job to make sure such a meeting is in her best interest."

"First of all, nothing I write about her will see print until two years after the trial, at the earliest. It can't influence anyone until the case has been decided."

"You'd be willing to sign an agreement that you will not reveal any information gained from interviews with her and with her family until the trial process is completed?''

''What's the trial process?''

''Including appeals.''

''That could drag on for years.''

''There's no death penalty here. Basically if she's convicted, I or somebody else will find a technical point to appeal on. The State Supreme Court will hear it or they won't. I can draw up an agreement specifying exactly at what point you're free to use the material.''

If she did not agree, no book. He was the gate to Becky. She could not see trying to write the book without interviewing the subject. ''Draw up your terms. I'll have my publisher's lawyer go over it. I see no reason we can't come to an agreement quickly.''

''It happens I've already drawn up an agreement.'' He laid it on the table. ''Take a copy along and let me know.''

''You'll hear from my publisher very quickly.''

''So what good will you do her?'' He put his hands on the table, palms down, leaning toward her.

''If she gets off, the book may never come out, unless they do want her story and hers only. If she's convicted, it's her opportunity to express her side of the events.''

He shrugged. ''She's interested in seeing you. Her family likes you and they've talked you up. They're naive people and not hard to impress.''

''I don't think they're that naive. They have a strong sense of loyalty toward Becky, and they know how she's been portrayed in the media.''

He grimaced. ''It's a pisser, all right. It's going to be tough to find a jury not tainted by pre-trial publicity . . . Lunch?''

It took her a minute to realize she had been issued an invitation. She accepted, of course. She had to get through him to Becky as soon as possible.

Over a pleasant Italian lunch in an old-fashioned dark restaurant and bar where he was known to the waiters, he seemed to relax and expand. He told her she could see Becky; he would arrange it for Saturday afternoon. ''I know you'll be sympathetic to her.'' His hand fell heavily on hers.

''I'm open-minded. I have no reason to prejudge her and every reason to hear her side.'' Gently, she disengaged her hand. Suddenly she realized he wasn't touching her to underline his caring for his client; he was actually flirting with her. She could scarcely believe it. She could not remember the last time any strange man had treated her as a sexual being. She was flustered but aimed to maintain an impervious façade, as if she simply did not grasp his intent. She had the strangest feeling as she sat there that her emotional disengagement from Nicolas had penetrated her whole body and her being, so that she appeared to this lawyer as unattached, available. But who would have expected that to make any difference?

"Becky's cute," he said, "but I make it a point never to get involved with clients. I like big women. They have more to offer, don't you think?"

"I never thought about it," she said honestly. "Certainly you have unfashionable tastes, and I commend that. But I must be getting home soon. My husband will be expecting me."

Somehow she didn't think he believed her, but he contented himself with squeezing her hand as they parted outside the restaurant—where she insisted on splitting the bill. He did not fight her long. It didn't matter, being deductible for both of them. "Stay in touch," he said. "Let me know what you think of my little client. We can have a more leisurely lunch when you have some time." He actually winked.

Driving back to Cambridge for a faculty meeting, she kept shaking her head. Who would have expected Becky's lawyer to make a pass at her? She found the incident not entirely displeasing. He had not been overly aggressive and had backed off promptly. She longed to tell someone, but there was nothing to tell: nothing had happened.

That evening she had supper with Jane at a Chinese restaurant near the school. The report of a committee evaluating their department's curriculum in terms of multicultural fairness was coming up, and they needed to map a strategy for what was going to be a bloody fight.

"I love Emily," Jane was saying as they sat over tea and fortune cookies. "But this instant motherhood or fatherhood is a bit demanding. I'm sure that's what happens to married couples. Sex gets crowded into the wee hours when you're too tired to play hard. They're always around, Leila. I spent a great deal of time out of the house when I was young—didn't you?"

"Cities are more dangerous now—or perceived so. Parents don't tend to put their kids out like some people put out cats."

Jane sighed. "Boarding school always seemed heartless and upper-class, but I'm beginning to understand the rationale."

Was it coming unravelled? Poor Emily. She was the lover and Jane, the beloved. Wouldn't it be nice if people would just love each other equally and forever? What an original thought, Ms. Landsman. "I'm rather detached from Nick myself. I don't know about my marriage." It felt disloyal to be talking about it openly with Jane. "It may have run its course."

"With David gone, the flaws and the bare places must stand out."

She found herself telling Jane about the lawyer; exactly what she'd sworn she would not do.

"Why are you surprised? You dress without the wee-est touch of flirtation or style, but you're an attractive woman. He must have climbed across the table and tried to squeeze your tits for you to notice. I've seen men and women flirt with you and you haven't paid the slightest attention."

"I never was interested. I'm the naturally monogamous type—too lazy, too timid, whatever." She opened her fortune cookie carefully. " 'You will face difficult business decisions, but you will conquer in the end.' That's our next departmental meeting, and we're going to rout the forces of reaction."

"You got the wrong one. Here's yours. 'You will meet an attractive stranger who will treat you as you deserve.' I hope that's not the lawyer. He doesn't sound like a compatible addition to our social circle."

On her answering machine was a call from Nick. "Sweetheart, I'm disappointed you're not home," his voice said as she kicked her shoes off and unpeeled her pantyhose. "At a movie with a friend? I miss you. I'm wondering if you've decided to come down? Seems silly, I'll be home so soon. Let me know."

She did not feel like letting him know. Let him worry. He had not rushed to return her calls for the last two months. She thought of Robert Green and smiled. It was not that she felt attracted to the tall lawyer with the hair implants; rather, his interest was a little toy she carried around to amuse herself, to enlarge her ego at will, like a tiny portable pump.

There was also a message from Cathy, Sam's mother, which she promptly returned. "Oh, Leila!" They were on a first-name basis, almost gossipy. "I'm so sorry about Zak invading you. He confessed to me when we were going to see Sam's lawyer this morning."

A day for lawyers. "I'd like to meet him. And of course, Sam."

"You aren't mad at us about Zak? He's such a fussbudget. I mean, he's a caring person, he really is. I can't imagine my own family coming through the way he has. You'd think Sam did it to upset them. The scandal, they keep saying, it's all over the papers. . . ." Cathy trailed off.

"I wasn't pleased to see him unannounced on my porch Saturday morning, but I never thought to blame you. Obviously you don't control him—just as obviously as he does try to control you." Dig, dig, Leila thought.

"He disapproves of my boyfriend, even, and Steve is a real gem."

"About meeting Sam, when do you think that can happen?"

"Zak and the lawyer aren't convinced. But I'm working on them, Leila. Sam likes the idea. Oh, could you have your publisher send him the book you gave me? You can't give him the book yourself and I can't."

"I'll take care of it."

There was a call from Belle, which she also answered, wanting to know how the meeting with the lawyer had gone—wanting to be praised again for having made the arrangements. Leila wondered if Becky had had the same hunger for approval, for pats on the head from someone she viewed as being above her.

When Leila finished with the answering machine's demands, she still did not feel like talking to Nick or to his machine. She got into bed to read with Vronsky lying on her chest staring in her eyes. She realized she was feeling almost happy. She was not missing Nick. She was not bored. Her life seemed pleasantly full of people to ponder and try to understand, obstacles to overcome, friends to pay attention to, many small tangible and ineffable goods.

They were in some museum—not Boston—Melanie and Leila. They were in light loose summer shifts with toddlers in tow. Melanie had pointed to a caryatid, a Greek woman holding up a building, a woman in the form of a structural column. "That's you, Leila. Caught in stone."

Yes, and now, at least for a short time before Nick returned, the weight of the building that was her marriage was off her shoulders, her back, her head. It felt good to move freely, even if she wasn't moving very fast or very far.

CHAPTER 24

BECKY

Becky and Terry had been going out for a year, and she was beginning to feel the relationship was stagnant. They had fallen into a pattern, which at first had been comforting to her, the dependability, knowing that she would see him on certain evenings, knowing what they would do and what was demanded of her. They went to a movie Saturday night or once in a while to a club with Chris and his current girlfriend—they changed with the months. They went out to pizza and for clams, for Mexican food, for Chinese. She watched him play tennis and occasionally, golf. They swam together at his parents' country club. She felt she had mastered most of the complex program that was pleasing Terry, what to wear, what not to wear (of the clothes available to her). He preferred her more demure than sexy.

Laurie graduated as a dental technician; Belle had moved to a better beauty salon where she got good tips. Scalloping had been good for Papa. Tommy was making money and wedding plans. She could spend a little on herself, and Terry sometimes bought her a present, usually jewelry or perfume. Mrs. Burgess would comment on her clothes from time to time. "Goodness, Becky, you must be very fond of that blouse, you wear it so often."

She tried and tried to please the Burgesses, particularly Mrs. Burgess. Mr. Burgess did not seem to mind her, particularly if his wife was not in the room. Once or twice he even smiled at her, and once he paid her a compliment, telling her she looked quite pleasant that evening. He had said it quickly and softly while his wife was putting dinner on the table. Mrs. Burgess would never like her; she had become resigned to that. They had reached a sour modus vivendi. Mrs. Burgess confined herself to little slaps, two or three an evening, and Becky pretended not to notice. Each intended to outlast the other. Mrs. Burgess had stopped trying to force her friends' daughters on Terry, and Becky was less eager to please—since it had proved altogether impossible. Terry stood not between them but off to one side, more amused than offended if he noticed anything. He seemed to consider it natural that his mother should dislike his . . . girlfriend? fiancée? his lover, who seemed no closer to marriage than she had last month or six months before that.

She was desperate. She had seen too many relationships in her own family and around her drag on and on, kids even, and marriage never took place. Eventually the couple went their separate ways, the woman doing worse than the man. Tommy was fighting to break that pattern; so was she.

She considered faking pregnancy. But she was on the Pill, and he had been at pains to stress to her that she must watch out. She did not think he would automatically respond to pregnancy with wedding invitations. More likely, he would blame her and expect her to have an abortion. Indeed, she thought pregnancy a stupid way to launch a marriage. No thanks.

Sylvie was home now with her baby. Becky had to wait until little Frankie was nursing or sleeping before she could depend on Sylvie's undivided attention, and even then she had to speak fast, because Sylvie was always nodding off. She never got a night's sleep. "Jealousy," Sylvie said with a yawn. "Jealousy is the answer. If he thinks some jerk is going to grab you, then you become more valuable. Then he'll want to make you his, all his, et cetera. That's how the male ego works."

He knew she was crazy about him. She couldn't hide her adoration, and that was half of what kept him with her. So how would he become jealous? She drew up characteristics of a man who would inspire jealousy. Older. He should be fairly well off. He should be offering marriage right off the mark.

After a year of her calling her boss Mr. Taffy-hands, Terry would scarcely credit a sudden growth of interest on her part. She could not spruce up the image of anyone at work, since she had long ago described them all with malicious intent. Sylvie's uncle had lost his wife, but Terry would be as amused at the prospect of her getting involved with a portly middle-aged plumber, as at her faking interest in the fishermen she knew. It had taken her years to meet a man like Terry. Where could she find another to threaten him with? If only Sound Cable would hire someone new, but they were not hiring. They were getting few new customers. She considered inventing a man, but she did not think she could bring that off. Terry would not spend time brooding about what was not in his face. She was convinced by his often crusty and prickly exchanges with his brother Chris that he was susceptible to jealousy, but she could not figure out how to engage it.

Instead she concentrated on making herself indispensable. She pumped his ego, up and up. She told him he was a great lover, that he was handsome, distinguished-looking, elegant, graceful. She watched him play tennis and did not once yawn. She laughed at his jokes, usually the same she had heard in the office. She soothed him into complaisance when the increasingly frequent quarrels with his parents set him on edge.

They were fighting about her. The elder Burgesses grew alarmed as time passed. Like her, they were conscious marriage must figure soon or the relationship taper off. They were also pestering him about getting a place of his own. Both boys were still at home. The Burgesses were paying off the boat on which she spent boring hours sitting and squinting at the water, getting burned through her sunscreen without complaint. They were talking about Mr. Burgess's retirement in five years. They wanted to move to a smaller house, still on the water but in a development for older people that had its own golf course and medical facility. Brochures for that and similar golden-age communities were thick on the coffee table. It was a topic of avid interest to them, and of boredom to the sons. The Burgesses were aimed at retirement the way she wanted to get married.

Chris was not earning much on commissions, so there was no chance of his moving out. The parents thought that Terry should get an apartment, nearby but out from under their roof.

The boys were spoiled. They never picked up after themselves. They never volunteered around the house. They seemed to feel that food magically appeared and dirty clothes or spilled coffee drifted away into the great beyond, bringing cleanliness and order to areas they had abandoned to dirt and chaos. When they were married, finally, she would have to change Terry's attitudes. He would have to understand they both worked, and if they were to live in a house or apartment, they would both have to be equally responsible. That was clear to her, and she would gently, lovingly, tenderly make it clear to him. Mrs. Burgess seemed to have little to do but pick up after her sons and make supper. A cleaning lady came in twice a week. "One of the local Portugee," Mrs. Burgess said, looking sideways at Becky.

"I understand," Becky said quietly but clearly. "My mother used to do that." Did they expect her to disown her mother?

"How awful for you. Did you ever clean?"

"My parents sacrificed so that I would have a college education—so that I would have a good job."

"Are you looking for something better?"

"I'm always looking for something better," she said.

Terry was watching a basketball game with Chris through all this. He never noticed when Mrs. Burgess was digging at her, and Becky had learned to say nothing. Someday she would get back at them. She would never forget how they had treated her. All those insults and innuendoes were put away like pins in a metal box, for the time they would be needed. After Terry had married her, she could afford to take some quiet long revenge.

She felt more and more desperate as the spring heated toward summer, but she remained solicitous and agreeable. Since he too lived with his parents, they had a choice of making love in his car, possible although never comfortable, and going to an inexpensive motel. She figured out that he would probably save money if he moved into an apartment, over what he was spending for a motel three times a week. She joked about it occasionally.

It was Saturday night, and he was late to pick her up. She wondered what that meant. She hoped it was simply traffic. Friday and Sunday could be heavy near the bridges to the Cape. Mama could see her watching the kitchen clock. "So many cars on the road. Don't worry, Becky my rose. He's crazy about you. He'll come. What's a few minutes?"

Had she made too many jokes about the price of the motel? Had she talked too much about the marriages of people she knew? Had she failed to please in bed or in conversation? Her stomach clamped on itself. She could scarcely swallow. Every muscle in her body was tensing into hard knots. She walked from room to room, dodging toys, dodging her siblings.

Finally forty minutes late, he arrived. He looked upset, angry, but he did not say anything to her in the house after he had greeted her, Mama, Gracie, Belle and the little ones, the audience that attended his arrival.

He hustled her out to his Subaru, a graduation present from his parents five years before. She knew he wanted a new car; she had to make him want her more than a gleaming bright red Subaru without a mile on it, without a scratch or a nick on its sleek flanks. She waited till they were inside. Then she put a tentative hand on his forearm. "Is something wrong, Terry sweetheart?"

"My mother is a . . . witch!"

She entirely agreed, although she found his language mild. But she knew better than to let on to her hostility. "Why, Terry, what happened? What did she say to you?"

"She started in, Don't you have enough self-confidence to go out with a girl from our own background? One who can stand up to any kind of scrutiny? How long are you going to live on us? You're twenty-seven years old. When will it end? As if apartments didn't cost just about everything I make." He drove furiously down the street, but he did not squeal around the corner. He always drove carefully; it was instinct to him. No matter how furious he was or how he gritted his teeth and mumbled curse words under his breath, nonetheless, he stopped at stop signs; he signaled before he turned. That kind of polite civilized core made her trust him. When he got them to a road that led to the water, to a pier with a clam shack that had just reopened for the summer, he parked carefully. Then he banged on the wheel with his fists and glared ahead. "If they want me out, fine. I'm moving out! Tomorrow."

"Where will you move to? Will Chris leave with you?"

"I don't want to live with that loudmouth! He makes me sick. They aren't driving him crazy, nagging him to get a place. They know the stupid jerk can't afford it, because he's just a failure. Do you know how he's managed to sell insurance? I'll lay it out for you. There's a two-hundred-thousand-dollar policy on my father, there's a two-hundred-thousand-dollar policy on my mother, there's a two-hundred-thousand-dollar policy on me. If we had a dog, the fucking dog would be insured for a hundred thousand. He sold an annuity to my Aunt Kate. He sold supplemental health insurance to my Uncle Rodney. We've run out of relatives, so he's run out of sales. And they don't ride him around the room, digging in the spurs and complaining how much money he's costing them. He's cost them a fortune. For what they're paying in premiums, they could have bought me a damned condo on the water. For two years, he's been selling insurance, and he's never sold a policy to anyone who wasn't a blood relative. He ought to get married and then he'd have in-laws to hit on."

The policies were for so much money, they were enough to buy houses, to base a life on. Her parents had probably never seen that much money, even if every penny they had ever made was to be heaped up in a pile in the yard. She was a little staggered at the thought. How much did such a policy cost? It seemed a lot better than playing the lottery, because people died all the time. If her parents had a policy on Joey, their money troubles would be over, it was that simple. "Why do they want you to move out? It would be wonderful to live with you. You're mature for your age. You're thoughtful. You work hard in an important and growing field—"

"They always spoiled him. I never had a car till my senior year of high school, after guys with half the money my old man makes all had theirs. It was a wreck, an old Honda Civic. But when he turned sixteen, he got his first car. They always expected me to get A's and then made a fuss over him if he managed a couple of B's. It's a double standard!"

"Being the oldest, they leaned hard on you. And they still do."

"Right! You see it too."

"I see everything that happens to you, because I love you, and so I care about how people treat you. You're a good person, and sometimes people don't appreciate you, just take you for granted."

"I hate being taken for granted. I'm always the good one. I'm the one they made the rules for. Don't bring girls home when we're out of town. Be careful never to get a girl in trouble. Stay away from drugs. Don't drive and drink. Don't overdraw your account. Don't borrow or lend. That's a joke. My brother owes money on four credit cards. He's overdue on all of them."

"By tomorrow, they'll calm down and everything will be normal."

"No it won't be! I'm sick of her nagging me. Let's see how they do without me to fix things that go wrong. I'm the one who, when the plumber doesn't fix it, calls him and asks him to come back and do it right. My mother talks a tough line to us, but she gets phobic on the phone when she has to complain."

"Honey, you'll feel better if you have something to eat. Let's go get fried clams and some chowder and sit on the pier."

He let himself be led. They sat at a rough wooden outdoor table watching the fishing boats and the pleasure boats passing each other in the narrow channel. A big herring gull stood on a piling and watched them eat. She imagined it was a wise old female waiting to see if she was reeling in her catch successfully, of if she was going to let him slip away.

"Baby, I think it's real easy for parents to take you for granted, and in fact not see who you are. They knew you before you could speak, before you could walk, before you knew how to take yourself to the bathroom, even. They get confused between what you used to be when immature, and what you are now. Someone who meets you sees an attractive, bright together very mature young man who makes a wonderful appearance and speaks thoughtfully. Your mother sees a ten-year-old with his pants falling down, sitting on his own pair of glasses."

"That's it. They don't see me. They don't even know me, but they think they know everything about me. My mother's always telling me that she knows better than I do what I want."

"Eat your spinach, it's good for you."

"I never minded spinach. I always hated peas."

"So do I," Becky said. What did she care if she ever ate a pea again? "Isn't that funny? I hate the smell they make cooking."

"That's it. It turns my stomach." They walked back to the car pressed side to side, his arm heavy around her shoulders, walking very slowly. It was beginning to cool and quicken toward night, a breeze rising off the water, the lights from the channel beacons blinking green and red. The gull flapped off. Becky wondered what the old gull thought of her progress.

He started the engine. "Tomorrow morning, I'm going out and get the Sunday papers. And I'm looking at apartments."

"I know where we can get the real estate sections tonight. We have to drive to New Bedford, but my corner drugstore will sell us that part of the paper early. It comes separately, and they put them together."

"Really? We could look at it together and mark prospects. . . ."

Sunday morning he picked her up at nine. The first two places were impossible, but the third, even though it was above a row of stores just off Main Street in Hyannis, was nice and light. The three rooms had been redone in a pleasant, up-to-date look. It was just a ten-minute drive from Terry's home office. Terry put his arm around her shoulders. "We could share this. You could move in."

She moved deliberately away from him and made her eyes large. "Terry, you know it would break my mother's heart if I lived with you without being married. I could never receive Communion. In the eyes of my family, I'd be damned." She followed Sylvie's old rule of presenting herself a good Catholic girl. Of course she went to bed with him; he was her fiancé.

"You don't want to live with me."

She decided to take her big chance. "I'd love to live with you, I'd love that more than anything in the world, but I can't do it. We're not married."

He looked around the apartment he had decided to rent, absolutely bare except for the refrigerator, stove and sink and the bathroom fixtures. Even the windows lacked shades. It was empty, a box to fill with some as-yet-untried, unlived life. "So we'll get married. I'll show them I can manage without them. We'll take out a license tomorrow."

Once again she found the strength to say no. "We're not ashamed. And we need presents. We'll set a date. What about the last week in June? That gives us six weeks. We'll get married from your family's church. Once the date for the wedding is set and invitations go out, my parents will ease up. I can start spending nights, so that I'll be living with you in a couple of weeks. I can fix this place up right away. No more Naughty Pines motel for us."

And it was so. It was the beginning of her dream come true.

CHAPTER 25

LEILA

Leila tried to examine Becky without staring. She could not tell whether the wan, drained quality was a result of being in jail. She looked thinner and more angular in person. They were sitting at a battered counter with a low grill between them, in the Barnstable House of Correction. To their right and left were a mother-daughter pair having a sullen, mostly silent session, and a husband and wife arguing about him bringing their children to his mother's. A female guard stood with her arms folded, watching and chewing gum.

Becky began by apologizing for being in the correctional facility. "My family is still getting the bond money together. I'll be out soon. But my husband and I had gone through our savings—and Mr. Green is expensive. I despise being in here, but it's a matter of cold cash." Then Becky asked Leila about herself, who she was, where she lived, the nature of her work. Leila decided as she patiently filled herself in for Becky, that it was partly caution that prompted the extensive questioning, but it was also simple curiosity. Becky seemed less impressed by her academic credentials than by her infrequent appearances on local news programs and public affairs programming, as an expert on women and violence.

Leila was trying to see in the woman before her, a good four inches shorter than herself and one third lighter, someone who could bash in her husband's head. Certainly a good-sized man would have had no trouble defending himself against her. She decided to take another look at the description of the body from the coroner's report. Leila wondered if Becky were physically able to commit the crime she had been charged with.

"How did you feel about those women, the ones in Framingham who let you interview them?"

Tricky question. Oh, I just loved every one of them? She was dealing with a fairly shrewd young woman, although one capable of great folly. "They were markedly different individuals. Some I disliked, but I tried to be fair to them. Others I felt that I understood pretty well. Some became my friends. I'm still in touch with them."

Becky nodded. "Suppose you don't like me?"

"I don't think that's going to happen," Leila said gently, giving Becky her best smile. "I think we can communicate—at least I very much hope so. If we can't, I promise to drop the project."

"I don't want to spend my life in here," Becky said. She added quickly, "I didn't do it. I didn't kill anyone. I'm going on trial because I went to bed with a high school boy. I mean, he was a senior but they speak about him as if he's someone I was baby-sitting, really."

"I agree. You're being tried for sexual crimes."

Becky sighed, her chin in her propped hand. She looked into Leila's eyes. "No matter what those sleazy tabloids say, I wasn't taking advantage of Sam. I was crazy about him. Honestly. I didn't see him as a boy. I saw him as a better man than my husband."

"Then why didn't you leave?"

Becky looked surprised. "Sam couldn't live with me. He was going to college in the fall. He had a scholarship. He had obligations to his mother and his uncle, who were supporting him. I understand family obligations. A month never went by that I didn't hand part of my paycheck to my parents, to help them out. They never put that in their dirty stories."

"Your family's loyal to you. That doesn't always happen, you know."

Becky's face spasmed into an odd small quirky smile that looked involuntary. "We . . . have to stick to each other. Anyhow," she added in a lighter tone of voice, "Sam's family is sticking to him too. They'd cook and eat me to get him off. The Burgesses would like to execute me themselves."

Leila saw a flash of anger there. "You didn't get along with them?"

Becky ran her thumb and forefinger along the sides of her pointed chin, reflectively. "I remember the wedding. Now you have to understand, there was no way my parents could afford that wedding. I didn't go for a great big splashy one, although I wanted to. I mean, how often do you get married?"

Becky seemed to be awaiting an answer, so Leila said, "Actually I've only done it once."

"How old were you? Did you have a big wedding?"

Becky was questioning her again. She made herself answer patiently. "Twenty-one. No, we were married by a rabbi in his study. But you were married in church, weren't you?"

Becky nodded. "His family's church. I thought it would be more real to him that way. But it made everything more expensive. Did your husband's parents take to you?"

"Not at first." She wasn't about to explain to Becky the difference between German and Russian Jews, and why she had seemed uncouth to them, while to her they had seemed Jews bleached of Jewishness, besides the strangeness of Texas Jews who spoke with a drawl to one from Philadelphia. "After I had my son, things got better. You had trouble with his family at the wedding?"

"Nothing was good enough. His father kept glaring and snorting and looking down on my parents. Mrs. Burgess kept making these acid comments. At one point my mother started to cry, not like mothers do at weddings, but because Mrs. Burgess was making her feel bad for her dress, for her hair. I could have slapped her. I felt she was going out of her way to poison my wedding day, and I couldn't even call her on it without making things worse."

"Did your families get along better later on?"

"They never saw each other again. Ever. Tommy came over, but everybody else felt too uncomfortable around Terry. He made it painfully clear he didn't want to deal with them. He acted as if he expected me to dump my own parents, my whole family, and pretend they didn't exist."

"That must have been hard. Did you try to change his mind?"

"I just saw them without him. But sure, I resented his attitude. I resented the little digs from his mother, and Terry never stepping in, never defending me. He took it for granted that his mother would look down on me. I never got used to that, ever. I mean, what had she done with her life?"

"Did they put pressure on you to start a family? Did he want to?"

Becky shook her head no. "It was out of the question, financially. Even when Terry was working, we had the condo to pay off. . . . Is your husband a professor too?"

"He teaches drama at B.U. But he's primarily a director. Of plays."

"What's his name?" Becky sat up, peering at her with a sudden visible increase of interest. When she was interested, her face had more color. She looked almost vibrant.

"Nicolas Landsman. He has a play now off-Broadway in New York, but usually he—"

"I know who he is!" Becky drew herself up. "Remember, I was involved in theater."

"Of course you were," Leila said gently. The truth was she didn't think a local production of *Dracula* as theater.

"I never grew up around plays, so it was exotic to me. But I took to it naturally, everybody said so. I'd love to meet your husband."

"When he comes back to Boston from New York, we could figure out how to arrange that." He'd adore meeting Becky; he'd dine out on it for a month.

"Really?" Becky sounded skeptical. Her mouth twisted slightly. "Oh, because I'm in all the papers—a depraved murderess who runs around seducing children."

"That's the up side to notoriety. Everybody wants to meet you."

Becky grimaced. "I always had a fantasy of being famous. But not like this. Did you ever want to be famous?"

"For me making a living was more important."

"But what about your husband? Doesn't he make big bucks?"

"He makes a living, but because he's on the road a lot and likes things nice, he spends a lot too. Basically I carry the house." It felt extraordinary to say out loud what she had concealed for years. Only Melanie had really known.

Becky's gaze rested on her, a little amused and a little resigned. "Doesn't it turn out that way oftener than you expect it to?"

"You didn't expect your husband to remain out of work so long."

Becky sighed. "I didn't. I felt as if he didn't really try to find work. He wanted work to find him."

Their time was up. "I hope," Leila said hastily as she was rushed out, "that we can talk again soon."

"I'd like that," Becky called after her. "I enjoyed our conversation."

In the car, Leila ran over the afternoon and realized how little she had gotten from Becky. Becky was going to be difficult to penetrate, for she was careful how she presented herself after her savaging in the media. Still, today she had finally met Becky; she was scheduled to see Sam. She was making progress. Traffic on the expressway into Boston was slow, because snow had begun to fall. It came down slantwise, small fast hard snow, more pellets than flakes. It piled up on the side of the road like detergent, coating the banks.

Once off the expressway, she had to drive slowly. The streets had not been swept and the pavement was slippery. She was glad David had taken the car to have snow tires put on. She dreaded dealing with mechanics. She could get around prison officials and police detectives, administrators and lawyers, but mechanics made her feel at once elderly and childish.

Vronsky was watching from the table that gave him the best view of the street. She could see him meowing at her through the window. When she unlocked the door, there he was. He attempted to lead her directly back to the kitchen. "A long time since breakfast, huh?" The little pebbles of snow slowly melted on her coat arm. She beat her hands together to warm them. "I want coffee, bad. What do you think of that?"

She turned on the espresso machine and checked her messages. Blinking light. Nick. "Since today is Saturday and I haven't heard from you, I gather you decided not to come. It's not like you to be so uncommunicative and to hang me up. Are you angry with me? Is everything all right with you? Are you depressed or is something bad going on with David or with Shana or with any of the fifty people you worry about? Give me a call and let me know."

"This is Cathy. This is Cathy on Saturday, I don't know what date it is. Zak has absolutely forbidden that you see Sam, so I'm afraid it's off. He's the one paying for the lawyer, and I couldn't afford that guy, he charges by the minute like a parking meter. So you have to fight this one out with Zak, please, and not with me, because I can't make him change his mind when he gets like this. My husband was the same way. I'm really sorry."

"Shit," Leila said. "Shit, shit, shit." She let herself down heavily in her desk chair and cursed for five minutes. Cathy did not have an answering machine, fortunately. "Hi, it's Leila."

"Leila, please don't be angry with me. Sam wants to talk with you. But Zak has forbidden it. Maybe once he's home, I can sneak you in. . . ."

"What I need is directions to Zak's. He descended on me without being invited. I intend to do the same to him."

Cathy did not argue but gave her the instructions. "But you won't tell him I let you know."

"Do you think he's likely to be there tomorrow?"

"Sundays the clinic is shut except for emergencies. I'm really pissed at him. He acts as if Sam is his kid, like he's taken over from Mike raising Sam. I think it's because he lost his own daughter."

"You said she died in a fire?"

"With his wife, Corinne. They lived in a big flashy house up in a canyon near L.A. She was a studio musician, gorgeous redhead. Sang backup, played electric violin. That's one bad-luck family. Anyhow, he ought to be home."

Zak might be good at getting dogs to obey, but if he thought he could get rid of her, he was going to learn differently. Tomorrow morning she was going to poke right into his life, the way he had appeared in hers, and she was going to stand there arguing until he agreed to stop interfering. She had learned years ago that, because she was a big soft-bodied woman, people often thought of her as more pushable than she was. When she stood her ground and fought back, often men and women both were taken by surprise. As Zak would be.

CHAPTER 26

MARY

Mary had never before stolen from her ladies, never anything but a yogurt or some jam or a slice or two of bread, some leftovers they wouldn't miss. But Mrs. Landsman had been getting rid of old clothes from her son's room. A lot of dust had come down with the boxes, and she asked Mary to clean the room.

When Mary was putting suitcases of winter clothes up in the closet, woolens she guessed he scarcely needed in California, she ran across something jammed in a corner. It was a tiny sleeping bag. It was the normal size opened up, but it squished into a small roll. No one would ever know she had it in her carry-all.

This has been a hard week. Snow was the worst, because she left tracks. She had to sleep in a church basement three nights. One night she spent at Logan. Another she slept in an unlocked garage behind the Anzio house, in their Volvo, curled in the backseat. If only she had a car of her own: she couldn't stop thinking about it lately. She'd have her shell like a snail to carry with her, and on nights like this week she'd know she could survive. When she got too cold, she could drive around with the heater on. Her savings grew with infinite slowness. Once or twice she dropped hints to Cindy, how an old car would make her life easier. Cindy wrote back that she was sure with the repairs and insurance, her mother was lucky not to have to keep up some old clunker.

All week she kept thinking about that sleeping bag. Her clients owned things that were exotic to her. Ten years ago, she had been an avid and knowledgeable consumer. She never used to buy a blender or a toaster without looking it up in *Consumer Reports*, to make sure she was getting the best for her family. Now she kept up with the latest consumer products by watching what her clients bought. The dishwasher at the DeMotts had to be programmed like a computer. It beeped when she touched the front. Their oven was the same.

Her desires were far more modest: a hot plate, a tiny refrigerator, a cot. Or just a car to live in. But she coveted that sleeping bag. All those freezing nights with her feet getting numb and her nose running, she kept thinking how snug she would be in that light warm little sack. The son didn't use it. Maybe he'd slept in it once or twice at some meeting or group event, but that was the sum of it. It still smelled new.

She couldn't get that sleeping bag out of her head. It was like being back in college and having a crush on a fellow she had met and talked with and knew would be just perfect for her, but he didn't acknowledge she existed. She had a physical longing for it. She bet it cost seventy-five dollars at least. She couldn't explain to Cindy why she would like a sleeping bag. Cindy wouldn't believe that she had taken up hiking, and then Cindy'd probably buy one of those big ones. She couldn't walk around Boston or Cambridge or Brookline or Newton with a sleeping bag in a roll on her back. Try carrying a sign reading HOMELESS. That bag would make such a difference in her comfort and safety these winter nights.

On her next day at the Landsmans, she didn't mean to do more than look at it. She cleaned the downstairs at a breakneck speed, scrubbing furiously, bashing that vacuum to and fro like a speeded-up video. Before she let herself touch it again, she cleaned the master bedroom and its bathroom. Finally she let herself go into the son's room. It was just where she had put it, at the very back of the shelf. She took it down. Then she pulled it from its little nylon sheath and spread it out. She couldn't resist getting into it. Oh, it would be heaven itself.

She couldn't put it back in the closet and walk away. It was as if she was holding life in her hands. This flimsy thing could keep her alive some cold night when her luck was bad. She felt ashamed of herself. Mrs. Landsman always paid the service promptly, always did her own dishes, had never asked her to do laundry or anything else she wasn't supposed to, that her other ladies tried to get away with. But Mary had to have the sleeping bag.

Every day she had been calling the hospital. Today they told her that Beverly Bozeman was conscious and off the critical list. She was no longer in intensive care and could have visitors at the regular hours. Mary was being foolish, but she could not help identifying with the woman lying there in the hospital bed, maybe remembering nothing, maybe sick to death with fear. Beverly must be terrified of going back on the streets and ending up dead.

She couldn't stop thinking of Beverly, maybe because her own life had been hard this week. The holidays were coming, and her clients would start to travel soon. Already today Mrs. Williams told her they'd be in Florida the first week of January. She apologized for not needing the house cleaned. "Oh," Mary said, "then you won't be having anybody stay that I can clean up after?"

So if she could survive the next three weeks, she'd have a roof over her head, a place she could spread out in. It gave her something to look forward to. She was waiting to see who was going away for Christmas. Last year she had a choice of two places.

Being Friday, she was going to try Logan again, a different terminal from last Sunday. Friday was a big tourist and family night, so they were used to people in all states of disarray snoozing here and there. Also if she was lucky and a storm hit as it was supposed to, the airport would be full of people sleeping. She could even lie down.

Storms were scary. They made people change travel plans. For those who lived on the streets, a storm could kill. She didn't feel smart this week, she didn't feel like such a great survivor. It was wonderful to sleep in her new bag. She felt secure that she wouldn't die of exposure. She'd always been afraid when she was sleeping in a very cold place that maybe she'd never wake. She couldn't afford to buy Beverly Bozeman flowers, but she brought some magazines Mrs. Williams was discarding and a nice wool sweater Mrs. Landsman had been going to give to Goodwill. She said perhaps it would fit her daughter's boy, and took it. She tried it on in the garage, but it was too big. The sleeves were too long and it hung below her belly. She couldn't wear something so obviously a man's and so obviously a discard, but she bet Beverly Bozeman could use it.

She had a supper of leftovers from Mrs. Williams—rather dry deli roast beef, a couple of slices of bread, an apple. It didn't quite fill her up, but she'd be all right. She went to Chestnut Hill Mall. It was nice to rest her feet. They had carolers and she sat and sang along. She had acquired a brand-new Bloomingdale's shopping bag, which she had at her feet along with her carry-all and her purse clutched on her lap.

Although she would rather have had someplace warm and secure for the night, and she would rather have had a meal instead of two bites for supper, she wasn't discontent. Free entertainment was something she loved. It was the season when she liked to pass time around Faneuil Hall shopping area too. But tonight promised to be a little cold for outdoor sitting.

They had poinsettias and baby evergreens all over and some white and pink camellias. She knew the Southern flowers from Bethesda. They had sometimes taken family vacations in the spring to Savannah or Charleston. She remembered touring those lush Southern gardens. She was never much of a gardener—more the petunia-and-marigolds-from-the-supermarket type, plus an occasional rosebush bought in bloom that died the first winter—but she loved the ambience of a well-planted, well-kept garden.

Nobody looked at her twice, sitting with her new shopping bag in her twelve-year-old wool coat still serviceable, her hat that Cindy knitted her, gloves she got from a lost-and-found in Logan last year. She hit the bigger lost-and-founds regularly, for umbrellas, mufflers, gloves. A plaid muffler always turned up, as would a pair of black fur-lined gloves. She had three mufflers, only one visible. The others were wound around her thighs to keep her warm.

She realized she wasn't going to arrive when visiting hours started. She was delaying going. It was warm and cozy in the mall. She loved hearing the carols. It took her back to her childhood in Centralia. Sometimes she found herself concentrating on her childhood, to feel happy briefly.

She got up and made herself leave. She knew it was superstition. She knew it was ridiculous to visit Beverly Bozeman. Beverly might be crazy. She might be a blithering idiot. She might be a hopeless drug-addict drunk who couldn't count past three. Mary recognized the foolishness of her quest but felt compelled to take the Green Line to the Red Line to Cambridge and trudge through the snow already beginning to come down jerkily and fast.

When they said a ward, she envisioned a huge room full of beds, but Beverly was in a smallish room with three other beds, all occupied by women. One, a black woman of perhaps thirty, was in traction. Another black woman had a head bandage on and seemed to be asleep or unconscious. The other white woman, even older than Beverly Bozeman, was watching the small television suspended above their beds.

Beverly Bozeman was sitting up. She did have flowers. Beverly stared at Mary blankly, frowning, and then a nod of recognition. Mary felt embarrassed, not sure if it was better or worse that Beverly knew she had seen her before. "You're the lady who talks to her in the morning or late afternoon, twice a week maybe."

"I came past the morning you were attacked. I thought you'd like a visitor. But I see you have a friend." Mary waved at the chrysanthemums.

"The rape crisis center gave her those."

Mary's gaze dropped. She could not think about rape and look at Beverly. It was too frightening. It was foolish to pretend that anything that happened to Beverly Bozeman could not happen to her. She was a little distracted by the way Beverly talked about herself, but not surprised. On the streets, people developed weird quirks, tics, compulsive routines.

Beverly looked tiny in the hospital bed. It was the hospital gown. She was no longer wrapped in ten layers of old clothing. Her grey-brown hair had been partly shaved and cut short, with a rakish towel-turban around her bandages. Her hands lay before her on the hospital blanket, small hands, very clean now and completely still. Bruises were just fading on her wrists, exposed by the gown.

Mary tried to think of something to say. "I wanted to see that you were alive. What happened to you is so frightening."

"Why would it frighten you? It's what happens to women on the streets."

"Any woman could end up on the streets," Mary said evasively. "Will you really be all right? What do the doctors say?"

"As little as they can." Beverly giggled. "She gets her information from the nurses. . . . How old are you?" she demanded suddenly.

"I'm sixty-one."

"Forty-seven."

Mary blinked, trying to keep her face from registering her reaction. "Forty-seven?" she repeated.

"You think she's twice that." Beverly grimaced.

"I thought you were . . . in your fifties."

"The nurses didn't believe her till they checked her records from Maine. She comes from Bath. They build ships there. Her husband had a job in the yards. Then he lost it."

"I was married too," Mary said. "I lost my husband to another woman, who lost him to another after that. He took my house, everything."

"She ran away from him. He used to beat her. He broke her jaw. There was a shelter and they took her in. But they can only let you stay thirty days. Then you have to find your own way. She didn't have money for rent. She ran out the door with the clothes on her back and the money in her purse." Beverly jerked her head at the Black woman in traction. "She's homeless too. She's been staying with a friend, but there's no more room because the father of her friend's kids came back. She was trying to beg, and somebody pushed her in front of a car. They called her a whore."

"Did they catch the man who hurt you?"

"Of course not." Beverly laughed dryly, convulsively, with the sound of an old car trying to start on a cold morning. "How hard are they going to look? They think he's crazy, raping her. It's not the first time, even."

"The same man?"

"No, the other guy, he was homeless too. He caught her sleeping under a bridge. But he didn't beat her up. That's when she left Jamaica Plain and decided to live around here. She figured it was safer."

"Generally it is."

Beverly leaned gingerly on one elbow and motioned her closer. "Why did you really come to see her? Why do you care?"

Mary suddenly found herself saying what she had concealed from the world. "I'm homeless too . . . Oh, I work like a dog cleaning people's houses. But I sleep wherever I can." She was shocked at herself. She stared from woman to woman to see if they had overheard, but no one was even looking.

"Thought so," Beverly said, nodding her head but unable to move naturally because of the bandages. "You're still in the fold. Meaning that you can pass. She used to be that way. She thought all along you were one of us."

Mary froze on the visitor's chair. How could Beverly tell? Something in the way she looked, the way she walked? How had she given herself away? She could not even bring herself to ask Beverly. It was too frightening.

CHAPTER 27

BECKY

Becky floated through the first four months of her marriage. It was delightful to wake in the morning in their firm queen-sized bed in the pale blue bedroom painted just before they moved in. There on the other pillow was not her sister Laurie with her snuffling and her sly sour smirk. Now Terry's corn silk hair was tousled against the pillow as he lay on his side in fetal position, innocent, vulnerable. The sheets had no stains, no history of sickness and pain. They were plaid or flowered. Even the pillows were fresh.

Only two of them shared the bathroom. It astounded her how long he could manage to spend there on mornings when she had to get ready for work. But one man, no matter how slow, was not nine other people, all in a hurry. Here when she did get the bathroom, it was clean—and she made sure it stayed that way. She had bought a toothbrush devoted to cleaning the grout. They had new fluffy towels and a rug on the floor, dark blue to match the tiles. The shower curtain had cute penguins on it. Everything was clean, everything was new, everything smelled fresh—just the way she had dreamed years before in the mall.

The girls at the office had given her towels and sheets and a green striped plant. She put that in a corner of the living room. They had two Danish-style chairs that had been in the Burgess household. They had the TV and the stereo from Terry's room at home. Gracie had given them a coffee table she had been storing in the basement. They didn't have a couch yet, but Sylvie had suggested Becky put some pillows on the floor.

The kitchen was small, but she was just learning how to cook, and by the time she got home from work, who could bother? They ate out three times a week. They got pizza or other takeout twice more, leaving her two meals a week to worry about. The appliances had come with the apartment, but the microwave and the toaster and the Mr. Coffee were wedding gifts. They had been given two blenders, an electric knife and an electric mixer, but they had turned those in on a VCR.

The bedroom was the best room, for the Burgesses had given them money for a pale oak bedroom set, a queen bed, a vanity with a mirror and two side-by-side dressers. It was funny to open the closet door. His side was crammed with sports jackets and shirts and pants, full of sporting gear, skiing and running gear; on her side the rod was barely half covered.

She heard him tell his buddy Lyle that she was unlike other women, just not interested in clothes. "When she moved in, she hardly filled a suitcase." He thought that her lack of clothes showed that she was not vain and frivolous. He had never gone without a video game or a pair of fancy running shoes or a certain type of bike. He could not imagine a life almost devoid of possessions, not through self-denial, but because they were not affordable.

Sylvie and she sewed bedroom curtains on Sylvie's machine. They were just oblongs—a print of yellow and blue and white sailboats—hemmed at top and bottom, but they made the room cheerful and kept out the gazes of people in the building across the street. They lived on a street with apartments or offices over shops. His parents were upset when they saw where Terry had moved, which Terry enjoyed. She thought it was marvelous to live in Hyannis, just like the Kennedys, at a famous address, but he called it High-Anus and said it was nothing but malls and doctor's offices and motels. She loved being able to run downstairs to ten restaurants. She had to drive to work on Route 28, and that was slow, but she found shortcuts. It beat commuting from New Bedford.

She savored the odd hours when she was home alone. His mother called him over to fix something from time to time. Becky went when they both were invited, but otherwise, she avoided Mrs. Burgess. The marriage had no impact on the scorn in which Mrs. Burgess held her. Sometimes Terry played softball with friends from his college fraternity, and weekly he played squash with his brother.

Those evenings she would visit her family or Sylvie. Other times she just stayed in the apartment, enjoying the space. The dry cleaner's downstairs was never open in the evenings, and on Saturday, only until noon. The really noisy times were in the morning when the truck arrived from where they actually did the cleaning and again at the end of the day when it returned. Then the sound of men yelling and banging things around rose through the floor.

She drifted through the rooms, touching the new objects, the lamp she had just learned she was not to leave in its cellophane wrappings. Sylvie had explained that was considered vulgar. She touched the newly bare lamp shade, she touched lightly the clean ivory wall, she stroked the Formica counter. When Terry brought a friend in, he always apologized and said the apartment was just temporary, and to be agreeable, she would smile and nod, but she thought this was paradise. Three rooms for just the two of them, everything so clean and sweet she could have popped the refrigerator and the vanity chair into her mouth.

Sylvie kept asking her if she didn't want to start a family, but Becky had never lived without babies and toddlers underfoot. To be alone was like the most powerful drug she could imagine, an ecstatic experience that reminded her of when Laurie had wanted to be a nun and gushed on and on about the presence of Our Lady. She had thought Laurie was making the whole thing up to get attention, but now she reconsidered. She was convinced that kneeling in the empty church, Laurie had experienced the joy of being alone and quiet for the first time in her life, and she had mistaken it for God.

Becky wished she could bottle the quiet in her apartment and bring it to her mother. But Mama could not even come and see her often. Becky had realized with a little shock about the third week of her marriage that Terry did not like her parents. She had always assumed that sure, her family home was a dump, but that anybody who loved her would see how sweet and long-suffering and hard-working Mama was, and would honor her for her virtues. But Terry was uncomfortable around any of her family except Tommy. He recognized Tommy's ambition, as he had recognized hers. Tommy too was marrying, and Terry thought that was a great idea. She did not know if that was because he felt that Tommy's marriage would make her family marginally more respectable, or because Tommy would then be living out of the house Terry refused to visit.

"Becca, don't fight about it," Tommy advised. "Just do what you want."

Mama noticed, of course; they all did. But Mama said it was better to have Becky come alone, because then they could have a real visit, instead of trying to be on their best behavior. Becky was embarrassed for Terry. He ought to have enough feeling for her to be open to her family. He ought to at least see what a good person Mama was, and Gracie, and how well-meaning Belle was too. It was a grave flaw in his character that he couldn't overcome his family's narrow-minded, middle-class prejudices. He would come around in time.

She admitted that when she walked in the old house now she noticed the smells, the utter chaos, the inevitable decay and disintegration caused by eight people living in a small space. That was because she had managed to snare Terry and clamber into the middle class. She was not a better person than Gracie or Belle, just shrewder and more selfish. She wanted her life to be nice—she wanted that more than anything else. Now she had it and she meant to keep it. Someday when she had more money, she would do something for all of them. Like Sylvie's aunt Marie, she would look and think intelligently about what her niece or her nephew needed, and she would provide it. In a quiet way Becky couldn't share with Terry, Aunt Marie remained her measure of the good life. The elder Burgesses lived in a fancier and larger house than Marie, but she lived more amply. Marie had friends; the Burgesses had acquaintances, associates. Marie had fun; the Burgesses did the expected thing.

For her wedding, Marie had given her a gift certificate to Saks in Boston with a note attached. Her message was, "Go buy yourself some good clothes. Men don't notice clothing, but they notice how you look. They want you to look like a million dollars without spending a penny."

Aunt Marie had made a transition to the middle class years before and could give useful pointers. Hardly anyone else could. Sylvie had been waylaid by starting a family. She no longer kept up with fashions or much of anything. Motherhood had closed over her like a warm salty tide in which she was afloat but swept along. Becky was determined to put off having a baby until they were thoroughly established.

Far from longing for a baby, the way two women in her office were trying to get pregnant, she had been burping babies since she was strong enough to lift one. She knew far more than Sylvie did about maternity, but she never volunteered advice, because she didn't want anybody telling her what a good mother she'd make. Someday, when the right sun rose over the right house on the right street. And they had the right bank account. Then she would have two children. Two only. They would get all the love she always dreamed of, the attention no kid in her family had ever been able to command.

In the meantime, Terry needed taking care of. He tossed his clothes when he undressed, and she had to pick up his socks, his briefs, his tees from the floor and the chair and the top of his dresser. He never thought about laundry or dry cleaning. He considered his clothes a self-enclosed system that functioned automatically: dirty clothes off, then the next morning, clean clothes appeared.

Still, she found his belongings cute. He had as fancy shoes as the kids who had run drugs in her high school. He had jackets with logos, outfits in which to play tennis or to ski or to ride a bicycle. It reminded her of a girl from middle school. The daughter of an ex-fisherman who had made money with The Guys on the docks, Tonia had everything. Her closets, like Terry's, bulged with special clothes for parties to which she was almost never asked, for she was nasty. Still, Becky played with Tonia sometimes because she had so many toys. Tonia had a Barbie doll and a Ken doll, each with dozens of costumes—just like Terry. Dealing with his clothes felt like playing with a Ken doll. But it was hard sometimes to do the laundry on a weekend. She had to drive to the laundromat and wait there.

Sometimes on weekends Terry just wanted to lie around and watch sports on TV. But some weekends they did something special. In August they went to New York with Chris and his current girlfriend Amy. They stayed in a hotel near Central Park and saw three movies and danced in a club. They went to the top of the World Trade Center and to Rockefeller Center. It was like a little second honeymoon, even though Chris and his girlfriend were along. On their real honeymoon, they had gone to New York too.

Becky was not fond of Chris. He was always putting his hands on her. He spoke too loudly and laughed boisterously at his own bad jokes. He was nothing like Terry, yet Terry said Chris was his parents' favorite. He was still angry that his parents had leaned on him to move out and let Chris live at home. Becky privately thought that the Burgesses had done her an incredible favor, so she was willing to put up with Chris when she had to. She just wished it were less often. Lots of times when she and Terry did go out, for instance to a Sunday Red Sox game in Boston, Chris automatically went along, sometimes with a girlfriend, as often without.

Saturday afternoon. Terry and his friend Lyle were sitting in the two decent chairs in the living room, eating potato chips, drinking lite beer and yelling at the TV set. It was the division championships for baseball. Becky was putting away clean laundry. On this warm September day, a fly bumped against the pane and she thought idly of killing it, but she did not. What harm was it doing? Just trying to escape. Why should she turn it into a mess on the screen? Instead she released the screen and waved it out with a dish towel. It buzzed off purposefully, as if to a secret meeting.

"Hey, Becky, give us another beer."

She took two more out of the refrigerator. Was Lyle staying to supper? She hoped they would go out to eat. There was nothing to feed him. She had done a little shopping when she was coming back with the laundry, but she hated hauling heavy bags up the steps. She always tried to get Terry to do the shopping with her, but he didn't like to. He said the supermarket was depressing. Also he would buy steaks and snacks and exceed their food budget. They were saving for a house. Supposedly.

After she brought the beers, she stood a moment, waiting to see if Terry would talk to her, but his eyes were on the screen. She carried a pile of washed clothes into the bedroom to stow them in their proper drawers. She heard herself sighing. She realized she was bored.

She tried to shake herself out of her funk. After all, if she was home, what would she be doing? Her old home. Doing housework. Doing laundry, just like now. But at least there was always someone to talk to. Sometimes when Terry was home, it was lonelier than when she was there by herself.

Maybe that was one reason people had babies so early. A woman wanted someone to pay attention to her. A baby at least would cry if its mother walked away.

Really, she had exactly what she had wanted. What on earth was wrong with her? It wasn't as if he didn't love her. Every night since they started living together, he wanted to make love. It was much faster than it used to be. Sometimes she came, sometimes she didn't, but what did it matter? It was over in fifteen minutes, and it kept him happy. That was the important thing, wasn't it? She had to figure out what she wanted that they could afford to buy, or where she wanted to go to eat. That was it. If she concentrated on that decision, she would be happy.

CHAPTER 28

LEILA

Zak lived off a road scattered with old Capes and modern ranch houses. SOLOMON the rusty mail box said. The sand road had been plowed, but it was still rough and icy going. The road twisted between two houses, dipped down past a bog, rose again up a hill of pines, snaked down the other side past two right-hand options. Finally it arrived at an old grey house among Norway spruces, not a common tree on the Cape and lending an air of slight gloom. Beyond the house was a small pond, surrounded by oaks and second growth—rum cherries, aspens, an occasional pitch pine. Two vehicles stood outside, a blue Toyota truck and a red Jeep sedan, neither new nor old, a hefty investment in all-weather vehicles; or did he live with someone? He was so involved in Cathy and Sam, she had assumed he lived alone. Maybe he had a visitor? She sat in her car feeling foolish.

She had a stomachache, that sour clenching with which her body registered a protest at being forced to do something she had no desire to go through. How often in her marriage she had envied Nick, who seemed to have little need to do what he did not want to. For him it was enough to explain blithely, I didn't feel like it. As if she had ever been in the mood to cart David to the dentist, looking pale and shrunken and with the air he wore so well of going to his execution stoically. She was forever doing things she felt had to be done. This book was an exception, an indulgence, to write about something at once as heavy and frivolous as murder. A hole in the social fabric, an individual aberration. Not so much a social problem of the sort she usually tackled as a slippage.

What galvanized her was the impression of being watched, a slight movement at the window. Resolutely she opened the car door, slammed it smartly behind her, and marched to the house, trying vainly to remember how annoyed she had been that this uncle had placed himself firmly in the way of her interviewing Sam.

She banged on the door, two fast knocks, and stepped back. The door opened at once. Dressed in a muted plaid shirt and jeans, he was smiling slightly, as if trying not to. It took her a moment to realize why he looked so different; in fact he looked more like the photo she had seen of his brother Michael than he did the man she had met before. "Where's your beard?"

"In the septic system. Sam's lawyer told me to shave it off. We obey our lawyers." He stood aside to let her in.

Quickly she marched into the living room. There was a fire in the fireplace, but confined in a stove with glass doors. This was a reasonable compromise she had considered for their porous house, but Nick liked the open fire. Once upon a time, they had used to sit in front of it embraced, legs stretched out, toes almost in the fire. Here two dogs, an unclipped poodle and a spaniel with its leg in a cast, a long-haired black cat and a tabby with a shaved belly were at various wary distances from each other on the Navajo hearth rug.

"Do you feel undressed without it?"

"Cold, mostly. I grew up here, but years in L.A. make me unused to the cold. Now I get wind burn." He waved her to an armchair, removing a cat. "She's blind. But I don't suppose you drove all the way out here to examine my naked face."

"You know why I'm here. You're blocking me." She decided to take off her coat. That would proclaim she was staying until she got what she wanted. She felt very watched. At least five animals were gazing at her. No, six. A bandaged parrot was also staring.

"Good morning, America," it squawked hopefully. "Pretty baby."

"You can't have found me without help."

"I'm a resourceful woman."

"And Cathy's a bit of a twit. She's mad at me. She can't see the larger picture."

"Can you? You're hurting Sam in the long run. I've talked with Becky, after all. I've talked with Terry's parents."

"Sam is still trying to shield her." His watch beeped. Out of his pocket he drew a vial, took out a pill, grabbed the tabby and got the pill down its throat in ten seconds. "Sam has to stop worrying about her and believe he's in real trouble himself."

"Do you believe he murdered Terrence?"

"Is this an official interview?"

"Do I have a tape recorder running? I tape all my interviews, for my own personal protection and in the interests of accuracy."

"I think about it all the time. Endless brooding, without issue."

"You don't know?"

"I can't imagine Sam killing anything larger than a mosquito. He's softhearted. He loves animals. I'd hoped he'd get his degree and go into practice with me." From somewhere a kitten had crawled into his lap. On the back of the rocker, the blind cat nuzzled his hair.

"The love of animals and the capacity for violence are not necessarily incompatible. Prisoners keep cats or birds, if they're permitted. A hit man may be a loving father and husband."

"I've told myself that. Yet I can't imagine, I can't picture Sam beating a man to death. It's going to be very, very difficult, if not impossible, for a jury not to convict him. I keep thinking that he's protecting her."

"Have you seen Becky?"

"A little fox-faced creature of infinite slyness." He paced slowly to the windows and back, the blind cat on his shoulder, the kitten in his hands. The floor was made of wide old boards, taking a nice polish. Scattered here and there were Navajo and Hopi rugs, bright against the dark wood. He paced in a wide circle around the chair he had motioned for her to take. Every time he passed, the dogs thumped their tails.

"Pretty baby," the parrot squawked. "Love me tender."

"She is not a big strapping woman. No jury will believe she beat her husband to death while Sam watched."

He sighed. "Do you think he's guilty?"

"I have trouble imagining Becky killing her husband, now that I've talked with her. I keep confusing Sam and my own son David. David is strong-willed but very gentle. Killing has always seemed to me to require a lack of imagination, a refusal of empathy. I can't imagine David willfully hurting anyone, given his capacity to extrapolate from his own feelings. He's always saying things like, We must have respect for all life forms." She wondered, shocked, how they had begun to talk with each other, instead of making speeches.

He sat down gingerly in a rocker some distance away. "I haven't been able to bring myself to ask Sam directly. I'm afraid of what he may answer. So far he's insisting he's innocent, but his friend Gene has talked and talked. The police may offer Sam a deal if he cooperates, but that assumes he did it."

"Once the papers and the evening news are full of descriptions of a murder and who they say did it, it's hard not to assume it's fact in the same sense as reportage of what the stock market did."

"I feel responsible for Sam. In loco parentis."

"But he has a mother, Cathy. And he's seventeen."

"In my head, he's still fourteen. Anyhow, seventeen's young enough. I was a real horse's ass at seventeen. I never made a right decision. I don't think I made decisions. I just toppled into things."

She looked at him, having trouble imagining him as an impulsive adolescent. He seemed, as Cathy had characterized him, a control freak. She must have smiled because he added, after a moment, "You doubt my memory. My wife—Corinne," he amended, with the air of correcting himself, "she used to doubt I'd ever been adolescent. She claimed I was born forty. That was when she was annoyed with me."

"She was killed in a fire?"

He nodded. "Would you like some coffee?"

"Thank you." Subject changed. She was warned off. While he slipped into the kitchen beyond, she looked around. She had not broken eye contact since arriving, so this was the first time she was able to observe. The fireplace with its inset stove took up much of one wall. The ceiling was low, the beams exposed. The room had been replastered carefully. The Southwestern decor of the Zuni vases and the rugs, a Mexican mask, sat oddly with the old Cape, obvious remnants of his marriage, his life in L.A.

The coffee table was almost hidden under a load of books and magazines, which she leaned to examined. *Science News*, *Science*, *Natural History*, *Audubon*, *Sanctuary*—magazine of the Massachusetts Audubon Society—*Archeology Today*, and various veterinary journals. A coffee-table book of Escher's drawings, inscribed *from Helen with Love*. Helen wasn't the wife. A girlfriend?

It was clean enough; but with the books all over the living room, several lying open as if he, like herself, read four or five books at once and left them wherever he sat or lay to read one of them, she suspected he lived alone. Wouldn't Cathy have mentioned a woman? Besides, Helen could be a sister, a sister-in-law left from his marriage. A colleague. His agent.

An intelligent man. Studious, curious. She wandered the room, picking up objects while the animals watched: a geode, a large pearlescent shell, an oblong of petrified wood, an old blue hand-blown bottle, Hopi pottery. He had the habit of taking off his shoes wherever he sat down so that under the couch were shearling slippers and one moccasin; near his chair were two Clark boots; by the door were snow boots from L. L. Bean, soaked through. Apple cores had been forgotten, desiccated among the books.

Most of the furniture was in earth tones, except for the strident mustard draperies on the windows. She was gazing at them when he appeared with coffee in mugs. "You're admiring my hideous drapes. My partner Josie made them."

"So you have to leave them up?"

He nodded. "I wish she'd asked me first, but she kept saying it was so dark in here. I wonder if I could bribe the dry cleaner to lose them."

She grinned. She was trying out various approaches, in a sense seeing what she could get away with, how far she could go in an attempt to lighten the atmosphere between them. "Why don't you throw them in the washer? A man isn't expected to know what's washable and what isn't."

"If they fit." He nodded judiciously. "I don't want my washer to break again. The repairman only works when he feels like it. He's a mad surfer."

"How do you happen to live out here?"

"It isn't out here to me. I grew up in this house."

"Really? What did your parents do here?"

"They left New York. My father had his first heart attack very young, and they changed their lives. We have wobbly hearts. My mother wanted to write, my father wanted to sit still and fish, so they bought a motel. It was never much of a living. They killed themselves all summer and closed it from the end of October until the beginning of April. My mother never did write."

"They're retired?"

"We're not a long-lived family. Cheer up, I might drop dead at any moment and then Cathy will conduct you to Sam with lightning speed."

"You don't trust Cathy."

"She means well. She's just . . . not too well stocked upstairs. You've got awfully chummy with her. A professional necessity, I suppose."

"I can find a lot to like in her."

"She's likable."

"At first I thought you might be interested in her."

His right eyebrow canted up. "Maybe you aren't so perceptive."

"I said, at first." She resisted the temptation to bond with him around Cathy's general flakiness. "Obviously you two basically relate about Sam."

"I tried to take care of her after Mike's death. Now she has a boyfriend, and she's his problem. But Sam will always be mine. She's too ditzy for me. I keep thinking she's playing little girl. But what you see is what there is, I'm convinced by now. Mike and I had very different taste in women. If as they say, men marry their mothers, Mike went for our mother's helpless side, and I went for her pretensions."

"I thought you were ordering Cathy around because you see yourself as the man of the house."

"No, I just see her as a little less mature and capable than Sam. I'm scared for him. Really scared."

She decided a statement was better than a question. "You're going to let me talk to him now."

He shrugged. His eyes seemed larger without the beard, more expressive, as if the beard had been a mask. "I suppose I am."

"I mean well. And nothing I do will affect the trial. By the time I start writing, the trial will be over. I'm not a reporter. I'm an analyst, long after the case is done with. What happened to that agreement you were having your lawyer draw up?"

"I decided it was just expensive bullshit. I have to trust you or not, on my own judgment. Which hasn't over the years proved much better than flipping a coin, but it's all I have."

"You're a master at self-deprecation."

He smiled wryly, meeting her gaze. "I'm someone who's made lousy choices. Typically I've pondered and brooded and weighed every alternative, and then taken the silliest. Here I am, age forty-three, back in my parents' house where I started. Back in my own pocket."

She tried to imagine herself in Philadelphia in Phyllis's old apartment. "It's hard for me to see myself returning where I came from. But this is a much nicer place of origin."

"I'm very attached. I've loved this house since I was a kid. I was always afraid my parents would move. In the summer, one of them used to sleep at the motel, in a little apartment. They'd take turns." He tweaked his nose between his fingers, frowning. "I'm eager to get Sam out of the House of Correction, but I refused to go through a bail bondsman. I'll breathe easier when he's out of that cage." He rose. "Time for lunch."

"Time for me to be going."

"Oh, I'll make you lunch. You've come a long way to work on me. I'm enjoying it. The least I can do is make you lunch. You can leave just afterward. I have to pass by the clinic. It's closed today, but I have a coyote in bad shape that got hit on Route 6."

"A coyote? Does it belong to someone?"

"No, it's a genuine wild predator and not happy at the moment. Somebody from the volunteer fire department brought it to me in his pickup. I think I can save it, but it's touch and go. These—" He waved his hand around. "Only the blind cat, Homer, is mine. All the others are boarding or in the hospital. They like it better here."

"I gather you don't treat horses."

"Not if I can help it. Coyotes are better behaved. What don't you eat?"

CHAPTER 29

BECKY

Becky and Terry had been married for a year and four months when they moved into a nearly new condo in Falmouth with a water view. That is, it was on the second floor and from the bedroom, a dip of blue showed between the buildings. His parents had co-signed the mortgage. The Burgesses dished out money to them now and again, money for a living room set this time. Terry bought the carpeting from the previous tenants, who were getting divorced. But every time the Burgesses paid for some object or gave them a check, Mrs. Burgess said, "We try to help when we can, since your parents never seem to do anything for you at all."

Becky wanted to say that her parents had done a lot for her: they had loved her more than she thought the Burgesses knew how to love anyone. But she kept still. She and Terry needed those occasional handouts. Without the help of the Burgesses, they would never have moved out of the apartment, which had proved hot in the summer and increasingly noisy after three skinheads had taken the apartment next door and begun staging drunken weekends.

Here they had off-street parking. There were washing machines in the basement. They had arrived in a place Terry no longer apologized for. Once again she regained that sense she had enjoyed right after marriage of things being perfect, unworn, unsoiled. Terry always said he lived in Old Silver Beach, the name of this part of Falmouth. It did sound inviting. There were not many condos around, but mostly single-family homes. She could take a shortcut across to work without going into downtown Falmouth and be there in ten minutes.

Tommy had given them a second TV for the kitchen. She never asked where he got it, as she suspected it was a perk that went with Tommy's relationship with The Guys. Tommy had decided to ease into that direction on the docks. It was not that he did not respect Papa, but that he felt he just could not get what he needed if he followed the straight and narrow. Becky did not think he was wrong. Tommy was her ambitious brother, and the older they got, the closer they felt. They understood each other better than anybody else in the family understood them. They were the outsiders, but they were loyal. Tommy was bringing in more than fish or scallops on his boat, but what did she care? He had married his girlfriend and he was taking care of his baby. Who could fault him?

She was expecting to move up at work too. She still had not got them to put her on the air, but she was going to become the director's secretary when his secretary left at the end of the year. Mr. Carter liked Becky, who fetched and carried for everybody and filled in every niche left vacant. Nowadays she had more and better clothes to wear to work. "You've learned how to dress," Mrs. O'Neill, the bookkeeper, remarked one day, totally startling Becky, who had never seen Mrs. O'Neill even look at her. "Your taste has improved."

Becky thanked her with pretended humility but she wanted to say, no, my pocketbook has improved, you horse's ass. Everything that people judged her by always came down to money. What she knew how to do, her makeup, her house, her furniture, her silverware, her dishes: it was all dollars made visible as objects of rank and what people agreed to call taste or beauty. She felt a deep rusty anger, but she suppressed it. Instead she said to Mrs. O'Neill, "Why, you always dress so nicely, a girl can't help but learn by observing you."

Mrs. O'Neill gave her a tight-lipped smile, the first that Becky had ever received. "You're a smart girl. Unlike most of them." From that time on, Mrs. O'Neill placed her in a higher category. Mrs. O'Neill was not only the bookkeeper but one of the people who had put up money for the original business. They were now part of a larger company, but Mrs. O'Neill had stock. She also had the most secure job in the office.

Becky quietly accumulated a mental dossier on Mrs. O'Neill, given name, Katherine. She lived in Sandwich, two blocks from her favorite daughter, and was said to have an entire room of tropical fish. In her office, she had an aquarium with angelfish. When Becky came in extra early or stayed late to finish up a report or a mailing, she would hear the *blub blub* of the bubbler in the aquarium. It was a soothing sound.

The other women who worked at Sound Cable made fun of Mrs. O'Neill. She was just this middle-aged bitch who had her own office and did the books. Becky, who always watched for lines of power, had been trying to cultivate Mrs. O'Neill. Now Mrs. O'Neill actually nodded to her with a little noise in her throat when she came in, something she had previously reserved for the three highest-paid men in the office.

She suspected maybe it was Mrs. O'Neill who had suggested she be promoted to be secretary to Mr. Carter, the director. There was only one higher position on the clerical side: office manager, and Gwen did not seem about to leave that position for another twenty years. Unless Gwen were to be run over by a truck, Becky was not about to become office manager.

But why wouldn't they let her on camera? Even something stupid like reading the local ads for service stations and restaurants or doing the weather or the weekly Adopt-A-Pet. She was more attractive than the women they had running shows, and she knew she could do a more professional job. How could she get them to think of her in the right way? Once they saw her behind a computer terminal, she was stuck as a clerical worker. They could not imagine her performing, conducting interviews, reading news.

Still, she could scarcely complain: three years before, she had started as a receptionist. The outgoing secretary would start teaching her the job right after Thanksgiving. She had not found the way to break through yet, but she never let opportunities slip past her. When Terry discovered that many of the people who had shows on cable were unpaid, he had begun trying to discourage her ambition to stand before the camera. Once in a while, he would urge her to ask for a raise, but she would be getting one starting the first of the year. She was not about to rattle the bars. She was too replaceable. Terry didn't seem to be trying to improve his own job situation.

She tried to get him to look for a better job, at a company with growth potential. He was not interested in job hunting. He said he had no time for it during the week, and weekends he needed to relax. She had liked it better when Terry was furious at his parents, but when they co-signed the mortgage, he moved back home emotionally.

Once again he was vying with Chris for their approval and their money. They doled out money like gold stars for pleasing them.

Over her reluctance, it was established that every Sunday they ate "dinner" at his parents. Dinner was served at two, which meant it killed the whole afternoon. They ate ham or turkey or a roast beef, big heavy meals. Afterwards she was expected to help Mrs. Burgess clean up, while the men took out the boat or just sat and watched a game on TV. It was not Becky's idea of a fun day, one of her two days of freedom.

"Becky, put the pickles back in the jar. On the counter. Wrap the roast beef. No, Becky, not in aluminum foil. In plastic wrap. How am I supposed to see through foil? Becky! Think for a minute now and then. No, Becky, don't save the salad with the dressing on it. It gets soggy. If you wish to save salad, you must wash off the dressing gently and then dry it just as gently. That's the correct way to save salad. You have a great deal to learn about running a house properly."

Mrs. Burgess would supervise every step she made around the kitchen, for Mrs. Burgess had one way and only one of doing any task. The top shelf of the dishwasher was loaded with glassware and bowls and cups and saucers. The bottom shelf was loaded according to a precise preordained pattern with dinner plates and serving utensils and pans. Everything in the kitchen had a niche. Becky was used to her family's kitchen where everybody stuffed things where they would fit; or her kitchen in the condo with plenty of empty cupboards. A shelf might have three boxes of breakfast cereal and some snacks on it. Above it would be a couple of cans of tuna and soup. Mrs. Burgess had racks of knives of all shapes and lengths, drawers full of mysterious gadgets, three sets of dishes. Becky felt like a recalcitrant slave. She did not want their heavy bland meals and she did not want to spend her Sundays cleaning up. She would have been happier with a hamburger or a chef's salad and some free time.

Saturday she had to clean and do the laundry. Once in a while she got Terry to go shopping for furniture and once they visited a street fair with Tommy and his wife. Saturday night, they went out to eat and to a movie. They always made love on the three weekend nights, and sometimes once during the week. For her, proof that he still wanted her was more important than the actual sex. She doubted that sex was ever going to mean a great deal to her, not compared to having a nice life.

She loved their tidy roomy condo. It had romantic casement windows. Cranking them open felt more dignified, prettier than raising the double-hung windows of her family home, always warped, always kept up by a stick or a beer bottle. She even liked the dove grey carpeting that had come with the condo. It was soothing, the color of the waves on a cloudy day. She liked being near the water. They had moved when it was warm enough to swim at a town beach nearby. It thrilled her to toss a little bag Belle had given her (it advertised cosmetics) over her shoulder and stroll along the road to the beach with a cover-up over her bathing suit, or if it was hot enough, nothing at all but the bright blue suit, the sunglasses one of Chris's girls had left in their car. Then she felt like an actress in a movie. She saw how men looked at her. They were not really seeing Becky Burgess. They were seeing a thin blond in a bright bathing suit. It did not matter. Their admiration fed something in her that was starving. When the fall advanced, she felt bereft. She had loved the sense of walking through her own daydream, perfect for once, prized, gazes following her like the train of a ball gown. All she lacked was a sound track.

Terry was not affectionate. She thought that perhaps neither of them knew how to be. Sometimes he picked up his mother's way of talking to her, as if she were stupid, as if she were on a lower plane of being. She felt that the Sundays they spent with his family reinforced attitudes she had thought dealt with and defeated. He had a way of saying, "Your family," that was just like his mother's. She could not challenge him. He did not say anything overtly bad. Who could prove a tone of voice? Who could touch an attitude that did not speak itself in open insults? It was like trying to locate a bad smell that no one else noticed.

He decided they should have his parents and Chris to a meal on his mother's birthday, the first weekend in November. "Why don't we take them out to a nice restaurant instead?" she asked.

"And drop a hundred fifty bucks? Forget it. No, they helped us with this condo. We owe it to them to have them over. Mother says every week she wants to see what we've done with it."

"But that's a lot of cooking, Terry."

"So, you've got all day. It's for my mother, Becky. It's her birthday, and it's what she'd like. You aren't trying with her."

"I am so trying . . . So you want to have them over this coming Sunday?"

"Right. And we have to get her a present. And a card. A nice present, but don't spend too much. It's tight this month."

"It's tight every month. Maybe you should pick it out. I don't know what your mother likes."

"She likes nice things."

Becky had never made a roast beef or a turkey, and the many types of hams in the supermarket confused her. Everything seemed enormous. Still, Mrs. Burgess put out a lot of food every Sunday, and the men ate huge quantities. She decided that a roast beef was perhaps the simplest. She would just put it in the oven, turn it on and let it cook.

She consulted Mama. "I put it in a pan with a little leftover wine, some tomatoes and onions and garlic and celery. I put the lid on and cook it for three hours, something like that."

"I don't think they eat onions and garlic. She just cooks it on a rack. The rack gets really dirty and sometimes I have to scrub it by hand."

"I never make it like that. You know, we don't eat so much beef. It's expensive. We like our fish."

Becky was shocked how expensive, when she went to the Stop & Shop. Twenty dollars for a piece of meat? She should wrap that up and give it to her mother-in-law in a box with a pink bow. She found a cheaper roast finally, a round roast. That sounded nice. She had to buy a pan with a rack in the supermarket. His parents were coming at two. She put the roast on at eleven, to give it the three hours her mother had recommended. She put potatoes in with it and made a salad. She bought cooked shrimps that cost fifty cents apiece and made a cocktail of them to start with.

Terry left the TV as she finished setting the table. He frowned. "It doesn't look right. Where's the fork for the appetizer?"

"Terry, we don't have extra forks. We only have settings for six."

"It doesn't look the way it's supposed to. Where are the flowers?"

"Go out and buy some if you want flowers."

"It's Sunday."

"Well, Terry, we certainly can't go pick them, can we? What do you want? Your parents have been married for thirty years and they own every dish in the world and real silverware. If you want us to eat like that, ask them for silverware and fancy china. Then I'll set a table the way your mother does. But silverware doesn't appear when you want it, and neither do fancy tablecloths and glasses with gold rims."

"You should have got flowers."

"Why didn't you? Remember me? I'm the poor kid from New Bedj your mother likes to wipe her feet on. What do I know about silverware and flowers?"

"My mother has been really good to you. She gave you that pearl necklace you're wearing."

And I'll always hate it, Becky thought. Like little teeth shining, the better to bite you with. Like wearing a necklace of tooth enamel. She took a deep breath. She must not lose her temper with Terry, especially not just before his parents arrived. At least the food would be good. And the beautiful blue scarf was wrapped and ready.

Half an hour later, the only sound was knives grinding against china. The roast was tough and Mrs. Burgess openly laughed. "Oh, Becky, poor thing, you've destroyed it. Did you start cooking it yesterday? You serve roast beef rare. That's the civilized way to treat a cow."

Mr. Burgess ate with an air of dyspeptic martyrdom. Terry would not look at her. Chris was the only sympathetic one. "I've had worse. Give us a smile, don't look so tragic. You tried. I never had a girlfriend yet who could cook. Nobody cooks anymore, except Mom. Mom's an old-fashioned girl."

About the scarf, Mrs. Burgess was polite. "What a surprise. I always feel a scarf is a perfect present when you don't know what to buy someone. I imagine you picked this pattern out? It's so . . . colorful. I do want to thank you, Becky, for thinking of my birthday."

It was a disaster, except for the salad and the ice cream. I will never do this again, Becky thought, I will never be forced into trying to imitate his mother. They can take us out to eat. I am not going to be tricked into making a fool of myself on their terms. Ever!

CHAPTER 30

LEILA

Leila had not spoken with Nick since he returned to New York. Hanging around a play already running was unheard of, unless there were rewrites in progress. It was not the play that held him in New York but Sheryl. She felt extremely distant from him—more than a couple of hundred miles. It felt as if their lives had disentangled. She was busy enough. Candidates for an open position were being interviewed at the rate of one a week, and that was an evening every time. She was considered deft at drawing people out in the informal dinner setting. The screening of candidates whose resumés looked good and whose publications were reasonably apt and frequent fell into a formal meeting in the department, and the wining and dining and careful scrutiny of the evening.

She was honest with Jane, with whom as always she ate lunch on Tuesdays and Thursdays. "I don't feel particularly married right now—"

"Are you looking around?"

"Don't be absurd, Jane. I find I've begun to enjoy living alone, although sometimes at night I can sense all those empty rooms around me, and it feels wasteful. When David and Nick were in the house, it never felt large."

"Nick's an expansive man," Jane said. "Won't he get round you when he comes back?" Jane removed a browned leaf from her salad, grimacing. "And why isn't he home? His play opened before Thanksgiving, didn't it?"

"His girlfriend's pregnant."

"Oh." Jane studied her salad carefully, frowning. "I know a good divorce lawyer. I have the feeling you're going to need her."

Even though Leila had been telling herself that her marriage might finally be over, Jane's voice resonated through her like a high dangerous tone breaking glassware in her psyche. She could not speak. Her eyes burned. She breathed deeply, quickly, as if oxygen could calm her. "That seems . . . premature."

"Does it?"

"I don't know any longer." She let Jane hand her the name on a paper napkin. She shoved it away in a compartment of her wallet.

Jane tilted her head. "Do you want me to go down to New York with you?"

"Would you do that for me?"

"Of course. I'd rather not, I won't lie, but if you need backup and you want to confront him and the live-in, I'm your second."

Leila was moved. "Thank you. Right now, I don't think I want to do that. I can see no advantage to operating on her turf—or his. The longer he stays, the more meaningful this separation becomes, but I am not in the mood to go and plead with him."

Saturday Leila met Zak for an early lunch in Sandwich, just before they were to go to the Barnstable House of Correction to see Sam. Leila was familiar with the building and the protocols, since Becky was upstairs in the same jail, but Zak looked pinched, nervous. "Are you regretting letting me come?"

"I'm apprehensive, but I always get this way when I have to go into jail. I can't help imagining what it must be like for him to be shut up there."

She nodded, understanding exactly what he meant. "I can feel my blood pressure rising whenever I go through the cage into the jail proper."

"It's different for white-collar criminals. Business criminals get stored in sort of golf-green facilities. I visited one when someone I knew in L.A. got sent up for pirating tapes."

He was picking at his food. She was finding him to be a more likable control freak than he had seemed at first, but still someone who suffered from twenty sorts of anxiety in the course of a day. "Why did you leave L.A.?"

"I have four standard answers to that, but the truth is, I'm not prepared to tell you yet."

"We don't know each other well enough?"

"Right."

"Why don't I get one of the standard answers?"

"I thought we were trying to be truthful in this mess. That's the only way we can proceed together."

"Amen."

"Where's your husband? He never seems to be around."

"In New York. He had a play open just before Thanksgiving."

"So he must be coming back soon."

Truth, mmm. She pondered truth in silence. Perhaps saying would make it less potent, less painful. "He's having an affair with an actress in the play, and she's carrying his child. That was what I learned Thanksgiving."

"Oh." He stole a series of glances at her. "It's starting to snow."

"I hope we aren't in for a storm."

"They said flurries as I left the house." He cleared his throat. "He told you about the affair?"

"He wrote a note and left it on my bed. But I discovered about the pregnancy myself."

"Oof." He shook his head. Again he was silent for perhaps five minutes. She was not feeling enormously talkative herself. "You sound as if you mind as much as I would."

"I'm furious. I don't know how to go on from this. I don't know if he wants to. I don't know if I want to."

"You know what would be novel? If we were truthful with each other. Something unheard of nowadays among friends or acquaintances, heresy between men and women. We wouldn't have to let anyone know. We could simply be quietly truthful."

"That takes trust," she said.

"But we aren't really in each other's life. We work in our little spheres. Maybe while we're trying to make sense out of this rent in the social fabric, this murder, this media-inflated scandal, we can share what we see. I suspect you don't have this habit with your husband, for instance?"

"Once we did. Long ago. Are you truthful with your girlfriend?"

"I don't have a girlfriend. We better get going. We can leave your car here and go in mine." He drove off slowly as the snow thickened, pelting down. The day was dark grey, dim as if they were inside some enormous ill-lit room. "I haven't let anybody far into my life in a long time. I have friends who visit now and then. Friends I spend a night with in New York or Boston."

"I have friends too, but they're women. My best woman friend died two months ago of breast cancer. I'm still missing her every day."

His voice grew so soft she had to lean toward him as he drove to hear what he was saying. "I left L.A. after the fire. It was a sudden canyon fire that bore down. When I could get into the canyon, the bodies of my wife and my baby daughter were found in the house. So was the body of another musician. A man. The au pair girl had been told to take the afternoon off."

"But if your wife was a musician, maybe they were rehearsing."

"They died of smoke inhalation. They were both naked."

"And you didn't know before?"

"I didn't know. I didn't even suspect. I was a fucking idiot."

"If you trust someone, why would you suspect her? If you don't trust, then it's over." She listened to what she had said and felt desolation wash through her. More than half her life. She was striking off onto a grey foggy plain alone. "We're both gloomy types at the moment. I didn't used to be."

"Me neither. Believe it or not, I was perceived as easygoing. I wasn't always mad as Chicken Little, not until my sky did fall."

"Now it's fallen twice."

"I didn't even live anyplace for five years after the fire. I did a stint being the vet at dog and cat shows. I shilled for a pet food manufacturer. I filled in for vacationing vets. I lived in Crete one winter and one spring in Provence, writing my dog book. When my mother died I came back here, spent a couple of weeks, moved my stuff in and took off again. It wasn't until Mike had his heart attack that I really moved into my family's house and stopped running. I started my practice. That nailed me down."

"You feel responsible for Cathy and Sam."

"I identify too much with Sam, that's my problem. I see myself in him—the adolescent nerd, oversensitive, overimaginative, living in fantasy. One of my fantasies was that some wise sexy older woman would take me in hand and teach me all about life and love. Maybe I feel guilty because Sam got his older woman, and look what he learned."

"Can you see Sam accurately? Mightn't your identification get in the way?"

They emerged from the grey box. The snow thinned and they could see all around again. They were still going slowly because here it had snowed several inches. Five cars ahead a snowplow lumbered along, a tail of vehicles behind it.

"Tell me about your son," he said. "It's hard to imagine we're the same age and you have a son in college. My daughter would be ten. You got married much younger than I did."

"Nick was my college sweetheart. David. Well, he's at Cal Tech now. . . ." She described David, she felt accurately, but also with her natural partiality. She finished the description, "I'm wondering if Sam will remind me of him in person as much as he does when Cathy and you talk about him."

Zak saw his nephew first as she sat in the grim waiting room; she was called as he came out. She went in nervously, with far more anxiety than she had felt before Becky. She feared, what? That Sam somehow would be too much like David? He was shorter than David but more muscular. In the photographs, he had looked slighter. Perhaps he had been weight training or filled out.

His skin had an unhealthy jail pallor—bad air, little exercise, bad food, anxiety early and late. He squinted slightly as if the light hurt his eyes, staring at her warily. "Mom spoke about you. I guess it's okay that Uncle Zak finally agreed you could come, although I don't know what good it can do." He whined a little. He sat limply, his muscles turning to water, his spine dissolving.

She did pity him. He was a good-looking boy in a gentle puppy mode. His hair was curly, like Zak's, dark brown. His eyes were hazel, bloodshot now, clashing with the greenish brown. It gave him a wild, slightly alien look. His nose was sharp but well modeled. He had once had acne, visible in the roughness of his cheeks, but he had already grown out of it. He looked slightly elfish, she decided. He gave her a tentative smile. "I don't know what to say to you. I don't even know who I am. I remember my mother, I remember Zak, I remember school, but it's as if I'm looking at it all from the top of a high mountain, and everything is tiny and miles away, you see?"

"Being held here is making you confused about who you are?"

"Reading about myself in the papers, watching them talk about me on TV. Watching them talk about Becky. We're villains in a soap opera, see? It's all there on the television, and I keep staring at it to find out who I really am. But it's like a movie about somebody else. I get scared sometimes that maybe I'm going crazy in here." He was watching to see how that went over.

She wasn't going to get involved in his riff about going crazy. "Do you love Becky, if you don't mind my asking?"

"I was crazy about her, you know? She was everything to me. At first I felt like I'd made her up, like she was the best dream I ever had."

"Do you still feel that way?"

"I barely remember her. The TV gets in the way, you know? We haven't seen each other alone for weeks. We haven't even been in the same room since the arraignment. Our cases were separated early—"

"Wasn't that your folks' idea?"

He nodded. He had a loose, rather heavy way of nodding, as if saying, sure, sure, sure. "Zak got me a lawyer he says is good. Now we don't even have the same lawyers."

He kept eye contact all the while he was speaking. He stared into her eyes. It was disconcerting and uncomfortable. Probably he had been told to do that by his lawyers, but it distracted her, it made her need to look away, and then to feel as if she had lost some minor contest. She would have liked to beg him to be more natural, but there was nothing normal about his situation. He was saying, "I read everything in the papers about us. Maybe if I read what everybody says, finally I'll understand it."

"What are you trying to understand?"

He visibly recoiled, squinted again. "Oh, just the whole thing. You know."

"Not really. I'm trying to understand it too, but you know more about it than I do." She was careful not to sound as if she assumed his guilt.

"Do you think I did it?" He asked point blank, as if reading through her careful phrasing.

"This is the first time we've met. I reserve judgment until I know Becky and I know you well enough so there's some basis for me to believe in your guilt or innocence. As it is, I put the media to one side and I try to see things freshly. I try to look at you as if I knew nothing about you, and you were a friend of my son's."

"Cathy, my mom, thinks because you're the mother of a boy my age, you'll be sympathetic."

"She's right, of course."

"You saw Becky, Mom said. What did you think of her?"

"I don't know her well enough yet. . . . I was wondering, how did you happen to join the theater group?"

"My high school teacher thought it was something I'd like. Budget cuts made the school drop the senior play. I think a lot of guys who have trouble talking to girls like to have a role to play, you know? I was brave on the stage. In class, at parties, I was totally scared to death of making a fool of myself. Up on the stage, I'm fearless. Like I can do a pratfall or kiss the girl and no problem."

Here he was in jail, worrying about being too shy. "And Becky was in the theater group?"

"She joined it six months after I did. We were both gofers at first. I helped with props and she worked on costumes and we did walk-ons. I remember playing somebody's grandfather in a white wig. It was totally ridiculous. But they started to give us parts finally." He started an inventory of all the parts he had played in various old chestnuts and Broadway plays his group had put on. She felt a sense of relief that she had not had to watch any of them, but she maintained an air of bright interest.

Talking about his time in the theater company, he was relaxed, animated, sometimes almost funny. He seemed a bright, sensitive seventeen-year-old, not one who could have bludgeoned his girlfriend's husband to death. She studied the two images and they did not balance. Not yet. He wanted to please her, to charm her. It was second nature to him to try to be liked. In mid-sentence, he would pause, staring to read how she was liking him. Adolescent anxiety cubed.

She did not attempt to bring the conversation nearer to her interests, but let him chatter about the theater. She believed in letting her subjects talk when she had enough time, and she would return next week, as she told him when the visiting time was up.

In the car on the way back to her own, she said to Zak, "I can't imagine Sam killing anyone. I felt the same way about Becky. Either the whole law enforcement apparatus is wacky, a hypothesis I'm willing to entertain, and this is a miscarriage of justice, or else my imagination is failing me and my empathy is getting in the way. I've known murderers before, and some of them were sweet and good women. They'd been driven to violence by brutality, by abuse. They were protecting their own lives, their children's. I can't get past that great lump of the fact of the murder."

"I have the same problem," he said. "Today I did the lawyer's work for him. I kept arguing with Sam that if he did anything, he has to talk to his lawyer. The State is offering a deal.'' He rubbed his eye hard. ''I'm sitting there arguing with him that maybe he should take the plea bargain, and then I think, what am I doing? The poor kid shouldn't be in jail. He should be home getting ready for college in the fall. He should be studying his trigonometry. He should be on the chess team getting ready for a match with Brookline. I feel schizophrenic.''

''Have you ever wanted to kill anyone?''

He snorted. ''Me, I fix broken bones. Oh, now and again, usually after the fact. Have you?''

She ran her hand through her short thick hair, tugging. ''I have trouble with anger. I just sit on it like a big hot egg. This is going to be some drive home today with the snow.'' At least Vronsky would be waiting. She thought she could almost say that to Zak, for he too lived only with his animals.

CHAPTER 31

MARY

Mary went to see Beverly Bozeman two days a week, while she was cleaning in Cambridge. She took to hanging around the old Sears store in between cleaning and visiting hours. They had made it into a mini-mall. It had toilets and she could sit down, move slowly from shop to shop. In the fast-food places, she was expert at passing by food someone had left on a table and snatching it up without pausing. Oftentimes women left French fries or cole slaw. When she was little, she thought it was *cold* slaw. Her family ate quantities of it, on the sweet side, also sauerkraut and potato salad. There were dishes none of her ladies ate that used to be common, like carrots in orange gelatin and vegetables in lemon, and the frothy gelatin desserts. Ham and shrimp in aspic. A standing rib roast had been one of her specialties. She hadn't seen one in ten years.

She amused herself by comparing clothing, hairstyles, what people said, what they did for fun. Card games. She remembered canasta. And Michigan rummy. Young matrons had to play bridge, as important as knowing about children's inoculations. It had been grounds for divorce if a wife couldn't hold up her end of a doubles bridge game. Maybe she liked the remember game because, without her memories, she was nobody. She had a sudden fierce need to call her daughter, to prove she had some connection, a real past, that once she had been part of a tight family. She called from a pay phone at the hospital.

They had a couple of old phones where she could sit, which she appreciated.

She identified herself to Cindy's husband Ron. He never recognized her voice. He sounded startled, as if he had forgotten she existed. There was a long pause. Finally Cindy picked it up. "Hello, Mom? Is something wrong?"

"Could you call me back at this number? My phone isn't working, so I'm calling from a pay phone."

She waited and waited, pretending to look for coins in her purse. Finally the phone rang. "Mom? I had to finish loading the dishwasher. Are you well?"

"I'm fine . . . All the Christmas decorations are up here. It made me think of you and the kids."

"We're going over to Daddy's for Christmas, you know that. What would you like for Christmas?"

"I'd love a wool jacket, a blazer I mean."

"What color?"

"Blue. Or navy. Just so it's roomy and warm. Winters up here are hard."

"But you like it up there. You always say how much you like it."

"It's just fine." She knew Cindy was terrified she would move back to the Washington-Baltimore area. "Is there something . . . something not too big I can get Marissa and Doug?"

Cindy launched into a list that went on for several minutes. Diligently Mary scribbled the list on a piece of paper, but she felt despair. She could not buy any of these things. She loved to send presents to her grandchildren, but all her gifts together could not cost more than eighty dollars. She never could put money away in her account for emergencies and her someday car during December and January, because of Christmas. She had to send something. She would be haunting Filene's basement, but even then, it was tormenting and humiliating to have so little to spend. She sighed as she said good-bye.

Beverly was a moody woman. Living with husbands and kids, women were always damping themselves down to make the household and family work. Then afterward, when they were alone, nobody put a check on them. A woman could let it all fly, with nobody she had to please or placate. When Mary walked into Beverly's ward, she never knew if Beverly would be glad to see her or if she'd be in a sulk. Her foul mouth upset Mary, but she couldn't blame Beverly, considering what she'd been through. "Beverly? It's Mary."

"She can see you just fine. She has got enough wrong with her without you deciding she's blind and dumb too.'' Beverly grinned. They hadn't replaced the tooth her attacker knocked out. She had a gap now, giving her a disreputable air even in the hospital gown.

''How are you doing? Guess you aren't seeing double any longer.''

''Once is enough, with what she got to look at, right?''

''That's so. Are they feeding you okay?''

''She's getting fat. Three meals a day, and some of her visitors bring her snacks. She don't expect you to, so don't look like that. She got plenty of visitors. The nurses are impressed. The police even came once, but they won't do anything. She bets they make jokes about it.''

''Anything that involves old ladies is good for a laugh.''

''She's old before her time. But she's filling out in here. She gained five pounds already, you know that?''

''Do they say when they're letting you out?''

''She won't ask. She'll stay as long as they'll let her.''

''I was never in the hospital except for the birth of my kids. After the first one, Cindy my oldest, I was dying to go home. With Jaime, I wanted to stay and stay and be taken care of a little longer. By then I knew what it's like to go home with a baby to a house that needs cleaning and a kid screaming where's supper. Two kids, and I hardly ever see them.''

Mary sat back embarrassed, flushed. She had talked more about herself in the last couple of minutes than she had in years. Because she had told Beverly her secret, she seemed to want to tell her whole life. Beverly listened, although Mary felt their lives had been so different when they were both ''inside the fold'' to use Beverly's phrase, that she was never sure what Beverly pictured. ''Sometimes,'' she said to Beverly, ''when I'm talking about Cindy or Jaime or my ex-husband, suddenly I feel as if I'm telling you about some woman I work for, or as if I made it all up. It's so far away. Do you ever feel that way?''

''She hates to think about her life before. If she does, she gets mad. Then all she can do is mutter and kick the curb, and then she looks even crazier.'' Beverly gave that gaunt gap-toothed grin. ''She gets scared when she thinks about when they discharge her. Can't go back to Porter Square. The police know her now. She got to find a new hang-around. But she sure wishes she could stay in here through the winter.''

''Winter is so hard.'' She wanted to tell Beverly about stealing the sleeping bag, but she was too ashamed. ''I always thought the streets were safe then, because of the cold.''

''Nothing's safe.'' Beverly laughed suddenly: a harsh dry laugh that caught in her throat, as if she were unused to laughing. "She was just thinking, Mary. She lost her home running from a man who was trying to kill her, and look what happened to her."

"Maybe you could get into a shelter. At least for a while."

"There's ten women waiting for every one of those beds. Women with babies, women they dumped out of crazy bins, old ladies who can't make it on the streets anymore. You ever been in one of those shelters?"

Mary nodded. "Early on. I couldn't hack it."

Wednesday, Mary dawdled, waiting to see if maybe Mrs. Landsman would come home early. Mrs. L. had a new pattern. She rushed in Wednesdays and changed, going out again for supper. Was she seeing somebody? She didn't dress feminine. She tended to put on a suit or a tailored dress. As Mary had expected, Mrs. L. arrived just before five, out of breath from rushing. Mrs. L. did not seem to be checking up on her, just in a hurry. She nodded at Mary and was about to run upstairs, when Mary stationed herself in the way.

"Mrs. Landsman, you seem to know a lot about women's facilities in this city and how to find things out."

Mrs. Landsman looked surprised. Visibly she shifted gears, sitting down on one of the steps and motioning Mary to do the same. "What's up? . . . Has this something to do with your friend who was beaten and left for dead?"

Mary did not think it was appropriate she should sit, although Mrs. Landsman kept motioning at her. As if she were the cat, Mary thought in annoyance. "She's still in Cambridge City Hospital, but they'll discharge her soon. She'll be back on the streets, and she'll have to find a new neighborhood. She'd like to get into a shelter, but she says the lists are long."

"Given her condition, maybe something can be done. I do know some people. I have to go right out, I have a dinner meeting. But tomorrow I'll make a few calls. Don't get your hopes up or say anything to your friend yet."

It wasn't as if Mrs. Landsman needed the sleeping bag. Maybe it had been used once. Mrs. L. would never even know it was gone, probably for years. Sleeping in a church basement, as she was planning to do tonight, she would be able to fall asleep instead of shivering all night in the damp. Curled up in the sleeping bag, she felt almost cared for, almost held.

But that night when she entered the basement, she heard a shuffling sound. She stood still in the dark and listened. An unfamiliar smell, a human smell, unwashed flesh. She heard someone stirring. Someone was waiting. Her heart thudded into itself like an ax striking soft wood. She backed away and then she trotted out as fast as she could. A janitor who had caught on to her? Another homeless person, a man?

She returned to the Anzios' car. They had the habit of leaving their garage and car unlocked. They had a long driveway for Cambridge, a long lot. Perhaps they felt their garage was far enough off the street to avoid notice. They had an old Volvo with a comfortable backseat. She could put up the armrest in the center and lie across, or tilt back one of the front seats. She decided to sleep in the back tonight.

It had been a long day, and for several nights, she had slept poorly. She curled up in her fine light warm sleeping bag, her lifesaver, and fell into an exhausted sleep. It was dark in the garage. Normally the light of dawn woke her, but it was the shortest day of the year soon, and no light had penetrated the garage when suddenly she heard the door going up. She woke in a panic, remembering quickly where she was, as she had trained herself to do. There was no time to slip out of the car, no time to do anything but roll forward onto the floor.

The door opened, the light went on overhead. She lay still on the floor of the back seat, still in her sleeping bag. This was the end. She was caught. She was trapped. She heard Mr. Anzio cough, start the car, stop to light a cigarette and then begin backing out of the drive. He turned the radio to a station with nothing on it but sports and headed up the street. She lay helpless in the backseat, trying to make herself as small as possible.

He seemed to drive forever. She did not dare look out of the sleeping bag. Finally he pulled into a building. He put out his fourth cigarette and turned off the ignition, not bothering to shut off the radio first. He grabbed his briefcase off the seat beside him, locked the four doors from the driver's door and took off. She was safe, shaking, but where?

At once, she got up, rolled up her bag and put it in her carry-all. She took the catch off the rear door, fixed it so it would lock when she shut it, checked that she had left nothing, and staggered out of the car, stiff and weak in the legs. She was in a cavernous parking garage. She was still wobbly and she had to pee really bad. No chance of that. She saw an elevator, probably where Mr. Anzio had gone, but she was afraid to appear in some office building.

A man was sitting in the booth beside the drive-in entrance, but he paid no attention to her as she trudged past and gave him a perfunctory wave. She emerged onto the icy street. She was downtown. She marched to the corner. Milk Street. She could get to the subway, although it would be a hike. Already seven forty-five. There were toilets in the Commons, if they were unlocked this early.

She was terrified how late she had slept. She had been exhausted beyond endurance. She must buy a little alarm. One of those travel alarms, but they started around ten dollars. She could not take such a chance again of oversleeping, but if she bought the travel alarm, she would have to cut back on food. More scavenging. She must never, never sleep into the active time again.

When she thought of Christmas coming, passing the decorations, there was always a tinge of melancholy, remembering childhood Christmases, remembering her family, the house full of Scotch pine and baking smells, everybody home. Actually it had been an edgy time, too many parties, too much eating and drinking, the kids never satisfied by their presents. They were always eying each other's gifts. She was always disappointed in her gift from Jim; she had not understood she was lucky to be given anything. She had wanted a romantic present that proclaimed he still found her attractive. Dream on. He had not.

Now she looked forward to Christmas because she would have a secure warm place to stay, when she could recover from this nagging cold, her throbbing back, her exhaustion. Her people were beginning to announce their plans. The Baers were definitely going to Florida the day after Christmas, until the day after New Year's. She was set for that week. Now somebody had to go away for Christmas itself: they always did. This week, she thought as she tried to hurry on the icy pavements toward the subway still seven blocks away, they would say, Don't come in Christmas week. Please feed Zurich or Griselda. Whatever, it translated into, *Mi casa es su casa*. Make yourself at home.

CHAPTER 32

BECKY

Becky's car broke down one January morning when she was trying to get to work. Terry had to drive her, making them both late. The estimate on the repairs was more than the car was worth. At this point, Mr. Burgess stepped in. Mr. Burgess and Terry, with Becky tagging along, went to a Toyota dealer and bought him a new Corolla. Terry wanted a Celica, but Mr. Burgess said it was not practical. They did not shop around, the way her family did for anything. Her mother would cover five stores to get a good price on a coat or a toaster.

With the Burgesses, there was always some connection. Sometimes it was someone for whom the father had installed air-conditioning; someone they knew from St. Thomas the Apostle or from the Lions'. Or who had been in Terry's fraternity, or with whom Chris had roomed in college. It did not seem to Becky that they got such good deals, but it was as if they required a proper introduction to a new riding mower before they could purchase it, or as if a mere stranger could never be trusted. The person from whom they bought had to belong to some large invisible club—a club of which she was not a member.

What it meant was that she drove Terry's old car, and Terry got a new blue Corolla. The best thing about getting his car was that even at five years old, it was eight years newer than hers had been and it had a tape deck. Driving to work or home, even just sitting in traffic or doing her errands, she would turn the music loud. The beat would fill the air. She would give her hair a toss and put on her sunglasses and rev up the engine. She would see herself, blond, slender, with her blue print scarf around her throat riding on the music as if it were surf, a perfect wave that those handsome boys rode in summer at the beach.

She had never spent much time at the beach before they had moved to their new condo, but she had fallen in love with it. It was a world where she was queen. She looked the way women were supposed to in bathing suits. She treated her suit like her face, carefully washing it in cool water as soon as she got home, letting it dry hanging over the tub. It was deep blue, cut high in the thighs and low in the back. In winter, she missed the beach. January seemed an infinity, and now February stretched before her, grey ice to the horizon.

Nowhere did men stare at her the way they did on the beach. On the beach no one paid much attention to cost and label of bathing suit, but only to the look, and she had it. The face was not as important as the body, and the body had to be thin and the hair ought to be blond.

On mild days driving this car with the windows open and rock music enveloping her, she felt the same sense of being really seen, of finding herself admired, wanted, held aloft on the gaze of others. When she stopped for a light, she could feel the man in the next car looking. Sometimes she enjoyed pretending she had not noticed, particularly if the jerk made noises. Sometimes she would raise her glasses and give him a melting look. She hated the days it was too cold, when she had to keep rubbing to be able to see out the side windows. Then she was just a dowdy wife in a wool coat, blowing her nose and waiting for a light.

She could never hope for that kind of attention at work. If she dared dress sexy or revealing, she'd be out on her ear in a week. Neat, that was the code, businesslike, no bright colors, no dangling earrings, no décolleté, skirts never too short.

Cautiously, she had begun dressing a little racier after work. To go to his parents, she dressed much as she did in the office, but when they went out to a movie or to eat, when they double-dated with Chris and his current girlfriend, when, rarely, they were invited to a party, then she put on one of two sexy outfits she had, one all black, one purple and silver.

She always wanted to stay longer than Terry did. She liked to dance, she liked to flirt, she loved the sense of being watched. Terry hated all that. He would say, "You were making eyes at Roz's husband, you were! Everybody was looking at you when you were dancing with Jack."

Why wouldn't he want people to look at her? "They just think I'm a good dancer."

"They just think you were acting like a slut."

"How dare you say that to me? I've never even kissed another man since we started going out!"

"I don't like the way you act sometimes. You get wild. Don't you see how people look at you when you dance that way?"

It was just the way the girls danced in the videos, the best imitation she could do. "Nobody but you thinks there's anything wrong with the way I dance. A lot of people tell me I'm a good dancer."

"If my mother ever saw you, she'd pass out."

"Have you ever seen your mother dance? Hardly. She couldn't dance if someone poured boiling oil on her toes."

If only she could go to parties, and he could stay home and watch TV, they'd both be happy. She didn't want any of those guys. She just wanted to have a good time and be watched, be admired. Too much of the time, she was just part of the furniture, at work and at home.

She never left off watching for an opportunity to get into the camera's eye. She considered trying to start her own program. When she came up with an idea (I could teach adolescents how to put on makeup: we could call it, "The Eyes Have It"), she could tell that her boss did not listen. Sure, he'd say, how's that letter to restaurants going? She remembered all the hours Sylvie and she had spent trying on faces before the mirror in Sylvie's mother's room. She knew that teenage girls would love a program like that, and she'd be the perfect hostess. She'd interview hairstylists and manicurists and give beauty tips, and every week her sister Belle would come on the program and do a makeover.

In the condo, most couples who became friends had kids the same age. The Higginses were a little older than Terry and Becky, but after they all went out to Chinese one night and the husband kept staring at Becky, the wife stopped being friendly. Holly and Brad Reicher lived next door, but she was a flight attendant and very superior acting.

There was an old lady just under them who was really sweet. Her husband was dead and Helen Coreggio lived with her dog. Helen had been a bank teller, but her passion was a community theater group, the Canal Players. Once in a while she acted a part, but mostly she made their costumes. She said it got her out of the house and gave her a whole group of lively people to be with.

Becky felt Mrs. Coreggio, who told her very quickly to call her Helen, really liked her. Helen kept telling her she was cute as a button and she was smart as a whip. Helen did not like Terry because he complained about the dog. Helen was crazy about her dog, Florrie, and claimed the dog had saved her life at the beach once, although the story was different each time Helen told it. Florrie was part collie and part Great Dane.

Helen had children and grandchildren, but they were scattered. Florrie was right there beating her tail on the floor and following every gesture Helen made with her great brown eyes. She was a big gentle dog, but she did bark whenever anyone moved in the halls. Becky could understand the appeal of Florrie for Helen: who wouldn't want to be looked at that way, gazed at, every gesture studied? Florrie thought Helen the most gorgeous creature in the world.

Becky only wished Terry would look at her that way, at least on weekends. But she was his old lady. "You're lucky," she'd hear him tell Chris. "You got it made. Nothing to worry about, nothing you have to do, nothing you're responsible for. Don't screw up. Just enjoy what you got, because it's the best time in life. Once you get hooked, once you're hitched, it's gone forever."

She felt furious when she overheard him, but she wasn't supposed to be eavesdropping, and what could she say? She had taken advantage of a fight with his parents to get him to marry her. She wasn't overjoyed with their life, but at least they had a clean spacious sunny condo of their own. She loved it. She bought dried flowers like Mrs. Burgess had and put them in two glass vases they had received as wedding presents. They had dishes that matched, they had a kitchen with tiles and appliances she kept without a fingerprint. The bathroom was sanctified by cleanliness and smelled of pine disinfectant, after shave and lilac bath gel. Even their towels were sets. The bathroom rug was fluffy and spotless.

Every morning she woke and looked at the beautiful unmarred ceiling and the curtains with the blue and white pattern of perky sailboats, and she sighed with pleasure. Every evening after a day at work, she tried to do one good thing for this precious sanctuary from noise and dirt and squalor. She kept the windows and mirrors clear. She scrubbed the burners and placed over the heating coils pretty covers with daisies. No matter if Mrs. Burgess peeked in her drawers and in her corners, never did she find dust bunnies. I am a good wife, Becky told herself, and he doesn't appreciate me.

Helen appreciated. Helen told her she was one in a million, just the kind of wife she herself had been, but her husband, bless his sweet soul, had adored her. "We always had love, you know what I mean? I mean loving, you know?"

Oh, they had sex on the weekend, hardly ever during the week any longer. It was fast and perfunctory. He barely touched her there anymore before he pushed in. She didn't feel special to him. She was convenient. She was afraid to ask him if he was sorry he had married her, for fear he would tell her the truth, that he would rather be back in his parents' home throwing his socks on the floor and having everything done for him just the way he thought it ought to be. They owed money on Visa and MasterCard and Diners Club. They were paying Sears for the blinds on time. Her car that had been his needed a brake job and new tires. The condo had a hefty maintenance fee, and their electric bills were scary.

Sometimes she had nightmares that he left her, and she would wake up shaking. She would be wandering around the streets looking for her home, and she would not find it. She would be lost, shut out. She would know that someone had promised to love her, but that he had stopped and he had gone away and somehow he had taken their home with him. She was alone and she tasted sharp and bitter despair like ammonia in her throat. She did not tell him those dreams, for fear she would put ideas in his head.

She asked her mama, "Did you ever worry about Papa leaving you?"

"All women do. Men up and go, it's their nature to be restless. Worrying don't help. You should pray to God. A family is the best hold on a man."

Helen was more helpful. "Inertia is your best friend. He's married to you, it takes effort to get unmarried. People are mostly kind of stupid, Becky. They get married, and then two years later, they say, Hey, I'm not single any longer. I got to support a household. I have to shop and cook and clean and worry about taxes. Then they have a baby, and they say, Hey, this is more work than I thought. I had the baby already last month and this month here I am still at it full-time, taking care of the baby. What happened to my life?"

"I don't really want a baby, particularly," Becky said softly. It wasn't a popular thing to say.

"Why should you? A smart pretty young woman, you ought to be free to seize opportunities. I see you have ambition. You have dreams. Most people just have routines. You keep your chin up and know I'm rooting for you." Helen was knitting her a long pale blue tunic sweater.

Terry thought it was weird that she was friends with Helen. "Hanging around with an old lady, decrepit enough to be your grandma. That's creepy."

"I like her. In my family, we all lived together. She's interesting."

"What's interesting about an old lady with a dog barking all the time? Don't hold up your family like some kind of ideal. Two and three kids sleeping in one bed—that's sick."

"If we'd had the money, everyone of us would have had her own bed and her own room. My parents aren't like yours—they don't dole out what they have and expect you to grovel for it. What they have, they give—generously."

"We're living in a condo my parents signed for. I drive a car they signed for. They bought the bed we sleep in. What did your parents ever do for us? Send some flounder and scallops by with Tommy? Give me a break."

To Helen she said, "I feel he's annoyed with me all the time. Like every morning I wake up and think, Oh, what a beautiful place this is to be, and every morning he wakes up and thinks, How the hell did I end up here with her? I'm afraid to say what I think half the time because I feel things with him are just tentative. Like he's still not sure he should have married me."

"After all this time? It's over two years, isn't it?"

Florrie put her huge head on Becky's knee and whapped her salami of a tail on the floor. "I try to think of things we can do together. But he doesn't have any interest in playing sports with me. When I try to watch a football or basketball or hockey game with him, he gets irritated when I start asking him to explain. Sometimes I sit there with the paper and I read him possibility after possibility. I say, Let's go to a play, let's go to a dinner theater, let's go visit Newport and see the old mansions, let's go dancing at that club by the pier, let's go to New York for the weekend, they're advertising a really good weekend rate in this hotel."

"You need to get out of the house yourself. You need some time apart. He never wonders for five minutes where you are. There's no mystery in that. You make yourself boring by always being underfoot."

"I do go see my family a couple times a week. He never comes."

"But where's the mystery, Becky? He knows your family. He despises your family—"

"It's not fair. They work twice as hard as his parents, and they get so little!"

"You need to do something for you. Why don't you come with me to the Canal? You'd love it." The Canal Theater Company.

"Plays seem kind of old-fashioned to me."

"You'd get out of the house, meet some people, have a good time. You'd get practice performing, even if you only do tiny walk-on parts. It gives you confidence."

"I'll think about it." Becky promised without conviction. She didn't see how putting on old plays was going to revive her marriage. She thought her marriage was like Nana's garden when she lay dying, little pale lettuce plants choked by jungles of rampant weeds. Becky hardly knew where to begin to clear out the weeds.

She sat at her kitchen table on Saturday morning before Terry was up and asked herself what could be wrong. She had most of what she had desperately wanted. She took letterhead she had swiped from the office and made a list. *What I Have* she wrote, then crossed that out and put *Becky's Assets*.

1. The right kind of husband.
2. A beautiful apartment.
3. Some good furniture.
4. A middle-class-type job.

Then she made a list of all the new pieces of clothing she had bought, the scarves she had been given, the jewelry, all their wedding presents. She managed to cover three sheets of paper. What was missing? How could she be unhappy?

CHAPTER 33

LEILA

"Vronsky, you're getting fat," Leila said as he lay on her chest. "You need more exercise."

"Mrrrmph," he answered, kneading the space between her breasts.

"What should I do about Nick?" She glanced toward the bedside table. In the back of her appointment calendar, she had the names and phone numbers of three divorce lawyers. She had called none of them. What did she want? The calendar rolled back. What could she have? Probably Nick part-time. Her husband having a baby with a young woman was not a situation she was prepared to ignore. They were essentially separated. He started teaching in January. Any moment he could appear and expect their life to continue and herself to act out ignorant complaisance; or he could appear and ask for a divorce. What she had to get straightened out was what she wanted: nothing she could have, surely, but of all the rotten options, which was the least unappealing?

But how did anyone just end a twenty-four-year marriage? How could she forget a man who had been the spine of her life? But she had formed her own center, and around her moved the concentric circles of her work, her colleagues and students, her research and writing, her informants, her friends. In recent years, Nick and she had not tended to form new friendships as a couple, but individually at work. Gradually, perhaps they had been letting go.

She still hoped for a miracle. Nick bounding back saying it had all been a mistake: Sheryl wasn't pregnant, he had been a fool, and he was ready to settle down to an intimate and loving middle age. She grinned at Vronsky, whose yellow eyes blinked back. "Fat chance, huh? I know Jane's right, but I can't seem to do anything useful about the situation."

Becky had been crying. It was the first time Leila had seen her frayed. "My lawyer told me Sam is saying I seduced him into killing Terry. He's plea-bargaining. They'll knock his charges down to get me. It's me they want, and they'll promise him anything."

"So you feel he's turned on you."

"Like a worm." Tears started slowly from the corner of her eye, one at a time, which she attempted to snuffle back and then scrubbed dry with her knuckle, roughly. Becky seemed ashamed of crying.

"That must be devastating."

"I loved him! I believed that he loved me. I really loved him. How can he turn and try to help them keep me in this disgusting dismal place?"

"You feel you trusted him and he's betrayed you."

Becky nodded fiercely. "I know so well what that feels like, so damned well. Excuse my language."

Leila realized that Becky never swore. To say "damned" was a major breach of her own self-imposed rules. She was soft-spoken and well-spoken, avoiding what she would probably call vulgar expressions. But today she had been wounded. "Why do you say you know what betrayal feels like?"

"Let's just say, it's not the first time I ever had the experience."

"In your marriage?"

"In every part of my life." Becky shrugged. "Look at me, waving my hands, shrugging my shoulders. I spent years with Terry learning to sit still and now here I am, acting like a peasant again, as his mother would say."

Leila understood that Becky had changed the subject, but also had given her a glimpse of old pain. "Was Terry the faithful type?" Leila asked as if offhand.

Becky shrugged. "Let's say the other woman in his life all the time we were together was his mother. She was competition enough."

"In what way?"

"Haven't you seen her on television? She'd like me fried. She'd like me hanged and quartered. She'd like to do it herself."

"What did she have against you?"

"You mean, before she decided I murdered her son? She thought I was déclassé. We're all Catholics, so it wasn't that. We're all the same kind of Catholics: make the kids to go to catechism and get confirmed. Go to Mass on Christmas and Good Friday and Easter and then again when you get into some kind of trouble. Otherwise you're on your own."

"What was it then?"

"My being from a Portuguese family. I mean, it's not like I know ten words of Portuguese. It's not like Terry has some kind of high culture. So he went to Falmouth Academy, so what? We both went to college. The reality was, him and me and all the rest of us, we're not Portuguese or Irish or whatever, we're all the children of television. That was my baby-sitter. That's who taught me about the world. So how was Terry better than me?"

"You're bright, Becky. It's interesting to talk with you."

Becky laughed sharply, a sound like a slap. "I am bright. And I'm not supposed to be. I'm supposed to be stupid. A lot of the time the people around me just haven't noticed."

"Was Terry bright?"

"I never considered he might not be before I married him. I assumed he was because I thought anybody who dealt with computers had to be smart."

"But later on, you were disappointed?"

"Men are always disappointing, aren't they?" Becky made a sour face and turned half away.

"Sam's supposed to be intelligent. Is he?"

"He's so smart, he's trying to kill me. I suppose if he confessed to killing Terry, he must have done it. But now he's going to pretend I had some part in it. He's turned on me. I can't believe he'd rob me. I always thought that kid did it—Gene, the friend of his who was caught selling my TV and VCR." Becky clamped down. She had arrived at a story and an explanation she would polish at her leisure. Leila let her talk on, nodding and clucking, aware she was going to get no further pushing Becky today.

As soon as she got home, she called Zak. "I saw Becky. She told me Sam has confessed and his lawyer is plea-bargaining for him."

"I don't want to talk about this on the phone. Would you come to supper?"

"It's five-thirty already. I can't drive two hours there and two hours back tonight, and I have a class tomorrow."

"What time?"

"I have a ten, an eleven and a two."

"All right, drive out after the two o'clock. I'll know more by then anyhow. I'm in a state of shock. Cathy was hysterical. Fortunately her boyfriend arrived and sat on her. She was making so much noise, there was no space for me to have a reaction. But now it's hit me. Sam really did kill Terrence Burgess."

"Why do you want me to come?"

"I need to make sense out of this. Don't you?"

"But can I help? Do you trust me now?"

"You seem to me somehow rock-bottom sensible—"

"Thanks. That's me. Rock-bottom sensible."

"Do you think that's an unattractive trait? I want you to bring your pragmatic nature and your pleasant self out here. I feel crazy. I feel as if all the people I think I know in my life turn into ax murderers or secret adulterers. I'm in a state of real paranoia. Will you come?"

"I'll come." Yet after the phone call, she felt strange. She felt as if she were doing something illicit. He was an informant like any other. Going to see him was not different from going to see Cathy. She had acquired this circle of more-than-acquaintances. She was still thinking about Zak when Cathy called. Leila was on the phone with her for forty minutes calming her down. Only after Leila had said good night did she realize she had never told Cathy she was going to have supper with Zak. Again she had the faint sense of doing something a little disreputable.

Her phone continued to ring as soon as she hung up. Jane called to tell her about an argument she had had with a colleague. As soon as they finished their analysis and strategy session, Emily took the phone. "Leila, I feel funny telling you this, but do you know your husband is in town? Janie thought you didn't."

"He's in New York."

"I saw him in Harvard Square this morning. He was eating breakfast with a young woman in the Charles Hotel. That's a place I take the boys when we're in the Square and they have to pee. I swear it was him."

"Thank you." Numbly she sat. Numbly she dialed the Charles Hotel. "May I speak to Sheryl Waters? She's a guest."

"That's room 440. I'll ring it for you."

The operator came back on the line. "There's no answer. Would you like to leave a message?"

"Please. Tell them that Leila called. I'll spell that for you."

At seven-thirty, her marriage was over. He was back but not with her. It was decided. She felt half-numb with shock. A great amputation had been performed, but the pain had not begun. She waited for the anesthetic to wear off.

She was on the phone with her mother—Phyllis often called Sunday night—when she heard the door unlock. "Mother, I have to get off now. I think Nick just walked in."

"You haven't had the locks changed?"

"Not yet, Mother. I'll be talking to you."

"You call me back after he leaves. If it isn't too late. We go to bed by ten Sunday night. And get a locksmith tomorrow."

After he leaves. After he returns to Sheryl. She would not cry. She sat at the phone as he called her name rather tentatively from below.

She came down the steps slowly, wishing she had had time to check her appearance. She was still dressed in her respectable visiting-prison clothes, for her hours on the phone had kept her from changing. Just as well, for she would simply have got into her nightgown and bathrobe and put her feet up. "Hello, Nick," she said coolly. "You got my message."

"I was just in town for a lightning visit. The play closed."

"Too bad," she said without inflection. "I'm sure it was a disappointment to you."

He looked sheepish, harried. "I should have stuck to my guns about New York. All I did was breach my own principles and give them a chance to go after me." He flung his overcoat on a chair.

She did not bother answering. She walked past him where he stood in the center of the living room and took a seat in an armchair. Vronsky jumped into her lap. "So you've brought Sheryl to Cambridge."

His face froze up and for a moment she could feel him grappling with the desire to lie. String her along. Then he sighed and let it all go. "I can't abandon her. She's out of work. She's pregnant. She's just a kid really."

She looked at him and she found she had great difficulty speaking at all. She could not seem to make words come out of her mouth. All the blood in her body was rising in a great hot wave to her head. One minute she was as cold as a granite slab; the next minute, she was cooking. Her brain seemed to be bubbling. Words were as distant to her as blocks of stone carved with runes she could not read. Vronsky lashed his tail to and fro. Perhaps her pheromones scared him. He jumped down and went to stand in the middle of the floor, howling.

"Are you annoyed? You didn't return my calls . . . I figured you understood I have to straighten things out. She wants the baby, but she doesn't see what's involved. I can't just dump her in New York without a job and with no means of support." He frowned at Vronsky. "What's wrong with that cat?"

She could see Nick's mouth moving and his eyes fixed on her. She realized that the thing in her, the force that was rising like hot thick liquid, like lava in her body, rising up to her brain, was rage. She was standing. She was making a noise. It was not words. It was a sound like a red banner coming from her mouth. Her hand closed on a vase on the coffee table, a vase of boughten chrysanthemums, and the vase was flying through the air. It hit his shoulder with a loud thwack. Flowers and water ran down his body. The vase fell on the floor and broke.

"Jesus! You could have killed me." He was rubbing his shoulder. "You hurt me. You really hurt me."

"Good! I wanted to." Now she could talk. Her throat was loosened.

He backed away, eying her warily. "What do you mean, throwing objects around like a kid in a temper tantrum?"

"Get out. You belong in the hotel with your pregnant actress."

"Leila, I'm ashamed of you. You're falling apart. You're out of control. You look crazy, do you understand that?"

"Get out of my house."

"It isn't your house."

"You don't live here any longer. You left."

"Leila, you're overreacting. I'm embarrassed, frankly. What I've always admired about you is that you've been a mature, stable woman—"

"Rock-bottom sensible. The bottom just melted. Rock melts if it gets hot enough. You didn't know that."

"Are you drunk? Have you been drinking this evening? Have you been sitting alone here night after night drinking?"

"I haven't been alone night after night."

"Are you telling me you have a boyfriend? I don't believe it. This is a cheap attempt to make me jealous."

"Jump to conclusions on your own time. I told you to get out and I mean it. I'll throw things until you leave." She looked around for something to grab. A fat book?

"Don't bother." He put on his coat, backing toward the door. "I've never seen you so out of control. You've lost it! You can cool down and then we'll talk. But I'll tell you, Leila, acting crazy and violent may impress your academic friends with how upset you are. It just turns me off. I hate bad acting." He slammed the door.

Slowly Vronsky came out from under the coffee table and glared at her. Well, is it over? he seemed to be asking.

"It's over. It's all over." Now she did cry, lying facedown on the couch. She cried and cried, for all the years gone, for the love that had burned up entirely, leaving only a charred smell, unpleasant, rank. Before she went to her ten o'clock class, she must make an appointment with one of the divorce lawyers. She realized not only was her marriage over, but she did not even particularly like Nick. They had become only an irritant to each other.

CHAPTER 34

BECKY

One evening in March as Becky and Terry were eating pizza and watching the news, she bit down and her cheek lit up and she screamed. The pizza fell from her hand and she rose, knocking her chair over backward. Terry gaped at her. "Are you choking?"

If she was, she'd be dead, for all he was doing about it. "Something's wrong with me." She realized it was her tooth, although the whole left side of her face throbbed.

It turned out to require a root canal, which cost four hundred dollars and used up four afternoons. The dentist also found three more cavities. She was shocked by the rebellion of her body. Would she be toothless soon like Mama? Mama had worn ill-fitting dentures for ten years. Becky began brushing her teeth zealously and even flossed. The idea of her beautiful white teeth crumbling away appalled her. Who would want a woman who kept her teeth in a glass by the bed? It was well into April before she was free of the dentist.

I'm getting older, she thought, and my life is standing still. I'm losing it. I've got to seize my life and do something. She tried to talk to Sylvie, who advised her to have a baby. She talked to Mama, who told her to pray and trust in God. She talked to Tommy, who said, "How about a vacation? Everybody gets dragged out. We all got bad teeth, anyhow. It runs in the family. Find some kind of deal on a vacation. I hate to see my favorite sis depressed."

She stopped at the travel agent's in a mall near her office and grabbed brochures of Jamaica, Trinidad, Grenada, the Virgin Islands. When she got home, before she could speak, she took note of Terry's slump dead in the middle of the couch. "What's wrong, honey?" she asked cautiously. The last time he'd been so down had been when the Celtics had got knocked out of the NBA finals.

"I got my pink slip today. In two weeks, I'm history there. They're down-sizing."

"You lost your job?"

"Isn't that what I said? We owe money on all the crap in here. We have payments that will use up our savings in two months."

She sat down and took his limp hand in hers. "You'll get another job. You're a bright man with a good education. You can find something better."

"In this job market? Every day I've said to myself, how lucky I am to have a job at all. And now it's gone."

"But there are lots of computer companies. Surely one of them will be glad to hire you. You just have to get out and get your resumé around."

"That's easy for you to say."

It turned out Terry was right. She began to understand he had minimal training. He had taken the job straight from college, and that was the sum of his experience: he had installed commercial systems, both hardware and software, at small companies around the area. He had never really done programming or design. There was a lot of competition for the kind of job he was prepared for, because anyone better trained could do that easily; and there were many better trained and more experienced people in his field who had been thrown out of work. When the installation base was rapidly expanding, jobs such as his were being created weekly. No more.

He had fifty resumés run off. He sent them out, he carried them around, he left them in offices. He had one interview the second week, two the third and then no more for two weeks. His energy dissipated. He did not get up when she did. He stayed in bed, annoyed if she made too much noise. Usually he was home when she got home, already impatient for supper. Sometimes he was out with Chris or Lyle.

Mr. Burgess played golf and began to bring Terry to his club twice a week, so that Terry would meet someone who might hire him. Terry now spent an increasing amount of time improving his golf, presumably to impress some mythical businessman who would hire him to install computers on the basis of his golf swing. Becky had observed growing up how quickly men thrown out of a job could settle into routines that filled their days and evenings, leaving little time to hunt for a job they became rapidly convinced did not exist. She was worried. They were scraping bottom every month. They were getting by, but just barely.

Terry always seemed to have money to spend on golf. She suspected his father was giving him a couple of twenties every time they got together, but since Terry did not tell her or put the money in the common household kitty, she could not prove it. She took to going quietly through his pants and removing a few dollars and some change whenever she picked his pants off the floor or a chair to hang them up or put them in the hamper.

All of her salary was going to maintain the condo, buy food and pay bills. She could not even give Mama a little money. They were rapidly using up their savings. He had always been careless with money and never knew exactly what he had in his wallet—a fact that astonished her. When she was shopping, she ran a tab in her head. She never used a calculator; she had never owned one before the bank had given them a card-sized calculator when they had opened an account. Secretly she despised him for being sloppy with money when they were having such a hard time, much as she was coming to feel contempt because he could not go out and get a job. Other men had been thrown out of work, other men in the same condo complex, and they had found jobs.

The neighbor who had angered his wife by flirting with Becky was laid off. He worked at Burger King for two months before he found a decent job managing a resort motel. Every man in her family had done odd jobs now and again. But Terry would not consider anything that wasn't "in his field."

She sounded out the women at work. Two of them had been through long periods with a husband out of work. Gwen's marriage had broken up. She had lost the house where they had lived, and she had been with her little boy in a tiny apartment ever since. Mary Lou got a pinched expression on her face. "It wasn't so bad," she said. "It was only a year. After a while we hardly talked. The worst part was, he kept getting mad. Screaming, yelling, hitting on me. I never saw him as a bad-tempered man before that year."

Just wait it out, Mary Lou said. Gwen came into her office the next morning. "I can tell you're pretty fed up, the way I was. But remember, you lose it all when you get divorced. One day you got a house, a nice car, a closet full of clothes, you're shopping for furniture and the newest gadgets. The day after the divorce, you're in a rented slum, you have big bills to meet and you wear your clothes till they fall apart. And you can't see any way out. Ever."

Mary Lou brought her a motivational tape her husband had used. On the way home, Becky listened to it. It made her feel energized. She would do something for herself. She would confront her fears and make lists, and each day she would conquer one thing she had hesitated to tackle. She would grow stronger. She would accomplish her goals. Yes.

She gave the tape to Terry at supper. "Are you serious? Chris and I used to make fun of people who played that stuff. I remember in my frat house, there was a guy who ate up that psycho-babble. He was always discovering his inner child, expanding his boundaries, all that shit. Come on, Becky, be real. Take that garbage back to the girls in the typing pool. I'm not stupid enough for those cheap psychologizing slogans to work on me."

"If you feel superior to anything or anyone who might help you, where will you find help?"

"I don't need 'help.' I need a frigging job. I have eighty resumés out. I go to every interview I can wangle. I pursue every contact I have a crack at. Get off my back. I can't create companies that don't exist, and I can't fix the economy single-handed. Although I bet you think you could."

He got up from the table where they were eating Stouffer's frozen dinners and stomped out of the apartment, leaving her the dishes of course. She decided she would just leave them, the way he did. She went downstairs to Helen's, to tell her woes to a sympathetic ear, but Helen was walking out the door. "I'm off to the Canal. The next production has an older woman, and I'm trying out for it tonight. Becky, why don't you come along? Give it a chance."

Becky got into Helen's car. Didn't the tape say, If you don't try new things, you'll be stuck with the old things? Don't lead a dust-collector life. Push on. She was pushing. If Terry was too smart to be smart, she wasn't. She'd take all the help she could get: from Gwen and Mary Lou, advice; from the tape, energy and a checklist on her progress; from Helen, an escape from the marriage that was shredding under stress like a cheap blouse bought at the mall when she was too young to know about clothing. She would go with Helen and pretend to be someone else.

The Canal Theater Company met in an old Masonic lodge that was underused. When the Masons met, the first Monday of every month, the theater group had to clean up for them. But then the building was theirs again. The honcho seemed to be a woman named Cecelia, about fifty and very lean, with henna red hair, long primitive earrings that jingled, a patchwork skirt that swept the dusty floor. She was called Ce-Ce and was quite self-important. Becky did not take to her, but she set out to ingratiate herself. She fetched and carried. Then she tried out for the smallest female part in the new play they were casting, Agatha Cristie's *Witness for the Prosecution*. Becky was to be one of the jurors, as was Helen.

It was a sizable cast. Becky was surprised, thinking they would do simple plays with only three or four characters, but Helen explained to her that the more people were in the play, the more people came. Everybody could coerce their family, their friends and lovers, neighbors and their co-workers into coming to see them play, even if all they saw was Susie in a wig pretending to be a maid.

The cast ranged in age from Helen, the oldest, to a high school kid playing a cop. His teacher had the male lead. Helen was right, it was fun. They all kidded around. Ce-Ce was dramatic and called them frequently to order, but Becky observed she did not really mind if they horsed around. A pot of coffee stood on a hot plate, and people brought in cookies and soda and potato chips. Becky, who had been too angry at supper to eat, filled up on potato chips. Everybody flirted. Nobody's spouse or significant other was around. Most of them were probably married, but this was time out. She wondered if any of them really followed through or if it was all flirtation.

Helen said on the way home that she would have to search the thrift stores for forties suits and dresses. Then there were the barristers' wigs and gowns. Becky perceived that Helen liked best having to struggle and sweat over the costumes, because that made her feel important to the group. Helen liked to be in a play but did not get frequent opportunities. Becky did not care about her part, although she would have enjoyed getting dressed up in something sexy or outlandish.

In the meantime, she would watch them all carefully and figure out how to make herself visible and important in the eyes of the other members of the company. She flirted a little with the high school teacher, Dick Berg, the male lead, but then she realized he had something going with the woman playing Romaine, a tall self-assured blonde who was married to an oncologist in Hyannis. They were always exchanging meaningful glances. When Becky left with Helen, she saw them kiss good night in the parking lot. A place for heavy flirtations, for a little fun, for stepping out of character and who would know?

"You're right," she said to Helen. "This hobby is just what I need."

CHAPTER 35

LEILA

Zak was patting a setter who had been partially shaved, stitches showing. "I've been trying to come to terms with Sam's confession, but mostly I've realized stuff about myself."

The blind tabby, Homer, was sitting in her lap purring. She was being stared at by an unblinking marmalade cat wearing an Elizabethan collar—to keep him from licking his wounds, Zak had explained. In front of the fire, a Great Dane was whimpering in his sleep. "Someday I've going to come in here, and you'll have a horse in the living room. What did you realize?"

"When I lost my wife and daughter, I replaced them with my brother Mike's family as soon as he died. We weren't close. We'd been rivals for my mother's attention. Cathy came with the territory, but the territory was Sam. I proceeded to make Sam up. I saw him as me. I had lost my daughter, but now I had a son, a younger me."

"How do you think you made him up?"

"He's lonely, insecure, bright. I saw him as wanting what I'd wanted, to be loved, to be respected in spite of not being the way young males were supposed to be. I cherished him as if I were making up my miserable adolescence to myself. You can't do that with somebody else."

"Do you think Sam minded?"

"I think he went along, enjoying the attention. But my need to see him as me kept me from understanding him."

"Because you couldn't have killed Terry Burgess?"

"I've acted like a complete asshole to get laid. Like a puppy in heat. But when Connie Roberts asked me to steal her the social studies exam—I was our social studies teacher's pet and dogsbody—I had sense enough to figure out it wasn't my body she was interested in. I had a lot of fail-safes built in by the time I was sixteen."

"You never thought he did it, not really, until he confessed."

"But do we really know he did it? He confessed, right, but he's miserable and confused. Maybe he's into pleasing them now. Saying what they want him to say. Maybe he's still protecting her. Say, he knows or strongly suspects she did it, and he's sharing her guilt." He shifted in his chair.

"No, come on. He involved her in the confession."

"Maybe he doesn't know any longer what he did. Maybe he's confused and despairing. He said he was losing a sense of himself."

"Zak, if he confessed, you don't really think he invented it."

Zak was silent. He went to poke at the fire. He squatted with his back to her, fussing. Finally he turned with an audible sigh. "I don't know what I think. Except I can't believe Sam was that violent. Ever."

"The murder still evades me. I can't see it."

"Have you read the reports? It was butchery. That man was battered to death. He was hit and hit and hit again. Can you see Sam doing that?"

"Or Becky." She sighed in frustration. "I should never have taken on this assignment."

"I just realized, I'm pissed at him. It's petty, it's egotistical. My feelings are hurt that he lied to me. I can't have seemed like a sympathetic listener if he had wanted to confess. I was dead set to prove him innocent."

"Loyalty isn't the worst virtue in the world, Zak."

"Sometimes it's the blindest."

She crossed her arms in the rocker, tapping her foot. "If you hadn't given Sam your love and your trust, right now you'd be blaming yourself for what he did."

"If he did it. If he even knows anymore if he did or not. He's just a kid in trouble. Look, sometimes I think a lot of what we call a person is a fictional construct. We say things about ourselves. I like this, I don't like that, and that makes us feel a sense of continuity. We remember certain things, although we forget ninety-five percent of what happens to us. But am I the same man who married Corinne? If I met her clone tomorrow, I'd never consider marrying her. In fact, I'd run the other way."

"So what are you saying? That Sam doesn't exist? That I don't?"

"Only that we're more fluid than we realize. Actually I don't feel fluid." He shrugged. "I seem to have an exoskelton of rigid expectations."

"If you thought Sam was you, I thought he was my son. I learned something unpleasant about myself too. Maybe I can understand Becky now, because I did something awful yesterday." She told him the story. "I too can be violent."

He shook his head, grinning. "Did you hit him with the vase?"

"I hit his shoulder."

"Would it have killed him if you'd hit him head-on?"

"Probably not," she said reluctantly. "Of course not. But it might have cut his face. Or broken his nose."

"It's a long way from bloodying someone's nose to bludgeoning him to death with a blunt instrument. Haven't you ever thrown a vase or a dish at your husband before?"

She shook her head no. "Have you?"

"I'm too inhibited against hurting anyone physically. I prefer to be nasty and sarcastic. But Corinne used to throw objects like pillows and books. Or she'd throw my clothes at me. A vase could do damage, but it's not exactly an attempt on his life."

She glared. Then he began to laugh, looking at her, and she began to laugh too. "I fancied myself a possible murderess."

"Why should you want to believe yourself violent? Perhaps it takes only a certain lack of imagination, of empathy, to kill a person."

"You think I'm romanticizing murder."

"Men kill women. Women rarely kill men. But women think because they imagine violence, they're capable of it. You feel guilty for wanting to hurt your husband. I hate to keep calling him that, by the way."

"Nick. His name is Nick."

"He isn't really your husband any longer. What did the lawyer say?"

"If Nick doesn't contest the divorce, it will be easy. I can't imagine why he would. The stickiness will be the financial agreement."

"I assume you are the principal breadwinner."

"How charming that you assume that. Nobody ever does. Yes. I've made about two-thirds of our joint income for the last ten years or so. But we own everything together."

"Isn't it amazing that a man and a woman start out with kisses, and twenty years later, the main tie is ownership."

"I have this drive to be free, now. Since I finally accept that it's over, I want it legally undone. I hate the idea that we're a couple under the law, that we're bound like convicts chained together."

"Drama in the afternoon! It's a legal fiction. Tomorrow, get the locks changed. Pack his stuff up and have it delivered to the Charles. Do you need help?"

"Part of me wants it all over and done with and part of me doesn't believe it. We've been together all my adult life."

"Do you still love him?"

"No. That's part of what I've been realizing. I've been afraid to see it, but this last shock was too much for a structure already seriously undermined. . . . This is boring. You've never even met Nick."

"Make a list of what you want out of the divorce and give it to the lawyer. What you must have and what you'd like."

"Are you always rational? Aren't you prone to guilt, at all? I bet you are."

"I was the younger son, but I have the classic oldest pattern. I don't feel guilty, I feel responsible. If you get a cold, I should have prevented it. I'm always trying to save people. To rush in, particularly with women, but it was the same way with Sam when I think about it, and fill a need. Plug a leak. Make it right. Good mind-set for a vet, right?"

"Was it that way with your wife?"

He frowned, petting the orange cat absentmindedly. "I'm trying to remember how it seemed when I met her. She was pretty but vulnerable. No sense of how to take care of herself—that was how it looked to me, good old sensible middle-class, did-you-remember-to-turn-off-the-stove me. The guy who checks the door twice to make sure it's locked. Who looks at his wallet before he goes out the door and again in the car before he drives off."

"After twenty years of being the responsible one, that seems sweet. I'd love somebody else to worry about whether the stove was left on." She yawned. "What time is it? I've got to leave. It's a two-hour drive, and I won't reach home till midnight." She stood, reaching for her purse.

He got up and stood in front of her. "Stay."

"Stay? Why would it be easier to drive back in the morning? It's true I wouldn't be so tired, but there'd be more traffic."

He put his hands on her shoulders. "I've always been terrible at this. Usually women make passes at me. Vets are always having women flirt with them. Something about the hands-on stuff. It's hard for me to ask for what I want. But stay with me."

Her mouth fell open. After a moment she remembered to close it. "I can't. . . ."

"You can if you want to."

"Why do you want me to? Oh, we've begun really talking to each other, and I like that a lot. But . . . why do you suddenly want to go to bed with me?"

"It's not sudden. We've been spending lots of time together. I find you attractive, and now you're available."

"You're saving me. I became audibly unhappy, and you're saving me."

"No, you can save me this time. You're a rock, Leila. Any sensible man would grab at you." He put his hands on either side of her face and kissed her.

It felt utterly strange, his face very smooth where the beard had been, his lips moving against hers and then his tongue entering her mouth. She almost panicked. She stepped back away from him, and he let her go.

"Zak, I can't do this. I'm not a spontaneous person. I haven't seriously considered another man in over twenty years—"

He smiled, still standing very close to her, one hand warm and heavy on her shoulder. "You have to imagine how endearing I find that. So seriously consider me. This isn't a now-or-never proposition."

"Please don't feel rejected. You don't understand how unsexual my life has been. It's been years since Nick and I made love often. It's hard for me to imagine another man even attracted to me."

"Because you're not young. You're not fashionably fleshless. You're a handsome woman who looks and acts solid. I find you interesting. You can stay on the couch if you like. I won't bother you."

"No, I feel too confused. I have to drive back and feed my cat and get my stuff together for class. I also have to call the lawyer and tell her I'm going ahead. Besides, Zak, you're Sam's uncle. I'm trying to write about him objectively."

"You aren't trying him. And do you believe, if we went to bed right now, that it would affect your opinion of his guilt?"

"Wouldn't you expect it to?"

"I can promise you, no. I have enough scientific training to respect empirical data and inference."

"Even when it leads where you don't want it to go? I'm not convinced. I'm not convinced I wouldn't be swayed."

He walked her to the door and gave her a brief farewell kiss, which she responded to, shyly, almost furtively. "Just promise you'll consider me."

"I promise."

It was only as she lay in bed that night with Vronsky curled into her side that she reexperienced the kiss with Zak, this time with pleasure. Remembering the feel of his warm mouth against hers, his lean body of almost exactly her height and weight, she felt a stir of response she had not in the moment. She had to make him understand she simply could not start another relationship. It would be a year, two years, maybe longer, before she was emotionally free enough to be able to respond to another man. She hoped that she could explain without alienating him, because she really did like his company. She could not possibly become involved with him while writing about his nephew. By the time she finished the book, in two years or so, he would probably be remarried. Too bad about the timing. A real pity.

CHAPTER 36

BECKY

Becky had never realized how much she prized the forty-five minutes to an hour she used to have between the time she got home from work and the time Terry arrived. It was one reason she tried to shop on weekends or her lunch hour. Sometimes she turned on "Hard Copy" or "A Current Affair" but she did not pay attention. It was just a benign presence, a buzz of conversation while Becky bustled about. After the stress of the day, she floated around the condo, picked up a stray sock of Terry's for the hamper, gave a little spray of polish to the coffee table. It was the time for her to make love with the condo she adored, to absorb its neatness, its cleanliness, its prettiness. Sometimes she just sat and looked around, imagining how she could place a chair she had seen in the Sunday *Globe* magazine, how she could hang something colorful over the couch.

Now every day when she arrived, Terry was waiting. Waiting for supper. Waiting to be amused. Waiting for someone to take out his frustrations on. Now the condo was never neat. His golf sweater flopped over the back of the chair. His clubs fell over when she opened the hall closet. Wrappings from a fast-food lunch lay on the counter and something sticky had spilled on the floor. An empty potato chip bag hid under the couch. *Sports Illustrated* had slipped halfway behind a cushion.

He watched all the reality shows that acted out crimes and captures.

She hated those programs. They were full of fat middle-aged cops and other boring people. At least when he watched the scandal shows, they talked about interesting things, like what Cher and Madonna were doing. That she could get into. She could see herself being a reporter on a show like that. She would get to meet everybody, and they would all be nice to her because they wanted good publicity. He also watched the boring, boring "People's Court" where the same judge droned on every day while losers tried to sue each other about plumbing that didn't work. She could learn a lot from television, but not from some program about a cop making a bust in a housing project that looked like where friends of hers had grown up, or two losers suing each other about somebody's dog being clipped wrong. Most of the time it was sports. They ought to drop cable to save money, but neither of them was willing to give it up. She got a discount anyhow. It would look cheesy in the office if she dropped it.

There was a new Burgess family song. His mother had launched it two weeks before at the Sunday dinner that had become the low point of her week. They seemed to sit there for at least twelve hours, before she was cooped up with Mrs. Burgess in the kitchen. "If only you children hadn't been so precipitous about getting married, there'd be no problem now. Terry could just move back in his room, and he'd have plenty of time to look for a new job, even to go back to school and get a master's."

"I thought you found it a burden to have Terry living at home so many years after college. I remember that it was a problem."

"Nonsense." Mr. Burgess snorted. "We're a close-knit family. That's just the way we are. Old-fashioned."

If she had not had the theater group to escape to, she did not know how she would have got through May with Terry still out of work. She was not convinced he was truly looking any longer, but seemed to be waiting for his father to conjure up a job for him with one of his golf buddies. Occasionally when the Sunday want ads had something likely, he cranked up a sputter of activity, but then it fizzled out. "If we didn't have this condo riding on our backs and all this furniture and gadgets and all this stupid crap, I could just relax. Treat this as a vacation. But we really put ourselves in hock, and for what?"

Well, if he wanted to feel that way, let him. For what? For her. So they could be together and married. Now that had become embarrassing, a mistake, an obligation. Sometimes he talked about unloading the condo, as he put it, but he didn't proceed because the housing market was static.

"I don't want to move out of here. I like this. I really like it."

He looked at her as if she was crazy. "What's to like? It's just a condo like a thousand others. It's not anything real, like a house." He seemed genuinely puzzled.

"It looks real enough to me." She knocked her fist on the door frame. "I like this place, Terry. So why don't your parents send you back to school, if that's what you want?"

"Maybe in the fall. If we can sell this. You could come to Amherst with me. Or maybe you could move back in with your parents and save some money."

It was a trap. He was trying to shove her back onto her parents. She was scared. He was lazy enough so that perhaps he would fail to act on getting into college, and his parents did not seem to be eager to spend the money. He was not going to sell the condo out from under her. She could carry it. She was carrying it now. "My parents don't have room for me. I see no reason why I shouldn't just stay here and remain at my job, if you go back to school. It's near work. It shouldn't take you long to get a masters in computer science."

"It's hard enough," he grumbled. "My parents are going to want to take the money from the condo and use it for school."

"I'm not moving out," she said. "If you want to go back to school, fine, but I'm not moving out."

"We'll see about that," he said.

Sometimes they had good times, sometimes they ate pizza and laughed and went to a movie. Tommy could still make Terry behave himself and lighten up. But much of the time they were engaged in a quiet war. Who was going to give in? Who was going to budge first? Not her, she swore silently. He was not going to take away from her the place she loved. They had wanted him out of the house; they were embarrassed by the apartment over the dry cleaner's. They had never really accepted the marriage and they were using his unemployment against her, when she was the one supporting him. She was carrying him on her back and she was tired of it, but she was not going to leave. If anybody was leaving, it was him.

Sometimes she felt she had become invisible. She gazed hard at herself in the mirror, and she liked what she saw, but Terry looked right through her. Even Taffy-Hands had stopped eying her since she belonged to his boss. She deserved to be noticed. She wanted so badly to be someone, she could feel that need throbbing the way her tooth had.

Friday, Dick Berg had the cast over after rehearsals. She was fascinated by his house. He taught high school. His wife was a chiropractor, and obviously between them, they did okay. The house was new and full of sharp unexpected angles. It was dark, so she couldn't see if they had a view, but they had several decks. It seemed to her that the richer people were, the more decking they had. Only people like her parents had a porch nowadays. The first time she had heard the Burgesses talk about their decks, she had felt like laughing. What did they think they were living in, a cruise ship? Now she was used to the word. The ceiling in the living room was high and sharply tilted. Dick Berg referred to it as a cathedral ceiling.

What impressed her was the decor. "See, isn't it great?" Sam murmured to her. "Everyplace you look, there's something to stare at. It's so intense here. I love it." She and Sam sat together on a low squishy couch and eyed everything. He was a kid whose father was dead and his mother was having a hard time. He had attached himself to her after the first couple of weeks, and she was happy to play big sister. He did not make her feel like an ignoramus. He did not pretend that the real paintings of wild colors and jagged shapes on the walls did not impress him, or the wiry things hanging down they called mobiles or the green elongated naked lady of pipes who lay on the wide wooden railing that ran around the top of the stairway down to the family room. Mr. and Mrs. Berg did not even have a TV in their living room. That was banished to the family room below, where the furniture was scruffy. This room was for impressing people, and she was impressed.

"Does your house have paintings and that kind of thing?" she asked Sam.

"It's full of stuff my mom makes. She's a potter."

Sam was cute, kind of wistful. He was shorter than Terry, but he wasn't skinny. He actually was built okay for a kid, especially his upper body. They made a cute couple in spite of the age difference.

Sam wanted to be liked. He was a lonely kid. He loved being in the play for the same reason she did, that the group made an instant warm pocket they could slip into. All of a sudden she had fourteen new friends. She had people she saw as often as she saw her husband, people she had a far warmer relationship with. They drank, they nibbled, they kissed each other when they met and when they left. She had never had so many friends, interesting ones.

There was a certain amount of casual pairing off, heavy flirtations. She found many of the men already spoken for. She was definitely not interested in Fred, who ran a bed-and-breakfast and seemed allergic to cats, dogs, strawberries, tomatoes, ragweed, roses, grass, wheat and everything else that was or ever had been living. Guy was gay. She knew that the configuration changed with every play, so she bided her time. In the meantime she flirted with Sam, who doted on her and followed her around like a good dog. Terry had looked at her with that intense preoccupation the first year. She could remember that gaze, and it made her want to cry.

She would come home from the theater group twanging with energy, and she would try to get Terry to have sex with her. The trouble was he began to notice the pattern, and to refuse, just to give her a hard time. They still had sex usually twice on weekends. The group turned her on. She wasn't a star, she wasn't even a featured player, but the group was fun. Helen and she gossiped all the way home like conspirators. Sometimes she completely forgot Helen was an old lady, and she talked to her just as freely as she ever had with Sylvie.

Becky prided herself on never forgetting a good turn or a bad turn. Papa never forgot somebody who'd helped him when he was down: those who had done him dirty, he swore he'd eat revenge stone cold, but he'd eat the last morsel of their heart someday. Only fools forgot and forgave, and only those without personal honor neglected to return a favor. She volunteered to walk Florrie and do Helen's shopping with her own. Helen was the only person besides Tommy and Belle she confided in fully about her marriage.

"What good is he?" Helen said frankly as she drove them to the rehearsal hall. "He doesn't work. He doesn't make you feel good. You do all the work."

"I keep hoping he'll shape up. When we first got married, I was so happy."

"If you marry a complete jerk, you're happy for six months. Then the glossy paint wears off and you look at what you've let yourself in for."

"If he'd only get a job, then he'd be out of my hair part of the time. His parents would get off our backs about how we're stupid to be married, it costs too much."

Sometimes Terry made sarcastic remarks about the theater group, but she avoided confrontation. She didn't ask, she just sailed out of the house. Much of the time he hardly seemed to notice. He went out sometimes with his old fraternity buddies or his brother Chris. He was drifting back into his bachelor habits. Some evenings, he went over to his parents' house.

Opening night Terry came and brought his parents and Chris and his girlfriend. They seemed to like the play okay, although the girlfriend said she had seen it on cable with Marlene Dietrich, and this was a joke by comparison. Becky was insulted for her fellow players. Afterward she wanted to go to the cast party, but Terry wouldn't. "All this way to see you say five words. This is supposed to give you experience for cable?"

"Confidence. This was my first part. I think it's okay to start small and work my way up to bigger roles. I'm learning from watching. And I'm learning to speak more correctly. Dick Berg always tells us when we don't speak properly."

"Really?" Mrs. Burgess laughed. "He must have his work cut out for him."

The next night, Sam told her, "I was so disappointed you didn't come to the party. How could you miss it? We had champagne." They were backstage during the first act, hanging out by the coffeemaker.

"Terry wouldn't stay. Next time I'm going to talk him into coming the second night, if we're in the next play, so I can go to the party."

Sam drew her into the empty dressing room. "We'll be in," he said authoritatively. "Everybody likes us. Ce-Ce said you had good ingenue looks. She means how pretty you are."

"Me, pretty? Why do you say that?" She turned a little sideways, giving him a look through her lashes.

"I think about you all the time, Becky. I've never known anybody like you." He was staring at her.

This is just an overeager kid, she told herself. He probably looks at all the girls that way. You can fall in love with a picture in a magazine at that age. You can get a mad crush on a singer just because you like his video. She just smiled. "You haven't known a lot of women, have you? I'm just me."

"I was done in when you weren't here last night. I'd been looking forward to the party. I knew there'd be dancing—I thought we'd dance. And I wanted to do this." With a look of half-frightened desperation, he lunged forward and kissed her.

She expected a quick buss, but he kissed her seriously and hard, his tongue parting her lips, his chest and hips straining against her. She thought of pushing him away, but why should she? It felt good. She was surprised and curious. She had not imagined he had the brass to hit on her. He did not feel like a kid either. He felt harder-bodied than Terry, shorter but better muscled. She wondered what his skin would feel like. His hands were splayed on her upper and lower back, just above her buttocks, grasping her hard. It excited her. Slowly, not breaking the kiss, she edged closer to him, feeling the tautness of his belly and thighs pressing into her, wedged as she was against a table. She could feel his erection then, and her breath caught. She felt that sharp ache between her thighs.

He was getting too excited. She was not about to do it with him right now, right here, among the scenery while the play was going on thirty feet away. She broke from him abruptly.

He stood a moment with his hands dangling. "Are you mad at me?"

"You took me by surprise. No, I'm not angry. I'm a little flattered, a little worried. I have to think about this."

"Becky, I'm crazy about you. I think about you all day, I think about you every night."

"Well, you go on thinking about me." She went past him out of the scenery. "And now I'll think about you too."

CHAPTER 37

MARY

Mary spent the night in a garaged car, but now she had her little travel alarm, so that she would rise early enough to be safe, and her lovely new sleeping bag to keep her alive and warm enough. It was Saturday. She would head downtown first thing. Filene's basement opened at eight during the holiday season. She needed a pair of cotton panty-hose. As the morning wore on, she would be able to sit on a bench outside if it wasn't too cold, and she could always find a seat in the upstairs waiting room. In better dresses, sometimes the fitting rooms had chairs.

Later on she'd go to Chestnut Hill or to Arsenal Mall. Malls were better for a winter day, but they didn't open as early as downtown. In between, maybe she'd visit Beverly. The holidays were a time of crowds when she could linger. Everybody had shopping bags, and the only problem with sitting was finding a place to do it.

But the holidays also made her feel her ostracism. She had no tree, for she had no room in which to put one up. The carols seemed to reproach her. No one was supposed to be solitary at Christmas. Everyone was supposed to have a family to go home to, to come home to them.

Sometimes she imagined moving to Hawaii, to be near Jaime. But he had warned her how expensive the islands were and how difficult it would be for her to support herself there. Still, maybe she should use the money she was saving for a one-way ticket to Hawaii, instead of a car to live in. She loved the idea of having a choice. There, she could always sleep outside. She would consider it. Yes. She had mailed off gifts to Jaime's two boys before Thanksgiving. It took forever for parcel post to get to her son.

His wife would go out and get her a purse or a scarf or something. She could not use a regular purse, as she had her huge carry-all. What she did was send them to Cindy or Marissa as a present. She decided to call Cindy. On Saturday, Cindy would be in her boutique by ten.

Her stomach hurt, and she kept wanting to eat. She imagined fried eggs. She had used to eat eggs once over lightly or poached with a nice thick slab of Canadian bacon and whole wheat toast. Jim hated his eggs runny. He wanted them fried until the yolks were solid and the whites, rubbery to her taste. His toast had to be close to burnt. On the other hand, she cooked her own bacon longer than his.

She would go to the grave remembering exactly how Jim had liked his sirloin broiled, the barbecue sauce he favored, the way he liked his shirts lightly starched, the kind of ties he would wear and the kind he would rather be beaten than put on. He could say nothing worse about clothing than that it was loud or bright. She knew his sock size and his pajama preference, what vegetables he would eat and his favorite flavors of ice cream—rocky road and strawberry ripple. He loved peanut brittle, but he could not eat it as he got older, for it hurt his teeth and got stuck in his fillings.

She wondered what he remembered about her. Did he ever think of her? Cindy said, Oh, he gets very upset if I mention your name. He doesn't like to think of me seeing you. He thinks you'll bad-mouth him, I suppose. Anyhow, Mother, he never asks.

She could not stop imagining the taste of eggs. She knew they weren't supposed to be good for you, although she had been told all her life that they were an almost perfect food, like whole milk. Every ten years, they changed the rules. She remembered the steak-and-grapefruit diet, it was named for a clinic even. That had been the standard diet on which she had tried to lose weight. Now steak was considered the equivalent of a double chocolate fudge sundae with whipped cream. Now she ate breakfast cereal or bread. But a proper breakfast would always be the kind she had prepared every morning for Jim and the kids: grapefruit, eggs and bacon, toast and coffee.

Her stomach was growling. She went into a bathroom on the second floor of Jordan Marsh and looked carefully through her bag, seeing if she had any food. When she had been staying at her client's houses, often she had some kind of snacks with her, fruit, crackers. Finally she went down into the second basement at Filene's and had a big caffè latte, which was just a glass of milk and coffee. She drank it slowly and very sweet. Someone had left part of a croissant and she grabbed it. Buying the alarm and having to eat in cafeterias and McDonald's this week had cleaned her out, besides the fact that she would probably have to stay in a motel tonight. She could not eat a real meal today.

At a pay phone, she called the cleaning service office, to see if anyone wanted her to walk their dog or feed their cat. Nothing. Why didn't her people start traveling? Why didn't they go off to Florida or Europe or Aspen? It was time. Tomorrow, the DeMotts were flying to L.A.

Finally she could call Cindy at the Goddess Shop. After the how are you's, she could not help asking, "Did Marissa like the sweater?"

There was a silence. "It fit her," Cindy said, as if desperate to think of something positive to say. "It fit her very well. It's very . . . practical. It's not the sort of designer sweater she usually wears, but I'm sure she can get some use of it. I rewrapped it—it came looking as if it had been run over. Did you get your present?"

"It came two days ago," Mary assured her daughter. Under her old coat, she was wearing the navy blazer Cindy had sent her: another layer of warmth and something good to show off. She would carefully hang it while she was cleaning and never, never wear it in her clients' houses, new, all wool with every button still on it. Whenever she wanted to look ultra-respectable, she went into a women's room, removed her normal layers of two bulky sweaters and stowed them away in her carry-all. Then she opened her coat and even took it off, never letting go of it, to show off her pristine new jacket.

It was not impatience that had made her open it at once at the post office. She could not carry around a box. One year, Jaime had sent her pineapples. It was hopeless. She had to give them away. This year she had asked him, which meant asking his wife, for one of those makeup kits. If she had makeup, it would be easier for her to pass as respectable.

"I do what I can for Marissa, Cindy. I can't afford the kind of clothing she wears. I can't afford that for myself, or anything like it. I thought this would fit her and she'd wear it maybe weekends?"

"Really, Mother, if you can't afford presents, you shouldn't buy them."

"But I want to give my grandchildren something for Christmas. I'll call on Christmas morning. Will you be home?"

"Until one. Then we're going to . . . out."

That meant Jim. "I'll call in the morning. I want to talk to both of them. I love you, Cindy."

"You too, Mom. I have a customer. Bye, now."

Talking to Cindy left her empty. She was always wanting more of the phone call than Cindy could possibly give her. It had to provide her with a sense of family, of connection, of her own past. She was simply not necessary to her daughter's well-being. Now she really wanted to see Beverly, the only person she talked with openly. They had a bond perhaps stronger than blood.

On the way from the subway to the hospital, she passed a 7-Eleven. She went in and bought a raspberry yogurt and ate it standing there. She did not care what they thought. Actually the man behind the counter looked half-asleep and could not care less if she ate the yogurt or rubbed it in her hair.

She felt a little better as she slogged on. The sun touched her arm with faint warmth. Tonight she would have to stay in a motel, or she would not survive. She would check in around four and not leave until check-out time at eleven the next morning. She would take several hot baths. She would sleep and sleep.

She would be warm and she would wash out her things in the sink and hang them in the bathroom. It would be nineteen hours of total relaxation. All day she would imagine it. She would even call and make a reservation. She knew how to check in, putting down a made-up license. She would use the Anzios' license plate, since she had just slept in their car.

Then Sunday she would go to the DeMotts'. She had examined their tickets in Mr. DeMott's sock drawer. They were leaving on a nine o'clock plane into L.A., so they should be gone long before she arrived around noon. She would simply walk in quietly. No neighbors would be lolling around outside in weather like this. They would leave the furnace on, lest their pipes burst. Just march on through today, and then it would be easy. As easy as it ever got. The DeMotts had no pets, so she must be very careful when they might return, but their house was big and well back on its lot. She would have until Thursday morning, four entire nights of warmth and rest.

CHAPTER 38

LEILA

Leila had vaguely noticed that Christmas was approaching as she passed through the Square and along Mass Avenue. The shops had been decorated for a month, and in some cases, since Halloween, so the imminence of the holidays did not impress itself on her until her students were all talking about what they were doing after finals. Suddenly there was no more time to get through the material, no more time to explain what she suspected the students hadn't grasped, no more time to open up the discussion, bring out the shy, shower them with information and insights to make their minds catch fire. A semester neither the best nor worst of her teaching career was in its last hours. Her book manuscript went off to her editor. She gave her finals and she was tediously grading them Thursday evening when David called.

"I thought I'd come home first, but then fly back early and visit Ikuko. She'll drive down and get me in L.A."

Leila was determined to hide how let down she was that his time at home would be truncated. "I hope you can change your tickets. It's kind of late. I think there's a penalty."

"I changed them already. I paid the difference."

He had done so before he had even spoken with her. "You seem quite serious about this Ikuko for the time you've been seeing each other."

"Well, I like her. And I'm curious about her scene at home."

He was not about to tell her he was sexually obsessed or crazy in love. No matter what he experienced, he would speak of the girl in that cool super-rational voice with her. She realized she was going to have to tell him her situation. "David, your father and I are separated."

"What do you mean? Like, he's in New York and you're in Cambridge?"

"Like, he's back in Cambridge with his pregnant girlfriend, and we're both seeing divorce lawyers."

"Why, all of a sudden?" He sounded aggrieved.

"You've said several times that I should leave him."

"But you didn't. You've been living with his . . . running around forever. Why break up now?"

"His girlfriend is going to have a baby, remember? That's quite a difference from going to bed with some actress a couple of times in Minneapolis. I never liked it, but it wasn't under my nose, and he always had seventy-five excuses about how tense he was, how insecure. I felt, since I couldn't go on the road with him, I had to forgive him what he did when he was lonely in other cities and under the stress of a play opening. This is different."

"I think you should go to a marriage counselor and work this out."

"David, it's past that. Neither of us wants to work anything out."

"Mother, you're going to be alone. I'm out of there. You can't live there by yourself. I'm sure he doesn't really want to leave you."

"I can't take it any longer. I don't get enough from him to put up with what he's doing. There's not sufficient feeling left. Not enough strength in the relationship. It's worn out."

"How could it wear out all of a sudden? You just have to try."

"I'm tired of trying, David. I thought you would understand."

"How are you going to manage?"

"Manage in what way?"

"Mother, how will you pay the bills?"

She was silent for a moment. "Is it possible you don't know I've basically supported the household for the past ten years?"

"I knew you worked, sure. But you never said you paid for things."

"Why would I say that?" She had assumed that David understood. What a family they were: David knew about Nick's infidelities, but they had both kept their relative incomes a deep secret from him. "Nick's half-time adjunct faculty, and the directing jobs never pay that much. This one is probably the best he's had, but it's over." She felt guilty finally saying it to him. Nick and she had never openly spoken of the situation, not even to each other, let alone David. It was a lot to lay on him suddenly.

David was silent. She held her tongue and waited. "It's a shock," he said finally. "After this many years, it seems sort of ridiculous to get divorced. Who is this bimbo? She's just some actress like the others. It'll be over any day now. If he's back in Cambridge, isn't she in New York?"

"She came with him. And it won't be over for twenty-one years. There's a baby on the way. Babies are awfully real, David. They change everything. You did. So will this one. It already has."

"Maybe we could just, you know, adopt it—"

"Why would Sheryl want to give us her baby? Be real. It's her power. And do you want to quit school and raise a child? I can't."

She heard a noise as if he were hitting or kicking something. "I just can't believe everything's gone to hell since Thanksgiving."

She had never been crazy about Christmas, a holiday that in her childhood had merely been a source of awkwardness and the knowledge of being an outsider, the same sort of feeling she had had repeatedly in her young adult life when friends began singing camp songs. She had never gone away to summer camp. She did not know where all these asinine songs came from, so that she had felt both grumpy, bored and excluded. In her childhood, Christmas had been that feeling times ten. Christmas was a whole industry: wrappings, cards, presents, wreaths, trees, ornaments, carols and carolers, cookies, television and school buzzing with it. Even the weather reports debated whether there would be snow for the holidays.

This year there would be no tree. Christmas had always felt like a conspiracy to use up her vacation time in between the work of finals and grading and the work of preparing for the new quarter. It was a plot to steal her reading and relaxing time.

She had thought David would understand her decision about Nick. He had always been on her side. She should have realized that the idea of his family changing would disturb him. Children always wanted their parents in situ, in stasis. The faster they changed, the more their parents should remain the same.

David was much on her mind at her next meeting with Sam. It felt odd to go to Cathy's to see him, but Sam was home on bail. He was looking brighter. His color was better, but his energy level still seemed low. "They won't let me see Gene. He's been out for a month already. He's my best friend and I miss him like crazy. And they don't want me back at school."

"What are you doing about classes?"

"I have a tutor. I got way behind. I have to study for hours and hours every day to catch up. Zak tries to help me, but he doesn't remember a lot of this stuff. It's totally dull to have to sit by myself learning all kinds of crap. At least they should let Gene and me study together."

He described Becky as seducing him to murder. Leila asked, "Everything was her idea?"

"It was an obsession with her. Once she talked about it, she never let up. 'Do it, or you'll never see me again. Do it, or he'll get both of us. He knows. He's going to fix us good. He knows, and we have to act quickly.' " Sam sounded deeply depressed. His voice rose as if dramatically, but there was no energy behind the words. He seemed sunk into a cold lethargy behind the façade of forced and obviously rehearsed statement.

She took a chance. "Do you feel guilty for having exposed her?"

"What's the point? We can never be together now."

There was something odd in that response. "Because you can't be with her any longer, you see no point in trying to protect her?"

"Protect her? Look what happened to me when I tried to protect her." He laughed bitterly. "My whole life has turned to shit. If I'd never met her, I'd be on my way to U Mass Amherst. My biggest worry would be what roommate I'd get. I thought I was this macho man."

Sitting back, she tried to imagine David so much in love with Ikuko that he'd attack someone, say, her father or an uncle who had been abusing her. She could not imagine this boy who had hair very like his uncle's and sharp, almost delicate features being passionate enough about Becky (who, she realized, had similarly sharp features along with a hint of fragility, the sense of being undersized) to kill for her. She could not imagine them that violently in love.

"Zak's upset because I confessed," Sam said, polishing his glasses. "But he kept after me to tell the truth. Finally what choice did I have? Like, they totally have me. It's a question of survival now."

"He needed to believe you're innocent."

"Then he's not a very good judge of character, is he? Or maybe he just never was crazy enough about a woman to know how much of a fool I could be for her. Becky." He seemed to have trouble saying her name.

"Are you angry, because he believed so strongly in your innocence?"

"I guess. Like it screws me up because it makes me feel I have to lie to him. I'm in enough trouble without worrying about how my uncle feels."

"You think he's being selfish?"

"Not really. He tries." Sam stared at her. "He likes you."

"I like him too. They say he's a very good vet." She sounded ridiculous even to herself. Defensive. Inane.

"Women come on to him all the time, but he hasn't been that interested. We really needed him, anyhow. Mom was messing up before he took over. She used to foul up the checkbook so bad I'd have to balance it. I was fourteen years old and I was trying to figure out a budget. Maybe that's why I'm a little crazy now." He looked at her hopefully.

She wanted to say she suspected he wasn't crazy at all, but she just nodded thoughtfully. "Where is she, by the way?"

"She's at work." He made a face of disgust. "The first week I was home, she was practically sitting on me. Like I'm going to run off to Colombia and join a drug cartel, right? Where am I supposed to go? I have like twenty bucks to call my own. So I'm going to run out of the house and go kill the guy at the gas station or something?"

"I think she's just worried about you. They both are."

"Zak acts like my mother's stupid—I mean, she's no genius, but a lot of the time the problem is that she doesn't want what he does. It's like telling somebody all the vitamins and minerals in some breakfast cereal, when they think it tastes like dog kibble, and they'd rather starve."

"Is he manipulative?"

"No, that's *her* talent."

"Cathy?"

"No, *her*. Becky. She could play me by the hour. I was such an idiot over her!" His face screwed into a mask of pain. "I thought I was so smart in high school, but I was stupid. I was the stupidest kid of all."

When she got home, her answering machine was throbbing with messages. Jane: "Do you need any support around the divorce? Remember I'm available." David: "Mom, I just had a weird conversation with Dad. I mean weird. I think he's lost it. I know kids my own age who have a better idea about relationships than he does." Zak: "I thought I'd come into the city tomorrow, Saturday. There's a seminar at Tufts on feline infectious peritonitis. Maybe we can go out to supper. I could swing by six or so." Student: "I know you said not to call you at home, but I got your number out of the book, and I have to know if I passed. I really have to know." Phyllis: "Personally Joan and I think Nick is a horse's ass, and his family gives me hives. I never thought he treated you like you deserve to be treated, and I wouldn't put up with half the shit you did. But how are you going to manage?" Nick: "We must talk. It can't be put off any longer. Changing the locks on the house was hostile and adolescent. I'll be over tonight at eight."

Her first thought was to leave at once. She would call Jane and ask her if she could spend the night. Then she asked herself, what was she afraid of? It would not be pleasant to see the man who had been her husband all her adult life, but probably it was necessary. Running away would only put off the conversation. The number he left was not the Charles. Had they found an apartment already?

His lawyer had talked with her lawyer. She wanted to be free, and presumably he wanted to cut loose from her. She found that she could not think clearly. Maybe it was better to see him and force herself to confront her choices and lack of them. Should she call him? No, let him wonder. Vronsky stood on her desk glaring. She had not been around much. She apologized to him and he rubbed against her hand. The holidays would certainly be peculiar. Maybe she would get a lot of work done.

By seven forty-five she had a bad stomachache and she had changed her clothes four times. She gathered up the paper, read two articles without any sense of what they concerned, turned on the TV and watched a program that was vaguely green. She got up, she sat down. She went upstairs. She thought she heard him at the door and rushed back down. She watched the numbers on the control panel of the dishwasher change from 45 to 38 minutes. She brushed her hair yet again. She picked lint and cat hair off the couch. Maybe she would start collecting cats, as befitted a nutty lady alone. She would have brown cats, black cats, striped, spotted, orange, yellow, white, grey cats, cats with long fur and shorthaired cats. She would have cats the way some people had mice. The idea amused her, as nothing had since she had listened to her messages. It was five after. Where was he? It would be just like him to drive her crazy by announcing his arrival and then changing his mind.

At eight twenty-two, she heard a car pull just into the drive. She did not let herself run in panic upstairs to brush her hair and check her appearance for the fourteenth time. She made herself go out to the kitchen and put dishes away. While she was fussing, the doorbell rang.

She found herself stumbling toward the door with a silly grimace on her face. Just before she opened it, she rubbed her hands hard over her eyes and cheeks to banish the smirk of anxiety. She composed her face into a politely inquiring mask, then jerked the door open. "Hello, Nick," she said evenly. At least her voice was under control. "Come in." She stood politely aside and beckoned him toward the living room, wishing briefly that she had redecorated or at least repainted.

He glanced around, nodded slightly and sat in his usual leather easy chair. "You're well?"

"Just fine." She took his coat and hung it on the coat rack, for the formality of the gesture and to give herself time to compose her façade. "And you?"

"It's all disturbing, of course." He saw the pile of his third-class mail. He had the first-class forwarded. "I don't want a war with you."

"You and Sheryl have found an apartment?"

"In Allston. It's only temporary. I want to put this house on the market. We can split the price."

Her first impulse was to deny him. Then she thought about the sheer size of the house, the taxes, the wasted rooms. "We can try to sell. It isn't exactly a mad mad market like the eighties, Nick. Melanie's house has been looking for a buyer since she died, and I don't think half a dozen people have gone through it." She was ready to look at him. In her mind he had been Nick of ten years ago. Now she saw a middle-aged man she knew very, very well, who was showing signs of too many late nights. His beard looked darker. She wondered if he was using some product to reduce the grey. Let Sheryl worry. That body need no longer be kept up by her.

"Don't hang me up waiting for the price that won't come again. I'd rather have one hundred fifty in hand than a potential two hundred apiece five years down the pike," he said. "Let's price it to sell."

She did not answer. She was in no hurry to move, and she did not much care if the house were to be for sale for a long time.

"We'll each keep our cars, I presume. Neither of them is new or fancy. Nothing to fight about there."

"Nick, these financial details are best worked out by the lawyers. I thought you had something personal to discuss."

"This is all depressing. I thought you understood my needs. Now I admit, things with Sheryl got out of hand, and she's fragile. Perhaps I shouldn't have chosen someone quite so . . . young and vulnerable. But she is having this baby, and I do feel responsible." He put his hands on his knees. "I'd imagine that you'd approve of a man feeling responsible."

"I find that line of argument cheesy. You're saying, I feel responsible for what I did, and therefore you will pay for it. Or it's like a murderer saying, But I tidied up, I cleaned the bloodstains. Surely you appreciate that I cleaned up after myself."

"Oh, did you ever meet Becky Burgess?" He asked in sudden distraction.

"I see her regularly," Leila said dryly. "Is there anything else you wanted to discuss this evening?"

"You needn't act hard as nails. You're a big woman, and with that confrontational attitude, you come off like a police sergeant."

"We're not on the best of terms now, Nick, and we don't much like each other. Do you want to see David when he's home?"

"Of course! I suppose you've been pouring out your anguish to him at great length, but he's still my son, and I certainly intend for him to meet Sheryl and I want him to understand my situation."

"You'll work out the details with him, not with me, please. What interests me is when you first thought of ending our marriage."

He looked at her with surprise. "Everybody thinks about getting out. Every time you're going into a new relationship, you think about leaving. It's natural. Things get dull. After all, what was I supposed to do in all those other cities? You were never around."

"You never wanted me around. Not only was I working, but even when I wasn't, you never wanted me there. I could have arranged my schedule to have long weekends. There's a woman in the psych department whose husband teaches at Yale. They spend half the week together and half the week apart. They've been living that way for seven years, and I believe they're faithful."

"You're not tempted by men, because you simply don't much like men."

"I'm asking you when you decided it was the end."

He rubbed his beard, frowning. "Last spring, I thought about it. When I went out to L.A. in May and started comparing my life with Tim's. He has a house in Malibu, goes to all the great parties and the headwaiters greet him by name. He has a fucking personal trainer to keep him in shape. We're the same age, we went to to N.Y.U. together, we were both in *Measure for Measure* in Central Park. . . . I felt I was standing in mud up to my chin."

"Last spring!" She was stunned. All those months when she thought over the summer that he was settling into a more tranquil middle age with her. Nothing she could give him had anything to do with that vision in his head. She did not belong in it. She could not even relate to those desires, for they were as alien to her as if he wanted to become a goldfish or a kangaroo. "Nick, what are you doing here tonight? What do you want?"

"For shit's sake, Leila, we were married for twenty-odd years. . . ."

She was struck that he probably did not know the exact number. "Twenty-four years, six months, nine days." She shook her head. "We'll never be able to communicate about our marriage. It just looked too different—from the bottom and from the top."

"You've been so damned sanctimonious for years, as if I'm something to be endured. Sheryl loves me. She loves me passionately."

Leila stood up and fetched his coat. "That's enough, Nick. We'll see each other in the presence of lawyers, and we will not talk about love and passion and your justifications for fucking very young women. Good night."

"You're a ball buster, Leila. We could have stayed together if you'd been more forgiving and more giving."

"I've given at home and the office too. I'm all given out. You're getting what you deserve. Enjoy."

"I intend to." He slammed the door.

"So do I," she said to the door. "If I still know how. At least I know how to enjoy quiet." She would not see him again. It was too painful. It left her with the feeling of having dined on broken glass.

CHAPTER 39

BECKY

Becky wished day and night she had money to give Mama. Mama had been taken to the hospital with chest pains that turned out to be her heart. She looked ten years older and her skin was blotchy. Becky was scared for her. If only Terry would get a job, any damned job, she could slip a little money to her mother. Mama wasn't supposed to eat fat, but who could eat a fancy yuppie diet with a house full of grown-ups and children to feed? Fried dough was one of the easiest things to fill the kids up in the mornings.

Tommy had his own wife and little one to support. Tommy knew he had to bring in more money than scalloping could. "I'm gonna do more work for The Guys," he told her quietly. He had been growing a mustache, very black, and he liked to rub it. It was large and glossy on his face, like the bow on a package.

"You don't want to do that! You know what Papa always says."

"Look where Papa is. You don't do well doing good. Somebody's got to sell their ass around here, right? Joey's dead. Somebody's got to keep the family above water, and I don't see no line forming."

"I wish I could help, Tommy. I wish I could help."

"You do what you can, Becca, I know. That paperweight you married, if he'd get up off his ass, then your life would be a lot easier."

A year ago, six months ago, she would have leapt out of her seat to defend her man. Now she just shrugged. "I don't know what to do with him. I got no assets, Tommy. He and his parents have tied up everything."

"You pay the fucking rent."

"But his parents co-signed on the condo. It isn't rent, it's maintenance and fees."

"I don't care if they call it tips, you pay it every month. He's one of those packages you buy something in like deodorant and it looks like you got a quart there, but by the time you open all the plastic and paper, inside is an itsy-bitsy little bottle that's not worth piss."

She laughed, she couldn't help it. "I made a mistake. I thought he was so special. Now if I divorce him, I'm out all the money I put in. Tommy, I hope Mattie knows what a good man she has."

He grinned. "She knows. She waited for me long enough, didn't she? Now you don't say a word about this to Terry."

"Why would I? We never say a word except to fight."

It seemed to her that for two years, she had spent half her time brooding about how to please Terry, how to attract, how to placate him. Now she seldom thought of him unless he was in front of her or he had left some mess to clean up. No, she thought about Sam. He was just a kid, she knew that, but he really revved her up.

She waited the next night they put on the play to see what would happen. Was he scared now? Would he dare try to approach her again? She neither moved toward him nor away from him. If he comes after me tonight, then I'll know it's real. The play was half over and they were both standing around backstage. She went off to the bathroom in the basement. When she came out, he was waiting. "Please!" he said. "Please!" His voice was thick and urgent.

The basement was damp and cold. He seized her arm and dragged her into a room they used to build sets. He shut the door and began to kiss her immediately, as if he had been thinking of absolutely nothing else. He held her tight against him as if he could pull her into his body through the clothes. He was strong for his size. They kissed and kissed, almost violently. She was sure he was a virgin. That excited her. She wanted to. But not here and now. She pushed him away. "We have to go upstairs. We'll miss our cues and that will be the end of this."

He heard her and let go. They went upstairs, tidying themselves frantically. She was astonished to notice that it was only the next scene. They had been downstairs no more than nine or ten minutes.

It made her feel hot just the way Sam looked at her. She did not wonder what she should do. She knew. But she wanted to make him wait. She would make him want her until he could not endure it. This fierce desire was the strongest thing she had ever touched in her life. It was like sticking her fingers into a socket of electric desire. The hairs of her head stood.

They would not meet again until Friday when the play resumed. Two more weekends. Then they would begin to rehearse another play. She would play any role. She would build sets, sew costumes, get down and wipe the floor.

That night Terry was not home when she got back. He must be out with Lyle or Chris. Still, the next morning while he was in the shower, she went through his clothing. His shirt and his jacket both had a scent. Not aftershave. Perfume. Sylvie's aunt Marie wore that. Cerissa, that was it. Well, whoever had left that scent on his shirt was not Aunt Marie, and it surely wasn't Chris or Lyle. He might have been dancing with somebody. He might have hugged somebody's girlfriend—but his kind were not huggers. At most they proffered a cheek for a peck. She helped herself to a five and two singles and some quarters. Almost every day she taxed his pockets. She felt a sharp searing contempt that he never knew how much money he had. In the midst of their difficulties, he never bothered counting his money. His parents gave him money and he shoved it in his pocket. There was plenty more where that came from.

She was going to watch Terry carefully. If he had a girl, she was in real trouble. But she also took it as a sign she could proceed with her heart's desire, or maybe it wasn't her heart. She had never before experienced pure lust, and this was pure enough, simple as sugar, burning as the moonshine the locals sometimes cooked in their garages. She had always wanted other things from men, a marriage, a home, an education, nice things. Sam couldn't give her a thing besides sex and adulation.

Friday she told Helen she was going to have to take her own car to the play, as she had a couple of stops to make on the way. She did not go downstairs with Sam. Instead she muttered to him, "Tell Dick Berg your mother is picking you up. I'll drive you home."

Afterward, Becky had thought she might have to make an excuse to hang around till everyone had left, but Dick Berg was involved in being fussed over by ex-students who had come to the play. Becky simply got in her car and waited till Sam joined her. She drove off at once, before he could touch her. She drove him almost back to his house, making polite conversation. He seemed very nervous. She enjoyed that. She loved the way his emotions showed in his body, like Helen's dog Florrie. He quivered with his feelings. It was marvelously exciting; she felt in total control. She did not pause in her driving until she judged they must be near his house. They were on a dark road. She pulled over to the side and turned out her lights. Then she turned to face him. "Do you want to kiss me?" she asked unnecessarily.

What he lacked in finesse, he made up in enthusiasm. He was a fast learner too. His tongue-kissing had already improved. It was great to be kissing and not have to worry about anyone walking in on them or about missing a cue. She dug her hand into his curly hair, like the pelt of a fine animal, ran her hands across his back. Compactly built. Strong. He felt much solider than Terry, denser. It would be fun to take his clothes off, but she wasn't about to do that in the car. They would go one step at a time, with him never being sure she would do it or not. She smiled against his shoulder.

This desire was like the strong, strong black coffee Mama made for Papa. She had it as a child diluted with milk and thick with sugar. She remembered the first time she had had it the way her father took it early in the morning. It had snapped her head back, scalding and making her heart beat fast at once. Yes, she had thought, this is real. This is what it is really like. Taking hold of Sam was that way.

She put his hand on the top button of her blouse. Unbuttoning, he was less clumsy than Terry, a lot more eager. He touched her briefly through the lace of the bra, then reached behind her and unhooked it. He was quick with his hands. She smiled, catching her breath. Would he be disappointed she was not larger? He did not seem so. She did not think he was about to make comparisons. They had the windows down. The night was mild and something smelled faintly sweet. The little leaves rustled seductively, like taffeta.

She was beginning to liquefy, so after a few minutes, she drew back and buttoned her blouse. It was time for words. "You know I'm married. You saw my husband, Terry."

"I love you!" Sam said fiercely, trying to pull her back to him.

"I think I love you," she said, wondering what it really meant. She had thought she loved two men, and she had grown to hate both of them. "But if my husband finds out how I feel, he'll really make a lot of trouble, I mean it." She chose her words carefully. She did not want to scare him off, but neither did she want him to think this was going to be easy.

"Would he hurt you?"

She nodded. "We have to keep him from finding out."

"Why can't you leave him?"

She wasn't about to give him a lecture on economics, not yet. "He'd never let me go. Not willingly. I have to take you home now."

"Tomorrow? Can we do this tomorrow?"

"I'll try." She liked the idea of keeping him in suspense. But nothing would have prevented her. She asked him about his schedule. She wanted to know where he was after school. His sister had married and left home. His mother had a studio where she threw pots and taught classes. She came home around six Tuesdays through Saturdays. His father was dead, his mother had a boyfriend.

Becky decided to have sex with him. She wanted to more than anything, but she wasn't about to let him know that yet. But where? She wasn't ready to fuck him in the car. Kissing and pawing each other were fine for the car, but she wanted a real seduction scene. She wanted to take his clothes off slowly and look at him and have him really look at her. She had some nice underwear that Terry didn't notice any longer, a reserve of sexy lingerie from her days at Lady Grace. A couple of times, Terry had brought home a porn movie along with the usual action films they rented. But they had never done the things she had seen in those films. Basically Terry watched them till they both got hot and then he just climbed on top of her, as usual.

She was convinced that Sam would do anything she asked him to. She felt immensely powerful. She felt as if she had grown huge and almost menacing as she drove too fast home, to make up for the time with Sam.

Mid-afternoon Saturday while Terry was at his parents, she called Sam at home. She hoped he would be there, because he had told her he used the weekends to catch up on homework. Still she felt cramped with anxiety until she heard his voice.

"Are you home alone?" she asked him.

"Yes. Is *he* with you?"

"He's at his parents. He's always there. Never mind him. Where are you?"

"I'm in my bedroom."

"I'm lying on my bed. I have on a black teddy with tiny straps and you can see through the bosom. That's all I have on."

"I wish I could see you."

"Close your eyes. I'm lying on a blue bedspread. Now I'm sliding the straps of my teddy down. I'm circling my breast with my fingers, very lightly."

He moaned and she smiled. "Now I'm squeezing my breast hard. Can you feel it? Harder. Now light again. Now my hand is moving down my belly. Now I touch the hairs. My hand just grazes them. My hand is moving over my mons and squeezes it. You know where that is?"

"I want to touch you. I want to touch you everyplace."

"Now I'm sliding my hand between my legs." No use getting too technical. He wasn't acquainted with the scenery. He'd learn. "I'm touching myself. I'm thinking of you and touching myself."

"Becky, Becky, let me do it. Let me do it to you."

"Maybe. Maybe not. I don't know. Would you tell anyone if I let you touch me?"

"I'd never tell a soul. Not my best friend. I swear it."

Suddenly she heard Terry's key. "Husband," she said and hung up, grabbing her clothes and running for the bathroom. She dropped the teddy into the hamper and pulled on her jeans. She felt uncomfortable in her pants. She had intended to make herself come, but not until she had Sam really, really worked up. She washed her hands and burst out.

"How're you doing?" she asked heartily. "How are the folks?"

"Chris wants me to go golfing with him next weekend in Waterville. A guy where he works has a time-share condo we can have next weekend for . . . next to nothing." He glared at her, expecting her to scream about wasting money when he was out of work. "With two other guys. Chris says one of them might have a job for me. Even if it rains all weekend, I can work on him."

She didn't believe that for one moment, but she did not care. Pro forma she asked, not to seem too eager, "It's not too expensive, is it? Maybe you could meet this guy some other way?"

"How? I'd never run into him. This way I'll be with him all weekend, and I can really impress him. I'd ask you to go, but it's guys, and you don't play golf."

"You were going to teach me. But I can't go. The play. That's the last weekend."

"You really like this play-acting?" He asked that with less sarcasm than he had shown in weeks.

"It gives me confidence, and it gives me experience so maybe I can finally get my boss to give me a chance on camera."

"Sounds great," he said with obvious insincerity.

She thought, he wants to go away, maybe with whoever wears Cerissa, and I want to get Sam into bed. A perfect weekend for both of us. I just have to get his schedule straight in my head. "I'm so glad you haven't given up, and you're trying to make new contacts. Would you like to go out for Mexican tonight before the play? I don't have to be there until a quarter of eight."

"Italian," he said. "Then I'll take in a movie with Chris and his new girlfriend."

"Oh, what's her name?"

There was a long silence. She could imagine him trying to decide whether to give her the name of the woman in question, who obviously was the Cerissa Sweetie. "Heather."

"That's such a pretty name," Becky said. "Heather who?"

"I didn't catch her last name."

He wasn't quite that stupid, to give her his girlfriend's whole name. He would dump her for this girl with his parents' help, if she wasn't careful. "I'll use the time next weekend to give the house a good cleaning, catch up on ironing. You know how I hate to iron!" She really was a good wife, as Helen was always telling her. She would make the condo perfect. She would also get Sam up here and into the bedroom. She felt her legs soften and begin to sag when she thought of him lying there obediently with a giant erection. Maybe they could work out a way for him to spend the whole night.

"I really appreciate your being good about this. It's important to me. This guy could be really useful." Terry put his hands tentatively on her shoulders. She could feel him begin to think about sex. She was agreeable. She was still turned on from the phone call. It was amusing to think of carrying that energy to Terry, who had seldom excited her in the last six months. She did not feel it was her he was having sex with, just a convenience.

She smiled seductively. "I want what's best for you, Terry, you know."

They beamed at each other and kissed in a tight embrace, for once totally in harmony and both, she was fully aware, lying their heads off.

CHAPTER 40

LEILA

Leila thought that David and she could have a good vacation together without invoking Christmas. She discovered that David was used to Christmas and felt deprived—or used that as a way of protesting the upheaval in their lives. Finally they went out on December 24 and bought a small tree. However, she had given the old ornaments to Nick. Last Wednesday, while she was at school, she had told Mrs. Burke to let him in. His study was stripped. His dresser stood empty. When she arrived home, his closet had contained only discarded clothes she packed up for Goodwill.

She had hoped that David's presence would cheer her, but he closeted himself in Nick's former study for long, long conversations with Ikuko. He then rushed out to see old friends home from college. Christmas, he announced, he was spending with Nick and Sheryl. "I can hardly refuse to visit my father, and he is marrying her. I want to see their scene, frankly, and there isn't going to be any Christmas here, is there?"

She felt sorry for herself. She called Jane, who invited her over. However, she had not backed off from a holiday meaningless to her, disappointing David, in order to partake with Jane and Emily. She thanked Jane profusely but declined. Then she sat stroking Vronsky, wondering what to do with herself.

The hole in her life from Melanie's death had had a strong influence on ending her marriage. She was needy, and she was not supposed to be. She was not the partner allowed to make scenes and demands. She had broken the silent contract of their marriage. Perhaps being the steady nurturer had depended ultimately on her being nurtured too, and without Melanie, she had fierce needs and sudden loneliness. She was still thinking as if she were married.

She called Zak. She gave him little time to question her, but told him what had happened and asked him if she could leave to join him right away.

"Come ahead. I've just been given half a bushel of oysters by my neighbor, after I let him chop down a young fir on my land. Do you eat traif?"

"Of course. Why live in Boston if you don't eat seafood? I'll bring a bottle of white wine."

She remembered that there was still the little wine cellar under the stairs, unless Nick had raided it. She had not been using it heavily. Actually, she discovered, he had taken over half the bottles, but she found a nice chardonnay and wedged it in beside the spare tire in the trunk, where it should chill on the way.

The weather had turned. Instead of a white Christmas, it was a grey and runny one. It had rained the night before and the temperature was sitting around forty. Everywhere snowbanks wept and puddles lined the clogged gutters. It was a sloppy mild day.

When she crossed the Sagamore Bridge, the weather cleared. Suddenly the ground was bare, although the Cape had more snow than Boston the week before. Battered grass emerged from the slush. The sky glinted a hard dark blue, busy with gulls rushing to some rendezvous or dinner. She almost turned around, wondering what in hell she was doing, but the idea of going back to the house where she felt utterly deserted would be a defeat, and what would she say to Zak? I changed my mind. I decided embarking on an affair would not be a great way to spend a day in which I was feeling sorry for myself, so I am reneging.

Was that what she was doing? She admitted it might well be, although she refused to decide. Still, she had been thinking about him a great deal. There were no other suitors. It was a choice between something and nothing; but solitude was a reasonable choice. After all, she had not exactly been sitting around learning to knit and purl during the past months. Her life was full, even if her bed wasn't. She was gambling, she who preferred security, the known, who had grown up despising people who took wild chances and depended on wild cards. Yet she was contemplating something way out of line.

Then there was sexual curiosity. She had been with only two boys before Nick and never anyone since she had met him. Her entire sex life consisted of an eighteen-year-old, a nineteen-year-old and Nick. She did not want Nick to be the last man she had ever been to bed with, but she did not want to pick someone up in the age of AIDS. The likeliest possibility was at the next big conference she attended, but she had always considered conference liaisons smarmy. Besides, she was always busy networking with other women. She really should not become involved with anyone in the case, but he was not a central actor. And she was not contemplating restructuring her life. A sort of friendship with sex, was that possible? A decoration rather than a core.

It was the kind of aberrant choice, a leap into another way of loving, that Phyllis had chosen. Zak was younger than Leila; he might well want a younger woman and another family next year or the next. It was unprofessional to become involved with him. It was also an opening, a lively possibility.

The day looked inviting here, unlike Cambridge. She had crawled from under a soggy wet wool carpet into bright air. Even if all she did was go for a walk, it would be worth it. From Shoot Flying Hill on Route 6, she could see dark water shining, the sea vibrating ionic possibilities unknown to life in the warrens of the city—even cozy, tree-lined warrens like her neighborhood. Sexual possibilities vibrated like ions under that brilliant sky.

She arrived at his little wandering side road in good time. Without snow, the woods looked more like October than late December, except for the angle of the sun, low and ruddy through bare branches of the oaks. He was outside, wearing a buffalo plaid jacket and swinging a maul, splitting logs. She called to him, and he strolled toward her, grinning. "Gorgeous day."

He took her on a walk through the pitch pines and scrub oaks toward the ocean. The path shone white even in the ruddy light. The trees grew shorter and more contorted. She thought of old Hasidim dancing. Finally they crossed a narrow asphalt road, followed it perhaps a hundred yards and then took a path through barberry and poverty grass over a dune, along a hollow and up and over to the ocean. She would never grow used to seeing it suddenly, much higher than she ever expected. It had eaten away the beach almost to the foot of the clay cliffs. "At high tide this time of year, there's no beach left."

A path was worn into the clay until it gave way to sand and they scrambled down. The clay gouged by winter storms looked like elephant hide.

It was chilly on the beach. She buttoned her coat to the neck and stuffed her hands in her pockets. The air electrified her. Her head tingled from the inside. Side by side, they strolled along with waves the color of iron filings lunging and crashing beside them while puffs of foam landed at their feet. "It's strange, being back here after so long. Of course I left for college, only back summers. But everybody I grew up with, they're all here," he said.

"Do they think it's funny that you've returned? Are you a success or a failure to them?"

"They don't think in those terms. And they don't find it odd at all that I should be back. It's as if I finally came to my senses. Maybe I have. Nobody ever gave me oysters in L.A. In fact, I've been given lobsters and I can get all the fish I can cook. Basically, I'm the vet, I'm useful, I fill a slot."

"I grew up in Strawberry Mansion, in Philadelphia. I can't imagine moving back. My mother left there as soon as she could afford to."

"I know that neighborhood. It's Black now—"

"It was then, too. How come you know where I lived?"

"I studied to be a vet in Philadelphia. I liked the city, actually. I liked going to school there." They arrived back at his house chilled. He made cocoa.

"I haven't had this since David was little."

"It does taste like childhood, doesn't it? The better part of childhood. The worst part tastes like a handful of frozen mud.".

The sun was dipping toward the little pond at three o'clock. She helped him bring in wood. It was getting cold fast, the air solidifying and heavier. Something looked at them from across the pond and then was gone, something large and grey about the size of a large German shepherd. "What was that?"

"Coyote." They finished bringing the wood in.

"Is that the one you had in the animal hospital?"

"Still mending. We have coyotes every place on the Cape. They're bold. Sometimes they come right up to the house in the daytime."

"So at night you hear them howling?"

"We have silent coyotes, as far as I can figure out. I've heard foxes bark, but I've never heard the coyotes make a sound. They're like spirit dogs. You see them and then they're gone. I found a fox with its throat torn out by one two days ago. Made me feel bad." He was working on the fire.

If she had not seen the animal, she wondered if she would have believed him. She was beginning to understand that Zak tended to be accurate. She suspected that unlike Nick, he might never invent or exaggerate a story to make dinner-party conversation. "Do you ever see deer?"

"Often at dawn. But I never tell any of my old buddies, because they all hunt. They're always asking me if I've seen any deer, and I always lament how they've disappeared since I was a kid."

She rubbed her hands to bring the warmth back. "I have the feeling when you talk about your childhood that, for years, you never thought about it." She curled on the couch with a blanket wrapped around her. "Maybe you had a rap about growing up on the Cape, friend of the fisherfolk, but you didn't think about it."

He was feeding logs into the fire. Finally he shut the glass doors. "It's a great place to grow up, but you're right, I put it out of my mind. I was the glamorous vet to the stars—anyhow, to people on the fringes of media. I was making twice what I make here and spending three times as much." He rose gracefully and slid his arm around her. "Upstairs, the heat is on. It's warm in my room. I could warm you up."

She had not expected his pitch to come so early. She had expected plenty of time after supper to decide, and David to serve as a perfect excuse for returning home, if she chose. But he was shrewd. He was not going to let her pretend that the question of whether to get involved was not hanging over them all of the time like a big question mark over the head of a character in the Sunday comics. She had driven a hundred miles and two hours to be with him. There was no excuse today about Sam or Becky or Cathy. She had simply come to see him.

For answer she gave him her hand and stood. "We'll try it," she said, her voice emerging so softly she was not sure he could hear her.

He did, for he smiled suddenly, a warm surprised smile that deeply creased his cheeks. "Well, don't say it as you might agree to try sky diving. I'm sure we can make it moderately pleasant! And afterward, you get to eat oysters."

"Aren't we supposed to eat them first?"

"First things first." Hand in hand they climbed the stairway. It was warmer on the second floor, as he had promised. She could not entirely lose a guilty feeling. Twenty-five years had passed since she had intimate contact with a man other than Nick. She could remember her two previous lovers, but not with any vividness. They had simply vacated her mind and her imagination when Nick took hold of her.

As they climbed the stairs and then went side by side down the hall, their arms around each other's shoulders and their hips bumping together with a sort of chumminess, she felt huge and awkward. What was she doing? But Nick was with his twenty-five-year-old soon-to-be-wife and mother of his baby-to-be. When Nick thought of Leila, he did not think of sex; he thought of real estate prices and tuition payments to be split. This man looked at her, a large ungainly academic who had never been beautiful and was no longer young, and wanted her.

His bedroom had probably been made from two old rooms, for set into the old flooring was obvious new work making a stripe down the center. Two dormer windows opened on the little pond, where a tall gaunt bird was stalking on the far side among the reeds, silhouetted against the tamped-down sunset, turning his head warily about, then stilting on. "Is that a heron?"

"The great blue heron. It's always a blessing. They have such a holy prehistoric look. I don't even try to sneak up on him."

The room was red and blue, two predominantly terra-cotta Hopi rugs on the floor, plain dark blue draperies, a red-and-blue velvet patchwork spread, a heap of pillows. He obviously read in bed, for the back was a bookcase jammed too full. The bed was king-sized with the headboard-bookcase and the low carved foot of beautiful light wood.

"Leila, are you frightened that I won't like you, frightened that you won't like me, or frightened that you will?" He stood near the bed holding her by the shoulders.

"That about covers it."

"You could worry I have AIDS."

"You can see how long I've been away from the meat rack, the whole dating game. That thought hadn't occurred to me yet."

"No, I like nice sane professional women who can talk to me afterward and don't require much saving. Who already know how to do things. I'm tired of running a finishing school. I'm finished. I'm not a high-risk partner. I never cheated on my wife."

"I think that's admirable."

"She didn't." He sighed and pulled her to him. "Enough self-pity. Let's please each other."

His body was entirely different from Nick's. It felt wrong for a moment, as if she were embracing David, because he was more David's size. But David was taller than she was. Zak was almost exactly her height and heft. She had always enjoyed the feeling Nick gave her of being a small woman, but she found she liked too the sense that she and Zak were evenly matched, paired like horses who could pull the same weight and went at the same speed.

Obviously he liked kissing, and even after they had moved to the bed and lain down, all they did for a long intense electric time was kiss. Her breath began to catch in her throat. His hands on her really felt her. Sex for a long time had been fraught with questions and betrayals and fears. This felt simpler. This reminded her of how it used to be for her, long ago, before David was born and before Nick took up with other women. Then sex had been a kind of conversation of the bodies, a luminous exchange of pleasure in which she had felt equal, cherished, confident, even radiant. Long ago. No matter what came of this, if anything, to experience desire again, to be simply with another body moving against her was a small but precious miracle.

Pausing to get undressed felt awkward. She turned away from him, embarrassed at baring her body. She did not look like the nudes in the movies, bone thin and with skin taut as a film of plastic pulled over a stick. She was a strong sturdy woman who walked a lot and ate reasonably. Her skin was good, but she bulged there and dipped here. Hers was a well-used body that did not conceal its history. She wished he had waited until after supper, until full dark.

She was still standing with her back to him, fussing with her clothes on a chair when he came up behind her and turned her to face him. "Leila, what's wrong? Come to me." He held her close, resting his cheek against hers. Her breath hissed as she felt skin on skin. She felt his erection against her and let out her breath slowly, almost dizzy. How had she used to breathe and make love at the same time? "You turned shy on me. Come on, let's get into bed before we freeze."

Gladly she slipped under the quilt and held tight to his body. He was taut and hard-muscled. It was not that he felt youthful. He had a belly and his chest was coarse with curly hair, but his chest, his arms, his upper back were firmed by all the wood chopping, and his legs were lean from walking. She liked touching him. She liked the way the skin of his back felt to her exploring hands. She liked the way his body fit around hers.

When he first touched her between the legs, she felt a twinge of pain, almost a burning like an infection. It was as if the excitement were too keen, too raw. But the pain passed and the excitement grew.

She felt as if each of them had in mind a scenario designed to show off their skills, but that they had scarcely begun moving toward tonguing each other when impatience or massive desire took them both over. She simply pushed him into herself and they started fucking. Within a minute he slowed, probably to keep control, and they continued and continued. Her body remembered old feelings, old tricks. She felt a rising quickening in herself, as if her body enlarged to fill the entire bed, the room, the universe. Unbelievably, because she had never come the first time in bed with any of her previous three lovers (with the first, she had never come at all), she found herself feeling the lava rush of pleasure, intense, with a twinge of pain again as if her body had half forgotten how to be pleased. She did not come strongly, but she was astonished that she was sure enough of him, relaxed enough, to come at all. Then he moved up in her, drew her legs around his hips and began driving for his own climax. Her thighs ached with stretching, for she had not had sex often enough in the past six months or longer to keep the muscles limber.

They lay side by side in contented silence as various animals jumped up to settle around them. A tail whopped on the coverlet. A cat purred near her ear. She wakened with a start in a dark room. The bedside clock read four-thirty. For a moment she did not know if that was A.M. or P.M., but then she realized that she had only dozed for fifteen minutes.

"Ah, you're awake," he said, reaching out a lazy hand to pat her shoulder. "This is one time I don't think it's an insult to put someone to sleep. You want to share a fast shower? Then I'll start supper."

He did not want her to help, but settled her in the living room with the Kronos Quartet on his CD playing sort of African music. She declined wine and had coffee. She felt cosseted, curled up in a rocking chair with the music and a book about seabirds anchoring her. The experiment seemed to have been successful. She did not feel guilty. She felt smug and clever, as if she had worked out some unanticipated way of enjoying herself. Really, she was thinking like the eighteen-year-old she had been who imagined she and her boyfriend had invented sex, unable to believe her parents had ever enjoyed this act or that all those aging fogies did it too.

After supper she would drive back to the city, not to escape Zak but to be home for David. She was sure Zak would understand. David would be with her only two more days, and then it was off to Ikuko. Oddly enough, she did not mind nearly as much right now. She was suddenly far more tranquil about almost everything in her life.

CHAPTER 41

MARY

With so many of her people gone, Mary had little work. However, she had places to stay. She would be owed money from dog walking and pet feeding when her clients returned. She figured that going in and out of the house much was asking for trouble. She was content to lie low and watch TV. She even made a pot of soup, something she hardly ever got to do. She drank hot tea all day long. She took two long warm baths a day, soaking her weary achy body until it shone. She tried a little of each bubble bath, gel and oil. Damask rose was her favorite. She washed her hair, laundered her clothes, polished her shoes and cleaned her galoshes. In damp cold weather, everything got wet and never dried out, till she smelled like a garage floor.

At times she let herself pretend she lived in the Anzio house. They had gone to Pittsburgh, where his mother lived. The day after Christmas, they were due back, but the Baers were leaving. She would clean up carefully early tomorrow morning and decamp. The malls would be mobbed, and she could hang out.

Today, Christmas, she must see Beverly. She had bought Beverly wool pants at Goodwill. The lining was torn, but Mary had spent the evening mending it. She had fixed the pockets too, so they would hold a lot. The pants were dark red and really warm. She would also bring Beverly a couple of chocolates from a party at the Millers'. She had discreetly hidden treats as she was cleaning up, including most of a plate of only slightly stale tiny sandwiches—canapés such as she had put out in her days as a Bethesda hostess. That had been her supper, although the pâté had given her indigestion. Her stomach must be more delicate these days. When she was younger, she could eat anything, no matter how fiery or spicy, and not even belch. Jim used to say, Mary has an asbestos tummy.

Catering must be a nice business. All that food to snack on. Marry a professional man, they told her when she was growing up; they should have said, be a caterer, buy a property and pay it off fast. Never mind the rest. Get a job around food and a roof over your head that belongs to you and you alone. Now that was advice no romantic young girl would ever heed.

The nurse's station was perfunctorily decorated, a plate of Christmas cookies set out on the counter. Beverly sat up in the half-empty room. Two of the patients had been released in time for the holiday. None of the original women with whom Beverly had shared the ward were still there. The others had been discharged; different women had come in their place and left again. Beverly's injuries had been serious, her condition bad, but they were also keeping her rather than discharge her to the street. Someone had taken an interest. A program had been found to cover her, but she was going to have to leave soon.

Beverly was fiddling with her cropped grey hair, growing back where they had shaved her head. "They're going to discharge her to Pine Street."

Mary nodded. She had worked on Mrs. Landsman to find a place for Beverly. "You can't go on the streets the way you are. Better to stay in a shelter till the weather warms up. As long as they let you stay."

"She always managed. She's tough. But she hates the noise and the prying. She remembers Pine Street in the old days. They took your stuff away at night. It's all the time waiting in line. They took your soul away."

"I didn't like it either," Mary said. "But if I was injured, I'd do it till I was strong again. They say it's nicer now."

Beverly loved the pants. Why could she do the right thing for her friend, but never for her daughter or her grandchildren? That night, lying on the Anzios' couch, she kept thinking about Beverly leaving the hospital. It was one of the worst days of her life when she had to leave her little apartment. Not that it was so wonderful—she had been ashamed of it, not understanding how lucky she was to have a so-called studio apartment, no matter how noisy and dilapidated and scurrying with mice that fouled her food. B.U. had bought the building to turn into student housing.

Her apartment and her job vanished together. She worked in a stationer's shop in the same block, and the renovation threw the store out a couple of months before she was evicted. Teodoro's Stationers could not find rent low enough so the marginal business could thrive. Mr. Teodoro was soon working at Stop & Shop, and she was running through her money in bottom-drawer motels.

Before she had been evicted, it had become evident she could afford nothing that existed, and the wait for public housing was forever and a day. Finally they had thrown her few things on the sidewalk in a pitiful pile she had had to walk away from, carrying her two suitcases and her raincoat and winter coat, her quilt. She was too stunned, too numb to cry. She kept looking back at her table, her chair, her bed, her pots and dishes. What would become of her?

There had always been neighborhoods of cheap rooming houses when she was growing up. When had they disappeared? Where did poor people live now? Everything she could find was beyond her income. She wrote to Cindy and she wrote to Jaime. Cindy sent her a letter full of advice on budgeting her income, a check for two hundred dollars and a long complaint about the cost of raising children in the Washington area. Two of her kids were in private schools. She simply did not have any discretionary income. What had happened to the settlement Daddy had given her?

Given me, Mary thought. I earned every penny, and he never gave me a cent more than the nasty judge made him part with. Where did it go? To relocate here. To pay bills. To buy medical insurance, now lapsed because she could not make the payments. To buy a winter coat. To put down as a deposit on phone, electricity, rent. To fix her car, while she had been able to keep it running.

Jaime put a twenty in an envelope and said he would send money whenever he could. The next month he sent another twenty. Nothing the next month. Then again. Once in a while he sent a twenty, always folded up neatly in a card with a joke on it. She forgave his failure to help her. Over the years he had probably given her more in his impulsive and disjointed way than Cindy with her lists and her excuses. And he had far less money to start with. Cindy made some money from her silly boutique, and her husband minted it.

Every day for the next two months, Mary looked for a job, but jobs were like ex-husbands: they wanted someone young and slender. She had had friends in the building, but they were scattered. Several had gone back where they came from, moving in with relatives in Tennessee or Kansas. Three women had moved together into a winter rental on Revere Beach, where they let her use their phone. She got into the Y for three weeks, then her money ran out. She could not find a job, and soon she was down to her last ten dollars. She was frankly terrified.

She had sold off her microwave, her jewelry, her good watch, her clock radio and most of her wardrobe. She had to winnow the artifacts of her life, the photos, the letters, the mementos. She threw away her old report cards and honors and diplomas. She tossed her wedding and divorce papers. Most of the mementos of her children she sent to Cindy and Jaime, keeping only a couple of photos. To Jaime she sent most of the photos of her parents, her grandparents, baby pictures, the record of her life. The letters she simply tore up.

She ended up with what would fit on her back, into a small suitcase and into a large fabric carry-all she had used to take to the beach all her kids' paraphernalia. On April 7 she walked out of the Y she had been calling home and into the city, with no idea what was going to become of her.

She was on the streets and terrified. She had no idea what to do with herself, where to go, how to manage. In six months she had gone from being a woman with a job and a little apartment and all the normal wardrobe and items—clock radio, electric toothbrush, microwave—that she had taken for granted as props of any normal life, to being a woman with a small suitcase she lugged about with her and a large fabric carry-all. She did not know where to go to the bathroom. During the daytime hours, she used the public library bathroom or the bathrooms in the department stores.

The first night she tried to sleep in a doorway, the suitcase was stolen. That simplified everything. It was the other street people who told her what to do. They thought she was funny, trying to sleep on the street in a peach-colored, satin down quilt she still had from her old life, carrying around a little pillow for her head.

The first days on the street, she kept bursting into tears. She could not believe this was happening. She was becoming dirty. She smelled bad. Her clothes were beginning to fray, stiff with dirt and wrinkled from being slept in. She was Mary Ferguson Burke. She had gone to college. She had raised two children. She had entertained the assistant undersecretary of commerce. She had belonged to a country club. She had had an all-electric kitchen. She had been photographed with Cindy, both astride on bays, for an article in a local paper on summer activities. She had owned forty pairs of shoes and eight coats and a dozen cocktail dresses. Now she was sleeping in a cardboard box in an alley, wearing filthy rags and smelling like garbage.

People would look at her and look away, they would stare through her. They would give her glances of disgust. She was a pile of dog shit on the pavement. She should be scraped off and put in a Dumpster. A younger Black woman named Samantha took her in tow. She had been hit by a car in an alley and walked stiff-legged, favoring her right side. She had lost half her teeth, but she still had a smile that made Mary feel warmed. Mary learned to stay away from her when she had not had a drink yet and again when she had too much, but in between, Samantha was kind and wanted to help. She decided Mary should try shelters and took her to the women's side of the Pine Street Inn. Samantha preferred life on the streets because she was crazy in love with an alkie they called Sly. She took Mary to Morgan Memorial, showed her the shelters, soup kitchens and where to get off the streets to keep warm, where to get water, how to pee in alleys without being seen. "Remember, honey, everything you got to do is wrong. It's against the law to sleep, to wash yourself, to pee, to take a shit. Everything you got to do, you can't do it if the law see you. Now, I can't pass no more. They know me. But you, you can still walk through a crowd, but you can't go along shuffling. You got to pick up your head and look like one of them tight white women. Then you can pass and hang out without them hassling you all the time. They like to beat on us. I can't get by no more, but you can. You just got to try."

Samantha, dead of hypothermia three Januaries before. She had seen it on the evening news while camping in one of her clients' houses. Samantha was the first Black friend she had ever had. Without her, she would not have made it.

Even now the smells overwhelmed her: sweat, vomit, urine, dust, disinfectant, the smells from the big kitchen. Always twenty people were coughing every moment. Stand in line to get in the door. Stand in the ugly lobby waiting to get inside. Get in line for your foam cup, your paper plate, your utensils, your starchy supper. Get in line for your towel. Line up for a shower. Line up to get your bed for the night. Line up if you want a locker, but there's a four-month waiting list. Get in line for your meds if they gave you tranks. Lots of the women were on Thorazine or something equally numbing or destructive. Stand in line to get clothes from the room, get a clean nightie.

The beds were a foot apart and she slept on her purse and wallet. She could hear this one muttering, that one in some kind of withdrawal, the other just crying. She could hear and smell them all and she could guess what she must seem like to others.

She could not let herself be pushed down into the faceless mass of "guests." She was not an alcoholic, she did not use drugs, she had not been abused beyond the ability to function. She began to volunteer. She wanted to distinguish herself in the eyes of the staff from the helpless hopeless women around her. But it was hard. It was hard to remember that she had ever had a real life. At five A.M. they had to be up and by eight, they were out on the street again to pass the day until late afternoon.

She had felt like a baggy body for which there was no room but this large storage bin. Many women were sick. Some were severely malnourished. Many had ulcerating sores on their legs or feet, sores that stank. It was not avoidable when a woman walked all day long on pavement in ill-fitting shoes and worse-fitting socks with holes in them.

There was no privacy, no silence, no place she could call her own. Every night that she managed to get into the shelter, never certain because beds for women were limited, she never knew where she would sleep. Nothing belonged to her. No space was her own. She was called a "guest" but she was on sufferance. Act up and you were excluded. The staff had changing blacklists of women who were no longer allowed inside. Life and death in the winter and sometimes in warmer weather. Life on the streets killed you slow, but sometimes people or the weather saw that it happened a lot faster.

She volunteered, she made herself useful, and the staff liked that. Soon she no longer smelled. She showered, she washed her hair. She began trying to get work again, but putting down the address of the shelter was iffy. Still, it was better than no address. She had been a secretary, she had sold in stores, she had been a cashier. She could find nothing. She looked far older than she had six months before. Her hair was scraggly and iron grey with an odd stain that had got into it one night when she slept on a grate.

She took pains with her appearance, but it was difficult. There were only three little mirrors over the three wash basins for the whole facility. The light was dim. Still she put on makeup Saturday and went to see her old friends in Revere Beach. They were scared too. They had to be out of their rental by the end of May, and they had no idea where they were going. They asked her where she was living, and she said, with a friend. I just sleep on her couch—it's temporary. They apologized and said they couldn't offer her their couch as Gigi was sleeping on it. But Gigi cut her hair and gave her a home perm. It felt wonderful to be with people who remembered her, who did not know she was no longer a person but a statistic, one of the despised who were thrust from the table and the room.

The shelter was a holding area to keep the women alive one more night. When she finally got a job with a cleaning service, she decided that she was rejoining the ranks of the living, however much stealth and subterfuge that took. She would hide like a mouse in the walls of the middle class. And she had.

CHAPTER 42

BECKY

On Saturday morning, Becky wished Terry a wonderful weekend, kissed him good-bye, telling him she was off to do the laundry. The day before she had switched cars with Sylvie. Becky had confided that she thought Terry might be having an affair, and she wanted to follow him and check it out. She had also borrowed a dark brown wig from Belle, saying it was for a joke at the office. With dark glasses and her wig, she was not afraid of Terry recognizing her. He was not the world's most observant guy. She was half convinced that if she followed him in her own car, he would not notice. Still, she enjoyed taking the precautions. It made her feel as if she were in a TV program about a woman detective, tough, able, efficient, with a gun in her glove compartment. Papa had a shotgun Joey used to take when he hunted rabbits. For years Papa kept an illegal .22 semiautomatic in his boat, but when the Coast Guard started getting excited about fishing boats and drugs and pulling searches, he had brought it home and kept it beside his bed in the end table. She had never used a gun. Maybe she'd ask Tommy to show her how.

She waited in Sylvie's car. She was betting he would turn right toward the Sound. He did. If he was heading for his parents' house, she would turn around. At the second light he turned left, toward his parents, and she shrugged. She would follow a bit farther. Maybe Cerissa/Heather was a figment of Becky's guilty imagination.

Then instead of going straight ahead, he turned off north. This was not the way to his parents. She followed him through two more turns into a development of winding streets with baby trees shivering alongside the curb before largish houses a little close to each other. She pulled over and watched him go another two blocks. Then she drove on, slowly. He was parked in the driveway of a house surrounded by shrubbery that must have been hauled in almost full-grown, for the house, like the others, could be no more than three or four years old. New rose bushes were in bloom along the drive.

She waited in the cul-de-sac. He came out with a tall girl in safari clothes, carrying golf clubs and a bright blue canvas bag. She was giggling and tossing her hair, just as blond as Becky's. Becky lowered her glasses to squint. The girl didn't seem any prettier than her. The house was even bigger than that of his parents, although not as well located, being in a development and not on the water. Still, this girl's family had bucks. Becky was being replaced by a more appropriate model. She was willing to bet, if his parents hadn't actually introduced him to Heather the Safari Queen, then they had certainly colluded in the affair.

Now he was going to his parents. She followed farther back, just making sure. He was taking Heather to his parents' house, probably to pick up Chris. She remembered bitterly when Sylvie and she had watched Ted Topper and found out about his fiancée. Ted and Terry merged in her mind into one man who had let her down. She was always being betrayed by men she trusted. She was always giving her love to men who turned out to be all façade and no heart.

She made a snappy U-turn, giving an old guy the finger, and headed back to the condo. She had just been given a license to screw the daylights out of Sam, but she did not fool herself that she wouldn't have done so anyhow. No, what mattered was the threat to her survival. She was not moving back home. She was not moving back tomorrow or the next day or ever. This was *her* home, not his. He didn't care about it. She loved it passionately. No way he was going to get her out. She'd fight him. She'd show him what it was like to try to drive her down, smash her back where she came from. She'd see him dead first.

She imagined him breaking his neck falling off a rock in the White Mountains. Dying of a head injury from a traffic accident. She imagined him paralyzed in a wheelchair unable to speak or move. She would screw Sam right in front of him. She would show him.

Sam didn't have a car. Just before noon, she called him to make sure his mother was out. She told him to walk to the end of his road and meet her there. That was safer. She was going to have to be very, very careful that nobody saw them together, because all Terry needed to dump her tomorrow was to catch a hint of Sam.

Sam was pacing back and forth looking at his watch and staring all around. As he got in, she drove off at once. "Is *he* gone?" Sam never used Terry's name.

"He's left for a golf weekend with his brother." She held back telling him about Heather. She did not want her value demeaned by infidelity. No, she wanted to depict Terry as the jealous possessive husband who must be defended against, so Sam would be scared of being careless.

"Do you like to play golf?" He was making nervous conversation.

"I've never done it."

"I went once with my friend Gene, we rented clubs, but we were lousy."

They had these inane conversations—what kind of cake do you like? Did you see TV last night?—and all the while he was staring at her breasts. She smiled slightly. He was really cute, her Sam. When she parked, she made him stay in the car and reminded him to lock it. He was to wait ten minutes and then walk up quietly.

She ran upstairs and tore off her jeans and shirt. She was wearing a fancy blue bustier and a blue bikini. Now she put on a matching negligee. This was the outfit she had worn for her wedding. She had not bothered in months. Terry scarcely looked at her. He had taken to fucking lately with the TV on. In fact, they rarely had sex recently. That was one reason she suspected he was getting it somewhere else.

When she opened the door and motioned Sam in, she could see him stare at her and almost flop over like a tenpin. He surged forward and grabbed her against him. She had planned to draw it out, to play games with him for a couple of hours, but he was kissing her so that she could hardly breathe and his hands were closing on her breasts already. The hell with the delay. She'd give him fun and games later. He was pushing her toward the couch.

"No," she said. "Let's go in the bedroom. It's nicer."

"Are we going to do it? Will you?"

She did not answer but only led him by the hand into the bedroom and shut the door. "Take your clothes off," she said. "All of them."

He obeyed her, blushing. He blushed dark red. It was wonderful. He could barely get his shorts off over his erection.

"Your socks too."

He had forgotten about them. Then he stood there looking embarrassed and foolish and gorgeous. "Lie down on the bed," she said.

He obeyed her, staring at her body. She loved the way he obeyed her. It made her feel high, the way people talked about drugs. She peeled the negligee off and stood there in front of him. "Do you like the way I look?"

"You're beautiful! Let me kiss you."

"Look at me. Keep looking." Slowly she reached around and undid the bustier. Then she slowly rolled the bikini down. "Keep still. Don't move."

He obeyed, but he was trembling. His erection stood up almost purple against his skin. Now she was naked and she climbed on the bed and knelt over him. She ran her hands over his chest and his nipples. She touched his flanks and his hips. She ran her hands up his thighs. He was visibly shaking but he obeyed her. She loved that. Finally she closed her hand around his prick and his control broke. He grabbed her, pushed her down on the bed and began to kiss her. She did not struggle. She was ready for him.

"Put your hand between my legs and touch me," she said into his ear. "Don't hurt me. Be gentle."

He touched her carefully. Obviously he was none too sure what he was doing, but he was groping his way. Finally his finger slid into her and he groaned, as if he could have an orgasm with his finger. She could. Very quickly she did. She did not cry out, but let it wash through her. Then she took his prick, spread her legs wide and brought him to her and into her. He gave a short deep cry muffled by her throat and began to drive into her. He came very quickly, as she had expected him to.

"My god, my god," he kept saying.

"You liked that."

He nodded dumbly. "You're so beautiful. This is what I dreamed about, again and again."

"We'll do it again and again, I promise you. If you're good to me."

"I love you, Becky, I love you so much. Can I look at you?"

"You can do anything you want to me, do you understand? As long as you're good to me and you do what I say."

"Anything I want to?"

She knelt over him, looking into his eyes. "Anything." She didn't think he'd come up with exercises that were too inventive, but she had ideas.

"Can I kiss your tits? Can I put them in my mouth?"

They began to explore each other, stroking, caressing, tasting. She seemed to be in a state of permanent desire. Ted Topper had been a far more skillful and experienced lover than Sam, but Sam pleased her. She felt she had never before really given herself over to sex, never really felt desire the way she did this afternoon. She taught him to eat her, and she took him in her mouth. He was pleasant to hold. He was cute, adorable. His skin was smooth and resilient. He was compact and tight-muscled. He wanted to please. He would turn himself inside out to please her.

Around two they got out of bed and sat at the kitchen table eating leftovers and what they could scrounge from the cabinets and the refrigerator. Then they showered together and went back to the ravaged bed. This was the way it had been supposed to be and never had been. Sam looked at her as the most important object in the world. He kept telling her she was beautiful, and he meant it. He made love to her without thinking about anything else. He was not worrying about other things. He was not fantasizing about some model he had seen in the swimsuit issue of *Sports Illustrated* or the last issue of *Penthouse*. He wanted her. He wanted her fiercely, the way a man was supposed to. He was always ready. This was how she had imagined sex with a man to be before she had gone to bed with the first one. It filled her up entirely, the way things ought to, so that she was never, for once, wishing to be somewhere else, to be someone else, to be part of the golden place in the TV where things really happened.

After they had sex again, they were both drowsy. She set the alarm, so that there would be time to eat before she took him to the performance. They fell asleep wrapped in each other's arms.

She awoke before him and gently disentangled herself, raising her body slightly on her bent elbow to look at him. He was hers. No man had been hers before in that absolute way. His mother did not know it, but she had taken him. He was no use at all for the sort of things she had looked to men for in the past. He would be going to college next fall. He did not even have a job. He could not bring her money or security or resources. Ted Topper had the most bountiful lifestyle and the most abundant resources of any of the men she had been with, but he had not been prepared to share with her. She was a rented motel room outside the house of his life. From Terry she had expected much, and she was getting nothing. He wanted to steal from her what she had worked years to create. What had he ever put into this condo besides his parents' money? She had picked out the furniture, she had made the curtains, she had cleaned the walls and decorated. At least Sam wanted more than anything in the world to make love to her. He looked at her with a wild hunger. He wanted her more than he wanted to eat pizza or hang with the guys watching a basketball game. He wanted her more then he wanted to go off golfing with some twit named Heather.

When he woke up, he asked her, "Can I stay over tonight? I told my mom I would probably stay with my friend Gene."

"Won't she check up on you?"

"My mom doesn't do things like that. I could tell right away she was thinking that her boyfriend could sleep over. She doesn't let him stay ever. She thinks it would be bad for my morals." He grinned. "Maybe I don't have any to lose."

"The important thing is loving each other, not your morals. Sometimes I wonder if you really love me. I'm risking a lot for you." She put her hand on his chest, tracing circles among the scant hair.

He seized her shoulders. "You have to believe how much I love you. I can't sleep at night thinking about you. I break into a sweat."

That was sex, but who cared? "You can stay. I think we're safe. But you have to understand, he's dangerous. He has a terrible temper." She almost found herself giggling when she said that. Terry was irritable and sulky but hardly dangerous. Without thinking too much about it, she was setting up Terry as a villain. She needed a way they could blackmail Terry into giving up the condo and just moving out. Scaring him. Forcing him. But how? His parents would still demand their money back.

It turned out that Sam could cook some. She had thawed some chopped meat and he made hamburgers for them, while she put together a salad. It was sweet. Terry and she never seemed to do anything like that. He didn't really want to keep house with her, that was the problem. He had left home reluctantly, married her in a rebellious mood. What he really wanted was just to live at home, be cooked for and taken care of, his clothes mysteriously vanishing from the floor where he tossed them, only to reappear clean and pressed. He liked dating. He liked going out with his brother and his old friends from college and prep school and his new friends from golfing. Being married and having his own life and his own home were just not priorities. He didn't want to grow up. Sam at the stove turning burgers seemed to her far more of an adult than Terry.

"Now at the play," she said sternly, "you are not to be making eyes at me. We are not sneaking into a room to make out. We are coming back here to bed, and you know that, so you'll behave yourself and act as if nothing is going on between us. This is vitally important. You have to listen to me. One of the people in the play lives just under us in this building, Helen."

"The old lady?" He looked at the kitchen floor. "She's right down there?"

"You got it. So we have to be careful. As long as I'm stuck with my husband Terry, we have to be awfully, awfully careful. Do you understand?"

He did his best at the play. She caught his eyes gloating on her at times, but mostly he tried to be good. He was always trying to do what she told him, and she liked that enormously. It was delightful to have him wanting so badly to please her. It was heady, it was stimulating, it was heavenly. She noticed Helen watching them both, but nobody else. They were all involved in their own scenes. She would have a little chat with Helen. Maybe Helen had caught a glimpse of Sam at the condo. If so, Becky would have to invent some cover story. What could he be doing there? Fixing something? Unbelievable. She was helping him with some assignment? She would come up with something. The best lies were believable and dull. The funniest thing is that she hardly had to lie to Terry. He just wasn't interested enough. Himself, he tended to stonewall her rather than lie.

She liked sleeping with the kid, waking with him. He even smelled good. His mother had trained him to be scrupulously clean about himself. She could nibble every part of his body with pleasure. In the morning, some inner door blew open in Sam. Suddenly be began to talk to her.

"You don't mind that I'm Jewish? There's so few Jews where I live, I always wondered how it would be when I really started to get involved with girls. I mean, I've gone out with girls, but it never meant anything. It was just, you're supposed to and so I did."

She was startled. "You're Jewish?"

"You didn't know? Everybody always does. I think only Jews are named Sam these days."

"I never knew any Jews. Why should I care? I mean, I've heard people say ugly things about Jews, but people say awful things about Blacks and Italians, and my best girlfriend is Italian. And I know what people say about the Portuguese. Did you know I'm Portuguese?"

"No," he said. "It's true, people say the Portuguese are dirty and stupid. People like to feel better than somebody."

She learned more about Sam in a few hours Sunday morning than she had the previous six weeks. He loved his mother; Becky thought that was good. He did not seem to expect much from Cathy. It was like Becky's attitude toward her own mother. He thought of himself as more capable, more together than Cathy, and rather than expecting much from her, longed to be able to help her out.

He had an uncle he was close to, a vet who probably did well. That must be how come he could go away to college. In the tenth grade, he had a girlfriend, Rachel, he really cared about and they had gone as far as touching each other through their clothes, sitting on the sofa in her house. Her father's gourmet store had failed, and they moved to Arizona. Until Sam met Becky, his big fantasy was getting Rachel back. They wrote, but less often than they had. Now he probably would stop writing Rachel, because it would be deception, since he loved only Becky. Before Becky, he had not known what love was.

Becky listened to his protestations of passionate love with silent skepticism but great enjoyment. That was how men ought to talk to women, even if they hardly ever did.

Suddenly the doorbell rang. She froze. It could not be Terry; he would just use his key. Helen? His parents, spying on her. She grabbed Sam by the arm and shoved him into the bedroom and shut the door. "Don't make a sound!" She ran to the door in her bathrobe. "Who is it?"

"Tommy, Becca. Let me in. Now!"

She opened the door. "Hey, Tommy. I'm not even dressed. What's up?"

He shut the door, locked it. "Listen, I need you to hold something for me until the middle of next week. Then I'll take it back. Don't ask me no questions, I'll tell you no lies." He gave her a book. "It's hollow, but don't open it, on your life. Just put it in your drawer and Wednesday I'll come by at five-thirty and pick it up."

Then he looked at the closed bedroom door. "Who's in there, Becca?"

"Nobody, Tommy. Terry's off in New Hampshire with his brother."

"What do you think, I'd come charging over here if he was sitting on his ass watching the TV like always? Who's in there, Becca?" He pushed past her.

Clutching her robe shut, she thrust herself in between him and the door. "This is none of your damned business, Tommy. If you want me to do you a favor, you do me one. Leave right now."

"I have to know who it is. You think I'm looking out for the interests of Mr. Couch Potato, the Happy Golfer? I come by here one day to see if he wants to make some money on the boats, I'm doing him a favor because he's hooked up with my favorite sister. He acts like I offered him a fat fresh dog turd. Now who's in there?" Tommy pushed her out of the way and flung the door open.

Sam was pressed against the far wall. He drew himself up and tried to look impressive. He had pulled his pants on and was fumbling with his shirt. "Jeez." Tommy backpedaled. "Who's the kid?"

"Tommy, mind your own business. His name is Sam and he's in the play I'm in. I was balling him, and so what? I never cheated on Terry or anybody else in my life, but I've had it. I need some love too."

"Are you Terry?" Sam asked, trying to lower his voice menacingly.

"If I was, you'd be in some trouble, huh? I'm her brother, Tommy Souza." He stuck out his hand and Sam hesitantly gave him a hand to shake. "Well, I hope you know what a good woman you got here. I don't know what the two of you think you're doing, but her husband is worth shit."

Tommy took Becky by the elbow out of the bedroom and shut the door behind them. He hissed, "You hide this and don't tell that kid anything."

"Of course," she murmured. "But you won't mention this to anybody, right?"

"Just take it easy with him, Becca. He's just a kid. Have a little fun, but don't take it too seriously. It's nothing you can lean on."

"He's crazy about me, Tommy. He'd do anything for me."

"At his age, he'll do anything to get laid. Promise me you won't fuck up your life just to spend some time in the sack with a high school kid. You better send him home soon anyhow. Terry could get back anytime."

She leaned close to Tommy to whisper, "Terry's with a woman. He has a girlfriend with some bucks. Name of Heather."

Tommy grimaced, one side of his mouth turned way down. "We got to get rid of him, Becca. He's no damned good for you."

"But I want to keep the condo."

He shrugged. "Sometimes you cut your losses and walk out."

"No." She planted her feet and shook her head. "Not this time. I'm not the one going to lose."

CHAPTER 43

LEILA

Leila was disappointed by David's visit home. He spent a great deal of time on the phone to Ikuko, long conversations behind closed doors. Afterward he was moody and distracted. While there had been girls in his life since he was thirteen, this was the first time one had taken up a central position. She supposed that she should be pleased that his emotions were finally engaged, but she wanted a little more attention from him than she could command. Coming home was a duty he was discharging. His mind was fixed on Ikuko.

Nonetheless, he had been displeased when he returned the night before and Leila was not yet home. It was good that she had not spent the night with Zak, very good. "Who is this guy?"

They were at breakfast. "He's a veterinarian. The uncle of one of the alleged murderers. Sam. A kid two years younger than you."

"He killed because he was crazy about this older woman. That's fascinating. Ikuko is a year older than I am."

"I hope you don't plan to murder any of your professors for her."

"It's so off the wall and extreme. What did he think when he was doing it? Did he suppose he'd never be caught? I can't imagine not realizing that if you can figure how to do it, somebody can figure out how you did it."

She pushed her bowl aside, propping her elbow on the table.

"What's strange is that they're both likable, Sam and Becky. Both plausible and personable and interesting. And in contradiction. One of them is lying."

"Which of them is better at lying?"

"I think Becky's had more practice." Becky after all had carried on an affair with Sam while married to Terry. Sam had only to confuse Cathy, a task no ten-year-old would find taxing. "The strange thing is how little sense I have of Terry. He's the missing man. Often in murder cases, the victim looms over the scene. But Terry is like somebody who got hit with a falling tree. He was just a guy who was in the wrong marriage at the wrong time."

"But it wasn't a drive-by shooting, Mother. He must have been pretty obnoxious. Maybe he secretly beat her or shot up."

"She drops hints he beat her. But I've known a lot of battered women, and she doesn't fit any of the profiles."

"Maybe they just all had a screaming fight and it got out of hand. For instance, would you like to hurt Father if you could?" He was looking at her from under his lashes, a sly glance.

She felt a slight chill. "What did he say?"

"That you attacked him."

"I threw a vase of flowers at him."

"Oh. Is that all? He made it sound so dramatic."

"Drama is your father's business."

"I knew he was exaggerating. Listen, I want us all to have supper together tonight. I promised Father and I want us to sit down like a family at least once." He leaned forward, as if to persuade her from a shorter distance.

"Your father and I are not seeing each other."

"You can't pretend Sheryl doesn't exist. Aren't you curious?"

"I vaguely remember her when she was Nick's student." She couldn't openly explain to David that she felt she had met Sheryl before and before and before. They were always thin; they were always in their twenties. They were not the ones going to shoot into sudden or long-term success. They were the ingenues who would fade, if lucky into character roles; otherwise, into whatever they would do with the rest of their lives. They were a little desperate, frantic to please. They saw in Nick a chance to clamber up, to become visible, to move on to other roles and regular work. Sheryl differed from the other ingenues in one striking regard. She had not aimed to improve her lot as an actress, not by becoming pregnant, certainly, not by deciding to have the baby; her desire had been not to use Nick but to possess him. Therefore the play had ended, but the affair had not. Why would Leila ever want to meet her?

"He's going to marry her, he told me so," David continued, fixing her with a benignly worried look, as if she were being dense. "You ought to look over the opposition."

"I'm not opposed to his marrying her. There's a baby on the way. David, I think you want me more involved in this mess than I care to be."

"Mother, you're in denial—"

"Denial of what?" She grimaced at the psych jargon. Was this Ikuko's influence? "I'm well aware of the progress of my divorce."

"Denial of pain. You're suppressing affect. Oh, today's the day I get divorced from my husband of twenty-five years, what else is new?"

"David, try to understand, I did my suffering while your father was having his affairs. Now he's Sheryl's problem, not mine. This is a resolution of a situation that had become increasingly intolerable. I was giving and I wasn't getting, and I'd rather have a cat."

"And a boyfriend?"

"I can't say about Zak yet. But if you insist I go to supper tonight—"

"I promised Dad you would."

"Why does he want this?"

"He said he misses talking with you."

"That's strange. I don't miss talking with him. I thought I would." She looked steadily at her son. She was disappointed in his reaction to the divorce; in fact, she had to fight a sense of betrayal. It was only fair to recognize that he had his own interests, quite different from hers. "You really want me to do this? Sit in a restaurant and eat with your father and his girlfriend?"

"You have to reopen a dialogue, Mother. You don't talk to each other. All you do is hire lawyers to negotiate. From what Dad says—you don't talk about it." He gave her a look of reproach. "You've worked out how to split things between you. You can't just pretend he's dead or something."

"I have no desire to see him for at least a year, frankly. But if it's so important to you, I'll get on the phone to Zak. I'd like him with me, just to balance things. If he's willing."

Zak was willing and curious. She was stuck. Was she afraid? She peered into herself with a cold skeptical eye, but could find nothing but a low-grade boredom with Nick, a desire to avoid pain and embarrassment, an ardent wish that the divorce be accomplished and sink below the horizon permanently. Still, she owed her son this awkward evening. He had grown used to thinking that she would put up with anything from his father, and that the marriage would endure regardless. She understood now that David's occasional comments that she should leave Nick had never been intended to be taken seriously. Probably it had been an indirect way of bidding her to stop complaining.

David carried out the negotiations for the supper and made the reservations. Leila could hear him consulting his best friend on the current favorite of Cambridge Chinese restaurants. As Leila went through her closet, she reflected sourly that every faculty member along with a parking space received an evaluation of the restaurants. It was a perk of working in any institution here. You shall receive an annual salary of X and the opportunity to eat first-rate Chinese food. She could find nothing she wanted to wear.

What she finally did was dash off to a boutique she passed on the way to school on Mass Avenue, buy a plum silk chemise and run back with it. Zak had arrived and he was chatting with David. She ran upstairs, showered, dressed and was back down on time, fastening her earrings as she descended. She could not justify what she had just done, but she was damned if she was going to show up in an outfit Nick had seen fifty times and might have actually selected. Buying a dress on impulse felt dangerously immoral, as if she might become Debbie. Debbie got married on impulse, got pregnant, left a man, bought a horse, quit a job, moved someplace. Debbie's life had always put Leila in mind of a room in which a fight had just taken place. The way her own bedroom must look right now.

Zak greeted her with a quick kiss, chaste but proprietary. David and Zak had settled on animal life as their topic, both with a peripheral interest in natural history. They were obviously nervous with each other but trying to act civilized in an unprogrammed situation.

As Leila expected, her party arrived first at the restaurant and waited. And waited. Finally they asked to be seated anyhow and ordered dumplings. Half an hour later, Nick swept in, prodding the woman whom Leila remembered. Sheryl was a bit shorter than Leila and much thinner. She had straight ash blond hair cut off just below her ears, high cheekbones and smoky grey-brown eyes, a face in which the features seemed a little spread out. During the introductions, Leila remembered her voice. It was the most attractive part of Sheryl, low, throaty, thick as hot caramel. She was carefully made-up and dressed in a beige coatdress, not yet visibly pregnant.

Nick seemed startled by Zak. It took him three tries to get Zak's name straight. He was not pretending to forget, she thought. He really was not absorbing the name. He was too surprised. Whatever he had expected, her turning up with a new boyfriend was not on the list.

Zak was dressed in his city clothes, no buffalo plaids, no outdoorsman's denims and flannels. He wore a green washed-silk shirt, a black cashmere sports coat. He seemed slight beside Nick. He had seated himself so that he was on one side of Leila, and David on the other. Under the table his knee touched hers. He was a quieter presence beside her than Nick. He did not demand attention in the way she was used to.

She tried to figure out why Zak seemed much younger than Nick; there was only five years' difference in their ages. Zak was slighter, yes. Zak sat back and watched a great deal and commented lightly. Nick boomed. He always held forth. He played the patriarch at every table.

Surreptitiously she glanced at her watch. An hour and a half, maximum two hours, and she would be out of here. Tomorrow David would fly off to his girlfriend. She was doing this for him, but she hated every moment. Ordering was a long wrangle that made her want to run into the street screaming. Any garbage you want, she felt like saying. Tell them to sweep the kitchen and serve it. What a dismal time killer to sit at this table looking at her ex-husband and his new girlfriend and comparing herself, comparing everyone with everyone in all combinations and permutations of depression.

Zak was explaining who he was. "Oh," Nick interrupted suddenly. "Leila brought her fat cat to you. She dotes on it. And you cured it of hairballs."

Zak sat straighter in his chair. "Actually I practice on the Cape. Leila and I met through a mutual interest in a murder case."

David said, "Zak's the uncle of that guy, Sam, who's just a little younger than me and who killed for love. He was a good student too. And Jewish. Imagine how obsessed with her he must have been."

Zak spoke softly but his voice was like a snake giving a warning with its rattles. "Sam may or may not have killed or hurt anyone. He'll have his day in court. That's where these matters are supposed to be decided." He turned back to Nick. "So how did your play do in New York? I think you had a play opening there recently?"

Zak knew perfectly well that the play had closed, because she had told him. Leila thought of going to the women's room and sitting there for a little while, say an hour or two. At the moment she would have liked to spank her son. Had she really been married to that disagreeable man? Love was a disease. Love was a long and tedious delusion. It was a one-person brainwashed cult.

"I ran into Meryl just the day before we left Manhattan," Nick said to her. "You remember Meryl from my days in summer stock. Meryl Streep," he added to Zak.

"I wonder how her corgis are doing these days," Zak mused. "They all had respiratory problems."

Was this bout being conducted on points or did someone expect a KO? They retreated to safe ground, the weather, winter storms, global warming. After that they earnestly discussed the difficulties of apartment hunting. Sheryl described with brittle animation the seventeen totally unsuitable apartments they had toured. David answered questions about Cal Tech. Comparison of the two coasts was batted around. East was east and West was west and the Midwest was someplace else, they all agreed.

"You're unusually silent," Nick said suddenly. "Are we boring you? Perhaps you were hoping for an evening alone with your new friend."

She was so startled that she dropped some Szechuan beef into her lap, staining the new silk dress. "I'm a little tired," she said more softly than she had intended. "Finals, my book, the one in production, all that."

Zak took over the conversation with a rap about how he never had fun when he tried to eat out on the Cape, because people would buttonhole him about their pets' symptoms and foibles. She tried to figure out what had upset her. The implied accusation? How dare you be having an affair. No, it was that hard poking voice. In the days when she had sometimes planned to go with Nick for a week or a weekend, when David was a baby and could be packed up and taken, she had realized finally that, before he left, he always managed to quarrel with her and storm out, so that she did not end up accompanying him.

Zak's hand closed on her knee under the table. It was not a sexual gesture, but intended to steady her. "So," she addressed Sheryl, who had managed to avoid looking at her all evening, "how do you feel about being back in Boston after four years?"

"It's a better place to bring up our children. I miss my life there, I miss my friends, but after all, Nick will be bringing plays to Manhattan again."

David was finishing everything. "Do we want another dish? Or have we had enough?"

"I think we've had enough," Zak said dryly. "It's been delightful. I was quite curious to meet you, of course." Looking at Nick.

"I didn't know you existed."

"Ah, you know Leila—deep and discreet," Zak said, grinning.

She realized that Zak was having fun. Sheryl had perhaps expected to enjoy the evening more than she had. No doubt Nick had presented Leila as loud and opinionated, the faculty feminist at bat. She decided she was not going to ask Zak to drive back to the Cape. Since David had set this up, he would have to endure Zak staying over with her, for neither was she about to exile him to the drafty guest room. She felt that through his nudging, David had pushed their relationship forward another step that neither of them had decided upon. Zak liked being her champion, she could tell that. But once David left for school, they would have to sort themselves out.

CHAPTER 44

BECKY

Becky put Sam to work late Sunday morning changing the bed linens and helping her clean before she took him home at noon and then exchanged cars with Sylvie. When she returned to the condo, she immediately ran to do the laundry. In a wild frenzy, she had the place looking unused and smart by three. She was sore from having so much sex. She took a bath and then she stood in the middle of the living room. They always went to Terry's parents' house on Sunday. She hardly missed that but felt derailed. Her life had been riding along in its ruts. Now she had plunged into open space, dangers, pleasures, the exciting and terrifying sense that she could do anything whatsoever.

She had stuffed Tommy's package in her underwear drawer. She could not imagine Terry going through her drawers, as she was about to do to his.

First she searched his dresser. Condoms. He wasn't using those with her. She was on the Pill. Something far more interesting among his socks. Insurance papers. The car insurance, insurance on the condo, medical insurance his parents had been paying since he lost his job. His life insurance Chris had sold him, that had her as beneficiary since they married. There it was. Two hundred thousand. But under the policy was a manila envelope full of papers from Chris.

She pulled out an application for changing the beneficiary. A memo in Chris's handwriting told Terry to complete steps one to six for changing the beneficiary from Becky to his mother. Terry had started to fill out the forms, putting on his name and birth date, but had not finished. He really was planning to dump her. She took Chris's instructions from the packet, tore the memo into twenty little pieces and flushed it down the toilet. That should slow Terry down. She did not dare dispose of the papers until she had figured out what to do.

Terry was certainly worth a lot more money dead than alive. Alive he was costing her, and he was about to cost her more. If only he'd have a nice tidy accident. But he wouldn't. He was lucky that way. He hardly ever cut himself shaving. Sam was always getting excited and knocking things over or running into a table in his haste, but Terry never even spilled coffee. He wasn't about to have some convenient accident.

In his pockets of his sports jackets and his casual jackets, she found receipts from restaurants and ticket stubs from movies. She had better take a careful look at the MasterCard bill. She also found a paper parasol from a rum drink. While she was off to the theater group, he had been going out, obviously. She was in deep trouble.

She toyed with the idea of making him jealous with Sam, but looking at the accumulated evidence, she doubted he would get usefully jealous. He'd be relieved to be able to dismiss her. She must be careful. But she had to keep Sam on line too. She needed Sam. She had to figure out how to keep a close eye on Terry while finding time for sex with Sam. This week there would be tryouts for the next play, which Ce-Ce would be announcing Tuesday. They would be back to rehearsing weekday evenings, and she would have her weekends free. She had to turn all that to advantage.

Two hundred thousand dollars. That was an enormous sum. She could invest it. That was what smart people did. She would pay off the Burgesses, buy a new car. When Sam went to school, she could drive up and see him weekends. It was only three hours. She'd pay off the rest of the condo too, so that she wasn't making payments on the mortgage every month. She'd still have half the money left. She'd go to conferences and seminars about media and make contacts for a real job.

No use daydreaming about that money. No use. It would change her whole life. It would fix everything. She would be as independent as Aunt Marie. She could afford Sam as a lover. She would not have two suits she alternated, but a closetful. She could help her family with open hands. It wasn't as if Terry was any use to anybody. If he dropped dead tomorrow, his parents would care—but who else? Even they hadn't wanted him around all the time.

But what could she do? She was almost out of time. Could she get around Terry and buy herself some time to think, to figure things out? She dressed carefully. She did her nails and put on perfume. She was all nerves, as if this were a big date instead of her despised husband who was with another woman and planning to dump her cold. Her stomach was so tight she was afraid she was going to be sick. She had a tension headache banding her forehead with steel.

Finally at seven-thirty she heard his key. She jumped up, forcing a big smile. "Terry! How did it go?"

His eyes narrowed. For a moment he looked mean and suspicious. Then he walked in, tossed his gear on a chair and stretched. "Lot of traffic. I was just two over par on the course."

"What about the guy who might give you a job?"

"He didn't commit to anything, but it looks promising. I'll talk to him again."

I bet you will, she thought, in bed. Never mind. "Would you like some supper?"

"I ate." He sat down on the couch and fumbled for the TV wand.

"I missed you this weekend," she tried, sitting down beside him. "I was thinking I'd love to learn to play golf, so I could go with you."

"You wouldn't like it. It was just guys."

"I just want us to spend more time together. I really started thinking about our marriage this weekend, and how we can make it better. You mean so much to me." She was looking at him. He had the strangest chin. Not that he was chinless in the usual sense, but his chin sloped into his neck. She was talking sweetly to him, in that baby voice she used in their romantic moments, but she was looking at him as if he were a stranger she had sat next to on a bus. She could not remember why she had initially found him so attractive. He seemed washed out, anemic, plain-looking. She had an image of taking the wand out of his hand and pushing it into his mouth. That made her smile.

He looked into her smile and his eyes shifted away. "Yeah? I don't know. As Mother says, we got married in an awful hurry. Don't you think it's kind of a mistake?"

"Never! I love you, Terry," she said with her best attempt at sounding passionate and solemn at once. "I've never met a man who was so special to me. It isn't a mistake to me. It was the best most wonderful day of my life when we got married."

He shifted uncomfortably, his eyes going to the blank TV screen. "Don't you think maybe we're . . . incompatible? Like we come from such different backgrounds."

You just noticed that this weekend, jerk? "I think we complement each other, the way you said when we were getting married. I thought that was very insightful, Terry, and I think it's still true. If you're a certain kind of person, why marry the same thing? What do you learn? You know what the other person knows. But you, you still surprise me. And I think maybe I can still surprise you." She put her hand on the back of his neck and started kneading.

"Aw, come on, Becky. I'm tired. I was on the course all day."

Screwing all day is more like it. She certainly had no urge to have sex with anyone at the moment, least of all him, but it seemed like a good idea. However, he was completely unresponsive under her hand. If she did that to Sam, he'd be undressed already. She let go and moved away. She had made her point. "I understand," she said, tremolo. "It's just that I find you so attractive, and I've been missing you all weekend."

"You have?" He looked halfway pleased. "What did you do?"

"I was in the play. This was the last weekend. I did the laundry, gave the house a good cleaning. I saw Sylvie and my brother Tommy. A nice quiet restful weekend. I thought about you a lot. I thought about us, and how I want to make it better."

He looked embarrassed, shifting his shoulders. Poor bastard probably spent the weekend telling Heather how he was going to break the news to his stupid soon-to-be-ex-wife, and how the marriage was over anyhow. She was not going to make it easy. She wanted time to figure out what to do, time to work on Sam. She doubted if she could keep Terry, and she was not sure she wanted to. She winced at having to play Devoted Wife seven days a week, while he permitted himself to be adored. If it wasn't for the condo, she'd just wave him out the door. Even the old car she drove was in his name. She owned nothing but the clothes in her closet. She would walk out of the marriage twenty-five and broke.

She saw herself back home, working at a job where she could never get ahead. She would be looking for a place to live, like the one over the cleaner's. She would have to buy her own car, because she could not even get to work without wheels. Unless they let her keep the wreck she was driving. She had grown used to comfort, to a clean bathroom where she could shower whenever, to quiet, to space of her own. She loved her family, but she could not shoehorn herself back into that dirty noisy overrun house.

She sat smiling at him on the couch as he hopped from channel to channel. You don't know what desperation is, she thought at him, smiling, smiling. You're trying to kill me. But I won't go down easy. I won't lie down and let you shovel me off the porch. This is war. We'll see who can fight harder, we'll see who can fight dirtier. We'll see who can win.

The next play they were doing was *Dracula*. Ce-Ce said vampires were very hot. This time both Becky and Sam had bigger roles. Sam was Renfield, the madman under the spell of *Dracula*. He had fun acting weird and pretending to eat flies. Becky was Lucy, Minna's friend who turned into a vampire and attacked little children. Every one was paying more attention to her now. She was going to wear a long dress and then a peignoir when she came back from the dead. She got to scream bloody murder when they killed her again with a stake to the heart. Dick Berg, of course, was Dracula. They had a torrid scene together where he fondled her and bit her neck.

After rehearsals, she drove Sam home and they stopped on the side of his road. It was second best to have sex in the backseat, but it was good enough to keep him crazy about her. He wanted to see her every evening, but they couldn't until the weekend, when his mother was in her studio. Saturday afternoon Becky drove to his house.

She liked doing it in his room. It wasn't like any bedroom she had seen. He did not have to share it with anyone. When his sister had lived at home, she had her own room too. That was how people should live. Sam's house was not for show. It was homey and clean enough, but not the way Becky kept her space. There were newspapers and books scattered about, overgrown houseplants, begonias, African violets, herbs. The paintings did not match the furniture.

Sam's room had books in it, weights and a pulley and a computer. He had a surfboard and ice skates and a miniature basketball hoop. The posters were not of rock stars but of dinosaurs, geologic periods, plants and animals of the salt marsh. A mobile over the bed was a model of the solar system. It amused her after they made love to set all the planets whirling around the sun, all the moons whizzing about their planets. She felt like that with Sam: that she was immensely powerful and could make him go through his paces anytime. It was a wonderful feeling. She adored him for making her feel so strong.

Instead of pinup posters and girlie magazines, he had guides to seashells and birds, to reptiles and amphibians. A bird's nest he said had belonged to a chickadee sat on his bookcase. He had a perfect conch shell from Mexico and a row of slipper shells. He was cute, he was adorable. He was much more fun than Terry. He was getting better in bed. He would do anything she asked him to, and after the first time, he could fuck longer. But the major difference was out of bed: he looked at her when she spoke, and he listened. It was that attention lapping her around that kept her primed sexually. She felt as if her whole life she had been wanting to be regarded, listened to, to be the center of somebody's total focus. That gaze electrified her. It was like the camera seeing her in the video after Joey died; it was like the men looking at her on the beach in her bathing suit. It was that, times a hundred.

She loved to explain things to him about men and women. She could care about Sam without losing herself, without pretending to be softer or simpler than she was. She did not have to flatter him. She did not have to pretend an interest in anything she did not care about. It was Sam who had to do what she wanted. It was Sam who studied how to please her. It was Sam who begged, who waited, who hoped. She had never been happier in a relationship; perhaps she had never before been happy. Oh, her condo made her happy, but she could not remember a time when things with Terry had not been fraught, when the space between them had not been a minefield to trespass on with care.

That week she began coming home at noon. For one thing, she didn't want Terry bringing his girlfriend to the condo. She hoped Heather worked someplace too far to get there at lunch hour, but she was taking no chances. This was part of her Devoted Wife campaign. She was coming home to make sure he ate. "Because of rehearsals, I want us to have some extra time together." It made for a frantic lunch hour, but this wasn't forever. Nothing in their lives together was going to survive long.

She sat across the table from him nibbling a salad bar plate she had picked up, while he ate the cheeseburger and fries she had brought him. She imagined him choking on the meat and her sitting there smiling as if nothing were happening. She thought, Suppose I pushed him down the steps. He'd probably just break a leg and be furious. Suppose I did something to his car. What? I don't even know what's under the hood of my own. My two-hundred-thousand-dollar man, going to waste. How to cash him in?

Every day she stole a look at the forms in his drawer. He had not filled them in yet. But he would. He would. She could not wait until he sent in the forms; it would be too late then.

Quietly after Terry had gone to bed that night, she got up and went into the kitchen. She bashed her arm with the electric iron. It was the heaviest thing she could find. It was awkward and hurt. Then she bashed her thigh. That should look impressive, and she could keep those bruises covered at the office.

That night at rehearsals, she showed Sam the bruises. "Look. Terry's suspicious."

"He did this? He hit you?"

"He's always hitting me, but this time he really hurt me. I don't know what made him suspicious. You know, I won't go to bed with him anymore. It makes me feel too bad. I belong with you, not with him."

"I hate him. I'd like to beat the shit out of him. I'd bash his head in. I'd knock him down and show him."

"I'm afraid he's going to do something worse. He's threatening me. I might not be able to see you any longer."

"Leave him, Becky. You have to leave him. I can quit school. I can get a job. I bet I'm as strong as he is."

"I know you are," she said, running her hands over his shoulders and arms. "I can't let you ruin your life for me. You need to finish high school and go to college. I want to do what's good for you. I want to be proud of you. Now we have to go back. I just don't know what to do. He'll never let me leave him. He said that he'd kill me first."

"Do you believe him? Would he really hurt you?"

She held up her arm, smiling wanly, bravely. "What do you think?"

"What are we going to do? I can't live without you, Becky. I can't!"

"I can't live without you, either. Maybe we should kill ourselves. Because if we don't and he finds out, he'll kill us."

"This can't be real, Becky. People leave marriages every day. He just has to accept that you love another guy and let you go. Then we can see each other every night. We can go out on dates."

"He doesn't love me, Sam, but he's very possessive. He won't let me go. He's said so time and again. If things go on this way, we can't be together. It's too dangerous." She held up her arm and then swept out. Let that cook on the back burner overnight.

The next day she rode with Helen. She told Sam that Terry was very suspicious, and she did not dare drive him home. He looked ready to cry. In the car on the way back, Helen put her hand on Becky's knee. "So, you got tired of the kid? Or what?"

Becky could not speak for a moment. She was too scared. She thought of trying to pretend she did not know what Helen meant, but Helen lived under her. Who knows what she had heard? Becky finally said, "How did you know?"

"Suddenly you got to drive yourself? Suddenly I notice he's getting in the car with you? You think I don't notice he's had a crush on you for weeks? Come on, I'm not blind and I'm not stupid. Look, he's a cute boy. You haven't got much going with your husband, that's obvious. So you're playing around a little. It's safe. He was a virgin, wasn't he?"

Becky nodded, too upset to speak.

"So you won't get AIDS from him. He's like a little jackrabbit, right? He was with you all last weekend, I kept track. Don't worry. I wouldn't tell your husband. You deserve better than you're getting from that lump. Out of work six months and going golfing. That's disgusting. If he was my husband, I'd throw him out."

"I wish I could."

"I saw that bruise on your arm when I was measuring you for your costume. Did he do that? Your husband?"

Becky nodded.

"He found out about the boy?"

"No, he doesn't suspect anything. But he's very possessive. He has a terrible temper lately. . . . I think maybe he's been taking something."

"Drugs?"

"I don't know. I've never taken anything. You know, I hardly even have a beer once a week. Nobody in my family ever did drugs, so I don't know what it's like. Maybe it's just the unemployment. He has such a short fuse lately." She was trying out various stories about Terry. She watched Helen to see if she was buying this one.

Late the next afternoon Tommy came to get his stash, but Terry was still hanging around. The three of them sat awkwardly in the living room making empty conversation. "Why don't you go out for pizza or something?" she asked Terry. She had to leave for rehearsal at seven-twenty.

"I'm not the one invited myself to supper," Terry said.

"Listen, I'll eat later. Never mind. I was just in the neighborhood, and I'd thought I'd stop by and see my favorite sister and her old man. Hey, Becky, you got that. . . . that blouse Mattie wants to borrow off of you?"

"Sure, Tommy, sure." She ran into the bedroom. The package was in her dresser. She pinned it inside a blue blouse she had never liked and brought it into the living room on its hanger. "Here, Tommy. Mattie can give it back to me next week."

"What's this about?" Terry grimaced.

"Mattie's getting her picture taken with the kid and she wanted something blue and simple."

He got up off the couch. "Isn't that the blouse my mother gave you?"

"Yes. It's such a nice blouse, Mattie will look great in it."

"I don't think you should go giving away things my mother gave you." Terry took hold of the blouse. "What is this?"

Tommy lunged, but Terry had found the package pinned inside. "What in hell is going on here?"

Tommy took the blouse from him, removed the packet and slipped it in the pocket of his leather jacket. "It's just business. I needed a place to leave something for a couple of days."

"Are you both crazy? You get that fucking dope out of here! Are you trying to get me busted? Are you trying to destroy me? I just don't believe this. I just don't believe this stupidity!" Terry was pacing and screaming at the top of his lungs.

Tommy made a fist. She could tell he was thinking of decking Terry, but decided against it. "You don't know anything about this. Neither does my sister. Just keep your mouth shut. It was an emergency, and it won't happen again."

"You bet it won't happen. I don't ever want to see you in my house! You get out and you get lost. Take your stupid sister with you."

"You don't mean that. Becky didn't know nothing. She's never done drugs in her life, and neither have I. This is just something I'm holding for a friend because frankly we all need the money. Don't you? Times are tough and everybody has to help each other out. Now stop squawking at my sister and chill out."

Becky was motioning for Tommy to leave. She figured she could handle Terry better if Tommy got out. He seemed reluctant. "Are you going to be all right?"

Becky nodded fervently and waved him out the door. Terry glared at her. "You stupid bitch! Are you trying to put us both in jail?"

"Terry, I know you're right. But I had no idea what was in the package. He just asked me to hold it. He said it was a surprise for Mattie. And he did ask me to lend him the blue blouse." She wrang her hands, glancing at him out of the corner of her eye. This was a total mess. Just when she had been getting him softened up. Here he had his excuse to dump on her. "I figured he'd bought Mattie some jewelry. I never looked in the package. Maybe I was too trusting, you know I'm inclined to be way too trusting. I really ask your forgiveness. But I never did anything wrong. All I did was believe what he told me."

"Then you're as stupid as he is! Your whole family are a bunch of stinking Portuguese lowlifes off the docks. You all smell of fish. You live in a shack that smells like the men's room in the subway. You probably grew up fucking the family goat!"

She could not speak. She could not open her mouth. Tears came to her eyes and ran down her face. He turned away with a snort of disgust and slammed into the bedroom, shutting her out. But her tears were tears of rage. She had no more time to act. She had to get Sam to help her, and if that failed, then Tommy. She had to get rid of Terry before he could hurt her anymore. She would never forgive him what he had said about her and her family, never. Now he was the enemy. She had to turn him into money.

CHAPTER 45

MARY

Beverly stayed for a while in a shelter. Then she moved back onto the streets. It was well past the holidays and none of Mary's people were traveling. When Beverly wanted to see Mary, she would leave a message with the cleaning service. Beverly knew Mary was having trouble finding a place to sleep. It was down to the teens every night. Sunday it snowed five inches. It was a hard time to be sleeping in church basements and unlocked garages. Mary had slept so little she was rapidly approaching a state of nodding out while standing, not only vividly unpleasant but dangerous.

Tuesday evening they met in the Symphony station at six. They sat on a bench sharing what they had. Beverly had some day-old doughnuts she had been given at the back door of a Dunkin Donuts. Mary had a can of sardines she had slipped into her bag in Mrs. Baer's kitchen, an orange, two carrots, two apples she had bought, and the end of a loaf of rye bread Mrs. Baer had been throwing out.

Mary had thought maybe Beverly put up with her in the hospital, where she was helpless in the hands of a bureaucracy she mistrusted. But the women went on meeting. They shared food. They knew each other's problems. To no one else could Mary talk honestly and openly about her life. She talked and talked, and so did Beverly. They described their marriages to each other, without making things nice or pretty. If Mary's life had been lived in the middle or even the upper middle class and Beverly's had been working-class, that did not matter now.

People glanced at them oddly. Beverly was no longer cleaned up. Her hair was a scraggly grey-brown mass under her greasy orange hat. She had picked up a set of clothes in layers, odd washed-out colors poking through. Mary was respectable, as always, her hair combed, her wool hat on straight, her carry-all and her newish bag in order.

If Beverly had been sitting alone, people would have walked by without looking at her. Mary remembered that invisibility. Passersby almost never made eye contact. They pretended not to see that the odd bundle of rags in the doorway was alive. She remembered how that avoidance and scorn made her feel unworthy. She had begun to shun contact. She had looked down. She shuffled along with her chin lowered so she wouldn't see people who pretended they could not see her.

She sat up stiff and straight and tried to shut out the curious glances. "So where are you staying?"

"That's what she wanted to see you about. You're welcome too."

"It's too late for a shelter." It was too late by the time she got done with work. To get a bed, she would have to be there before four.

"This is a place of our own. It's a great abandoned building. Houdini found it. You know Houdini, don't you?"

"I've met him." Houdini had lived on the streets for ten years. He was famous for being able to get into locked-up structures, into vans and buildings. He had been caught often enough and done time, but he was always back on the streets and looking for a place he and whoever he let in could camp.

"He invited her in on this new crib. She'll take you there."

"Are you . . . with him now?"

"Houdini? He's married to a bottle. The guys are upstairs, Houdini and a boy they call Mouse. She's downstairs. She got an apartment of her own, even a mattress. Wait till you see."

From the station, they walked south and east. The empty building was past the edge of the gentrified district. It was boarded up and marked with big NO TRESPASSING signs, but Beverly led the way around to a basement entrance. The door was closed by a chain with a rusty padlock on it, but the chain had been cut and simply hung together loop into loop, so that the break was not obvious. Rats scuttled away as they came in. Mary used her flashlight. Red eyes caught the beam and then were gone. Beverly led the way to the stairs. The basement smelled like a toilet, and Mary gagged and shivered. It felt as cold down here as it was out in the street, minus the steel edge of the wind.

They went up quietly, listening for danger. If a building had been opened by the homeless, Mary knew it could also be used by dealers, crack-heads, runaways, anybody who wanted to get off the streets. But they seemed to be the first ones in tonight.

The first-floor apartment had its door off its hinges. "We think they did that to get rid of the tenants," Beverly said, once they had made sure they were safe. "See, there's a chair and a counter in the kitchen. There's her mattress. You can sleep on it with her. She got her own blanket."

"I have a sleeping bag." Mary unrolled it. "It's my treasure."

"That's great. Did somebody give that to Goodwill or the Salvation Army?"

With Beverly, she could tell the truth. "I took it from the closet of one of my ladies. She wasn't using it, and her son is spoiled rotten. He only used it once maybe—"

"Don't apologize. You'll be snug in it tonight." Beverly squatted in the bathroom on the tile floor where she had put down a hubcap. The floor was black and white tiles, cracked and dusty now. The bathtub had been taken out, but the sink was still there and the toilet with a broken seat. But there was no water anyhow, Mary remarked.

"There is too water," Beverly said. "We got everything here to be comfortable. They left a bucket. She filled it with snow and it melted. See? We got water to drink. Now see what else. You're her guest. We can have hot water." She rummaged in her bag.

Mary said proudly, "We can have better than that. I always carry tea bags. You heat the water and we'll have tea."

"Real tea! This is more like it."

Beverly had a cup of Sterno and some matches. She set the Sterno burning on the tiles and over it she rigged up a tripod with an old coffee tin she was using as a pot. It even gave off a little warmth. Mary took off her mittens and rubbed her hands together near the flame. She felt happier than she had since she had stayed in a nice house over New Year's. It was cold, it was dirty, it was dark, but she had a friend and they were company and a little protection for each other.

She had not had anyone to chatter with in years and years. She had talked to her husband in the old days, she had friends in the neighborhood, other housewives married to professional men, she had talked to her children until they entered that stage of adolescence when they protected their secrets from her as if her knowledge of something emotional would cause that crush or wish to instantly implode. Her ladies sometimes talked to her, but she did not give them anything personal back. Her revealing to Mrs. Landsman that she knew Beverly was a one-time risk, never to be repeated.

Now she had a friend who understood. They compared notes on all the places they had slept or passed a night without daring to sleep. In many public places, it was forbidden to sleep. You could sit in the library, you could sit in a bus or train station, but you were never supposed to have to sleep. Nothing you really needed to do when you were homeless was supposed to happen. You were illegal. You were wrong to be alive and there.

About nine-thirty, they heard a stir below. The Sterno had long since gone out. They hid against a wall and waited. "It's Houdini," Beverly said with relief. "Hey, Houdini."

It was dark in the hall and Mary could see little. Houdini was a small man, as she remembered him, but she could not see his features. He gave off a strong smell of piss and alcohol. The kid with him was skinny, a little taller than Houdini with light brown skin, and kept behind him. "Hi, Bev my darling, how are you? Who's your friend?"

"We met years ago, Houdini. I'm Mary. I met you once when I was with Samantha. Do you remember Samantha?"

"Yeah, sweet Samantha." He crossed himself. "Well, welcome to our humble abode, Mary Contrary, and remember, home is where you make it. We'll be upstairs if you need us, ladies. Come on, Mouse. Pick up your end. See, we found ourselves a great piece of wood. We're going to have ourselves a little fire to warm up. We got a door from an old car we can use as our stove." Houdini and Mouse labored upstairs with their find. Houdini called down the stairwell, "This is the Ritz, ladies, and welcome to it."

"She hopes we can stay here for a while," Beverly said. "These must have been nice apartments. She bets the people were sorry to get kicked out."

"I hated to leave my old apartment. I expected to live out my life there," Mary said, crawling into her sleeping bag.

They talked about food and weather and clothing. They talked about neighborhoods and cops and the Others, the people with homes. They laughed and giggled a lot. Mary thought she hadn't carried on this way since she was a teenager and had her girlfriends to sleep over at her parents' house.

It was cold in the apartment, but with the windows boarded up, the wind did not whistle through. Mary put her sleeping bag next to Beverly's mattress and blanket. Upstairs they could hear Houdini laughing and once something fell.

"You're not afraid of Houdini or that kid?"

Beverly laughed dryly. "She's scared of most men, but not Houdini. He's okay. The kid is retarded. He wouldn't hurt a flea. Houdini has a good heart. When he's got a squat, he lets his friends share it. Some guys would keep a crib like this to themselves. She's going to look for a piece of carpet tomorrow. She figures this is good for a while. We can fix it up a bit. Maybe find a table or something. Some pans. We can make it nice for ourselves. See if you can score some matches today. She's running low."

Before they went to sleep for the night, Mary took her flashlight and went downstairs to use a corner of the basement as a toilet. It was always necessary to be extremely careful when relieving herself in the dark and the cold. It was easy to stain garments or get her hands dirty. A bad smell from an accident or carelessness had to be avoided. She could not simply wash herself, her clothes, even her hands.

She was squatting in the dark just finishing when she heard a sound nearby. She shone the flashlight and then charged before she had time to think. The body of a cat lay on the floor. She did not bother to check what had killed it. The rats were eating it and they had freshly killed two kittens. What she heard was a third kitten hissing as it lay back against its mother's quite cold body. She seized up the kitten, clawing fiercely, and wrapped it in her coat. Failing to think of anything else to do, she meowed at it. It slowly stopped struggling and clung to her. She carried it upstairs.

"I found a kitten downstairs the rats were attacking. I brought it up."

"You can't keep it," Beverly said. "What will you do with it? They're always coming in these buildings, the same as we do. They don't live long."

She carefully unwrapped her coat. The kitten clung to the coat, shaking. It was small but complete, perhaps six weeks, perhaps eight weeks old. The rats would have made short work of it as they had of its siblings. She looked under the tail. Her siblings. "I can't put her back to die. She's hungry."

"Who isn't?"

Finally Mary gave the kitten some leftover crumbs of bread. The kitten ate them. What else could it do? It crawled into her coat and curled against her body for warmth, kneading her with its tiny sharp claws like a row of pins, kneading for milk that she could not give. She crawled into her sleeping bag with the kitten still holding on and tried to sleep.

In the morning her alarm woke her in the dark. She tidied herself up as best she could, taking a small amount of the melted snow for necessary washing. The kitten did not venture far, too weak perhaps from hunger. It sat on the sleeping bag crying occasionally in a faint voice. She gathered up her bag and her carry-all and tucked the kitten into her coat. At the corner 7-Eleven, she bought a can of cat food and fed the kitten on a stoop, holding it enclosed in her coat. Her coat was going to smell of cat food.

Fortunately she was going to Mrs. Landsman. That was a woman with a soft heart for cats. Mrs. Landsman was going to come home to a note and a kitten. If Mary got fired, she got fired. She would say she found the kitten outside in the street, alone and starving.

She hadn't been able to stay there in months, anyway. They were getting divorced, and the house would be on the market soon. Mrs. Landsman would either keep the cat or send it to a shelter, which would be a more merciful death than being eaten alive by rats like Kitten's sisters. Kitten was purring now, her little belly distended with food. She had managed to eat half the can in five minutes. Mary promised to meet Beverly at the Symphony T station. She would organize some supper. Mrs. Landsman usually had something she could help herself to, and she would buy tuna fish and bread. Then they would go to their new hotel for the night, Houdini's Ritz. She belonged somewhere. She had a friend, almost a family. They could fix that apartment up, they could. This weekend she would look for furniture and useful things people threw out. For once she had something to look forward to: a home of her own with Beverly.

CHAPTER 46

LEILA

The night was pleasant, if somewhat hushed. In the morning, Zak left before David had organized himself for breakfast. Then all was frantic until she had him packed up, delivered to Logan Airport and on his plane west. She came back to the house empty but for the expectant Vronsky on the rug where he always met her. Once she had bundled the tree she had not wanted into the trash, she felt more relief than sadness.

David was growing up and he was rushing off to his first real relationship with a female. Whether it worked out in the long run or not, at least this strong attachment to Ikuko was a good sign. Sometimes she worried that she had held him too closely to her, that she had partly replaced the absent husband with the present son. Now he had pulled free. That was one reason she had not concealed from David her connection with Zak.

Zak had come through for her. As the week went along, she thought from time to time of calling him, yet she did not. She tried to examine her lack of urgency. She sat up in bed surrounded by her notes on Becky, one hand on Vronsky's nape, and considered. She felt a more comfortable distance from Nick. He was seamlessly absorbed into coupledom with Sheryl. It was peculiar to her how Nick and she could have slept in the same bed, put parts of their bodies into each other, been intimately involved in the details of daily life, and now have almost nothing to do with the other. He was drawn into a new couple and about to hatch a different family.

Perhaps she was putting off seeing Zak exactly because he had been so protective and useful. He had acted . . . husbandly. He had done it well. But she didn't desire a husband. She was still getting rid of one who had sucked up a good half of her daily output of energy for two decades. "You and I have reached a pleasant accommodation of wishes and needs," she said to Vronsky, scratching him gently under the chin. "I don't know if I can do that with Zak, frankly." It occurred to her that Zak had not been on the phone proposing a rendezvous. Did he also have the sense of becoming a couple much too quickly?

They both had skills for a serious relationship, but perhaps they were too ready to stick it all together and let it run. She could end up living with him because they both knew so well how to live with a partner. He was, for all his travels, a thoroughly domestic man.

Another week went by, and still they did not talk. Becky was opening up. At one point on Saturday she said to Leila, leaning close, "You think I did it, I can tell, but you still like me. Don't you think that's kind of crazy?"

"If you'd hurt someone I loved, I'd hate you. But I never knew Terry, and his parents have been unpleasant. I try not to make a judgment about whether you did it, but simply to keep an open mind."

"I know you have to say that, but neither of us believes it for thirty seconds," Becky said, wrinkling her nose.

"Try to believe it. But I'm glad that you know I like you. I'm not supposed to like or dislike you, but I find that I can't help but respond."

"People like me better now, unless they've already decided to hate me," Becky said, staring at her hands. "It's fascinating. Don't you think it's because I'm famous now?"

"Do you think that's it? Or have you changed?" She thought of the people she had interviewed who had known Becky. Her family mostly adored her, but people she worked with did not. "She was a manipulative little bitch," one of her teachers, a radio announcer, told Leila. She noticed that people often spoke of Becky in the past tense. "She was cold. She didn't care about anybody but herself," a woman in Becky's office said. "You'd have to keep after her to pry loose a few bucks for pizza or a shower or a going-away present."

"She was efficient, but she was always trying to get on camera," her boss said. "She never gave up. Thought it was glamorous."

Her previous boss said, "She wasn't the friendly type. She did her work but she didn't give much of herself."

She found Becky reserved and careful, but also capable of charm. Perhaps murder had improved her self-confidence. Gently Leila probed in that direction—how Becky might feel she had changed.

"I've always been too trusting," Becky said, looking at Leila from under her lashes.

Leila did not believe this. She thought that Becky was always on guard. She had to be.

"Well, what worse can happen? My husband's murdered, and I'm going on trial. My own boyfriend, my ex-boyfriend, is accusing me. I might as well relax, because I've already been run over by a semi."

They both knew what worse was likely to happen, so neither mentioned it. Instead Leila asked her what she would really like to do. "Oh, I want to get off, of course. Then I think I'll move into Boston, to escape all the fuss and the gossip, you know?"

"Then what, if everything works out?"

"Well, remember that woman who had the affair with the guy running for president? Gary Hart. She was on every talk show and then she was a spokeswoman for jeans. I'd rather be an anchorwoman, but I wouldn't mind being the spokeswoman for something glamorous, like designer jeans or perfume or whatever, while I'm so well known."

They were in the visiting room at Barnstable House of Correction, as sad and bleak a setting as Leila could imagine, but Becky was smiling now, her sharp chin dug into her hand. Becky was running through all the talk shows, the ones she liked and the ones she thought tacky. Leila felt oddly moved. Becky was Leila without books, without the resources of the library to open a world beyond the tube. Without a cultural background, any girl's dreams could sound tawdry. Leila had learned to dream correctly.

Leila arrived home with the first urgent desire to see Zak she had experienced since the night with Nick and Sheryl. She felt awkward, uncertain what the silence on his end meant. Obviously they had both gone farther and faster than they meant to, but had he responded by deciding to quit? Their times together had been extraordinarily pleasant and rather easy. Yet both reacted with fear. She found she could not make herself call him. The coward's way: she wrote a note. "Dear Zak, We seem both to have fallen down our own rabbit holes. Would you like to get together? I would love to make you a meal for a change, if you're in the mood for coming in the city this week or next," was what she wrote on the fourth revision, copied into a perky card. Then she sweated how to sign it. Finally resolved upon: *Warmly, Leila*. That shouldn't scare him too badly, and it was tentative and casual enough, she hoped. Maybe taking a chance with her, risking a new and real relationship had been as out of character for him as it was for her. For once, she had broken her own rules and gambled.

Sunday morning she answered the phone, half-expecting Zak, and Mrs. Burgess greeted her. "If you could come today—it would have to be early—I could talk to you about my son."

Within fifteen minutes she was driving toward the Cape, quick, before Mrs. Burgess changed her mind. She had no idea what had prompted the call, but she was delighted. Mrs. Burgess greeted her at the door and ushered her this time into the downstairs family room, an area of beat-up sofas, overstuffed chairs, a big TV and stereo with CDs and newspapers scattered about. "My husband and my son Chris are off at the boat show today, so we have a little time."

"You don't want to talk about the murder in front of your family?"

"My husband has had two heart attacks. We've kept the boys . . . I mean we kept it from both of them and now from Chris. They both happened while the boys were in college. Francis can't get excited. I try to stand between him and all the scandal and gossip, but I'm not always able to keep it from him." Mrs. Burgess was a woman without animation, someone who had perhaps been sat on so hard in her childhood or adolescence that she would always speak almost without inflection and certainly without raising her voice, but what she was saying carried conviction.

Leila moved so that she could see past the reflections on Mrs. Burgess's glasses, to see the woman's eyes. Mrs. Burgess did not allow many expressions to touch her face. "You thought that talking with me in front of your husband might excite him dangerously?" Here is a secretly emotional woman, Leila thought, without outlet. Would she someday explode?

"Exactly," Mrs. Burgess said. "We live under that cloud. That was why I've been trying to sell this house. We need something easier to manage. We need to live in a senior community with a medical facility right there. It breaks my heart, but I was never able to make Terry understand why the two of them had to stand on their own feet. I didn't want them far from me. I just wanted them to settle in their own nice little places nearby so we could sell this white elephant. The taxes are huge and so is the upkeep."

"But you haven't sold it."

"The real estate market is slow. And after what happened to Terry, I just couldn't ask Chris to move out. I was afraid. My son only married that vixen because he felt rejected. I never meant for him to feel that way—I was only trying to protect his father."

"Why have you decided to talk to me?"

"I keep brooding over what happened to my family. I thought talking to you might help. But I don't think anything ever will. I live for the day the trial finally is over and that woman gets a little of what she deserves."

"Won't that just wake up all your feelings again? Going over the murder, what led to it."

"I can't let go. I can't forget for a single day. I just go over and over it again and try to imagine what I could have done to keep him from marrying her. I tried—I really tried. I hope I'll feel some kind of resolution at the trial. Sometimes I think I'm going crazy with anger and no way to speak it aloud."

She had a phone call from David Sunday night. "Mom, remember that sleeping bag you gave me a couple of years ago?"

"The super-light bag you wanted desperately from L. L. Bean and have used exactly once. I remember it, not very fondly."

"I used it more than once, come on. I need it. A bunch of us have a primitive cabin in Big Sur for a weekend. Please send it off tomorrow."

She looked in his closet, but she could not find the sleeping bag. Then she emptied everything from the bottom and the shelves. She could have sworn it had been there when they had cleaned out David's room after Thanksgiving. Maybe she had put it away in the basement with his skating gear?

Over the next two days, she looked in the basement and in the storage under the eaves. Wednesday morning she left a note for Mrs. Burke, asking her if she had put the bag away someplace. Leila briefly wondered if Nick could have taken it, but she couldn't imagine him going through David's closet. If the bag did not appear, courtesy of Mrs. Burke, she would call L. L. Bean and have one sent to him overnight. Somehow she would produce a damned sleeping bag, but she did wonder what could have become of it.

When she got home after working in her office at school all day,

Vronsky was not on the rug to greet her. She was immediately worried. Had Mrs. Burke accidentally let him out? She called him as she hung her coat to dry and pulled off her boots. He did not come. She ran through the rooms of the house and upstairs to her bedroom. There he was sprawled on the bed. Sick?

No, he was curled around a small black-and-white kitten like a dust-ball, who was holding on to him. At the sound of her voice, the kitten stirred and would have bolted, except that Vronsky put his heavy paw on the kitten and held it down. His wise yellow eyes looked at Leila and he purred loudly. Thank you for the present? Like Adam, had the kitten been made from his rib while he slept? Really. Only men would invent stories about babies popping from daddy's foreheads or coming from the clean and sexless side.

"Where did you get her?" Leila asked. The kitten's belly was distended and it looked ratty. Vronsky had been cleaning it. Leila sat on the bed and cautiously examined the kitten. Female, emaciated, but recently fed. There was an ugly sore on the neck. "You should never have been allowed in with Vronsky. Fleas, dozens of fleas. Tomorrow you go to the vet."

Downstairs she found a note from Mrs. Burke on the kitchen table.

> "Dear Mrs. Landsman: I'm sorry I don't remember about a sleeping bag. I hope that wasn't among the old stuff from your son's room we gave to Goodwill?
>
> "I found this kitten this morning in an alley with a dead mother cat and two other kittens who had just been killed by rats. I couldn't leave it to die, and my daughter is allergic. If you don't want it, take it to a shelter and they will dispose of it. I hope I didn't cause you any trouble. See you next Wednesday, Sincerely yours, Mrs. Mary Burke."

She dropped the kitten off at the vet's in the morning. Vronsky followed her to the door complaining loudly. In the late afternoon, she picked up a flealess cat with a dressing on its neck and all its shots. "It's a female," her vet said. "Suffering from malnutrition and what I suspect is a rat bite."

Obviously she was keeping it. Vronsky would never forgive her. She brought the kitten home to him and he sniffed it all over. She worried he would not recognize the kitten's smell, but he picked her up by the scruff of the neck as a mother cat would and carried her up to the bed, where Leila had changed the sheets and bedspread lest they have fleas forevermore.

She fed the kitten the milk substitute the vet had sold her, along with a special kitten food from the same source. The kitten ate everything and began to purr in a deep bass voice. She had not heard it meow at all. She did not hear any voice from it until she took it into the bathroom to put a new dressing on the wound, shutting Vronsky outside. At that point, the kitten burst into contralto despair. On the far side of the bathroom door, Vronsky sang a baritone lament. She called the cat Waif.

She was in bed that night reading when the phone rang. She expected Zak. It was Phyllis. "Leila, you've got to go to San Diego. Debbie's over her head."

"Mother, what are you talking about?"

"I can't do it. I can't just take off work. They'd love to fire me, a woman my age. And I don't have the strength to cope with it."

"Mother, what's happened to Debbie?"

"That yutz has taken off. He's left Debbie with three kids, chickens, horses, dogs, goats and a mortgage. And she's very pregnant, as you know. She called me up crying her eyes out."

"But Mother, I'm in the middle of a divorce myself—"

"About time. What did he ever do for you? You're better off alone. I always thought he was the worst kind of luftmensch. You'll do just fine, Leila. You're the strong one."

"Maybe I'm tired of being the strong one—"

"Like hell. You wouldn't trade places with Debbie for five minutes. You just hop on a plane and go straighten things out. Debbie can't do anything but sit there and tear her hair."

"I'll talk to her. But I have responsibilities, Mother. I can't just fly off because Debbie's in trouble again."

"Leila, I'd go myself but for my job. I can't risk losing it. Soon they'll get rid of me for good, and then all I'll have is my social security and a nest egg. Joan and I save more together than we could on our own, but I can't dash out there."

"Mother, can you imagine Debbie dropping everything and coming out here because my marriage just fell apart?"

"Would you want her to? You're who you are and she's who she is. I'm the one who supported the family and your father was the one who fell apart. Now I have a partner who goes fifty/fifty with me, but how long did it take me to strike gold? It'll get your mind off your troubles, right? And you can drop in on David."

"I'm not sure how he'd feel about that." She saw before her endless phone calls, to Debbie, who would cry; to David, who would not be in the dorm, and then would call back after she had gone to sleep. She had to call her travel agent in the morning and leave a message at the cleaning service for Mrs. Burke to feed the cats. And when she got to California, what could she do? She had spent her early twenties instructing her sister how she should live, to no end except to make Debbie angry. Her ordinary response to any statement of Debbie's was disbelief. How could you do that? How could you believe that? What else did you think was going to happen?

Looking at her younger sister, she saw a woman who did not believe in the laws of gravity or of cause and effect. Looking back at her, what did Debbie see, except a busybody dull hausfrau who counted every penny and measured every response. She found Debbie chaotic and Debbie found her controlling. It would not be pleasant, but she did not doubt that Debbie needed her.

She remembered other years and other crises. Debbie had been abandoned with her first baby in Cincinnati in what turned out to be a cocaine deal gone sour her unemployed husband had run out on, leaving know-nothing Debbie and her baby to face two angry hoodlums. She remembered when Debbie had left Robin's father everything except two kids and one suitcase of their clothing. Debbie intended to go to Phyllis, but her purse was stolen in Chicago.

Phyllis was right: she resented being the strong and sensible one who had to pick up the pieces and pay whoever had to be bought off, but she would not live Debbie's life for a day.

CHAPTER 47

BECKY

Becky walked in Friday night to find Terry glaring at her. "I wonder why that hag downstairs gets home from this play business a full forty-five minutes before you do."

"Simple, Terry. She's just the wardrobe lady. I have one of the important roles this time. She can leave before we're done rehearsing. She just has a walk-on in the first act." She carefully folded her cardigan. "It's not like you to worry about me." Normally he didn't demonstrate enough interest to work up a decent suspicion. On the table near the door she spied an envelope, addressed to Chris's insurance office.

"I'd be a fool not to get suspicious. I saw what a fuss you made about that Berg guy the night I went to your play."

"He's married, and furthermore, I think he's a ham. I have absolutely no interest in him. I don't even particularly like him."

"Then how come you hang around those people so late?"

"I'll quit immediately, Terry, if you want me to. I only want to please you. I'll tell them Monday to get someone else."

He shrugged, losing interest at once. "Why should I care? I just wanted to know where you were so late."

"Terry, it's just a way of getting some practice at being onstage. I was a gofer in the first production, but I have a substantial role in this one. I'd be happy to quit. I'd rather spend more time with you."

He seemed deflated. He had been working himself up to fight. She felt as if she were crossing a river on thin black ice. She had to take every step carefully, always ready to retreat or dart ahead. He wanted out, but he did not know how to get rid of her. She was playing a conciliatory game, backing down at once, offering anything to prevent the confrontation he sought. She smiled slightly to think that if he was planning to get rid of her, she was also planning to be rid of him.

He stood staring at her. He had a habit of staring at her lately as if he had just begun to see her and did not like what he saw. "Have you been hanging around your dope-dealing brother?"

"He was just holding that for a friend. He'll never do it again. And no, I haven't seen him all week. I know you're mad at him."

"Why should I be angry with him? He's just like the rest of your family. My parents warned me, but I didn't listen."

"I've tried to please your parents, you know I have."

He slumped into a chair, his mouth twisted into a sour grimace. "We can't make it together, Becky. We should never have got married. This is just shit. You belong among your kind and I belong among mine."

"I thought we became each other's kind by marrying."

"We'll both be better off out of here. You know there was a break-in this Tuesday, downstairs on the end?"

"Helen told me."

She imagined a bullet entering his forehead above his eyes. But she had asked Sam casually if he knew how to use a gun, and he did not—a pity, because she was sure she could get one from Tommy. Tommy would do anything short of killing Terry. He wouldn't go that far for her. Nobody but Sam would, if she could make him.

She sat down on the arm of the chair Terry was sprawled in. "I'm tired," he said, guessing she wanted to make love. Guess again, she thought, but stroked the hair back on his head. What a strange flat head he had. They would have to fake a robbery. A break-in, like the other one. During the daytime, the burglars had entered from the porch and taken a TV, a VCR, money and jewelry. Now suppose they had found someone at home. Maybe if Terry confronted them, that was a scenario. So if they didn't have a gun, what would they do? Hit him with something.

But Sam was no bigger than Terry. The two of them could surely manage to knock him down and then do it, but it would make a lot of noise. She was still coming home every day to make him lunch. She tried to vary the time a bit so that Terry would not feel safe about having his girl over. It was critical that he not start bringing Heather to the condo, or that would burn her chances.

"Becky, it's not working. Listen to me. Do you want to move out? It doesn't matter. I'm putting this place on the market as soon as I talk to a lawyer."

"You're going to see a lawyer?"

"My dad knows one. You should see one too, I guess."

"When are you seeing the lawyer?"

"I have to call him."

Good. He hadn't done it yet. "Please, I want us to go to a marriage counselor first. Please. I'll find the name of a good one. If we can't work it out with a marriage counselor, then I'll give you a divorce without fighting you. But please, let's try. We were married in church. Do you want to try for an annulment?" That could take months.

"My mother wants me to go that route. She says there's never been a divorce in the family."

"Ours too. We could see a priest. The Church will counsel us."

"Becky, what's the use? I don't want to be with you." He pulled away from her in the chair.

She stood and walked to the center of the room. Then she pivoted. "You'd rather be with Heather?"

His mouth dropped open. Then he shut it with a little click. "How did . . . Heather?"

"I even know where she lives."

"How do you know about Heather? Who told you? Did you hire a detective?"

"Don't be silly, Terry. I wasn't even suspicious. I'm just too trusting. It never occurred to me you were cheating on me."

"Who told you?"

"I can't tell you that. . . . It would cause too much trouble. I just want things to be good again between us."

"Fuck you, Becky. Who told you?" He stood up and clenched his fists at her. He charged forward and shook her shoulders hard so that her neck whipped back, then dropped his hands as if she were hot to the touch.

Was he actually going to hit her? She didn't think so, but he was red in the face. His eyes were bulging, his lips drawn thin and white. "I can't tell you. I didn't believe it, but he told me all the details. How you went away with her last weekend. Everything." She edged toward the door, in case he was angry enough to attack.

"Who could tell you that? Nobody but Chris knows."

"Chris has always liked me, Terry, no matter what he may say to you. He says you don't appreciate me. He was worried about me."

"That bastard introduced me to Heather. He went out with her first! No, you're lying." He pounded his fist on the table. Everything rattled. "You're a rotten liar, Becky."

"I'm not saying who told me. But she lives on Seagull Lane. I even know which house. I know you went to Giuseppi's with her. And how would I pay a detective? I just know what this person told me."

"You're lying! Chris wouldn't talk to you. He'd never tell you."

"Believe what you want to." She sauntered off to the bathroom. When she came out, he had torn a sheet and blanket off the bed and he was lying on the couch with his head under the covers. She went quietly into the bedroom, but she did not sleep. She plotted. She was happy now solely when she was with Sam or when she was imagining Terry dying in front of her. Only by staging his punishment again and again could she endure him.

He was finicky in the morning, objecting to the milk, claiming it was turning, as if he wasn't home all day and couldn't just go and buy some. She smiled. It was marvelously bracing to her patience to think of bashing his head in soon, very soon. She must act fast. She had volunteered to walk Helen's dog. She said she'd get milk. She waited till he was in the bathroom, then took the forms from the table and ran out. She tore them into tiny bits and flushed them down Helen's toilet while Helen was putting on Florrie's leash. From a pay phone she called Sam and then Tommy. When she got back, he was fuming about the forms from the table.

"Oh, that letter? I just mailed it. I thought it was something that ought to be mailed. I'm sorry."

Once again he looked deflated. "You mailed it?"

"Didn't you want me to?"

"Sure," he said. "Sure. Thanks."

Saturday afternoon she drove to Sam's house. She waited till they had made love, on his narrow bed under the poster of the tidal marsh. Then she began to mimic weeping. "This is the last time, the last time," she said in his arms, her voice trembling. She really did feel like bawling. Everything was difficult and tense, and time was running out.

"What do you mean, the last time? Don't you love me any longer?" Sam gripped her arms.

"Of course I love you. I love you more than I love living, believe me. If it was just me he's threatening, I wouldn't hesitate. You're worth any amount of pain, any amount of danger."

"What do you mean, he's threatening you. Terry? Is he hitting you again?"

"He told me I have to quit the theater. He's suspicious. He sees I don't ride with Helen any longer and I don't come home the same time she does. He was sitting up last night. Then I noticed he was following me this afternoon, but I got away from him. He's going to do something violent, Sam, I'm telling you. It's my life or his, I swear it."

"What do you mean, your life or his?"

"He's going to kill me. If you really care for me, then you'll help me get rid of him the only way I can. He'll never give me a divorce. He'll never let go of me. He'll kill me, and if he finds out about you, he'll kill you too."

"You don't mean it. You're upset." He let her go and sat up with his back to the wall, frowning helplessly.

"I mean it, Sam. It's my life and maybe yours. If we don't kill him, and do it this week, I'll never be able to see you again. He's making me quit the theater. He's watching me all the time. Tonight or some other night this week, I'll go home and you'll hear about it the next day. I'm a small woman."

His hands moved convulsively. He shook his head as if trying to clear water from his ears. For maybe half an hour they argued. He wouldn't believe there was no other option. She argued doggedly, watching the clock out of the corner of her eye. She had to persuade him before three-thirty, when she must leave. She was meeting Tommy, who had promised her some sleeping pills. If Terry was groggy, if they could catch him in bed, it would all be easier.

He said, "We can run away together. We can hop on a bus tomorrow."

"What would we do for money? I have less than two hundred dollars. Do you imagine he couldn't trace us? There are only two bus routes off the Cape."

"We can take your car and run away."

"You think he couldn't trace that car? He'd probably report it stolen. It's in his name, not in mine. His parents bought it for him years ago."

"We could go to Canada. Montreal."

"First, we couldn't work there. Second, understand his family has money. He can afford to hire a detective, and he will. We'd be fugitives.

And you'll never be able to see your mom or your uncle. You'll quit school and never finish. You'll never go to college, the way you deserve to."

"I can't bear this," he said, his hands digging into her shoulders. "There's got to be a way. We can't give up! Nothing matters except you."

"I don't believe you. Or you'd have the courage for what we have to do."

"People go to plastic surgeons and get their appearance changed. People even get their fingerprints changed, I've read about it."

"Who pays for all this surgery? No, you just want to play games with me." Finally she tore the sheet away from herself and embraced him. "One last time together, and then never again. Take me. Make love to me so that I remember you. Because I'll never be alone with you again. Ever."

She half expected him not to be able to, he was so upset, but at his age, she guessed nothing could get in the way. She had not been able to bring him around to her plan, but she would see what a few days without sex would do. This was the first time she had not come with him, but she was annoyed that he was resisting her. Men were always disappointing her. Even Sam. But she still hoped that she could bring him around.

CHAPTER 48

MARY

Mary was glad to have the abandoned building to stay in and Beverly's company. Tomorrow, Wednesday, she was to clean Mrs. Landsman's and feed her cats the next few days. She had not yet told Beverly she would be gone for four nights. Mrs. Landsman was finally traveling again. She was off to California early tomorrow; she would be gone before Mary arrived to take possession of the house.

This was going to be a cozy squat. Mrs. L. always had plenty of food in the refrigerator and the cupboards, and she did not keep a tight inventory. There were comfortable places to sit and draperies to draw. The kid and the husband were off the scene. She would take care of Bronskee and see how Kitten was doing. She thought of Kitten as her own kind, ill-treated, unwanted. But at least Kitten might have a home. Mrs. Landsman seemed to have forgotten about the sleeping bag, at least Mary hoped so.

She had to figure out what to tell Beverly. She wanted to ask Beverly to come to the house and stay with her, but Beverly smelled. She was obviously a bag lady. She could not slip through the streets of residential Cambridge as Mary could. People who would not glance at Beverly when she was squatting by the curb or huddled in a shop entrance, would stare and start asking questions if she ambled along Garden Street with her shopping cart heaped with her bags and blanket.

The homeless were either invisible in their expected hangouts, or stridently visible if they appeared beyond their grates and doorways.

Mary's trick was not looking homeless, a task that had been difficult for the past ten days, sleeping in the abandoned building. Usually her clients were not at home when she arrived, and the first thing she did was clean up, wash her clothes. She had improved life in the squat by pilfering matches, an old pot, two plastic jugs to tote water.

Beverly panhandled some, but she hated it, and she was terrible. Houdini had a routine down. He could still do card tricks when his hands did not shake. His sidekick Mouse was illiterate, but he could heave and haul for cheap movers. Once or twice a week, they would need somebody extra for a heavy job. Mouse and Mary brought in money regularly, while Houdini and Beverly worked trash and garbage cans and the alleys in Back Bay. Gradually they were furnishing their squat. Mary and Beverly had two broken chairs and an old Formica kitchen table. They had several lengths of carpeting over the windows to keep the cold out. They slept on another old rug, placed under Beverly's mattress and her sleeping bag.

Every morning Houdini, Beverly and Mouse, if he did not have a job that day, went the round of Dumpsters, looking for returnable bottles and cans, items they could eat or scavenge. After lunch, they would hit the fast-food places again and the areas where office workers had lunch.

"Found a whole bag of doughnuts on a bench at the Arlington T stop. Some fool went off and left them. Not day-old either," Houdini boasted.

"In the women's room at Filene's, she found a scarf. You can borrow it, Mary, and in a phone she found twenty cents. Also that candy machine in the Washington Red Line station is broken again and if you jiggle it right, it gives you what the last person bought. She had a lovely candy bar with nuts for lunch." The wages of Beverly's day of ceaseless scavenging.

They all went through the streets alternately looking down, hunched over to see a safety pin, a bobby pin, a comb, a good butt, a half-eaten sandwich, a useful bag, pennies, cans or bottles that could be turned to cash; and quickly looking around to make sure no trouble was about to land on them, no kid was going to attack, no cop had picked them out to bother.

Although they had tried to come and go quietly, some of the neighborhood kids noticed them. Two days before, someone had come in and messed with their stuff, urinated on one of the rugs, broke some bottles. Beverly had been hassled on the street and had taken to carrying a heavy stick she had whittled to a sharp point. She was afraid of rape, afraid of mugging. She was afraid of the kids, but kids were everywhere, and this was a good squat.

Mary could not tell if Beverly's fears were justified, or leftover paranoia from her rape and beating. Mary had never been raped, although she had been chased down the street several times, propositioned, slapped around. Beverly said most of the bag ladies had been raped. The police generally thought it was funny. No one had ever been charged in the assault on Beverly.

No, Mary could not bring Beverly back to Cambridge with her. She would depart the squat for the four nights she had secure at Mrs. Landsman's. She was fighting a head cold anyhow, probably from the smoke and being chilled all the time. But she could not figure out any way to insert Beverly into her scam and take her to Mrs. Landsman's large and comfortable house. She felt guilty that she could not share her squat, as Beverly was sharing, but Mary had the feeling that would be the end of everything.

Gingerly Mary raised the issue over coffee made in a misshapen aluminum pan over a fire of Sterno. "One of my ladies says I can stay in her house for the next three nights." Later she would say she could stay one more night. "Then I'll come back. She had a family emergency and she wants me to sleep in and take care of her kids."

"Is she paying you extra?"

"Some. You know how they are." She felt guilty lying to Beverly, lying and keeping the warmth and the good bed to herself, but Beverly had been twisted out of shape by life on the streets. She talked to herself and she swung her new stick menacingly as she strolled. Mary was afraid to leave her scant possessions in the squat, in case the kids came again.

"I'm saving for a car," Mary confided. "I know I can't make enough for an apartment, but if I could buy an old station wagon or an old van, then I'd have it made."

"She'd like one of them mobile homes," Beverly said, leaning back on her greasy blanket. "Winnebagos, they call them. You could just sit yourself down and live as good as in a house. Follow the sun. Now wouldn't that be something? One time, a bunch of us a got a site at a campground on the Cape and we slept there for a week. Now, that was grand. Then for another week, we slept out in the woods. Then it started raining all the time and we had to come back."

"All those off-season houses, sometimes I think about them. I met a woman like us last year in a mall, we started talking. We recognized each other. She spent two years in Maine. She had stayed in rich people's summer houses.'' Rich people. Mary smiled. With Jim, people like those had dined at her house. They were not rich people. Only to the poor. They were affluent. "But she got caught. One of the kids came up suddenly and called the police on her.''

"What did they do to her?''

"The kids roughed her up. The cops kept her in jail overnight and then one of the local ministers put her on a bus to Boston. She was looking for another resort. She was thinking about the Vineyard.''

Beverly rubbed her sore feet. "Now, where in Maine? She knows Maine like the back of her hand. Don't you love how we can sit up and talk here? This is real freedom, Mary. We can make it nice here, our own.'' Beverly sounded calm, content.

Mary had worked for Mrs. Solano today, and she had some leftover bread, nice Italian bakery bread, and a couple of apples they split four ways. Also a few biscotti and some walnuts and carrots. She took what would not be missed. Houdini could not chew the walnuts or the carrots, since he didn't have enough teeth left, but he soaked the biscotti in water. She had stopped and bought hot dogs, which they boiled in the battered pan. It took forever over the Sterno, but the smell was great. They ate them with the bread.

"Sometimes I dream about food,'' Houdini said. "Roast chicken. I used to love chicken at Sunday dinner. And chocolate cake.''

Houdini's feet were bothering him. Mary could not stay in the room when he unwrapped his feet, it made her gag, but Beverly helped him. Mary was ashamed that she could not stand the smell. He had foot ulcers, and his socks had worked into his skin. Finally Mouse and Houdini retired upstairs. Sometimes she wondered if they were lovers, but she didn't think so. They both drank in place of sex. If they were, they had a right. It was small-enough comfort they all were able to give each other. Years ago, she would have thought an old man (if Houdini was old, in fact) and a kid together, both male, were a terrible sin and a scandal, even worse because of the mixing of races, but she did not think so any longer. They took care of each other as best they could. If she had learned anything on the streets, it was to judge people by their kindliness, not by their looks or race. Jim, who called her Holy Mary when she was scandalized at people's carryings-on around them in Bethesda, would now have been shocked by her easy tolerance of what he would have called deviates.

Staying here was flirting with life outside the pale, life on the streets, yet she had not felt so at-home with anyone in years. She was honest with Beverly and the boys, she was herself. She could let herself begin to care for Beverly. She would miss her friend's company tonight. A friend: how could any of her ladies in their comfortable houses understand how rare and precious it was for her to have a friend? When she had lived in Bethesda, friends were women with whom she played tennis, went to the beauty salon, played bridge, exchanged recipes. With Beverly she shared the truth of her life, she shared security and danger, she shared what food and warmth they had between them. On the streets, friendship could mean life or death. Samatha's friendship had saved her life eight years before.

"Her head bothers her sometimes," Beverly confided. "It hurts where they worked on her. She gets terrible headaches. She sure wishes she had that stuff they gave her in the hospital. But she never did see pills like that lying around the street."

"I'll look through my ladies' medicine cabinets and see what I can find." Mary crawled into her sleeping bag, fully dressed, and fell asleep in spite of the cold. She always woke up three or four times during the night. She had to pee. Somebody in the street would scream, or a car would hit another with a resounding crash. A fight would break out. Bottles would smash against the house. She did not take that personally, as the house looked deserted. She never peered out, for fear of being seen. Neighborhood rivalries and quarrels were not their business. Only survival was.

She woke up sweating. Her first thought was she had a fever. It was strange to be too warm. Then she was choking and she realized it was smoke. She struggled out of her sleeping bag and stuffed it in her carry-all. Then she shook Beverly. "The place is on fire!" she screamed.

Beverly did not wake up. She moaned and turned over. Mary grabbed the bucket of water they were using and poured it on Beverly, who sat up then, cursing. Mary had accidentally poured water on herself. Her feet were sopping and she had splashed herself up the front. "What the fuck are you doing? Woman, are you crazy? She's soaking wet," Beverly screeched.

Mary ran into the hall, shouting upstairs, screaming to Houdini and Mouse. The stairway was full of smoke. "Beverly, we got to get out now." She tried to remember if there was a fire escape. "Come on, Beverly, now!" She ran up the steps yelling for Houdini and Mouse. The downstairs was on fire. She smelled something. Gasoline. Somebody had torched the building. "Beverly, come on, it's going up! Now!" She ran back and dragged Beverly upright and tried to pull her along.

"Leave her alone, she got to get her stuff," Beverly said between hacking. Coughing and fumbling for her stuff, she punched Mary. Mary went over backward and struck her hip hard.

"Now, Beverly, now!" Mary stamped her foot in frustration and grabbed her purse and carry-all. Most of her stuff was in the corner and it was too late. She ran for the stairs with her coat half on and plunged into the smoke. Her eyes burned and she could not breathe. She kept running. Her coat was on fire. She let it fall and kept running. The fire had been set on the first floor. She ran through it and down the steps to the basement and through to the street. Whoever had set it at least had not locked them in. The door swung wide. She ran out. Her sweater was on fire. She remembered about falling down and rolling. She rolled on the filthy wet ground. Then she picked up her stuff, stamped out the cinders, the sparks that had landed. She was without a coat. She unzipped her sleeping bag and draped it around her shoulders. When she turned back, she could see flames even through the boarded-up windows. "Beverly! Beverly!" she screamed. "Houdini! Mouse!" She called till she was hoarse. Somebody pushed up a window and yelled for her to shut up.

"Call the fire department," she croaked back. "The block is burning."

She kept coughing. She had breathed too much smoke. She felt dizzy and short of breath. She could not get enough oxygen into her lungs. She was freezing and wet, but she could not stand anything against her arm. Her right arm was badly burned. It hurt so intensely that tears kept running down her face. Maybe she could go to an emergency room. Maybe they would take care of her. She had to work in the morning.

Still it felt like half an hour before the fire truck arrived. "There's three people squatting in that building," she said to a fireman, tugging at him.

"Get out of the way, lady. Go home. If they're alive, we'll find them."

But of course they weren't.

CHAPTER 49

LEILA

Leila got off the plane in San Diego to a temperature of seventy-two under a dry sun, but her sister Debbie did not meet her. Instead, at the baggage carousel, a tall big-boned woman with a shock of stand-up white hair was waiting for her. "Howdy. I'm Debbie's neighbor, Babs. She asked me to bring you from the airport. I got my pickup outside in the lot."

Babs was not talkative on the drive to Santa Ysabel. Leila learned that Babs had never been East, was that rare breed, a born-and-bred Californian from Mecca, where dates were grown near the Anza-Borrego desert. Babs had been married, had four kids, all grown up, and was a widow. That was the sum of what Leila, who had interviewed murderers and battered woman, attackers and victims with remarkable success, was able to pry from the taciturn woman at the wheel of the old red pickup. That and a few attitudes. Easterners were not much use. Debbie was hopeless but good with horses. Her kids were okay, especially Robin. Her husband Red had been a pain in the butt.

When they reached the remarkably green mountains, patches of snow began to crust the ground. These southern coastal mountains rarely rose above three thousand feet, but that seemed enough to change not only the climate but the season. Leila thought it would have been nice if somebody had warned her. She had brought clothes suitable for

L.A. in January, but apparently not Santa Ysabel. She was nervous and annoyed that Debbie had not come to see her.

"She hates riding in the bumpy truck. Scared of losing the baby."

Debbie already had three kids by three different husbands/boyfriends. Only one of the exes, the therapist Bruce, paid his child support regularly. Once in a while a check came in from the musician. Leila had never been to this place. The last time she had visited Debbie, Debbie was living in Pomona, in the Valley, where she had been into compulsive spending and had racked up six thousand on her credit cards.

After the therapist husband had decamped, peppering the financial landscape with letters that he was no longer responsible for her debts, Debbie had decided that she had been corrupted by consumer culture. She had been ready for the suburban cowboy, Red Rodgers. Red had parked Debbie here, where the battered pickup jounced over deep ruts of mud and rock, back among the pines to a raw-boned ranch house that looked pried from a development.

Surrounding it were a paddock where a horse and colt stood in the shallow snow, outbuildings, sheds, a chicken run, a barn, the remains of a vegetable garden, a couple of dead vehicles, all fading into the surrounding forest. The woods were pretty, but the house was a faded pink with aluminum gutters. An upended tricycle lay beside the remains of a snowman. Why did she feel so depressed? Why did she want to turn and run back to Cambridge?

Debbie was waiting in the kitchen. Three children and a fourth on the way, and she was still thin. Her belly was big, but the rest of her stayed childlike. Standing near Debbie always made Leila feel oversized, huge, baggy, sagging, bursting with flesh. Never had there been a problem in childhood or adolescence in differentiating between her clothes and Debbie's. Hers were the economy size; Debbie's, the petite, cute things.

The two older kids, Abel and Robin, were at school. The toddler, Ben, glared at her from Debbie's side. He was blond and skinny and fierce-looking. He tugged hard on his mother's arm, his teeth bared, almost growling. Leila collapsed in a chair. "I left home at four-thirty your time. I'm wrung out."

Debbie appealed to the ceiling. "Really, Leila, anybody would think you don't enjoy traveling! You travel more than anybody I've ever known—except for Bung, of course." The musician. "I'm just a stick-at-home."

"Same with me," said Babs. "Got a little java on the fire? That would hit the spot."

"You know I can't drink coffee, Babs. It wouldn't be good for my baby." Debbie patted her stomach.

Leila started a list in her head of things she had to go to town to buy. Without coffee, she would not survive the day. Debbie rose to brew herb tea, which Babs said she would accept as a last resort. As Debbie stood, the contrast between her rounding belly and her almost spindly arms and legs, her long slender neck, was even more marked, almost spidery.

Leila was annoyed at herself for complaining. She must not start off wrong with Debbie. They had such a long and messy history, offering little satisfaction to either. Now that she had just lost a husband, she should try to make a meaningful connection with her only sister. Debbie had been the flake with the broken relationships, while solid Leila rotated within her marriage.

When Babs had finished her tea and lumbered out, Debbie at once burst into tears. At the kitchen table she wept with her head on her hands. Ben glared at Leila harder, blaming her for his mother's upset. Finally he began banging on Leila's knee, the easiest part of her to reach. Debbie stopped crying. "Ben, behave yourself! You don't just walk up to your aunt and hit her."

Ben took refuge against his mother. "Ben, at Thanksgiving, you came to my house. We ate turkey and you played with my cat, Vronsky. Remember?"

Ben stuck his thumb in his mouth, looking confused.

"Debbie, why did Roy, I mean, Red leave? Is there any chance he might come back?"

"He was going to San Diego all the time, he was supposed to be involved in some development. But he had a girlfriend, it turns out. She manages a hotel in Del Mar. She makes a good living and she doesn't have any kids."

"An older woman?"

Debbie shook her head in exasperation. "Older than who? Leila, I'm forty-two. Why do you always imagine I'm still a kid?"

"He picked a great time. What is it, fifth, sixth month?"

"You don't understand, I like having babies. Maybe this is the last one I'll get. I feel like you look at me, and you think, Oh, Poor Debbie! Another man's gone and left her. But what I see is, Well, that lasted a couple of years and I got this great kid out of it. I got him to give me a kid. And the kids are really all mine, except for Ben. His father Bruce, you remember Bruce? relates to all of them."

"He's a saint. Is Red giving you any money?"

"He's been good about that. This new woman, she's loaded, so he's being generous. And like I said, Bruce sends child support every month."

"Does he still have partial custody?"

"He comes and gets them for a weekend every month, all except Abel. Abel won't go. He and Bruce never got along. Robin likes Bruce. So Robin and Ben go every fourth Friday. He spoils them." Debbie shrugged.

Leila made supper. "Why do I always take over the kitchen when we're together?"

"You like to run things," Debbie said. "Why should I care? I have to get supper on the table the other three hundred sixty days in the year."

"I don't do that much cooking when I'm home."

"I don't believe you. You've always liked playing Julia Child."

"Debbie, I'm alone. Nick is living with another woman. David's off at school. I'm in the process of selling the house in Cambridge."

"What are you planning to do?" Debbie looked dismayed. "You're not planning to come out here, are you? You're not thinking of that. I know Mom is capable of trying to talk you into it."

"Debbie! I'm tenured faculty at Lesley. I don't even plan to leave Cambridge if I can find something affordable. That's where my friends are."

Debbie looked skeptical, a way she'd always had of tilting her head slightly, looking from under lowered lids. "With Nick gone and David out here at school, what's to keep you?"

"My life, Debbie, my life. I don't want another one. I just want to improve the one I have."

"I do need help, but you and me under one roof, it would never work out."

Leila felt like bellowing that Debbie was the last person she'd live with in the entire country. "Absolutely not," she contented herself with saying. "Debbie, let's try to talk with each other this time instead of at each other."

"That would be some kind of change."

"What do you want me to do while I'm here?"

"Just listen to me and don't be so damn judgmental. Help me figure out the finances. Get me a lawyer. Those kind of things." Debbie jumped up and wiped her face briskly. "My four o'clock will be here any moment."

"Can you still do it pregnant?"

"I don't lift them. I can handle it. I know how to move."

Debbie called herself a massage therapist. She gave regular massages for sore muscles and stress, relief from pain after accidents and over-exertion, but she also gave advice. She was good at the massage and the advice must be acceptable, because whenever she stayed in a place long enough, she built up a clientele. She could set her own hours, work at home. Sometimes she made two hundred dollars a day, once she had settled in; sometimes she made nothing.

"Why can't she save money?" Phyllis complained. "She makes more than I do, with all my years of experience. So why can't she put some away?"

"With three kids? Don't fool yourself, she can't get ahead."

That was a conversation they'd had over the past few years again and again. Phyllis could do little for Debbie aside from buying the kids an occasional toy and sending them a small check and a videotape from Grandma now and then. Phyllis had bought herself a video camera and taped everything from bowling with her cronies to family greetings.

Robin came home from school, dropped at the end of the road by the school bus. She climbed into Leila's lap. Robin was eight and very dark, her black hair in braids with red bows. She clung to Leila. "Where's David?" She had a crush on her cousin.

"David's in college."

"He isn't coming?"

"Not this time. He has to stay in school."

Abel was the last home. He did not arrive until Debbie had finished her five o'clock and Leila was holding the spaghetti sauce on low. She forbade herself to say, How you've grown. She remembered David's spurts of growth. It embarrassed him to be exclaimed over. Abel had dark brown curly hair like Sam, but he was much taller and exceptionally thin. He had his basketball gear in a canvas bag. She stopped and did her figuring. Abel would be fifteen in three weeks. Had his father been tall? She could no longer remember. She watched him at supper, remembering David at fifteen.

Abel was at the sullen age, angry because he needed a car where they lived and he was still too young and there was probably no money for one anyhow. He was angry because there was one sex too many in the world and he hadn't figured out yet how to relate to that. He was angry because he was growing so fast his body hurt and his voice was uncertain and sometimes betrayed him. He was angry because he was six feet one and still didn't need to shave. He was angry because he was secretly convinced he was some kind of pervert monster and he did not know what to do with himself, and it must be somebody's fault—probably his mother's. Leila recognized the age and the stage.

She was ridiculously surprised that Abel was as large and as old as he was, as if Debbie's children should grow more slowly than David had. Debbie was right, she thought of her sister as younger than she was. She was still waiting for Debbie to grow up, whereas Debbie had made consistent choices for years that always diverged from what Leila would have wanted.

She sat down with Debbie, her checkbook, her mortgage book, her tax returns, her estimated income. Debbie got cranky fast. To her budgeting reeked of calculation. "I like to take each day as it comes," Debbie said. "I don't believe in pretending we can know the future. The earth could blow up tomorrow. We could all die in a nuclear accident. Why pretend I know my income next year? I could be in an auto accident on the freeway. I could win the lottery."

Here was Debbie who had no idea how much she earned in a year and where the money went, sitting over the kitchen table with Leila, who always knew exactly how much money she had in the bank and what expenses she expected to cover that month. Here was Debbie, who made perhaps half what Leila earned, saying that frankly she never worried about money, to Leila who had spent the last month trying to work out her post-divorce budget. Through the door from the living room came the clamor of the TV and the squabbling of the two older kids. Why did Debbie make her self-conscious? She felt defensive about traits that ordinarily she took for granted or felt proud of.

As the next day bumped along, she failed to help Debbie much, for old annoyances caused them both to bob and weave and duck imaginary punches as well as real ones. It was also clear that Debbie was not going to make it without help. It might be that she would quickly find another man. But not that quickly. She was too pregnant. With four kids, Debbie would have a harder time finding a new man than she had with three; yet Leila wasn't sure that was the problem. Lack of a man might be part of the solution.

She had thought of Red the suburban cowboy as having saddled Debbie with his dreams, lugging her off to the backwoods and leaving her with a dozen bellowing farm animals. But Debbie insisted on riding still, although the doctor advised against it. She said her mare was gentle. She tried to get Leila up on a horse, in vain. Instead Debbie took her daily ride with Babs, who cantered over from the next house, a quarter of a mile away. They stood around in the yard and talked horses and goats and weather.

Debbie had always been far better at mothering than Leila. Leila had never been the sort who made cookies fresh and created beautiful Halloween costumes and masks. Leila was usually trying to get David to eat apples and oranges instead of cookies, and Halloween costumes were either bought at a novelty shop or up to her son's ingenuity.

Now she saw Debbie the mini-rancher. The colt was to be Robin's. Robin and Debbie curried their animals side by side in the later afternoon, gossiping about horses. Leila could not even tell what they were talking about, a local competition in some obscure horse art. Abel's job was taking care of the chickens. He also sold eggs. Red might be gone, but Debbie had put down roots here as she never had in Pomona or Cincinnati or St. Louis or Atlanta, any of the cities she had sojourned in. The mare, far from being a burden, appeared to have introduced Debbie to many women: some ten years younger; several, like Babs, much older. Debbie had always connected to other mothers through day care, through school, but now she had other ties. Women with horses appeared to befriend each other.

She wasn't going to scoop up Debbie and bring her to Cambridge, as she had imagined. Whatever she could do for Debbie, it would have to be done here. If Debbie had help, she could work more, and the financial situation would ease. At least they could count on goat's milk, cheese and eggs.

"Have you considered taking in another woman to live with you?"

"I put an ad in the paper, but the women who came, they wanted someone to take care of them. You think I'm romantic, but even I could see that."

"Isn't Red trying to make you sell this place?"

Debbie shook her head no. "He feels so guilty about leaving me pregnant, he's giving me the house. Besides, his girlfriend's got a house he likes better, just three blocks from the ocean. He just wants me to keep quiet through the divorce and not bug him about the baby."

"I guess that's convenient, in its way."

"See, he changed his mind about living up here last winter. He found the winter boring. He started talking about moving to San Diego then. I knew it was trouble. If I'd been willing to pick up and go to the city with him, he'd never have taken up with that woman." Debbie ran her hands nervously through her hair. "When it came to choosing between him and this place, I want this place. I know you think I'm crazy, but that's how it is. I'd rather be poor living here than in a little house or apartment in the Valley." Debbie glared, expecting to be read a lecture, but Leila only nodded.

"I understand."

CHAPTER 50

BECKY

Becky called in sick to rehearsal Monday evening and spent it virtually sitting on Terry. She had bought two books on saving a marriage and insisted on reading aloud the choicest bits to him. His eyes glazed over. She almost felt pity for him. If he could be bored to death, he would be dead.

"Becky," he said, a beaten look on his face. "Why do you want to stay with me? You can't like the way things have been going any better than I do. Why not hang it up?"

"Divorce is immoral," she said, something she was sure neither of them believed for two minutes. "If you want an annulment, I'd agree, because then we each could marry again. But why not try? We loved each other. I still love you." She could hardly explain the truth to him, that she wanted the condo far more than she wanted him; she wanted to stay in the desperate middle class, as opposed to the desperately poor.

"Becky, this is crazy. We don't even really like each other. You don't ski or golf, you don't watch sports, let alone take part in any. You don't like my family or my friends. You want to go dancing and to parties. I don't see any point in that if I have a girl already. To me, the only use is for picking somebody up. We don't have a life, don't you see that? We're like roommates. We eat pizza five nights a week."

"I tried to cook meals. I'm tired when I get home from work."

"You tried to cook a meal exactly once, for my parents, and you hated every second of it. It was a bad joke. Becky, I feel as if everything I do here just messes up the condo for you. If I put the sports section down, you pick it up and throw it in the trash. I take off a jacket and you carry it away. You're always cleaning up behind me like I'm an old dog, don't you see? You look at my things as if they're covered with dog shit."

She was surprised that he had caught on to her physical distaste, because she was sure she had covered it up. Ever since she'd been with Sam the first time, Terry seemed disgusting. "I'm just trying to keep our home neat—like your mother."

Tuesday night he urged her to return to rehearsals, he almost begged. As if reluctantly, she agreed. She gave herself a choice bruise across the hip. She had to pull down her jeans to show Sam, backstage while Dracula was engaged with Minna.

"No, no, I can't see you," she said wistfully. "It wouldn't be fair to you. It's too dangerous. Every night I lie in my bed and think about you. Sometimes I even do things to myself, Sam, thinking of you. But those afternoons and those nights are gone from us. Terry stands between us now."

Sometimes she feared she was overdoing it a shade, but Sam did not respond badly. He was overwrought. He pleaded. He begged.

Finally Thursday, the last rehearsal before Monday night, she told him she would try to slip away Saturday. If she did not come, he would know that Terry had stopped her—forcibly. Her voice trembled. Maybe she really could be an actress. No, she would rather be on a show like "Entertainment Tonight" or Barbara Walters. I just want to be myself, she thought, the best of what I am. If I can just get Terry out of the way. This was the first week Sam had gone without sex, and he was simmering. He kept trying to drag her into the basement, but she found excuses. She was not about to ball him in the basement.

Saturday she did slip off to see him, presumably while Terry was with Heather. He had promised her he would not see Heather while they were trying to work things out. She did not believe him, but she had to nail Sam. She couldn't let him get unhooked. That afternoon she was wild. She had put on her best Lady Grace bustier and tap panties in blue satin, with black fishnet pantyhose. They were uncomfortable, digging into her crotch, but she knew they would boil his blood.

The bruise across her hip stood out against her fair skin. He kissed it, his face creasing as if he would cry. "How could he do this? How?"

Lying under him she began to weep. She hardly had to fake it, only a little, because she was too nervous, too tightly wound to get excited, and he was actually hurting her. "I'll never seen you again. Never! I can't bear it. This is the very, very last time."

"I'll do it." As he drove into her, he groaned, "I'll do it. I'll kill him. I'll do it. I'll show you I'm a man. I'll do it."

There was just time after she washed to explain her plan. He stared at her, amazed, as if he thought his saying he would do it would satisfy her and that would be the end of it—as if it were some nonsense he could say while fucking and then forget when he got off her. "If you're really my man, you'll prove it Monday. You'll show me you can do it. You'll show me you really have the guts to do it."

Tommy would find a car for Sam to borrow. She met her brother at the bridge, and they walked the canal embankment together. It was a warm June day, sultry, with clouds that looked made of cement. The mosquitoes swirled around them. She opened up and told Tommy what she was going to do.

"Be sure to take the right kind of things. Any cash. Any gold. The TV, the VCR, good watches, cameras."

"What about golf clubs?"

"Take them. Anything that can be resold. Just don't let anybody see you. Mess up drawers and toss things around. You want it to look like they don't know where things are." Tommy put his hand on her shoulder. "If we had the cash, we could just put out a contract on him. But people get blackmailed that way. Do it yourself and do it right. You can't do it too soon for me. It makes me nervous, him walking around ready to blow the whistle on me. I don't need that piece of crap on my case."

"It's my only chance in the world, Tommy. He wants to take everything away from me I've worked so hard to get."

"The kid, he can drive? He's got a license?"

"Sure. He just hasn't got a car."

" 'Cause the last thing we need is him wracking up the car, rear-ending somebody or taking a curve fast and ending up in some picture window. He's got to drive careful. Can he do that?"

"He's the careful type, Tommy. He's a good kid and he's crazy about me. He'll do what I tell him to."

"That's the way we like them, you and me." He squeezed her shoulder hard. "Good luck, Becca. We both have to take on things we never thought we'd have to do, just to keep from drowning. It's a nasty life and they don't give us a thing. I'll be seeing you."

Monday noon she mixed two sleeping pills into the soup she was heating for Terry. Then she rushed back to work. She had chosen Monday, because in mid-afternoon she had to pick up two thousand new brochures from the little print-Xerox shop they used. They were offering cable service to a new area. With luck, nobody would notice exactly how long she was gone. Also she didn't want to give Sam enough time to brood, to change his mind. She was sure he could talk himself into inaction. She headed straight for her condo but parked before she got there and went in to the back of the building. Sam was waiting just inside. She had had a key made for him. "Whenever you look at that key and think of putting it into a lock, think about putting your sweet cock into me," she said, squeezing his balls gently as she kissed him. Sam was sweating, although the day was only mild.

"We can't do this. I mean, not for real." He grabbed her arm tight.

"No?" She glared at him. "Then stop toying with me. You don't care. Just go and leave me to him. Go!"

She thought for a minute he might leave. He looked miserable. He kept wringing his hands till she felt like kicking him, but she remained huddled against the wall.

"Becky," he moaned. "Becky, we can't do this."

"If we do it, I'll be able to see you whenever you want. I'll have enough money to follow you up to school." She flung herself forward and threw her arms around his neck, grinding her body into his. "We have to do it! We have to!"

He held her tight against him, half sobbing into her hair. Embracing him, she could feel the hammer she had told him to bring inside his jacket. She ran her hand along the hammer and then down to his prick through the rough tent of jeans. "We'll be together, Sam. For us! Because I love you. Because you love me." She pulled free, stepping back. "We have to hurry. We can't afford to loiter on this." Without looking back, she took the chance of starting upstairs. Then she heard him behind her.

She opened the door cautiously and peered out. As she had expected, nobody was around. No one was home in the daytime except Helen, and she could explain away anything to Helen. Helen was conniving at the affair. Helen would hear nothing suspicious, she was sure. She went quietly along the corridor and up the steps at the far end. Their door was the second. She unlocked it and motioned Sam inside. Then she pushed past him. Inside she could hear the sounds of a soap opera from the TV in the bedroom. She hoped Terry had fallen asleep watching the soap. The pills should have knocked him out. She hoped he'd be laid out snoring.

She was terrified as she stood just inside the living room with Sam behind her. What she was doing seemed absurd. She could not possibly do it. She felt vulnerable taking another step toward the bedroom, where the TV was blaring. Helen had told her that Terry watched soap operas half the day, but she had thought that Helen was exaggerating. Terry acted so damned superior to Tommy, but Tommy was out their scalloping, which was no picnic, ever, and if he was bringing in drugs for The Guys, it was only for his family. People did what they had to do to make a living, the way Joey and her uncle had gone out in bad weather, because they needed to. Only Terry was too good to take any job that wasn't fancy enough for him. His parents slipped him money. His parents told him to ditch her and let her drown, sell the condo and run back home. Terry would not work and he would steal from her the fruit of her work. But she could turn him into money. She turned and glared at Sam. "Now!" she mouthed. "Fast. There's no going back. Now."

Sam looked as if he might get sick. He swallowed. He stood as if all his muscles had seized up, one foot forward, his arm slightly raised from his side.

"Take out the hammer," she muttered. She found Terry's golf clubs in the front closet. She took a big one with a metal end. Let him be asleep. With two sleeping pills in him, he ought to be out. She had a moment's terror that Heather might be with him, but she was sure the woman had a job. He wasn't going to take up with anyone who didn't have income. Sam was following her as she crept toward the open bedroom door. In her head she could see Terry sprawled on his back on the bed with his arms flung out, the way he slept, his mouth open, snoring softly. Sam would bring the hammer down on his head. He would never waken. It would be over. A quick and merciful death. He would never see what hit him. The whole thing would happen under the cover of "General Hospital." Then they would fake the robbery and clear out. Swift and clean. Five minutes and it would be done.

CHAPTER 51

LEILA

Leila spent the last night in a Sheraton near the San Diego airport, since her plane left at eight in the morning, and she would have had to rise at four to be driven in. She felt ashamed at her contentment, putting on her silk kimono and ordering room service, turning on the TV to "Sixty Minutes" and running a deep bath. The hotel seemed peaceful after Debbie's house, the room sinfully ample. She felt herself slowly uncurling from the defensive posture she assumed around her sister. Everything about her had been on display, from the robe she wore to the coffee she drank and the eggs she did not eat.

On the plane she prepared for classes and went over the interview notes she had printed out before leaving home. She was exhausted, for she had slept badly at Debbie's, where she was sharing a bed with Robin. She longed to be home. Mrs. Burke was reliable about feeding Vronsky, but she worried about Waif. Kittens at that age were fragile, and this one had suffered quite enough. There was no way the kitten would be fed the number of times a day she really needed, but at least the food should be put out in ample portions.

The ride was rough and disagreeable. The connection left late and arrived in Boston late. The cold seized around her as she looked for her car. She had missed rush hour, so she made decent time through the tunnel and to Cambridge. The light was on in the vestibule, as she always left it. Vronsky greeted her in a state of high agitation. She did not see Waif. "Where's your kitten?" she asked him.

He took her immediately to the kitchen, where Waif lay on the stove, curled up to a pilot light. She looked ghastly. There was no food down. The bowls had been licked clean. A bag of dry food was lying on the floor. Obviously Vronsky had pulled the bag over and out. However, the kitten probably could not chew the dry food. She was breathing slowly, dehydrated too, for the water dish was empty.

"What happened to that fucking woman?" Leila said to Vronsky. "You poor creatures! I can't stand people who don't carry through their responsibilities to children and animals. She's fired!" She filled a water dish. She ran into the downstairs bathroom for a medicine dropper. She began putting water down Waif's throat. Waif could swallow. She mewed faintly.

Letting her luggage stand, her coat lay where it had dropped, Leila fed Vronsky regular cat food. Then she opened a can of chicken and turned it into mush with water in the blender. She began dabbing it into Waif's mouth, holding her on her lap at the table. The kitten swallowed. She began to lick her chops. Little rascal wanted to live. She was extremely weak but she began lapping the watery chicken mash. She ate and ate until she was exhausted and fell asleep.

Leila stopped in her office to listen to her messages. Jane. A student begging an extension on an overdue paper. Phyllis wanting to know if she was back yet. Zak. A polite query if she was available for dinner a day before. Oh dear. Cathy, very upset about something. No Mrs. Burke. The woman had not had the courtesy to call in and say she couldn't make it, although, when Leila thought about it, it was pretty silly to call an empty house and say you couldn't come. Who would the message be for, the starving cats?

Vronsky was still talking. He ran upstairs complaining. Leila followed him with her suitcase, driven to unpack at once, so that she could return to her life rapidly. Something smelled bad. There was an odor—urine, vomit, something burned. Had the cats been sick? It was stronger as she approached her bedroom. She heard a sound, a moan. She froze. Vronsky ran ahead of her into the bedroom, calling her loudly, an impatient mrowing. Cautiously she proceeded, pausing in the doorway. The bed was made but someone was lying on it in David's sleeping bag, the one that had been missing. It was filthy and looked as if it had been in a fire. It was Mrs. Burke lying on the bed.

Mrs. Burke opened her eyes and tried to sit up but obviously could not. She moaned again, her head tossing back and forth. The room reeked of something charred and a strong odor of sickness. The woman was wearing a nightgown with her arm in a dirty bandage. As Mrs. Burke stirred, she began to cough spasmodically, deep choking coughs from the bottom of her lungs. Leila, stunned by the sight of Mrs. Burke in her bed, could find nothing whatsoever to say. Guardedly she touched Mrs. Burke's sweaty forehead. Burning up with fever.

"Water," Mrs. Burke managed to spit out. "Sick."

Leila brought her a glass of water. Discreetly she picked up Mrs. Burke's enormous purse and carried it out of the room with her. "I'll be back with some soup. Do you think you can keep it down?"

She opened a can of chicken soup. She checked on Waif and moved her to a pillow by a radiator, turning up the heat, giving her a little more chicken mash. While the soup heated, she sat at the kitchen table and began going through Mrs. Burke's large purse. Makeup in an old jar, scarves, some large underpants, two bras, socks, pantyhose, gloves and mittens, a long slip, two rolled blouses, aspirin, safety pins pinned together, a hand mirror and hairbrush, a receipt from the emergency department of Boston City Hospital, marked *paid cash for treatment of burns incurred in a fire*. That was dated the night before Leila left for San Diego.

She began to guess what had happened. Mrs. Burke must have been in a fire at her daughter's house—that's right, she lived with her daughter. Her married daughter who was ashamed of her mother's cleaning. Obviously after the fire, Mrs. Burke had decided to go to work anyhow and then had collapsed. She looked for the daughter in the shabby address book. Most of the addresses were in the Washington area. The only Burkes were a Jim Burke in Virginia and a Jaime Burke in Honolulu. The daughter was obviously married and had taken her husband's name. She phoned the cleaning service. She got an answering machine and left a message.

All right, once Mrs. Burke was coherent, she could get the daughter's phone number. Right now a doctor was required. She called Emily.

"In your bed. That must have been a shocker. Something like the three bears coming home, but this was hardly Goldilocks. It sounds like pneumonia to me. Tell you what. I'll come by in half an hour with my little black bag and take a look. In the meantime, you should go on trying to find the woman's family. I wonder if they reported her missing."

She fed the soup to Mrs. Burke, whose head could scarcely remain upright. "A doctor friend of mine is coming. She thinks you may have pneumonia."

"Got to get up," Mrs. Burke managed to say, between coughing fits. She was coughing up a terrible green scum. Leila felt a little ill, but she held on. Mrs. Burke, her bed, the entire room reeked.

The only thing to do was call Honolulu. It must be afternoon there. She got an answering machine. "My name is Leila Landsman," she said, giving her phone number. "This is about your mother, Mary Burke. She's very ill. Please call me as soon as possible. It's very important."

She spooned a little more mash into Waif and tucked her into her blouse. Then she sat down and ate the rest of the soup. It did look as if Mrs. Burke had cleaned the house before she collapsed. She gave Waif to Vronsky to wash and made up the bed in David's room, where it appeared she would be spending the night. As she was finishing, the doorbell rang.

Emily was gentle and efficient. "One oh four point eight. It's pneumonia all right. I'll give you some antibiotics, Mary. What's the burn from?"

"Fire," Mrs. Burke said. "Building on fire."

"Your daughter's home?" Leila asked.

Mrs. Burke did not answer. She only coughed.

Leila wanted to ask Mrs. Burke what she was doing with David's sleeping bag, but it hardly seemed an appropriate time. She did not want to embarrass Mrs. Burke in front of Emily. It was possible that Mrs. Burke had taken advantage of her absence to search for the missing sleeping bag, had found it and then, when she collapsed upon returning to feed the cats, had made use of it as bedding. Perhaps it would be best to agree on that story and not find out if Mrs. Burke had stolen the sleeping bag. She hardly seemed the type to go off on weekend camping trips.

Emily gave Mrs. Burke an injection of penicillin. She worked the dressing off the injured arm and put on some ointment, bandaging it again. She left three prescriptions with Leila, whom she motioned downstairs. "Something's not right here. She has signs of mild frostbite on hands and feet. Her body is covered with old scars, sores that healed badly. Her feet are incredibly swollen. Those are all signs of a hard life, and I do mean, hard."

"Do you think her daughter abuses her?"

"I don't know what to think. Keep her in bed. See if you can locate her family, but check them out. There's something off. Maybe her daughter was hurt in the fire. Maybe she was killed. I never read the papers except on Sunday. Otherwise, why haven't they gotten hold of her? They must know where she goes to work. Normal people leave their schedule, phone numbers, in case the daughter has to reach her in an emergency. Maybe they're in the hospital."

"Maybe they're out of town. On vacation. At a convention."

"What does her daughter do?"

"I haven't the faintest idea. Mary Burke was not one of your casual chatterers. She protects her privacy something fierce. The only time she ever opened up to me at all was around the time a homeless woman she knew was brutally attacked."

"I remember that case. Raped too." Emily rubbed her nose thoughtfully. "It just seems odd that her daughter doesn't have the police breaking down the door."

"I'm beginning to wonder if the daughter exists, or if there's some secret. The daughter's a prostitute, say. Something like that." Leila tried to pay Emily, but Emily refused.

"I don't do house calls for money. Only for friends. Besides, I think you've got yourself a whole lot of hassle. I think she's in real trouble."

"Is she in danger? Should I put her in the hospital?"

"Better to take care of her, or find the missing daughter. The pneumonia should start responding to antibiotics. She's a tough old bird, Leila. I'd like to talk to her when the fever comes down. I'll try to come by tomorrow at noon. If you find the daughter, call me at my office and let me know."

After Emily had left, Leila sat in her study with her head in her hands. It was nine already. She called Zak, half expecting to get his answering machine. Nobody in the world was home or bothering to respond to her queries. She tried to think of something nice to do for Emily. Something for the boys?

"Zak Solomon here."

"I just got back from California—my sister had a crisis. I walked in tonight to find my cleaning lady in my bed with raging pneumonia and no way to contact her family. And my new kitten was almost dead of starvation and dehydration. So you see my overture wasn't hollow. I just got derailed."

"I thought you'd changed your mind."

"No."

"A sick cleaning lady in your bed, a sick kitten and a sick sister? What are you, Typhoid Mary?" He was laughing.

"I don't always live in a state of crisis. I think of myself as a rather dull woman. My sister tells me I'm scared to take a chance on anything."

"When I met you, you were just starting divorce proceedings."

"I won't comment on *your* family. And yes, I'm feeling swamped."

"All right, what did you do for the kitten?" He waited while she described her attentions. "Tell you what. Invite me to supper tomorrow night. Even if your cleaning lady is still occupying your bed. Maybe you should get a nurse in temporarily. It seems you're footing the bills anyhow."

"I have to go to school tomorrow. Come at seven . . . Zak? I'll be very glad to see you. This has been a rough period."

She called Emily back for a nursing recommendation, called a woman Emily knew, got shunted to somebody else who might be available, and finally, forty minutes later, she had a nurse coming in the morning. Then she ran a bath and afterward, sat with a bottle of Beaujolais and began idly reading through the newspapers of the last five days, delivered but untouched.

She was catching up on the political news, but also she was watching for items about fires. It was after eleven, but she was still on West Coast time. She started with the most recent paper and worked her way back. She was on Friday when the phone rang.

"Yeah, is this Leila Land? Your message said this was about my mother."

She told him briefly. She had not got far when he interrupted. "No, you got it all wrong. Are you sure this is my mother?"

"I got your phone number from her address book. You have the same last name. Her name is Mary Elizabeth."

"That sounds like my mother, but I only have one sister, and she lives in Chevy Chase. Her name is Cindy."

"What's her last name?"

There was a short silence. "We aren't a tight-knit family. I'm trying to remember. Austin. That's it! Her husband's name is . . . Ron Austin. But Mother never lived with her. They didn't get along."

"You have no other sisters? Maybe a sister-in-law?"

"I was married before, but Mother wouldn't have anything to do with my ex-wife. No, you got the facts wrong. Mother never lived with Cindy."

"So how do you reach your mother? Do you have a phone for her?"

"We write letters. I have her address." He read off the number of a post office box in Kenmore Square. "Once in a blue moon, she calls me, but she's not much for the telephone. Says all she can think about is how much it's costing."

While he was talking, she checked out the address book she had taken from Mary Burke's oversized purse. Ron and Cindy Austin were listed, at a Chevy Chase address. "What do you want me to do about your mother?"

"It seems to me you're doing just fine. It's hard for me to do anything more than cheer on the progress from this distance."

"Well, frankly, you could send her some money. I don't know when she'll be able to work again."

"I'll see what I can do, but I have a family, and business here is pretty slow. I'm trying to keep a small business afloat, and it's not easy. I'll see what I can do, but I'm not a rich guy. I have a wife and two little kids, and child support from my last one. Now my sister, her husband rakes it in. They live high. It's them you should be hitting up for some money for Mother."

After the call was over, she pondered. No doubt this guy was mildly upset about his mother, but Mary Burke was too distant from his present life. She was not a priority. It was late to call the daughter in Maryland; that was for tomorrow. Hit up, huh? She wondered whether when she was Mrs. Burke's age, if she needed help, would David think she was hitting him up?

She was not overjoyed about having a sick and feverish woman she barely knew on a personal level lying like a beached and dying whale in her bed. She felt petty in her objections, but she also felt invaded. Further she could see the responsibility for resolving the situation landing right on her head. Tomorrow she must call the daughter. Sons could slough off obligations more readily than daughters, and perhaps Mary was closer to her daughter?

Maybe there was some relative in the Boston area she referred to as her daughter. Families had different branches. Maybe a child by a previous marriage or even a child borne out of wedlock in the scandal that would have represented forty years ago. One she had given up for adoption? Perhaps Leila was being too dramatic. This daughter might turn out to be a cousin, or the daughter of a close friend. Whoever the woman was that Mary lived with, Leila would track her down. She wanted her bedroom back.

She scanned the newspapers until the day she had left. There was a fire. Abandoned building, homeless squatters. Suspected arson. Woman identified as Beverly Bozeman. Leila sat up abruptly and Vronsky stared at her. That was the name of the woman who had been raped and left for dead; the woman Mary Burke had taken an intense interest in. Three killed in a fire. Too much coincidence here. She was beginning to wonder about this invisible home.

Carrying Waif and followed by Vronsky, she went to bed in David's room. She felt uncomfortable, invading his privacy. She rarely entered his room, unless he asked for something. She tucked Waif into her armpit and Vronsky curled against her thigh, but she was awake long after they dozed off. She felt like an overworked and understaffed social service agency, with more clients than she knew how to handle. Her life had become a series of external catastrophes. She had not had time all week to think about the end of her marriage and what she wanted, how she intended to live now. She had a sudden great urge to see Zak, to bury herself in him. She longed for some warm and intimate and very personal comfort. She wanted to be something more than a resource, at least for an evening.

Tomorrow she would tackle the problem of the daughter.

CHAPTER 52

MARY

Mary came out of her burning fever gradually. At first she had no idea where she was. Then she remembered and she tried to bolt. She struggled out of bed and made it halfway across the room before she fell. A strange woman appeared, a nurse, and helped her back to bed, scolding her as if she were a retarded child. "Now, now, Mary, we mustn't do that. If we want something, we have to call out or ring this bell. You see? On the bedside table. Mrs. Landsman left us a little bell."

"I've got to get out of here."

The woman muscled her back into bed. "What you have to do is rest, drink lots of water and get better. You had pneumonia and your lungs were full of fluid. You were dangerously ill."

"I'm better now."

"Yeah, you're better. You can talk like a human being instead of groaning and moaning and carrying on. Right. But if you try to push your body, you'll have a relapse." The big woman snapped her fingers. "Just like that."

She was frightened but she could not stay awake. She sank into an exhausted sleep, waking to her coughing. The room was dark. This time she remembered where she was. It was a disaster. She vaguely remembered Mrs. Landsman coming into the room and talking to her.

When the nurse brought in soup on a tray, she asked, "You came here this morning?"

"Honey, I been taking care of you, this is the third day. You sure you don't recollect? You told me all about your son." The woman was perhaps a few years younger than Mary, not as big as she had appeared at first.

"My son? I don't remember. I have to leave here."

The woman put a bony hand on Mary's shoulder. "You don't have to do anything but mind me and rest. Now drink your soup."

"Where is Mrs. Landsman?"

"She'll be home later on. She and her boyfriend're out eating Chinese. She's paying for me, you know. You got a good friend there."

Mary didn't feel up to explaining that Mrs. Landsman was not her friend, but her part-time employer. She was surely fired. The service would not put up with her disappearing for days. "What day is this?"

"You finish up that bowl of soup, and I'll tell you. No way otherwise."

Mary slowly spooned the warm soup into herself. Sweat broke out on her forehead. She slid further under the covers.

"It's Wednesday. Mrs. Landsman found you here on Sunday. I been coming in every day since Monday A.M.."

"I have to call the service I work for."

"Mrs. Landsman already called them. She called your son and your daughter too. Called the doctor. Remember her? A strong-built lady."

Mary frowned. "I think so. . . . Mrs. Landsman called my daughter?"

Nodding, the nurse carried out the tray. "You ask her about that."

The whole card house of her life had collapsed. Now what would become of her? The service must know she was homeless, and they would never keep her on. Her daughter must know too and would not let her see her grandchildren ever again. Cindy would pretend that Mary was dead before she would admit to allowing her mother to be homeless. It would be shameful. It was all too shameful for everyone, including herself. What was going to become of her?

She would have to go back to a shelter and start over again. But she was older. It would be harder. Still, she had her nut put away. They couldn't touch that. If Mrs. Landsman thought Mary was going to pay her back for a nurse and doctor, she would never admit to having that account. Unless Mrs. Landsman had found the checkbook. She looked for her carry-all and her bag. Mrs. Landsman must have taken them, or how would she have found Jaime and Cindy? She imagined Mrs. Landsman going through her things, all that she owned in the world, her precious, pitiable things. And the sleeping bag. Mrs. Landsman must have seen the sleeping bag.

Wednesday she had come from the emergency room over here and slowly cleaned the house. The next day she had cleaned for Mrs. Anzio in Watertown. She had already been coughing hard, weak and feverish. That night she had returned to Mrs. Landsman's, giddy and sick. Friday she had not been able to get up for work and then everything blurred.

She hauled herself up on the pillows in the bed. It was Mrs. Landsman's bed. She was scared. What would become of her? She heard voices downstairs. The nurse strode in. "Mary, I'm leaving now. See you tomorrow. You keep drinking that water beside your bed, you hear? Mrs. Landsman is back."

Mary thought she was going to pass out. She kept wishing she was still sleeping in the squat with Beverly beside her, safe together, cold but in good company. She would wake up from a terrible dream and it would be last Wednesday. Her only friend had died. Houdini and Mouse had never wakened. They were all dead. Only she remained to mourn. She wished she had died in her sleep, that she had never, never roused to her bleak hopeless life. She was tired of fighting disaster. She was exhausted. She wished she had died over the weekend when she was raging with fever lying on this bed that belonged to another woman—as everything belonged to somebody else.

Mrs. Landsman came into the room. "Ms. Odell says that you can talk now. That's the nurse who just left." Mrs. Landsman was wearing a blue silk dress with a V-neck, not the way she dressed for work or around the house. She had nice legs, Mary noted with surprise. Mrs. Landsman's face was flushed. She seemed nervous and stood just inside the door. A man entered behind her. He was only a little taller and about her age, slender, with curly, almost kinky hair and glasses. Was this what the nurse called her boyfriend? Mary didn't believe it. Middle-aged women who were dumped didn't show up a month later with a boyfriend, believe her, she knew.

Mary didn't say anything. She felt the less she said, the better.

Mrs. Landsman came reluctantly, cautiously into the room. "You had pneumonia, as I'm sure the nurse explained. I found you here very, very ill when I returned from San Diego Sunday night."

Mary realized she had to say something. "I'm sorry about being here. I collapsed when I came to feed the cats after work."

"I understand. But where else would you have gone?" Mrs. Landsman came a few steps farther and pulled up a chair beside the bed.

The man leaned against the dresser that had used to be Mr. Landsman's. He looked interested and mildly amused. Mary kept glancing at him, waiting for him to speak. She was not used to men who hung back and kept quiet when women were speaking. Maybe he just felt it was none of his business and he was better out of it. So why did he stay in the room? He made her nervous. "I'll leave as soon as I can. I tried to leave today, but I couldn't make it across the room."

"I'm going to move you into my son's room tomorrow. I have to come and go all the time in here to get my clothes. . . . But if you left here, where would you go?"

"Home, of course."

"Nobody has an address for you. Even your daughter only has a post office box."

"You talked to my daughter? What did you tell her?"

"Mostly I tried to get information from her. She doesn't know much about you, does she?"

"She has her own problems. She has two kids, one in college and one in prep school. They have a big mortgage and they have a lifestyle to keep up."

"I gathered as much." Mrs. Landsman sighed.

"Mrs. Landsman, please leave my children alone. I'm not their responsibility. They have their own lives. I don't want anybody interfering between me and my children."

"You should call me Leila. And I should call you Mary. After all, we seem to be living together, for a time. You don't have a home, right?"

Mary said nothing. Her heart was constricting in her chest. She could feel the sweat breaking out on her forehead. "I have to rest. I can't talk any longer."

Mrs. Landsman stood. "Don't be frightened. We'll figure out what to do. Frankly I'm ashamed that I didn't realize you were in trouble long ago."

"Did you tell the service?"

"Only that you had pneumonia and couldn't be back to work for some time. I said you'd call them when you could work again."

"They won't stand for this. Disappearing."

"They obviously didn't pay you enough to live on, anyhow."

"When I get better, I'll look for a job as bank president." Mary began coughing spasmodically.

Mrs. Landsman laughed. "Rest. I assume Ms. Odell gave you your antibiotic before she left? Great. Okay, good night."

Mary tried to think what to do, but even her fierce anxiety could not keep her awake. She had dreams of running, of being hunted, of danger and pursuit, but she slept on. When she woke, she heard soft voices in the next room. They were murmuring, laughing. He was in there with her. Mary was shocked. She had not thought Mrs. Landsman that sort of woman. She wasn't even legally divorced yet.

Still, Mary thought, women survived as they could. Who knew where Mrs. Landsman had found him, but she did seem to have a boyfriend. He didn't look sleazy. Maybe she'd landed on her feet. Mary was astonished. She would swear on a stack of Bibles that Mrs. Landsman hadn't been fooling around. Yet here she was showing off her legs and going to bed with another man.

It wasn't that Mary didn't understand trying to make another marriage. She had come up to Boston with a man she had known for years through Jim. Doug had been divorced two years before. Doug had been taking her out to dinner now and then for a couple of months, when his firm transferred him to Boston. He wanted to bring someone he could trust who would help him get settled. She had no office skills beyond simple typing, but she knew how to organize. She had become his personal assistant at the Boston office of a chain that sold and installed office equipment, making decent money and wearing nice clothes and having a sweet little apartment.

She had not been with Doug in Boston more than two weeks when he pressed her to become intimate with him. She had not been comfortable with the idea, but she understood she had little choice. She wanted him to marry her. She could see herself in the nice house she had found for him in Waltham. At first Doug was uncomfortable in Boston. He had been living in the Washington area for twenty years. He knew how to do business there. In Boston he was lonely. He found the climate harsh. He missed the Tidewater area. He seemed to have no idea how to re-situate himself physically or socially.

She found the house, she arranged for his things to be moved North, she waited for the movers and unpacked him. She bought the household things he needed. He arranged for her to have a credit card so that she could buy for him. She felt almost married again. For the next two years, she had constantly hoped he would marry her, but did not feel that she could push him.

Still, she had her own nice little apartment in Allston, near the

Green Line. She was covered by medical insurance. She was making enough to get by comfortably, to go down and visit her daughter and the grandchildren. She was saving to visit her son in Hawaii. She was making a new life.

Then Doug got interested in a woman at an interior decorating firm they were working with. The relationship between Mary and Doug tapered off gradually. About two months after he had stopped seeing her, she got her pink slip. Reorganization. Her position was being eliminated.

Eight months passed before she got the job in the stationery store in Kenmore Square. By then she was living in that one-room walk-up. She had thought she had come down in the world. She complained to her daughter, until Cindy stopped taking her calls.

Mary caught on. She stopped complaining. She stopped describing her tiny walk-up to Cindy or worrying aloud about her lack of medical insurance (the storekeeper couldn't afford to give it to her and the job didn't pay enough for her to buy it on her own) and how badly she needed a car. She shut up about herself, and Cindy was once again willing to talk to her from time to time about the children and how well they were doing and her own problems with making ends meet in her upscale household. The kids always had to have what the others around them, often from more affluent families, had, whether it was clothes or a car or sporting equipment.

She asked herself if she had loved Doug. Certainly she had been fond of him. She had been dependent on him, while believing him to be entirely dependent on her. She was replaceable. He was not.

She could recall Jim's slightest inflection, the way he had of scratching the back of one ankle on the front of the other. Mosquitoes always seemed to bite him on his ankles. She remembered walks they had taken in Shenandoah, the rustic cabin where they had made love. She remembered buying apples and apple syrup in the fall, and how he had loved cider that was just turning fizzy. She could close her eyes and see the nape of his neck or his knees.

She could scarcely call up Doug's features. All the photographs of both of them and almost everyone in her life except for a couple of snapshots of her children and grandchildren in her wallet—they had gone the way of her other possessions. She had lost her mementos, but not her memories.

So she understood what Mrs. Landsman was grasping at. She could not blame her. Mrs. Landsman had just been much faster about it.

Maybe it was the difference in their eras of growing up. Also she had been older than Mrs. Landsman when Jim had left her, forty-six. She did not know Mrs. Landsman's age, but she was probably in her late thirties. It made a big difference, those eight or ten years.

It did not bother her to hear little noises through the wall. She had not been interested in sex for years. What she dreamed about was much more elemental: to have a place she could call home. She remembered a homeless man who had moved into a park on the border of Newton and Brookline undetected for years. He had built himself a rude shelter, but he had lived there peacefully, bothering nobody, among the deer and the rabbits. But the park authorities found him. They tore down his lean-to and thrust him on the streets, all in the name of conservation.

She had reached the end of her road. It would be back to a shelter for as long as they would let her stay, and then on the streets, sleeping on the heating grates, looking for an abandoned building to squat in, hiding in basements and garages. Living like that little kitten she had picked up, like the starving strays that had been flung out into the grim savage streets to die fast or slowly, as luck would have it. She would be joining them shortly. She might as well lie in this soft warm bed now and sleep while she could, for people like her were forbidden sleep.

CHAPTER 53

BECKY

Becky came quietly into the doorway with Sam immediately behind her. She could feel the leather of his jacket rubbing her elbow. He was finally carrying the hammer. His breath whistled past her ear.

Terry was not asleep. "General Hospital" was blaring from the set. He was sitting cross-legged on the bed with the pillows propped up behind him talking on the phone. "Well, you tell Chris to call me back as soon as he comes in. This is his brother and this is the third time I called today." He slammed down the phone. The soup she had doped was sitting only partly eaten on the bedside table. A box from Domino's pizza lay on the rumpled spread, the pizza about two-thirds eaten. The ungrateful bastard hadn't even eaten the lunch she had come home to make him. She was terrified that he would say something that would reveal to Sam she had been lying to him. Terry might suddenly say, I want a divorce, I want a divorce now. Then all her careful work on Sam would be lost. She was frozen. She felt as if she could never move.

He was dialing again. Sam made a noise in his throat and lurched forward past her. Terry turned and saw them. "What the hell? Who are you?"

Sam came at him with the hammer swinging. Terry bellowed and rolled away. The hammer hit his shoulder and Terry screamed. The pizza remains went flying onto the carpet. It would stink of cheese and oil and tomato for weeks. Terry started screaming. Sam was swinging the hammer wildly. He caught Terry in the side of the head and Terry rolled off the bed, still screaming. They had to shut him up. He was making enough noise to bring the police, to bring everybody for a mile around. Becky rushed around the bed and swung the golf club. She got him in the head but he only screamed louder. He was rolling to and fro, kicking out. His foot caught her in the ankle and she fell against the bed. Then she stood up and hit him with all her strength. He was bleeding all over the carpet from a wound on his ear. She brought the club down again. This time she caught him in the face and she could feel his teeth give. Blood came pouring out of his mouth along with an awful scream. "Shut him up!" she screamed. That sound had to stop.

Sam stood over Terry and swung the hammer down. This time he caught the skull sharply on top and the bone seemed to give way. He kept swinging the hammer, making a weird sound like a crying baby. She could not get the club in again until Sam paused. Then she smashed the club down again where Sam had been pounding. The scalp was bleeding all over everything. Finally Terry lay still on the carpet. Blood was all over the good blue spread and the beige carpeting. He had wet himself through his terry robe. Then Sam dropped the hammer and staggered into the bathroom to throw up.

She did not want to touch the body but she made herself feel for a pulse. She could not find one. Finally. She stood up and looked at him. He was a real mess, blood all over and a bad smell. Sam came back drying his face on a towel. "Take the towel with you," she said. "We'll get rid of it. Put it on the floor now and put the hammer in it."

Sam did not want to touch the hammer where it had dropped. There was blood and hair and something greyish on it like slime. She picked it up and put it on the towel.

Sam was rousing himself. "I have to go out the deck doors and make it look like a break-in."

"Break the glass. Use anything. Use one of the other golf clubs. We'll take that along too."

While Sam quickly broke the glass and then unlocked the door from the outside, she picked up the bowl of drugged soup, poured it down the sink and put the dish in the dishwasher. Lazy Terry hadn't even turned on the dishwasher loaded with the morning and noon's dishes. She started it.

Then they moved the TV set and the VCR, Terry's watch, what they could grab, downstairs to Helen's storage area. Helen kept her boxes there from moving and her off-season clothes, but little else. Becky had Helen's key. They would store the stuff there until it was safe to move it out in a day or two. They could take it at night. She was careful to empty Terry's wallet and remove his credit cards and all the money in the dresser. Quickly she pulled out drawers and dumped the contents, like someone searching for valuables.

The clubs and the hammer in the bloody towel Becky tied up with string. "Drop it in the Canal. It'll sink. Be home before your mother. Don't call me. I'll call you as soon as things quiet down. It won't be long."

She got into her car and drove back to work, quickly but watching for cops. She did not want to have an accident. She did not want to be stopped for speeding. In ten minutes, she was pulling into the lot and ran to her desk. She began processing the mailing at once. Nobody seemed to have paid attention. She worked feverishly.

Her boss came by at four-thirty. "Is that the mailing? Ready for once?"

"I got it around two. Then I ran the labels."

"Great," he said without inflection and strode off.

She decided to make an appearance in the room where the two pool girls worked. "What a Monday. I'm exhausted."

"Every day's a Monday around here," Gina said. "You've got something on your skirt."

Becky almost fainted. Had she got Terry's blood on her? She glanced down. For a moment she thought it was his brains from the hammer. Then she realized it was pizza. "Sloppy lunch."

"Don't you go home to lunch these days?"

"I like to make Terry a warm lunch. Otherwise he just eats junk food. And being in this play, we haven't had enough time together. I'm going to quit. I promised him this weekend. Enough is enough."

"What harm does it do, if you enjoy it?" Gina asked reasonably. "Guess what I did Saturday? I went to the Ice Capades with my niece."

"You liked it? Maybe I'll ask Terry if he wants to."

In the john, she flushed the piece of pizza down the toilet, sponged her skirt and examined herself. She decided to change her shoes in case she had stepped in anything. She always kept a pair of cheap shoes in the office for use if it started to rain. They were just imitation leather and cracking, but she would take no chance. She washed the soles of the shoes she had been wearing carefully, scrubbing them. It did not do to be careless.

She worked on the mailing until everyone had gone home but Mrs. O'Neill. Mrs. O'Neill had a ritual of going around the office and checking everything before she left. While Mrs. O'Neill was busy, Becky cut up Terry's credit cards with the scissors in her desk. Then she put them all in an envelope and into her purse. She felt calm and organized. She loved to feel organized. No one had ever really appreciated how smart she was.

She had to act normal. She stopped at the mall and ordered a pizza, the same as she did three times a week. The guy behind the counter always winked at her. He called her Blonde Ambition, because she often worked late. "You ever get tired of your husband, you know where to find me," he said, taking her order.

She did not feel hungry and it was a waste to buy a pizza she would never eat, but she had to do everything the way she always did. She dropped the credit cards in little pieces into a Dumpster, being careful to handle them with her gloves on and to take them out of the envelope from her office. That she folded and put in her purse. Then she picked up their dry cleaning. Again it felt like a waste to pay for Terry's jacket and his pants, but she was establishing her innocence. She stopped and got her mail. As she passed Helen's door, she knocked. Helen opened it a crack to look over the chain. Then she swung it wide. "Becky, what's up?"

"I'll ride with you tonight."

"Oh? Things quieting down?"

"I ended it last week. I'm ashamed of myself. Terry's trying harder. I think we can make it."

"It sounded as if he was having a party this afternoon. First he had that damned TV on loud. Then he had a noisy party."

"A party?" Becky made herself look skeptical. "Terry's not a party boy. I can't imagine that. Maybe he was straightening up."

"He had friends in. They were yelling and jumping up and down."

"I'll talk to him about it."

"At one point, a picture fell off my wall. I just don't like that kind of rowdiness."

Becky picked up the pizza. "I'll speak to him, I promise." She climbed the steps slowly. When she unlocked the door, it felt eerily quiet in the condo, where the TV was always blaring. She did not feel like going to the bedroom at all. She had the bizarre feeling that, just as earlier he had not been asleep, now he would not be dead but sitting on the bed and furious.

She made herself act out normality. She hung her coat in the closet. She put the pizza on the table in the kitchen. Then, reluctantly, calling, "Terry, it's Becky," she crossed the living room to the open door of the bedroom. It smelled. Blood was all over the carpet and the bed. She did not look at him except out of the corner of her eye. She backed away and screamed once, for practice. Then still backing away, she began screaming as loud as she could. "Help! Help!"

She ran next door. Holly Reicher answered, her hair wrapped in a towel. "Hi, Becky, what's up?" She sounded bored and a little annoyed, as if she expected Becky to try to borrow something.

"Something's wrong! My husband's lying on the floor bleeding."

"Did he fall? Call a doctor."

"I'm scared. Everything's thrown all over the place. Something's wrong." She covered her face with her hands and let herself slide down against the wall of the corridor.

"Brad!" Holly bellowed. "Brad!"

He came out in the hall. "What's the matter?"

"Something's wrong," Becky howled, trying for hysteria. "He's lying in his blood!"

"Who's your doctor?" Brad reluctantly walked into their apartment. "What happened in here? Did you have a fight? Where's your TV?"

"I just got home from work! I just stopped and got us supper and walked in," Becky wailed. "The TV was here this morning."

Brad walked across the room and looked into the bedroom. "Oh my god," he said and blocked the door. "You don't want to look at this. I think you've been robbed. We'd better call an ambulance. And the police."

Becky sobbed hysterically, rubbing spit surreptitiously on her face. She could not make herself cry tears, but she could fake it pretty good. She scrubbed at her eyes until she was sure they would look red and swollen. "What's wrong with Terry? He's hurt bad, isn't he?"

"He's hurt real bad," Brad said, guiding her along to his apartment, his hand on her elbow. "Come on and sit down. Holly! Call the police. Right now. There's been a break-in next door."

She threw herself down on their couch and faked sobbing. In the kitchen she heard Brad say to Holly, "He looks dead to me. There's blood all over the place and he's not moving. . . . Hello, yes, I want to report a break-in and . . . and the person may be dead but I didn't want to touch anything, so I didn't check him out. . . . Next door."

Becky gave herself a rest while Brad and Holly talked in low voices in the kitchen. She messed up her hair. She rubbed her eyes harder and managed to make them water. She decided it was time to be a little more dramatic. She staggered into the kitchen. "I'm going next door. He needs me."

"Becky, he's past needing anybody. Sit down," Brad said not unkindly, pushing her shoulders downward. "The police are on their way."

"Did you call an ambulance?"

"I think it's past that."

"What do you mean? He's unconscious. He lost a lot of blood."

"Becky, Terry's dead. Sit down and try to get yourself together. The police are arriving any moment. They'll have a lot of questions."

They retreated to the bedroom. She heard Holly say, "I just knew I shouldn't have answered the door."

Brad said, "She's hysterical, I had to help. But let's get dead bolts put on the door."

"You think somebody broke in?"

"Maybe he let them in. I didn't look around. I don't want to get mixed up in this. Maybe it's drugs. But they took the TV. I saw that right away."

"We're lucky they didn't break in here. Or did they? We better look around." Brad and Holly went dashing around checking their condo.

I hate them, Becky thought. Yuppie worms. It occurred to her it would have been a nice touch to have broken into another condo. She could have kicked herself for not thinking of it. Maybe Sam and she ought to do another job in a couple of weeks, just to reinforce the idea of burglars active in the area.

Suddenly Holly noticed her. "Oh, do you want a cup of coffee, or anything? The police should be here by now. Suppose we were being burglarized, what good would they be?"

Becky stayed on the couch, her eyes closed. Suppose she aped going into shock? Too complicated. She could do hysteria fine.

At last a police car arrived outside, siren whooping. Two patrolmen came upstairs, followed by Helen. Florrie was barking downstairs. "Yes," Helen was saying, "my dog did bark. But I thought he was having a noisy party. I heard thumps and bangs. The TV was on loud."

One patrolman stood at the door with his gun drawn, while the other went in. He came back. "Radio the captain," he said, and what sounded to Becky like a string of numbers.

"They haven't let me go in," Becky said to the one patrolman. "Can I see my husband?"

"I'm afraid I have to seal the premises." He guided her out in the hall. "In a murder investigation, we have to keep everyone out. Why don't you go back and sit down next door?"

"Officer," Holly whined, "we hardly know each other. I have work to do. I was just being nice. She can't stay in my condo."

"She can come downstairs," Helen said. "I'd be glad to have her. Some of us care about our neighbors."

"Go downstairs, lady . . . Mrs. Burgess? We'll talk to you soon."

Another police car arrived. Becky watched side by side with Helen at her windows facing the parking lot. Then another. An older man in a sports jacket got out of one. Two men in regular clothing got out of the other. Another police cruiser pulled up and two more patrolmen came. She imagined her condo jammed with police. One of them had a videotape camera. Helen and Becky could hear them upstairs. Becky did not bother being hysterical after the first five minutes. Helen said to her, "I know you're upset, and it's a real horror. I'm scared myself. We need better security around here. But sometimes good things can come out of bad."

"I know I'll miss him, no matter how he acted. He did love me."

"I'm sure he did." Helen patted her shoulder. "You never had any supper. Don't you want a bite to eat?"

"I'm not hungry," Becky said, but her stomach growled. She had been too nervous to eat lunch.

"You may not be hungry, but I am. And you have to keep your strength up. I'm going make a little spaghetti, and you can eat it with me or not."

Becky could hear them upstairs. What were they doing? Up and down they went, up and down. She could hear them laughing and talking. There were two men outside going over the grounds. Finally somebody came to the door, the older man in the sports jacket. It was a nice jacket, she noticed, a grey tweed. She dabbed at her eyes and snuffled. He had papers for her to sign so they could search her car and Terry's car.

"I need a list of everyone who's been in and out of your apartment in the past month," the man said. He was perhaps forty-five, with close-cut, pepper-and-salt hair. He was of medium height. Captain

Edelson. There was a finger missing on his left hand. She tried not to stare at the stump of the little finger. But he noticed.

"Shot off," he said. "Years ago. Nowadays, they'd probably sew it back. Now let's start that list. We have to screen out the fingerprints of friends and family so that we know whose prints don't belong there."

She decided to include Sam, saying that they had read together from the play the weekend before auditions. She included Helen, although she didn't think Helen had been upstairs. She included everyone in Terry's family, his friends and about half of hers. She wanted them to sound like a well-adjusted busy couple close to both families. He also asked her about valuables. He walked her upstairs to say what was missing, but he wouldn't let her touch anything or even take any of her things, like a nightie or a clean pair of panties. Then he hustled her down to Helen's again.

He had more questions. "Was your husband having an affair? Did he take drugs? Had he ever taken drugs? Were you having an affair? I don't mean to be insulting, you understand, we have to know these things. They'll turn up anyhow in the course of our investigation. Did he have alcohol problems? Had he ever had problems with alcohol? How about you? Where did he work? Was he fired? Was there an argument? How long had he been unemployed? What kind of relationship would you say he had with his brother? Would you say you'd been having money problems?"

She confessed to money problems, and competition and a quarrelsome relationship between the brothers Chris and Terry. She worked to present the picture of a loving young couple with little money but great hopes for the future. Planning a family but holding off until they were more secure financially. The police captain, Edelson, had the habit of asking the same question five different ways. He did not let her alone until one of the detectives came in to tell him the medical examiner had arrived.

When the captain left, Becky caught Helen looking at her hard and a bit strangely. Her stomach clenched. She gave Helen a big smile, before she realized that must be inappropriate. Helen said softly, "You did fine. Maybe you laid it on a little thick with the hearts and flowers, but you were fine."

Becky did not say anything. She felt frozen. Did Helen know? Was it that easy to guess? Or was she just reading too much in? She wondered how Sam was feeling. What was she supposed to do with herself now? How should she act? She wished she dared ask Helen's advice.

CHAPTER 54

LEILA

Leila and Zak were sitting at breakfast. They were both people who dressed and tidied up before eating. Perhaps she thought we are signaling a cloture to our vulnerability in bed. They were also busy people and people who liked being busy. Sitting around over the breakfast table was uncomfortable. She surmised each felt their new intimacy required extra politeness, but she suspected they would soon dispense with the long breakfasts and charge off into their separate days. He was saying, "You don't understand how amusing I find it. I'd say nobody but you could ever end up with her cleaning lady living in her bedroom—"

"If you find it amusing, perhaps you'd like to take her home with you?"

He held up a hand for peace. "What I was trying to say was that I'd say it wouldn't happen to anybody else, except that I once had a woman I had gone out with exactly four times move into my house with her daughter when she was evicted. It took two months to pry her out. I used to be a marshmallow."

"The universal donor. O Negative. That's what I am. Can receive from hardly anybody, but can give to almost everybody."

They exchanged wry grins. "Still," he said, "you're going to have to do something about Mary Burke. Clearly she doesn't like being here any better than you like having her. I don't think she trusts you."

"I can't do anything until Mrs. Burke, Mary, whatever I'm supposed to call her, until she's recovered. I can't turn her out onto the streets. Her daughter finally agreed to split the cost of the nurse, but it was a struggle. The daughter strikes me as capable of great ruthlessness without a flicker of remorse, because all that counts are her children." Waif stuck her head out of Leila's blouse and yawned.

Zak grinned. "You look ridiculous with that kitten in your bosom. I know, she has to be kept warm. Still, it's hard to guess who to talk to, since you have two heads and one of them is furry. . . . What about the son in Hawaii?"

"A benign loser. He means well, but he's too laid-back to get worked up over what's happening. He's six thousand miles away, and neither of them has the price of a plane ticket. He lives with his wife and his kids in an apartment. While Grandma could sleep on the couch for a week, it's no long-term solution."

"Suppose you just shipped her off to one of them, the son or the daughter? The son sounds kinder. Wouldn't they have to deal with her?"

"Zak, she isn't a package of old clothes I'm bundling up for Rosie's Place. She has strong opinions. She was furious that I called her kids. She had them convinced she lived in some rooming house without a private phone. She'd endure anything rather than be a burden to her children."

"Fierce pride. Lethal pride."

"Or simply defending her sense of self-worth against the discovery that if she did throw herself on their mercy, they might throw her right back."

"I wish you could come out to the Cape with me for a couple of days. We're both very aware we're not alone here."

"I can't till she's out of danger. Besides, I thought we'd agreed that we're going to take things slowly."

"We both have a tendency to act as if we're not only married, but we've been married for years." He laughed, shoving back his chair. "I never thought I'd meet anybody with some of the same virtues and faults I have in relationships. Still I wish you'd come."

"If I can get away, I will . . . think about it. I promise." She looked into his eyes that seemed greener than usual this morning. His eye color seemed to respond to ambient light and the colors he was wearing far more than hers ever did. Her eyes were dark brown all of the time; his eyes were changeable as weather. "We need to go slow. We live a hundred miles apart. That helps. I don't want to live with you and I sure don't want to live with Mrs. Burke."

"Maybe if you lent her the money for a deposit on a cheap place, she could carry it. She'd have trouble getting together the deposit money for rent and utilities, all that cash she'd have to lay out up front."

"She was on a list for public housing for three years till she lost track of it. They've torn down or rehabbed all that cheap housing that used to be in the South End. There are more abandoned buildings than there are the kind of rooming houses and SRO's people without money used to live in."

Zak began to get himself together to drive home. She was sure he empathized with her situation, but equally sure he was delighted that he could walk out and leave her to grapple with the problem to which she could find no ready solution. It was keeping her away from Becky and Sam.

When the nurse arrived, she and Leila moved Mrs. Burke to David's room. After Leila stripped her own bed completely, she went off to campus. Boston was enjoying a January thaw. The temperature had risen into the middle forties. The trees dripped, the houses wept from their roofs, the snowbanks sank into concave rotten mounds and the grass began to poke through the spongy crust of former snow. Her house did not feel her own, so she was glad to flee to her office. She made most phone calls from there now. She did not like having Mrs. Burke, but she recognized desperate need and she had, by default, to take responsibility. Maybe she would try to get her colleagues to sponsor Mary in a little apartment. She would start sounding people out about it today.

When she got home, Mary seemed better. She was sitting up in bed drinking English Breakfast tea and eating toast and jam. She had lost weight and did not look well yet. Ms. Odell had washed her hair. It was a lighter-looking grey and fluffy from the blow-dryer. She was wearing a flannel nightgown Leila had bought her.

"I called the service and they said, If I can't do the work, that's too bad. They took on another woman already. They're giving her my people. What's going to become of me?"

"We'll figure out something," Leila said with what she felt was empty bombast. "We'll find a place for you."

"Don't you be calling my kids again. I won't have that. I won't!"

She suspected Mary was talking strong, but feeling quite weak. "I won't call them again. They're both supposed to be sending checks, to cover part of the cost of the nurse. I won't ask them for anything else." Leila sounded sour even to herself. She resented these kids. She was inheriting their mother, just because they couldn't be bothered.

She retreated to her study. This situation could not continue past the next few days. She had to find another place for Mary. She felt spoiled and petty, but she was not comfortable in her home.

The next day, Friday, when Leila came home from school, Mary announced, "I told that nurse I don't need her. I can get to the bathroom on my own now, and I can dress myself."

"You're too weak to leave," Leila said, putting her hands on her hips and assuming her best matron manner. "You can't go back on the streets. If you don't want the nurse, I'll be happy to tell her that's all. I know you don't want to stay with me, and I'm not delighted either, but I'm damned if you're going out of here without us finding some answers."

"I've been taking care of myself for fifteen years. I've survived situations you wouldn't believe. I can make it. I know how."

"You almost died, Mary. You're in no shape to sleep in unheated places. You can't go into a shelter where you have to walk the streets for twelve hours a day before you can go back in. We'll find another solution."

Over the weekend, she left Mary in charge of the house. Mary was getting up part of the day, which meant she could feed the cats. Waif had taken to following Vronsky around, his little trotting shadow. If he leapt up on his favorite windowsill to watch the street, Waif would try the leap, miss it, and then skitter up the draperies with her tiny sharp claws to join him.

Leila returned Sunday afternoon, with a great deal to do for her classes. She had not gone to see Sam or Becky since the crisis call from her mother sent her to San Diego. She had still come up with no better idea than her plan of soliciting pledges from her colleagues to get Mary back on her feet financially and to her own apartment.

Mary was out of bed when she arrived, dressed and cleaning the kitchen. "This is silly, Mary. Don't feel you have to be scrubbing everything. Just sit down and watch TV or read the paper. Take it easy."

"I like to be useful."

"That's the problem with both of us, I think."

Sunday evening she had a call from David. "Mom, I went to see Debbie the way you asked me. Ikuko drove us down there yesterday."

"I didn't ask you to go, David. I just said you might want to."

"Well, everything is a mess! Aunt Debbie fell off her horse—"

"Is she all right?"

"She's still pregnant, if that's what you mean. She broke her ankle. So we spent the whole weekend feeding the kids and slopping the animals and it was grim! She has a bossy horsy neighbor who tried to tell us we should stay there instead of going back to school. It's like Little Appalachia with the kids crying and the animals bellowing and her lying there not supposed to get up. I don't see why Abel can't do more."

"I don't suppose you remember what you were like at fifteen?"

"I was into birds and computers. What's wrong with that?"

"Anyhow, you've just depressed me more than I can say. Do you remember Mrs. Burke? She cleaned our house every Wednesday?" She told him briefly.

"So she stole my sleeping bag?"

"David, I sent you another one. You have one, she has one, everybody's happy except me. I'm going to hang up now and drown myself in the bathtub."

It was too much. She was not flying back to California. She was not going to run a hotel endlessly. She had to sell the damned house and find someplace much smaller to live. She had to get on with her book. Sam's trial had been separated from Becky's. It was set for next week. She sat in a hot bath trying to turn off her mind and failing. She was so tired she wanted to weep.

A phrase Zak had used about leaving California came to her. 'I decided to consolidate my debts.' She marched in to see Mary, who was in David's room. "I just got into bed," Mary said defensively.

"How attached are you to Boston?"

"I can't go stay with either of my kids. That's out."

"I wasn't thinking about your kids. I'm thinking about my sister, who's seven months pregnant in bed with a broken ankle, with three kids, no husband, two horses, a goat, chickens and a dog. Once she gets on her feet after she delivers, she can make a living. But right now, there's not going to be much money. It's a good-sized house. It's up in the mountains—it's pretty, but it isn't in a city or even a town. She needs help desperately. . . . That's where I was last week, but I can't go back. I have my classes to teach."

"I've never been afraid of hard work. I know how to take care of babies and big kids too. I raised two kids. I can cook, I can shop, I can do anything that nurse did. I don't know about chickens, but I like horses."

"It would be a terrific favor to me if you'd consider letting me send you out there for a while."

Mary was sitting up, frowning, animated. "I never took care of a horse, but I've ridden them. I'm not scared of animals." She rubbed her hands together in nervous excitement. "If she'd have me, I'd go in the minute. I like it where it isn't so cold. I just need enough money to eat on. I just need a place to stay and something to do."

Leila called Debbie. She got Abel. She tried to chat him up, but he was feeling too sorry for himself to make conversation with a remote aunt. Then Debbie came on. "Debbie, I've got a serious problem you may be able to help out with."

"I can't do anything. I'm flat on my back with a broken ankle and I'm not allowed to lift anything heavier than a book."

"Then maybe this will be good for you too." She proceeded to lay out her plan.

"I don't know," Debbie said. "What is she like?"

Leila was calling from her study, so she wouldn't be overheard, but nonetheless, she lowered her voice: "I don't understand her. But she's hardworking. She's feisty and independent. She's honest," Leila remembered the sleeping bag. "In a way, she reminds me of Babs."

"Doesn't sound like your type."

"She isn't. If you don't like the idea, forget it."

"No, it might help. But she'd have to share Robin's room. Let me talk to her. I can tell if it'll work. You have no idea who I could live with and who I couldn't stand."

"No idea, right. I'll get her to the phone." Leila retired to her study with her heartbeat accelerated, her blood pressure on high. She felt like a matchmaker sweating while her clients engaged in awkward fraught conversation. Please like each other, please get married, live happily ever after. She felt guilty at trying to clear out her own life by pushing them at each other, but she had to work. It was manipulative, opportunistic and the only way out she could find.

The conversation was taking a long time. Perhaps that was good. Perhaps. She clung to Vronsky, who kneaded her skirt with his big feet, purring wildly. Waif sat on the desk with her head cocked, watching them. She was an observant little thing, affectionate so far only with Vronsky, but she was beginning to get the idea that Leila was the food source. Sometimes when Leila looked at her, she would purr, as if happy to be noticed. A little will to live with fur. No wonder Mary had saved her from who knew what filthy alley.

She was all black, except for a white fingerprint on her forehead just over her eyes and little white feet, like spats. Her eyes were becoming a clear light green. She would probably be a small cat, with a heart-shaped face and very pointed ears. Her whiskers were as white as her feet.

"My own life has been totally neglected," she explained to the cats. "I feel buffeted by other people's needs. I just want to live with you guys and my work and be quiet and peaceful and productive. For over twenty years I've been running my life around Nick. I want to stretch out and fill my own space. I want a part-time lover instead of a full-time relationship job. Neither Mary or Debbie likes me. I want them to keep house together and not even think about me."

CHAPTER 55

MARY

Mary could remember when she had first come to Boston with Doug, flying in and out of Logan at Christmas to see Cindy and her grandchildren Marissa and Cole. She had never been anything other than middle-class; she had never been anything other than comfortable. Of course she flew to see her children. Of course. Then for years, Logan had been only a place she spent a night, the gateway to nothing but the streets.

Today she had a plane ticket and Mrs. Landsman at her elbow to make sure she boarded. Mrs. Landsman had bought the ticket. Mary did not feel as if she were accepting charity, because Mrs. Landsman had been blunt about what was involved. "My mother has insisted for years that I be responsible for my younger sister. Now she needs help, and I can't give it, and she can't accept it from me. So I'm offering you to each other. You'll help each other if it works out, and if it doesn't, then I can't solve the problem."

"Is she like you?"

"Hardly at all. We don't even look alike. She takes after our father."

"You're sure you don't want me to take Kitten?"

"Waif and Vronsky are not to be separated. They've made their wishes known." Mrs. L. grinned and looked at the departures monitor again.

"You don't have to wait."

"I like keeping you company."

The woman wanted to make sure Mary got on the plane, that she didn't just take the ticket and turn it in for cash. Mary had thought about that. Here she was being shipped to the opposite end of the country, where she didn't know a soul. How would she get back, if things didn't work out? She wouldn't know the ropes. She would be helpless and dependent on Mrs. Landsman's sister, Mrs. Rodgers. Still, she remembered Houdini, God rest his soul, telling her that life outside was easier in California. You could camp in a park without freezing. You could sleep in the shrubbery, because it was always green and leafy.

Truthfully, if Mrs. Landsman did leave, Mary did not know if she would get on the plane. Once upon a time she had flown several times a year with her husband. They had gone to visit his parents, her parents, gone off on vacations to Florida. One year when the kids were in high school, they had all flown to London and Paris and Amsterdam in August. Now she had not been on a plane since she had lost her job with Doug.

The ticket had cost so much money, it troubled her. With her savings account, now in the form of a cashier's check pinned to her slip so that if someone stole her purse, her nest egg would be safe, plus the money from the ticket, she would have just enough to buy an old car. It bothered her to waste all that money on a six-hour flight.

The plane seemed huge, looming out there where she could see it through the window. It was the middle of the winter: suppose it went down? Who would care? She would die and no one would mourn her. She did not imagine Cindy would grieve long. Jaime would be sad, but she was not a potent force to either of her children. Maybe she could make herself necessary to this Mrs. Rodgers?

Mrs. Landsman was telling her about the place she was going, in the mountains. She could scarcely listen. The voice barked at her like a friendly dog asking for attention. She could not give attention. She was too frightened. What was she doing? Where was she going? She was leaving everything she had learned slowly and with great pain over the years, where to get free food, where to pass time safely, where she could doze for an hour, where she could get out of the weather in the morning, in the afternoon, in the evening. She would be no one in a new and terrifying place.

The streets were dangerous, but she knew the dangers. She knew her round of church basements and garages left unlocked, of clients' houses and bus depots and the public library and the subway, spots where she could escape from the heat or the cold or the rain. Now she would be thrown on the mercy of a strange woman way out in the country, where she could not simply walk away. She would be stuck. She felt a rising gorge of panic in her throat. They were beginning to load the passengers, starting with small children and wheelchairs. Soon it would be too late to escape.

"I'm going to go to the bathroom before I get on the plane." Her voice squeaked.

"Good idea. It's over there." Mrs. Landsman went with her, waited outside.

She could insist on simply walking away. But then what would she do? She had been let go by the cleaning service. There were dozens of women to supplant her, instantly. The service was not interested in her explanations of how she had ended up in Mrs. Landsman's house. She had missed work and she had been replaced. It was that simple. She was sixty-one years old, with no room, no resting place of her own and with $527 in savings pinned to her slip. She had lost most of her little possessions in the fire that had killed her friends. She was still short of breath.

She let Mrs. Landsman walk her back to the loading area and she got in line and she boarded the plane. She buckled herself into her seat and closed her eyes. What would become of her? She knew Mrs. Landsman had been good to her, but she would never like the woman. It was hard to like anyone whose house she had cleaned for five years. She had scrubbed Mrs. Landsman's toilets and floors; they were not friends. She found Mrs. Landsman bossy and unsympathetic. She was a little put off by the boyfriend. The doctor who had treated her turned out to be a lesbian; that made her feel funny. It was one thing to look the other way and never quite be sure about Houdini and Mouse; it was something else to have a doctor living openly with another woman, and her a professor. The more she saw of Mrs. Landsman's life close up, the less comfortable she felt.

Would the sister, Mrs. Rodgers, be as difficult? She sounded softer. The sisters did not get along. She hoped that was significant. She was in deep trouble. She had to make herself necessary. She had to fit in. She had to please and maneuver and adjust—as she had when she married. As she had with Doug. But this was adjusting to a woman, an unknown woman. She felt as if she were being flung through the air, like the girl fired from the cannon in the circus, but she was not altogether sure any net was going to be spread in California to catch her when the plane landed and she was discharged into a strange land.

CHAPTER 56

BECKY

Becky enjoyed most aspects of her celebrity. The "Local News and Views" program that aired every weekend from the cable studios featured her. Belle and Gracie were thrilled. Tommy was annoyingly lacking in enthusiasm. "You should keep your mouth shut, Becca," he muttered. "Every time I turn on the TV, there's your mouth going. Chill out. The less you say, the less rope they have to hang you with. And don't smile so much. You start out looking serious, but pretty soon, you're smirking like you just got the lead in the school play."

As if she didn't know how to behave on camera; as if she hadn't majored in communications in college. Tommy was out of touch. He didn't understand this was her opportunity. Her boss was actually considering a couple of the proposals she had submitted to him over the past year. He had pulled out of the files the beauty show she had suggested doing with Belle, and the idea for a weekend morning show, say at eight Saturday, showing houses in the area for sale. They could get backing from the real estate people for that. At the weekly meeting Friday afternoon, both proposals would be considered for fall.

Once this mess had blown over, she was sure she would have a show and then she would have her foot in the door. She would have videos as demos. She would start looking for a real job. Tommy was silly to imagine she would let this opportunity to become known to the media people in southeastern Massachusetts and in Boston slip past her. She had set up a robbery, and the police were looking for thieves. In the meantime, she was on channels four, five, seven and fifty-six in Boston on the news, and on six, ten and twelve out of Providence. Her photo was in the *Herald.* The photo made her nose too prominent, but she liked the way she came over on television. Tommy just didn't understand her game plan. People recognized her sometimes in the supermarket and at the dry cleaner's. Holly and Brad next door, who didn't speak to her for two weeks after the murder, now gave her big hellos and invited her to their next party.

The police came by on regular patrol every afternoon, when the two burglaries had occurred. But they could not afford to post someone there full-time. As she had planned, she had quietly taken the smaller things out of the storage area and buried them in pine woods halfway between the office and the house or tossed them in the Canal. Sam had taken the VCR out under his jacket finally, and she assumed he had disposed of it in the Canal where he had thrown the clubs and the hammer. The TV would have to wait for next week. The police had combed every inch of shrubbery and lawn in the area of the condo and the scrawny woods behind them. They interviewed everybody in the complex. Hardly anyone was home in the afternoons.

It was a real drag to have to camp with her family. She hated it. The police wouldn't even let her in to get her clothes for days, and she had to borrow Belle's and Laurie's—nothing she would normally wear. Sylvie said she could stay with Mario and her for a few nights, but it was crowded there too and she had never got on all that well with Mario. Finally the detective who'd been doing the most questioning of Becky, Sergeant Beaumont, told her she could come back and get the place cleaned up.

Detective Beaumont stopped by the night she moved back in. "By the way, Terry's brother Chris tells us he was having an affair. And he thought you knew about it."

Becky was scrubbing the bathroom. "My husband Terry was unfaithful to me once, on a golfing weekend with his brother. His brother didn't like me, frankly, and he invited this other woman along after I couldn't go. Terry confessed to me, yes, but I wouldn't call it an affair, exactly. It was something he was ashamed of."

"You must have been upset."

"I was! I felt betrayed. But I also felt it was my own fault for being caught up in that theater group. I promised Terry I was going to quit.

I felt I'd failed him by being busy weekends. He'd done something stupid, and I felt I'd done something just as stupid—getting so involved in putting on plays."

She had scarcely had a good night's sleep since they had shut her out of her condo. It really was a mess. They had taken some of the bloody bedding, but the carpet was stained. She had cleaners in and they charged her a bundle. She was desperate to get settled again. Until the day the carpet cleaners came, she slept on the couch in the living room. The bedroom had a bad smell. She was going to have to do that room over. The bedspread was gone, the curtains she had sewn herself had been torn and the bedside lamp broken in the struggle.

She did not want anything around to remind her of Terry. The sight of his jackets and trousers on his side of the closet, his skis, his dresser with its drawers of socks, underwear, sweaters, his sports gear, all brought back her anger. She cleared his shaving gear and aftershave and pimple cream out of the bathroom and tossed it. She had put up with so much from him. Finally she had responded to abuse with abuse. She had thrown his anger back in his face. She had served him right. He had promised to love her, he had promised in church, and then he had taken up with Heather and treated her shabbily, insulting her parents, her home, her family, insulting her. She bundled up his clothing and brought it to his parents' house. Maybe Chris would take some of it. She wanted it out. She wanted him utterly gone.

She felt she was being thoughtful and generous, but the Burgesses acted really weird, as if she ought to keep his old sneakers and his grey flannel pants around for souvenirs. "These are Terry's clothes? In garbage bags?"

"I didn't have enough boxes. I thought you might want to give them to someone. I don't wear men's clothes, Mrs. Burgess, and I thought you'd rather have them than for me to give them to Goodwill. I thought Chris might want something to remember his brother by."

"I just can't believe you're getting rid of all his things."

"A therapist I've been seeing for trauma suggested I might be less depressed if I did that."

Mrs. Burgess's face twisted. "This is all that's left of our Terry. In garbage bags!"

Becky restrained her impatience. "Mrs. Burgess, what should I have done with them? I was trying to do the best thing for all of us."

She was enormously relieved to be back in her condo again, but she could hardly relax. Sergeant Beaumont was always coming around in the evenings and weekends. He never called first. He was a skinny man with a shock of black hair that looked greasy. His eyes were a light color, pale blue or pale grey. He had a thin sharp nose and long-fingered hands that were independently active, picking up objects, a pen, a vase, to examine them, turning them over and over. It put her on edge. He always called her Becky and he spoke as if he knew all about her, a sort of imitation uncle manner.

Sometimes he turned up at work, which was irritating. She felt it did not look good for the police to keep coming around. But it was even worse never to know when he was going to appear in her living room. She had scarcely been able to see Sam, who was complaining bitterly. She had dropped out of the theater. It didn't seem right to be onstage with her husband just murdered. Mama had told her to stop the play acting for the time being. She had carried that as far as she cared to, anyhow. What was the use playing vampire in a company that performed in a Masonic temple on the Cape? Really. That wouldn't do anything for her advancement, especially now that she was becoming known to the local media.

She did manage to see Sam every Saturday afternoon. She went to visit her family and then she went to Sam's. "You said we could be together all the time, and I hardly see you. I can't study. I can't work. The counselor called me in today to talk about my grades. I can't concentrate. I just keep thinking about you and what we did."

"The police are sitting on me, but they don't know anything. It'll blow over soon, and then we'll be free. It's just a matter of being patient for a couple of weeks." She could not believe how immature he was acting. It had been a mistake to get involved with someone who was practically still a child.

"But how can you stand it? Don't you want to see me?"

"Of course I do! I can't sleep at night. I think about you every day. But I'm scared of the police. We have to take it easy, just for a couple of weeks more. Then we can do anything we want. Anything." She gave that word a lot of spin, staring into his eyes, her hands on his shoulders.

The truth of the matter was, she thought as she drove home, that she found Sam less appealing. In comparison to Terry, he had shone. He had been so sexy and affectionate and focused on her. But now she needed to get her life together. She didn't long to spend an enormous amount of time with a seventeen-year-old who had a crush on her. She really ought to improve her skills, to work on concrete plans for the two programs her boss was considering. She needed to write a pilot script for the beauty program, her favorite. It was time to replace the broken lamp in the bedroom, the bedspread. Friday both her proposals had been discussed. The boss seemed to be leaning toward the real estate program, as a potential money-maker.

She wondered how long the insurance money was going to take. The insurance company would drag their heels, that was sure. Anyhow, she was going to dress a little more sophisticated. A widow could have a certain cachet. She looked great in navy. A black suit seemed elegant if she wore light blue next to her skin. Being involved with a seventeen-year-old, no matter how devoted, did not fit in with the new image she needed to build for herself.

Still, she had to keep Sam happy until he went away to school. Then he would become involved with someone his own age and forget the adventure with her. Not that he would really ever forget her, for she was his first love. Things would slowly peter out. In the meantime, she had to keep him satisfied but out of sight. The police were making that juggling act hard. Why couldn't Sam understand the potential danger they were in? He couldn't see farther than the end of his prick. Every time they had a few moments alone, she tried to talk to him about being careful and he wanted to jump on her.

Tommy asked her if he could stash some stuff in her apartment, now that Terry was gone, but when she told him how often the police came around, he abandoned the idea. She didn't want to be involved in Tommy's schemes. Terry had been right: having anything illegal in her condo was idiotic. She wouldn't let Sam come over either. She went to his home Saturdays, and twice she met him after school when she managed to get off work early. If she hadn't quit the drama group, it would have been easier, but she took Mama's advice seriously. People would not think that looked good, for a widow to play a vampire. She had a notion too that even acting something wicked was a bad idea. She shouldn't stand up in public and suggest duplicity or violence.

She spent a lot of time buttering up Helen. She walked Florrie every morning before she went to work. She spent a couple of evenings a week with Helen watching TV. Helen did not have a role in this production but was only making costumes. Becky volunteered to help. Helen knew more than she ought to, and it was important to keep her close. Helen enjoyed cooking. They were like a little family. In a way, Helen was her best friend now, as Sylvie had been for years. They understood each other very well, she felt.

Oddly she sometimes missed Terry. Although she had imagined how wonderful it would be to come home from work to a house empty of him with his stuff thrown about and the TV blaring, she found it a little bleak. She was used to companionship. Never in her life had she ever slept in a place alone. It was unnerving. Sounds scared her. She began to think about whether she shouldn't move as soon as the insurance money came through. Helen told her she should get herself a dog, and she considered it. Not a mutt like Florrie. She wanted the right kind of dog. She began to ask people what kinds of dogs were the best.

Captain Edelson appeared Saturday about eight. She knew he was just trying to see if she was out Saturday night. How obvious! Well, he found her with Helen working on costumes. He asked her to come upstairs so he could talk to her. She followed him obediently up to her condo. It was neat and clean. He would not find anything out of order, nothing he could poke his nose into. He wore a different jacket, this one a district check, with khaki pants. His hair was light grey, cropped short. The veins were prominent in his hands. He wore a wedding ring on the finger next to the missing one. His eyes were brown, rather nice eyes in a face she would never have looked at twice. He was one of those men the gaze passes over. Still, he was better dressed than Sergeant Beaumont and he didn't keep handling her things all the time.

"Have you learned anything," she started in at once. "Have you found any suspects?"

"We're working on several leads," he said in his dry voice. "How are you doing? Mrs. Burgess was upset you brought Terry's clothes over in garbage bags." He sat at her kitchen table and motioned her into the other chair.

"I don't have enough suitcases or boxes! I was trying to be nice."

"Becky, you know a young man named Sam Solomon."

Becky's heart and stomach closed on themselves like metal fists. "Sam . . . Yes, in the theater group I used to be in."

He held his silence a moment, gazing at her. She recognized the device. It was supposed to produce drama or suspense. He'd have to be better at acting than he was to manipulate her. "We've been told that you had an intimate relationship with this young man."

"Sam?" She made her eyes wide. She let her mouth drop open. "He's in high school! He's a kid."

"He's almost eighteen. He was in the theater company with you."

"Right. And I liked him. I was closest to my downstairs neighbor Helen and to Sam. I helped him read his parts. We all just had bit roles, but we encouraged each other . . . But *intimate*? That's ridiculous. Who would say such a thing? Who would even think something like that?'' Helen wouldn't tell on her. But who had, then? Nobody had known. Nobody except Helen.

Captain Edelson shook his head sadly. ''I understand you might feel embarrassed about such a relationship. But it's important for you to tell us the truth, Becky. Lying to us makes you look bad in a murder investigation.''

''First of all, I'm not lying. I can't imagine who would even think such a thing. I was nice to the boy, yes, but I'm just as nice to Helen, even nicer. I walk her dog all the time. Sometimes I run errands for her.''

''Other people in the theater company noticed the relationship. They saw you embracing. One of Sam's high school teachers became suspicious.''

''Embracing! Everybody there was always kissing each other. That's just theatrical put-on. It doesn't mean anything.''

''We'll be talking to you again soon, Becky. You might consider whether there isn't more you want to tell us about your relationship with your husband and about your relationship with Sam Solomon.'' He stood.

''Instead of talking to idiots who make up stories about every blonde they know, why don't you find out who broke into our condo and stole our stuff? That's what killed my husband, and you haven't come up with a single suspect.''

''Don't be sure of that, Becky. I'll be seeing you.''

As soon as she saw his cruiser leave, she called Sam. His mother answered. ''Who is this?'' She sounded suspicious.

''I'm in his physics class. I need to ask him something.''

Clunk. His mother went to fetch him. ''Sam, the police were just here.''

''Becky? Is that you? When can I see you?''

''Shhh. Don't say my name in front of your mother. The police were just here, and Dick Berg told them about us. How did he know?''

''He wouldn't tell them. He'd never do that.''

''He did. Sam, did you talk to him about us? Did you?''

''One time he was teasing me about you. That's all.''

''I can't believe this. We're in real danger.''

''What does it matter? That doesn't prove the other.''

''But it gives motive. It makes me look bad. Now you listen to me,

Sam, you deny it and you keep denying it. We were friends. I helped you with your parts. That's all. You admired me. You don't know anything more. You hear me?"

"Why do you sound that way? I feel as if you don't care anymore."

"I love you, Sam. Watch what your mother hears of our conversation. I'm just nervous about the police hanging around. We have to be careful. It's only for a short while longer. If we can go on fooling them."

"I just don't feel you care about me."

"Sam, I'm scared, and you ought to be. We have years and years. We just have to get through this tunnel. It's tricky. It's dangerous. When they come to talk to you, you have to watch everything you say and how you act and your littlest reactions. You understand?"

He said he did, but she knew he was just too young to grasp what was at stake. She dreaded the thought of having her fate ride on Sam's interrogation. She had never imagined they would trace her to him. Who besides Helen knew? Tommy, of course, but he would never tell. She did not think Helen had betrayed her. It was that damned Dick Berg, with his paternalistic attitude toward Sam, trying to protect him from her. As if Dick Berg didn't smooch around with that woman who was playing Minna, Beryl, who was married to an oncologist. He was allowed to fool around, but Becky wasn't.

She also suspected Ce-Ce. Ce-Ce had never liked her. Ce-Ce liked women who sucked up to her, flattered her, told her how remarkable she was. Becky didn't thick Ce-Ce was remarkable, just bizarre. With her hennaed hair and her jangling bracelets, she looked like something out of a time warp. Ce-Ce thought all women should make a fuss over her and envy her and all men should flirt with her. How could a detective take Ce-Ce and Dick Berg seriously? Perhaps he didn't. Perhaps he was just fishing, trying to get a reaction out of her. All Edelson had were suspicions and gossip. Did he think she was going to act guilty? She had done only what was necessary. She had had no choice. There was nothing to regret, nothing.

CHAPTER 57

LEILA

Sam's trial, severed from Becky's, was mostly a formality, since he was pleading guilty to second-degree murder and no jury was involved. He would be sentenced after Becky's trial. Leila thought that was unusually overt manipulation on the part of the State. Help us convict her and your own sentencing will be lighter. She went with Zak to see Sam. He was back in the Barnstable House of Correction. She had her twenty minutes first.

Leila looked at Sam with pity. She could not help confusing him at times with David. He seemed, like many bright boys, a combination of extreme sensitivity and total callousness. She did not think that the man he had killed, Terry Burgess, occupied him except as a problem. Before the judge, Sam had delivered a speech well rehearsed by his lawyer about his shame and guilt and how terrible he felt about the Burgess family. He had delivered it earnestly and properly, but she did not believe a word. She sensed that he was truly remorseful for the pain and trouble he was causing Cathy and Zak. The Burgess family he called the lynch mob. He could not extrapolate from his mother's anguish to that of Mrs. Burgess. When he was forced to mention Terry, he usually broke eye contact and grimaced. "I don't care what anyone says, he was a bastard. He used to beat her. I was a fool to get involved with her, but he deserved it."

The Burgess faces were on the evening news as Becky's trial began with the selection of jurors: a tight shot of Mrs. Burgess with her long sharp chin and her perfect teeth uncovered in a snarl; Mr. Burgess, with an ill-fitting mask over flesh grown watery, eyes popping with rage; Chris, looking sullen.

Sam's anger was directed at Becky. He leaned back from the flimsy wire barrier, clenching his fists. "She lied to me. She told me he wouldn't give her a divorce. He did beat her, I saw the bruises. But he wanted a divorce, his parents say so. But they'd say anything. She made me feel like I had to save her, I had to. She seemed so afraid of him. I'd only seen him once, at the play. I thought he was this heavyweight. But he wasn't strong. He was taller but he wasn't as strong as I am. She could have got a divorce anytime, and I'd be going to college. Why didn't she just get a damned divorce like everybody else and leave me alone?"

"How did you come to accept the idea of killing him? That was a big step, wasn't it?" She asked aloud the question she had asked herself again and again.

"It was like there was really nobody in the world but her and me. I wanted her so bad I can't tell you. My grades had taken a dive. I couldn't concentrate. I'd sit in math class, I'd be in gym class, I'd be in study hall, and all I could think of was being with her. In bed, I mean. Not that we had a bed very often. We mostly used the backseat of her car. I just wanted to be alone with her and for everything else to go away."

"So he wasn't real to you?"

"I couldn't even remember what he looked like. I still can't. I'd never spoken two words to the guy. You have to see, from the moment I kissed her and she let me, and she kissed me back the way nobody ever had, it just wasn't real. I was in a movie, understand, I was in a dream. It was too totally good to be real. Nobody else and nothing else got through. I couldn't even hear what other people were saying to me."

"Sam, why did you and Gene pawn the VCR and the TV? Did you need money that badly?"

"I know it seems now like I was an idiot. But I couldn't throw good stuff in the Canal. It felt too wasteful. I was raised to finish all the food on my plate, to wear clothes until they wore out, to think about what things cost. And Mom recycles everything. I just couldn't throw that stuff in the Canal, you know? I couldn't do it."

"But why did you involve your friend?"

"*She* hardly had time for me after the murder. She kept saying we'd have all the time in the world soon, soon, but in the meantime, she wasn't trying, she wasn't trying at all."

"So you turned to your best friend?"

"I felt crazy. I felt kind of lost. Like I couldn't believe we'd done this thing, and now I couldn't even be with her. I had to tell Gene. And he said, well, you can't just keep that stuff under your bed. Let's sell it. Maybe we can get enough for it all to buy some kind of wheels we can share. So then at least I'd have something. And then I could go see her when I wanted to."

A few minutes later, he was talking about his plans. "Zak says maybe I can get a degree inside. Then when I get out, I'll at least be a college graduate." Leila looked at him, young and unformed-looking with his life gone into the ditch. He terrified her. She could not bear to think that David could make a stupid mistake—hit someone with a car, whatever—and everything would be utterly changed for all the years he lived.

Six months ago, Sam had been at the center of Cathy's life and Zak's; now he was a hole they moved around. Sam belonged to the State, to the assistant district attorney, who was coaching him daily, going over his testimony. Sam worked at his testimony the way he must have done for his classes, before Becky. He had been a good student.

While Zak was with Sam, she walked among the cars of the parking lot. The day was mild. The snow had melted, laying bare the dead grasses and sodden leaves of fall: a dank monochrome world, all beiges and browns and greys. In the distance, Massachusetts Bay looked made of zinc.

For Zak and for Cathy, there was a deep embarrassment in thinking about Sam. He had ruined his life. He had grossly spoiled his own plans, and that act of unimaginable violence had severed him from his intimate family. Cathy loved her son, certainly, and Zak loved his nephew, but that love had a sore hidden side. That love had lost its trust. There was an unspoken feeling that there was something wrong with Sam that they could not grasp, that they were somehow responsible for but would never know how or why. He was more of a stranger than they had realized, and now they could not forget.

Zak was always quiet on their return from Barnstable. Often they saw Sam separately, because Barnstable was much closer to Zak than to her. Other times, she knew Zak appreciated the company, even in silence. For weekend visits, they linked up. Then mostly they went to the Cape. With her house being shown to prospective buyers, she found it pleasant to get away. Today, however, they were headed to Cambridge, since they had tickets to Mark Morris, along with Jane and Emily. Jane was cooking supper, an interesting if sometimes harrowing experience. Jane liked dinners to be authentic, even if that meant eating a Berber dish with one hand and no utensils, squatting on the floor. Leila was not worried about Zak. He took such things in stride. She was mainly worried that Jane might plan something so elaborate they would be late to the Wang Center.

The real estate market was sluggish, and so far Leila had not received an offer she could accept. Nick was far more eager, but she wasn't dragging out the process to annoy him. She simply wanted to come out of the sale with enough money to buy something. She wanted a yard; she wanted two bedrooms; she wanted to be within walking distance to work—a mile-and-a-half radius.

When they reached her house in their separate cars, Zak dropped into a chair. "I wonder if I could have killed Corinne. But this was premeditated."

She turned on the coffee machine and sat on the couch. "Do you believe a lot of thinking went on in Sam's head?"

"I find myself staring at him while we're talking and trying to imagine him bashing in someone's skull with a hammer. The police never recovered the weapons, but according to Sam, he used a hammer and she used a golf club. It wasn't one of your antiseptic executions from across the street."

Leila had read the same reports. "Would you feel better if it was?"

"I'd understand it. If you could press a button, wouldn't you wish for your ex-husband to cease to exist?"

"I can imagine it," she said grimly. "*Poof* and he's air."

"Well, this wasn't *poof* and Burgess didn't vanish. They must have stood there beating the shit out of him for ten minutes. I see myself walking in on Corinne and that loser she died with. I see myself making a scene and calling her a bitch and a whore. I see myself breaking things. I can see myself vindicative as hell, trying to take Lauren away from her. But I can't see myself beating her to death. That's a boundary I can't cross even in my imagination."

"In my life, there's a point where I give up and cut my losses. Becky didn't have that point. Her feelings are really hurt that Sam has turned on her. She keeps telling me she trusted him, and now he's just like the other men she knew. What did she think he'd do under pressure? Take the blame?"

"We're both unwilling to know what it would feel like to decide to kill someone and then to do it. Yet in war young men and boys, just as gentle and as thoughtful and as sensitive as Sam, commit atrocities against combatants and nurses and ordinary wives and mothers."

"Maybe you just learn to make a big Them/Us division. Us hurt. Them get hurt. Us count. Them don't count. Us can eat Them."

Zak rose and held out his arms. "It's this enormous burr we keep rolling uphill. Let's let it go. We can agree we're not going to kill each other."

"I think I could make an absolute promise to that effect." She stepped into his arms and for a moment they just held each other, hard. "Would you like it in writing?"

"Sometimes, Leila, I feel like a herbivore, a sort of buffalo at best, compared with a sleek predator. We admire predators—panthers, lions, tigers, even wolves. Maybe to be naturally thoughtful and hesitant to use violence is to be somehow second rate. To be in the middle of the social food chain. Especially if you're a man. This society thinks real men are violent."

"I don't want to be a predator—I don't want to be involved with one either. I'm not surprised when a man's violent. I'm pleased when he isn't. But I have mixed feelings when a woman's violent. On one hand we feel she's giving us a bad name, bringing down our moral real estate values. On the other, she made it into the big time, we can do it too. That's part of why Becky fascinates me. She broke the rules in all senses."

"Do you wish you could? Secretly?"

"The rules I want to break are the unwritten ones that say that now I will be lonely, that my life after divorce will be desolate and bleak." She pressed closer to him, feeling his body real, limber, firm against her. "I want to begin naively and freshly with you. I want to figure out how to be together, as if there were no expectations and no unwritten rules of success and failure. I want to figure it out without prejudice, without old habits."

"That sounds meek, but it's a huge demand. It's trying to rewrite our social DNA."

"I never asked you what happened to that coyote you had in the clinic?"

"I healed him and let him go at the dump . . . I don't think I want to know your line of thought. Look, out of our gentleness, we can just grub along and try to love each other." His hand closed warm on the nape of her neck.

She stood very still. That was the first time either had mentioned love. But, she thought, I loved Melanie as much as I loved Nick, and she didn't eat me up. She didn't make me feel lumpy and asexual. Maybe we can work at loving each other weekends in a careful and easy way, two creatures of glass and gristle. Then she leaned back and smiled at him, her hands sliding down to his buttocks. "We can only try."

CHAPTER 58

MARY

"You can't tell me what to do." Abel glared at her. "You're not my grandmother. Besides, my grandma's a dyke."

"What kind of nonsense is that?" Mary was nervous, standing in front of the overflowing pail of compost it was Abel's job to take out. Her authority was flimsy, invented. He could simply refuse her, and what could she do?

"Red said so. Before he left. And I'm glad he left, because he was an asshole. My friend Lobo says he was a con man and that my mother was conned."

She decided to ignore his foul language for the moment. She was in enough trouble. "Love makes people see the best in each other. Your mother wanted to believe in her husband—the way she wants to see the best in you. You shouldn't believe everything a man says about his in-laws. I never met your grandmother, but I know she's a nurse. She was married and had two children, so I'd just forget what Red Rodgers thought about her—and most other things too." Mary kicked the pail, lightly.

"You can't make me do anything."

"You're getting to the age when nobody but the law and your own good sense can make you do anything," Mary said, trying to keep her voice from trembling. "Since I can't lift it, I'll just get your mother out of bed and she can take it out."

"I don't want her to do it. That's not fair."

"It's her or me, Abel, and I can't."

"It's a cheat," Abel said. "I'm always having to do the dirty work."

"That's what you get for growing up," Mary said. She actually could lift the pail, although it was plenty heavy, but if she did, she'd be doing that every time and all of his other chores too.

Robin, the little dark child with the Indian eyes, was easy. She was starved for love. She was the only girl, the child not of a marriage but of an affair. Mary suspected the father was Latino but no information on him had been given her. Robin just wanted to be held and fussed over. Mary won her right away. They were sharing a room and Robin came into her bed whenever she was scared at night. Mary cuddled her far more frequently than she had her own children. Robin was affectionate enough to wiggle through Mary's awkwardness. Robin had her problems too. She was not always truthful and she had a bottomless sweet tooth. If Mary did not watch, she would make herself sick on candy and on cookies. Robin adored Abel, who largely ignored her.

Ben was difficult. It would take time. He hung on his mother. The baby would force him away a little. She would bide her time and work on him then. Abel was causing her the most problems. He was in rebellion against his own mother, and he saw her as an ersatz mother come to try to coerce him into toeing the line. If she did not win him over or at least neutralize him, she would not be able to stay, once Debbie got on her feet. She would be more trouble than she would be worth to Debbie, without Abel's permission, essentially.

She studied him. One strategy was to ask nothing of him, to smile and let him go, but she had a strong feeling that would not work. For one thing, it ran against her own character. She had never let her own kids get away with murder, and she would not be able to control herself. Second, she felt that laxity would simply fertilize Abel's contempt.

He was pushing against the boundaries, but he still needed and wanted them in place. She had to get him on her side, but she had no idea how to manage that. He had been uprooted too many times; he had too many pseudo-fathers. He was sick of people who came into his life, grabbed some authority, took over and then vanished. He was not lovable, but she did not mind his sore pride. She thought she probably understood it better than his mother did. Debbie was having trouble with her oldest son, and if Mary could only get around him, Debbie would be better disposed toward her.

Debbie was mistrustful of her. "If my sister thinks she can control me through you, she's crazy. I don't want anything from her and I don't need anything from her. She thinks she's right all the time, there's one way to do it and that's her way." Debbie had been sitting up in her bed resting against a pile of pillows, frowning. Her ankle was in a light cast and crutches rested against the headboard. Debbie looked overwrought and miserable.

"Mrs. Landsman shipped me out here to get me out of her sight and you off her conscience. Now she's out of the loop. It's up to us whether we can get along okay or not." Mary spoke with a hearty false confidence. "I've restocked the kitchen and cleaned it and the bathroom. I've started on the laundry. Three kids sure make a mountain of clothes. I'd forgotten."

"I think Robin needs socks. Could you check her drawers after the laundry's put away?"

"Let's make a list of the kids' sizes—I mean as of this hour. I know how fast Abel's growing. I think he's got taller since I arrived." Five days ago. No one but Robin was more than tolerating her.

Debbie sighed. "Isn't he just shooting up? I can't remember exactly how tall his father was. . . ."

"Debbie . . ." Mrs. Rodgers had told her to call her by her first name. Mary had not resisted. Here her strategy was not to hold back but to press in to every available entrance and crack and vulnerable place. "Wouldn't you like me to wash your hair for you? I could bring a basin of water in. We'd probably get the sheets wet, but we could change them."

"I can make it to the bathroom, if I can sit while you do it."

Debbie softened while Mary washed her light hair. "My mother used to do that," she confided. "I remember she'd sing while she washed my hair, old pop songs. Tunes from *South Pacific.* She never could sing on key. Neither can I. Only Leila can. Don't you think she has a pretty voice?"

"I don't know her well."

"You don't like her all that much, do you?"

Mary pondered her answer. She was always having to figure out what was the best possible truth or lie to tell. Finally she said, "Not particularly. I hope you aren't insulted." She knew perfectly well that the sisters were not chummy. No more than Cindy and Jaime were. She had heard them sound off on each other too many times. Jaime thought Cindy opportunistic, calling her a weasel. Cindy thought Jaime a loser. Well, wasn't that what Mary herself was?

"I'm nothing like my sister. Why should I be insulted?"

"You're a much warmer person," Mary said, rinsing Debbie's hair gently. "You have such fine pretty hair and skin. Your coloring is like my daughter Cindy's."

"Do you have a picture of her?"

"Just one with me. I lost all my old pictures in a fire."

"That's so sad."

"I'll ask Cindy to send me some new ones when I write to her next."

Debbie never asked her why she didn't live with her daughter, because Debbie didn't want her family supervising her. Debbie hadn't heard from Red's family since he had left her, not one word, and she was annoyed with her own mother because of something from last Thanksgiving, Mary didn't know what. She would try to find out. Maybe Babs next door who also had to be won over, knew. She was the most important outsider. Mary sized her up. They could make friends around the horses. Fortunately, Mary was great with animals. The horses already nickered when they saw her and Min came trotting over to the gate. They had to be exercised. Min was grey with a white blaze.

With much trepidation, Mary got herself up on Min the next morning and went riding with Babs, full of apologies for her bad seat. But it began to come back to her. She and Cindy had ridden often, before Cindy got too adolescent to be willing to be seen with her mother. Here she must ride. It was something she could share with Debbie. Debbie loved her horses. She missed them. Mary was so sore after her first ride she wanted to weep, but she kept her mouth shut. Her muscles would stretch. Complaining was a luxury she could not afford, being on probation.

Mary began observing the horses carefully and then reporting to Debbie. They gossiped about the horses as if they were people, and indeed, Mary thought Min and her colt Sika were far nicer than most of the people she had been dealing with in recent years. They had a good relationship with each other too, a nice mother-daughter affection, although Min would snap at Sika's flank if she thought Sika was too frisky.

It was beautiful here. She remembered all her days cleaning houses with nothing to look forward to but a cafeteria supper and then a night in Logan or somebody's unheated garage. If she couldn't stay on with Debbie, she did not want to return East. She'd go into San Diego or

L.A. and try life on the streets. True, she didn't know anyone, but what did she have to go back to?

The air was clean and piney. She liked the smell of the animals; even the goat wasn't bad. There was always something to be done with the kids or the house—a leak to get fixed under the sink, a curtain to rehang. The animals always needed attention. There was shopping, laundry, cooking, cleaning, Min and Sika to exercise and curry and feed and water. The chickens, who surprised her with their strong personalities. The goat, who was affectionate as a dog and needed milking. Who'd ever believe this is me, she thought as she milked Nannie. She wished she had been able to keep Kitten and bring her here. Mrs. Landsman would never even let her outside in Cambridge.

If Mary had not been a strong sturdy woman used to a hard day and a harder night, she would never have been able to keep up with the demands. Things had piled up. The house had been dirty and neglected. The laundry stank. The refrigerator was empty but for some spoiled tofu and rotten lettuce, a few open cans and bottles. Eggs of course. They always had eggs and goat's milk. Debbie kept up with the mending in bed, but she was terribly, terribly bored. TV did not amuse her; she spaced out when she watched it. Debbie played games with Ben and read him stories.

"That's a neat sleeping bag," Abel said, when she was airing it. "But it smells burnt."

"It was in a fire. I was in a fire."

Abel looked her in the eyes, suddenly interested. "Like a forest fire?"

"No. A house fire. Three people died. I tried to save my friend, but she wouldn't wake up. I was the only one who escaped."

He looked at her sideways. "Bullshit. Right?"

"It was in the Boston papers. I could show you a clipping that Mrs. Landsman, your aunt, gave me. My friend died."

"Let me see."

"I'll show you tonight. After supper."

Had she backed herself into a corner? Abel had been fascinated by the idea of her being in a fire. She kept trying to reach him. How much truth could she tell? When she finished the dishes, Abel put himself in her way. "You were going to show me something about a fire. You said you would."

Mary went to the room she shared with Robin and found the clipping among her things, all put away neatly in two drawers of a dresser, the other two drawers empty. She passed it to him.

"That was you, who ran away?" Abel frowned, disbelieving.

"The other people were a woman named Beverly Bozeman, as it says. And two street people, Houdini and Mouse. I came to know Beverly Bozeman when I'd pass her on my way to work. She was a bag lady who hung around near the subway entrance. Anyhow, one night she was . . ." She hesitated and decided at fifteen he could handle a story about rape. ". . . attacked by a man who stabbed her, raped her and left her for dead. He threw her body in a big Dumpster—you know what I mean?"

"Just because we live in the woods now doesn't mean I don't know about cities. I've lived in Cincinnati, in Seattle, in L.A. I know about Dumpsters and what happens to women on the streets."

She doubted that, but she went on, smoothing the edges of her story as she talked. She told about visiting Beverly in the hospital, about being intrigued by her and becoming her friend. Then she described wanting to understand how Beverly actually lived, and deciding to spend a couple of nights with her friend in an abandoned building.

Abel was impressed. "You really did that? Took your sleeping bag and just went into a tough neighborhood and slept in a boarded-up building with all those homeless guys and the bag lady?"

Mary said, "I wanted to see what her life was like. How else would I ever find out? Sometimes you have to take a chance to learn things. It's like getting on a plane and coming out here, when I didn't know any of you. You have to take chances on new things sometimes, new people."

"Weren't you afraid of those guys? Houdini and Mouse?"

"They were friends of Beverly and very gentle."

"How come you could go and do something like that?" He squinted at her.

"Well, Abel, my own kids have grown up. I'm at the age where I can take some chances, and it's nobody else's business, right?"

"Like when you're my age, if you make a stupid mistake, it goes in your record and it follows you everyplace. But if you're an old lady, you can get away with it?"

She felt guilty as she straightened the kitchen. Abel had gone back to the living room to watch a basketball game, but first he had taken out the compost. She had turned her friends into fascinating characters in a TV drama, with herself as the visiting reporter, comfortably ensconced above them, descending at will and reascending to security. She was exploiting her friends as fodder to impress a rebellious kid.

As Mrs. Landsman had promised, she had been satisfactorily vague with Debbie about Mary's situation. All Debbie knew was that Mary had lost her job and her apartment because of having pneumonia, that she had collapsed at Mrs. Landsman's house. She did not think Debbie would ever press her for details. Here she had left her past behind as she had left the East Coast. It was like a parcel abandoned in a locker. She hoped she hadn't revealed too much in attempting to impress Abel.

Debbie liked to be praised, taken care of, fussed over. She liked to be told she was still pretty, but even more, she liked to be told she was smart, even that she was wise. Mary would oblige, daily. She watched for clues as to what she should make herself appear to be, so that she could stay. So that they would want to keep her. So they would not throw her back.

If she wasn't climbing to the top of the mountain, at least she was no longer sliding off. She was clinging with her nails and her teeth.

CHAPTER 59

BECKY

Thursday she stole forty-five minutes to see Sam and fuck him near his house, with the car pulled off onto a beach road. She faked an orgasm for the first time with Sam, because she was too nervous someone might come along, but Sam was pleased anyhow. He clung to her. "The police came. It was a Captain Edelson. They asked me all kinds of questions about you, like had I ever been to the condo. They asked about why I stopped riding home from the theater with Mr. Berg. I said his being my high school teacher made me nervous. I don't think they believed me."

"Next time, tell them he hung around so long afterwards smooching with his friend that you couldn't wait that late. It doesn't matter if they believe you or not, if they can't prove anything." She sat up and stared into his hazel eyes. "It's very important not to volunteer any information. Don't try to impress them. Don't make dramas, Sam—"

"You talk to me as if I'm an idiot. Why would I make dramas? You're the one who is always gabbing to reporters and interviewers. Everybody's talking about you and the murder. If you hadn't panicked and quit the theater group, we wouldn't have a problem seeing each other, if you even care."

"I explained to you, what my mother said about how it would look. I can join again once everything calms down. They're not going to go on hounding us. There'll be another juicy case, and we'll go on the back burner."

"Not if you keep stirring it up."

He was simply jealous because all the attention was on her. "It isn't as if I enjoy talking to them. I'm trying to manage the news to avoid drawing suspicion to us. I'm doing it for both of us."

She turned the radio loud as she drove home. If she were a cursing woman, she would have let go a few choice oaths, but her mother had not raised her to have a foul mouth. She was ready to wring Sam's neck. He was attempting to tell her what to do, the little snot. She was entirely dependent on his judgment, which was almost nonexistent, and his ability to keep silent, which she was beginning to doubt. She had not chosen well. Would Tommy have helped her if she had begged him? But she would have had to split the insurance money with Tommy and he probably would simply have hired someone who could have blackmailed her. Sam had not even thought about money.

When she got home, Captain Edelson was sitting in his car waiting for her. "Stop off some place?"

"I was feeling depressed. I went to the beach and took a little walk. It's hard to come home to empty rooms . . . Have you found anything? It's been well over a month since my husband was killed."

"We're working on the case. We'll figure it out, of that you can be sure." He followed her upstairs. If Sergeant Beaumont played the know-it-all uncle, Captain Edelson offered no such pseudo-warmth. He looked at her bleakly and talked in a dry monotone. She was weary of these men asking questions and staring at her slyly and snooping around all the time. They deprived her of a life. They haunted her evenings. They had appointed themselves guardians of morality and what people expected, and she was going to sit home and be lonely if they had any say in it. Didn't they have anything better to do than harass one already-harassed woman?

"We have a statement from Miss Heather Joyce of 148 Seagull Lane. Miss Joyce admits to a relationship with your husband, Terrence, known as Terry Burgess. She claims that your husband intended to divorce you and marry her. She said that he had asked you for a divorce."

"That's absolute invention. No, he never asked me for a divorce. That's the bimbo Terry's brother Chris fixed him up with for the golfing weekend I couldn't go on. Terry confessed to me. But far from saying he wanted to marry her, he said he never wanted to see her again. He said he was ashamed of getting involved with her."

"She claimed he definitely told her he was asking for a divorce."

"Captain, I'm not responsible for what my husband may have said to a woman he was spending a weekend with. He may have said that. He may have said he was single, for all I know. But that isn't what he said to me, his wife. To me, he said he was sorry. In fact, he cried."

"According to your brother-in-law Chris, Terrence was planning to change the beneficiary on his considerable life insurance policy. It amounted to two hundred thousand dollars, now payable to you. Chris said your husband planned to change the beneficiary to his mother."

"Captain, you don't understand. Chris sold insurance, or at least he tried to. Everybody in the Burgess family is insured for everything under the sun. I think they even have a policy on me. They did it to help Chris out. I don't know who the beneficiary on Terry's policy is. I thought it might be his parents, because we owe them money from buying the condo. A while ago, Terry said we should have insurance to cover if we were both out of work, so his parents wouldn't lose their shirt if we couldn't keep up payments on the condo. I think we had some sort of mortgage insurance. I was making the payments on the condo, but we weren't able to pay back his parents, you understand? We felt bad about that. But Chris is the one who knows about all that, because he wrote policies on every one of us."

"You claim you didn't know about the insurance policy on your husband with you as beneficiary?"

"Everybody in their family had insurance on everybody else. I never paid attention. You have to understand, my brother-in-law didn't like me and I didn't like him. I wouldn't have voluntarily taken out a policy on a dog with him. He caused trouble all the time in my marriage—or rather he tried to."

"You're suggesting that your brother-in-law is lying to us."

"Captain, I don't know what he's been saying. Chris and Terry always had a competition going between them. They were very concerned with each other, not always in a good or healthy way. I did think Terry had fixed the insurance so that it would pay off his parents."

"What do you mean by unhealthy? Drugs?"

"Terry never took drugs in his life."

"Are you prepared to swear to that?"

"He never did drugs. Ever!"

"Because his former fraternity brother, Lyle Sutter, claims that Terrence Burgess took cocaine on two occasions in college."

"That was before I knew him. I have trouble imagining Terry ever doing something illegal."

"You claim that your husband told you about Heather Joyce and expressed regret. Did he promise never to see her again?"

"He swore it to me."

"Can anyone corroborate your story?"

"Well, I told Helen Coreggio downstairs about the golf weekend. It wasn't the sort of thing I would spread across the countryside. If I'd told my family, I was afraid one of my brothers might have come and given Terry a very hard time. I felt he was genuinely sorry and wouldn't do it again. I also felt it was my own fault, because I'd gotten so involved in that theater group."

"That's the one with your boyfriend, Sam Solomon, in it?"

"He isn't my boyfriend. He's just a kid."

"A kid you were very nice to."

"I was nice to everybody in the group. Why wouldn't I be? I liked them. I liked being in plays. I resent what you're saying. Ask Helen Coreggio if anything funny was going on. She was almost always with me when I was with him."

"Except when you drove him home."

"Do you think Dick Berg was having an affair with him? He drove Sam Solomon home oftener than I did. Sometimes Helen drove *me* home."

"Your neighbor, Holly Reicher, recognized a photo of Sam as someone she saw around here."

"He brought me the script for *Dracula*, and Helen and Sam and I read it together, trying to figure out what parts to try out for."

"How often was he here?"

"I think he was only in the building once, and we were mostly in Helen's place."

"Mostly? What does that mean?"

"It means I don't remember, because it wasn't important. He's just a nice kid. Helen liked him too. Oh, it's possible he had a crush on me, but that was the extent of it. He was certainly too shy to make a pest of himself."

"It must have been flattering for you, a married woman whose husband was having an affair, to have a young man with a big crush on you. A nice-looking young man you were alone with after every rehearsal and performance."

"For all of ten minutes in my car. Really! I feel like you're making up a story that even you can't believe."

"What I may believe is irrelevant, Becky. It's what a jury will think has been proven."

They had Sam in her apartment. She had to make a move. "Perhaps he did have a crush on me. But I didn't take it seriously. Would you take a teenager's crush seriously? I thought he was a sweet and serious boy. That's all I thought about him. Maybe I shouldn't have been so nice to him, but I try to make people like me. I certainly have been nice to other people, like Helen in the building, who can tell you. I help her with sewing and walk her dog. I didn't think being nice to a boy in my theater group meant anything—to me or to him. If I was wrong and he had a big crush, I wasn't aware. He's just a kid."

She started out to see Sam Saturday, but realized a blue car was following her. Instead she drove to an outlet mall at the Canal. She called Sam from a pay phone inside. "Becky, the police were questioning my friend Gene."

"Why?"

"I don't know why," he whined, and she felt a chill of suspicion.

"You weren't stupid enough to tell him anything?"

"Maybe we can get together Monday afternoon when I get home from school."

"Did you tell Gene anything?"

Sam hung up. She wanted to strangle him. She wanted to pummel him. What could he have said to his stupid friend from school?

The blue car was still in the parking lot when she came out with some panty hose. She thought of strolling over and asking the detective if he was enjoying his Saturday, but she decided the innocent would not expect to be followed. It was hard to resist, because she could see herself, cool and collected like Sharon Stone in the movie, going over to the car and standing hand on hip. Why had they fixed on Sam? She had never expected them to bother Sam. What was visible to link them? And what did Gene have to do with all this? He was a short chubby friend of Sam's. They had most of their high school classes together and both planned to go to U Mass Amherst in the fall. She was getting very, very irritated with the police and she wondered if there wasn't somebody, like the sheriff or a selectman she could complain to. They were screwing up her life, interviewing more and more people at random. It was growing intolerable.

She was at work the next Tuesday when two detectives marched into her office, Beaumont and another detective whose name she could not remember. "Mrs. Rebecca Burgess, you're under arrest for the murder of your husband, Terrence Burgess. You have the right to remain silent. . . ."

It was just like the movies, except there was no music, and her boss and the girls she worked with were all standing around watching. "I'm sure I'll be back soon," she said to her boss. "This is all a mistake. Why they can't catch the thieves is beyond me."

Detective Beaumont actually put handcuffs on her, as if she were some violent criminal. As he led her out to the car, he said, "We did track the thieves, Becky. We found the pawnshop where Gene Wiggins and Sam Solomon pawned the TV, the VCR and a gold watch of your husband's. The Wiggins kid is very talkative."

"This is ridiculous," Becky said. "I wouldn't hurt a fly, let alone my own husband. This is insane. I don't understand how they managed to get my VCR or my TV or Terry's watch. . . . Unless they broke into my condo while I was at work! Maybe Sam Solomon noticed the stuff we owned when he came up with Helen that time about the *Dracula* script. I can't imagine why Sam and his friend Gene, who I only met once when he came to see *The Witness for the Prosecution*, would want to kill my husband."

She was scared, she was really scared, but they had nothing to connect her with the murder. She would deny everything, and it would be her word against some fat little high school boy she scarcely knew. She would out-act him, out-tough him. They had no proof. They could scare her and threaten her, but then they would have to let her go.

CHAPTER 60

MARY

Mary beamed as Debbie finished the chicken and the gravy. "That's the best chicken I ever had," Debbie said, lying back against the pillows. "Bruce—Ben's father—"

"The one who sends the money."

"That's Bruce. Reliable but dull. Anyhow, he could cook up really good Mexican food—do you like Mexican?"

"I like just about anything," Mary said tactfully. Mexican food gave her gas, but so what? "Do *you* like Mexican?"

"Not while I'm so pregnant. I keep wanting chicken and green stuff."

"Your color's much better." Mary thought Debbie looked ten times healthier than when she arrived. She looked rested, she had gained a little weight, she was sleeping enough. "I saved you out the other half of the breast, in case you want it."

"You know just what I like. I'll nibble on it."

No wonder the chicken was good. She had put three tablespoons of butter in the gravy. The low-fat margarine that had been in the refrigerator when she arrived was still moldering at the back. Debbie was too skinny. Mary did not approve of starving yourself during pregnancy. Cindy had hardly gained the weight of her baby, and Marissa had been born as tiny as a kitten. Debbie's kids were eating more too. They liked her cooking. No more tofu hot dogs and sprouts. Abel, who had been stuffing himself on Big Macs before coming home after school, arrived on time and called first thing, "What's for supper?"

After they ate and she washed up, Mary tended the animals. Abel followed her around. "And then after she has this baby, she'll get all silly again about some guy. You wait and see. As soon as the baby can walk."

"Maybe, maybe not," Mary said. "Four kids are a sizable family. Maybe she was lonely. Maybe we can make her feel better about herself and her life. Maybe she won't need another one."

"I wish I had one of those trail bikes. I think they're cool. But my father never sends any money."

"Maybe we can swing it after the baby. Your mother's going to teach me massage. I'm strong, you know. I'm stronger than she is. I can do it too. She thinks I should go for a license." Mary scratched Nannie's chin. "Now don't try to eat my pants, you goose!" She headed for the horse barn, Abel sauntering behind her. She could smell tobacco on him, but she had chosen not to fight that battle. Let Debbie take that on. Maybe they should ask his coach to talk to him. He admired his basketball coach.

Abel had decided she was on his side. She was what he thought he had always wanted his mother to be, asexual, a good cook, available, solid. Mary studied each of the children almost as assiduously as she studied Debbie. Abel did not understand that Mary quite agreed that Debbie should be done with men. Anyone moving in here would displace Mary. She couldn't let that happen. Debbie had four children, and that was enough. They could always adopt one if a baby was necessary. The kids looked different from each other anyhow. Abel was tall with dark brown hair, skinny, rangy. Robin was tiny and dark, with olive skin and Indian eyes. Ben was blond and chubby, with skin prone to burn and blemish. Who knew what the baby would look like? Probably huge and redheaded. She had seen photos of Red Rodgers.

They would collect more animals. They would take in stray cats and dogs, lame horses, crazy chickens, abandoned goats, cranky cows. They would fill the land with a menagerie until Debbie simply could not move. Debbie had a soft heart for children and a softer heart for animals. Debbie would not abandon her animals. She would be rooted here. It would be cozy and complete.

Every day Mary proved to Debbie and to the children how indispensable she was. She drove Robin to the dentist. She waterproofed Abel's boots. She played ball with Ben. She played dolls with Robin.

Now it was time for Babs to come over for fresh brewed coffee, a little Jack Daniel's and a lot of rummy and hearts. Babs was going to look for a fourth to play bridge. Mary had not played in ten years, but she had been notorious in her Bethesda circle. Everybody had wanted to be her partner. They moved their game into the bedroom and played on a tray put down beside Debbie.

"Spring's coming," Babs said. "Three ladies, how do you like that?"

"So early?" Mary asked. "Isn't that great?"

"It's God's country," Babs said. "Sometime I'll take you down to the desert. I love it in February. Desert's beautiful."

"After Debbie has her baby. In March."

"Right." Babs nodded approval.

"I want to go too," Debbie said. "It's not fair to go without me."

"You're not going to want to go, I'm telling you now," Babs said.

"I have easy deliveries," Debbie said. "My last obstetrician said I was a natural."

"I never had long deliveries," Mary said. "Of course we didn't have natural childbirth then and they knocked me out. I'd get to the hospital in a rush, lie down. They'd stick a needle in my arm and I'd wake up with a baby."

"Must have put you off sleeping for a while," Babs said. "Just kidding. I had four myself. It's a good number, but you got to stop while you're ahead."

"Days are getting longer," Mary said. "I noticed it tonight. Min's getting frisky. Do we have to breed Nannie?" Whenever she said *we*, she felt it right in her solar plexus. We ought to get a new jacket for Ben. We have to get the roof on the shed repaired. Each time she waited to see if anyone was going to challenge that fragile *we*.

She called Cindy. "Oh, that woman, Mrs. Landsman. She was hysterical. She didn't understand. I didn't like to give my number to the ladies I worked for. It was unfortunate I collapsed in her house—I had pneumonia. I'm really sorry she bothered you. It was all her imagination, the whole crisis. As soon as I got on my feet again, I decided it was time to leave Boston. Such long cold winters. Sure, you can call me here. I'm a nanny on a ranch in the mountains, very nice. I might go back to school in the fall, part-time. Maybe Marissa would like to visit me here. . . ."

Debbie agreed that Mrs. Landsman had butted in, getting all excited and bothering Mary's children. "The best way to get along with Leila is to stay away from her. She wanted to come out here and move in with me, but I put my foot down. No way, I told her, no way. We just don't get along. And I'm not hard to get along with. Do you think I am?"

"You have a gentle, deep disposition. People think they can push you around, but you're like a tree with deep roots. You bend but you don't break."

Debbie smiled, looking at herself in the mirror across the room. "Gentle but deep. . . . I see more than people think I do."

"Absolutely," Mary agreed. "That's why you do so well with the massage therapy. People trust you."

In the morning when Mary awakened in the room she shared with Robin, she looked out the windows and saw the live oaks and the scrub jays and the sun on the grass just starting to grow. The winter before, Red had begun finishing a room upstairs. Mary took over where he had left off. Babs showed her how to do simple carpentry. She could learn anything she had to, anything. The joists were all up and half the wallboard. The wiring was done. She would have her own room in a month or two, working on it at odd moments. It would be rough, but it would be her own.

Every day Mary rode Min. "I forgot how much I loved to ride," she said to Debbie. It made her feel powerful. It made her feel in control for once. "I grew up in the country." Well, sort of. Besides, this wasn't country, like real farms. It was vacation country and country where crazy women like them could play rancher and make a living at odds and ends. It would do just fine. She was beginning to create a past that would lead comfortably to where she was. Sometimes she almost forgot she had been homeless so long. Almost. Every time she washed dishes in the kitchen that was sort of hers, she remembered what it had been like never to know where she would lay herself down that night, never to have enough sleep, never to have more than she could carry with her at all times. To always be alert and on guard.

As she followed Bab's bay along the trail that snaked up a low ridge, she said, "I don't know why Debbie is so down on Bruce. I like him much better than the last one, Red. And he pays what he's supposed to. That's a great virtue in an ex-husband. I suspect he was the best of the lot."

"She's better off without them all, if you ask me," Babs intoned. "Not one of them's worth his weight in horse manure."

Bruce liked her too. When he had brought the kids back, they had a nice chat. Her politicking never stopped. She was running for election every waking hour. I am running for family member, will you vote for me? Do I have your vote this week, Mr. Abel, Ms. Robin? What's my score?

Debbie was so important to her, she could not have begun to say what she really thought about the woman. She wanted Debbie more desperately than she had ever wanted a boyfriend or a husband. Making Debbie like her, need her, trust her, depend on her: that was her major job. She worked at it unstintingly. She would never badger Debbie the way her sister did, trying to make her be strong and calculating and cold. No, she would encourage Debbie to be herself and Mary would be strong for her.

She was sixty-one, and here she was launched on a new life. She had a roof over her head. Maybe she could really go back to school part-time nearby and learn a new skill. She would make money. She would be able to buy her grandchildren presents like a grandmother should, when she was working at a real job. Maybe in a year or two, they'd let her visit.

She had opened a bank account here. Her checks had a picture of a cactus on them. She would be the perfect friend and mother and companion and caretaker and live-in nanny for Debbie. She would make them all need her, she would make them all love her, as she had failed to do with her own family.

Debbie said, "I love the way you cook. My mother could never cook. I've tried, I tried hard for the kids and every man I've been with. But I don't really like to be in the kitchen. It's not my style, you know? But I lie here and I smell your chicken fricassee. I never had a fricassee. I don't even know what one is, you know that? And those omelettes with cheese and home fries. I could die for them. You have the knack. You could be a chef."

"I don't want to be a chef," Mary said. "I don't like restaurants. I just like to see the boys and Robin packing it away." And you. I will feed you and take care of you and make you feel good, so that you'll hardly need to go past the front gate again. Anything you don't want to do, I'll do for you, and you'll be my perfect child. There was something in Debbie that had always longed to be taken care of, and Mary was homing in on that fantasy. She was going to take such good care of Debbie that Debbie would never even notice as the world slipped to a safe distance, away.

CHAPTER 61

BECKY

The moment the arraignment was over, Becky was grabbed by a matron and a male guard and rushed into a cruiser. She had no idea where they were going, but they only drove around the stone courthouse and through a parking lot, up a hill to a big brick building behind a wire fence. It was windy on the hill. The grass was turning brown, but from the hill, the bay was clearly visible, blue as freedom itself.

Over the glass doors, it said HOUSE OF CORRECTION. That was a laugh. Her whole life right now needed a lot of correction, but she wasn't going to find it here. They were buzzed in and went down a corridor, through a metal detector. They took off even her belt. They took her purse. Everything was emptied. A woman in a box in the wall behind a heavy glass panel buzzed them into the Trap, the matron called it, and they searched her right there, between the inner and outer grates. Those metal grates closing made a definite and terrible sound, like fate. Then the matron hauled her up through another barred door to the second floor.

Becky just could not believe that she was shut up in a noisy, dingy, stuffy box. Terry would have been laughing—no, sitting there with that smirk he put on when he thought he had been proved right. The whole Burgess family had that smirk: a super-tight, closed-in expression that said they were stuck on themselves and they felt superior, especially to her.

Bail had been set at fifty thousand, steep but the assistant D.A. had asked for no bail at all. He had stood there and argued that the crime was clearly premeditated. He said that a woman who could suborn a minor to murder her husband and carry out that murder brutally, he kept saying brutally, as if she hadn't tried to keep things simple and clean, could not be trusted on bail. Her lawyer argued that she had strong attachments to the community and her family and would not flee—and that the state's case was circumstantial. Her family had to bail her out. Maybe Tommy could raise some money. They had set the same bail on Sam, which wasn't fair because it was his fault they were in here.

Sam and his fat idiot friend from high school Gene Wiggins had not dumped the TV and the VCR in the Canal as she had ordered Sam to do. If he had obeyed her, nobody would be in trouble. Her ex-lover, whose primary virtue had been to obey her, had struck out on his own in a fit of greed. The little jerks had taken the TV, the VCR and Terry's gold watch, which had been a graduation present from some uncle, and pawned them in New Bedford. Sam knew perfectly well she came from New Bedford. As if two high school students could just barge in with a bunch of hot merchandise and nobody would notice. She was sure that had been Gene's idea. She was furious at Sam for involving his fat stupid friend. They had been friends since middle school and they studied side by side. They had been outcasts together in school, in the chess club together. They had cooperated on some weird astronomy project for a science fair. Oh, Sam had talked about Gene. He had even suggested that she meet his buddy. She knew he wanted to show her off to Gene, to show Gene he was getting laid, but she had put an end to those fantasies at once and firmly.

How was she to know he had told the whole story to his chess buddy? She had been worried he might confess to his mother, that he might open up to the uncle. Never had she thought Sam would be such an idiot that he would confide in a kid he went to school with.

This cell was too depressing to endure. At least she was by herself. Across the hall was a dormitory with eight women. The men's side was supposed to be more crowded than the women's side. She was comforted slightly to think of Sam stuck in there with a bunch of drug traffickers, rapists, child abusers, hit-and-run drivers and guys who had broken up the local bar. That would teach him to open his mouth and start telling her secrets to other greedy kids. That would show him the importance of being quiet about what he ought to keep to himself.

The best thing would be if she could talk to him and get him back under her supervision. Figure out how to cut her losses, what he should say, what story they should put out. Damage control. It was frustrating to know he was in the same building and yet might as well be in the next state. She simply could not get to him. They didn't even have the same lawyer. Tommy had gotten her a guy he said was the best criminal lawyer in New Bedford. Tommy said he was expensive. She told Tommy that once she was free and collected the insurance money, she could pay him back and her parents, no problem, so don't short-change her now.

Sam's uncle had hired some lawyer from Boston that Tommy said was even more expensive than Robert Green. Robert Green was an older man who was kind of weird-looking, tall and skinny with a funny, spotty forehead, but she liked the way he got right to the point. He told her the weak aspect of the case the state was closing around her was that they lacked direct evidence connecting her with the murder. Sam was linked by the pawning of the objects from the robbery. But as long as Sam didn't break, only gossip linked Becky to Sam.

Helen told the police nothing. Helen steadfastly defended her and claimed to disbelieve that Becky had been sexually involved with Sam. She was fiercely proud of Helen. That was how a friend should act, stonewall them. Maybe she herself had a better instinct with women, because she had surely screwed up with men. Still, if only she could put her hands on Sam, she could make him do anything. Maybe when they both were bailed out, she could get to him. She could work him around, she knew she could.

Green came to see her that afternoon. Her family could visit only twice a week. It was depressing not to be able to see them more often. Especially Tommy. Tommy made her feel safer just to look at him. But her lawyer could come pretty much when he wanted to. She didn't have to meet Green downstairs, where she saw her family. That was a dreary room with a stupid flimsy grill and a smell of despair. Everybody lined up, the women on one side in old chairs and their visitors on the other side and the guard in the middle with the sign-up book bored while everybody tried to wring some intimacy out of the couple of feet they had to themselves with the dirty counter and the low grill in between.

But Green could meet with her upstairs in the women's section, in the day room, where women went to get away from the TV, to write letters, to be alone. She liked him because she sensed he really wanted to win this case. She liked men who wanted to win. She tried flirting with him, giving him the look under her lashes and leaning forward the right way, but he stopped her cold. "Save that. And don't do it in front of the jury, ever. You hear me?"

She did not bother again. After all, she was just trying to please, to motivate him further, and if he didn't want that, she didn't need to make the extra effort.

To her question about progress on bail, he frowned. "Your family isn't about to come up with the money. They're going in hock to pay legal fees, you must know that."

She was silent a moment, clutching herself. Weeks in this holding pen. "What about Sam? Is he going to get out?"

"His mother has no money. They won't go the bail bondsman route, but his uncle, who's paying for their lawyer, is trying to raise the money in a loan on his practice or a mortgage. That's a slow way to raise the bail, but he'll get the money together eventually. Therefore, yes, Sam will be out, although not for a while."

"It's not fair for him to get out and me to be stuck in here where I can't do anything."

"The less you do, the better. You aren't thinking of trying to reach the boy, are you?"

She didn't answer him. He didn't understand that if she could get her hands on Sam, she could make him say or do anything. The problem had arisen from not being safe to spend a lot of time with him while the police were on her back. The problem came from not staying on his case.

"Because if you're thinking about that, don't. It's suicidal. Now, Helen and Sam have both said that your husband beat you. Did he?"

Green wanted that to be true for some reason. She acted as if she were ashamed. "He did hit me sometimes. I don't want to talk about it."

"If the boy starts talking, and you can count on that, then we might try using that in our defense. We'll see. It's hard, because you were supporting him and there are no children. The question then is why you didn't leave." He rose. "You think about every instance of brutality and make notes for me. I'll see you Friday, if I get out of court in time. Otherwise, Tuesday."

She sat in her cell with her face pushed into her hands. She was polite if someone spoke to her. She didn't want to talk to any of the women. The only people she wanted to see were all on the outside and she was inside, looking out. Robert Green didn't understand, she had to get at Sam to protect herself. If she didn't get to him and work on him, his family and his lawyer would turn him against her, she knew it.

Someone was throwing up in the bathroom next door. It made her nauseous. The women in here were a sorry lot. They reminded her of kids she'd gone to grade school with. They were caught for shoplifting, taking or selling drugs, prostitution, drunk driving. They'd hadn't an ambition among them. She sighed heavily, looking at her chipped nails. There was only one other woman in the place who was facing anything like heavy charges, and that was a joke by comparison. She'd driven a car when her boyfriend robbed a convenience store.

Becky was the star here. Everybody had seen her on TV. Nobody tried to hurt her or make her do anything. One big Black woman in a purple tee and sweat pants said to her, "So you killed your old man, big deal. Not one of us didn't think of that some time. You did it." The woman gave her a high five. Mostly the women cried a lot or were depressed. A number had kids they kept talking about. She was determined to stay on top. If only she could figure out how to see Sam; he was the key. She had got them to let her have a bleaching kit for her hair. It was important that she keep herself up—although she couldn't do her hair as well as Belle. She just had to get out of here and work on Sam, and then they would simply ride out the troubles.

CHAPTER 62

LEILA

After the jury selection, when Becky's trial finally began, Leila canceled all appointments and conferences and one day of classes. Jane would cover for her Thursday. There was no way she could manage to be at the trial every day, but she wanted to observe as much as possible. Zak would attend, and Cathy had closed her studio for two weeks. The trial was not expected to be lengthy. She missed the first day, but got there for the second.

The courthouse was a stone building with a tall imposing white entrance. The inside was old and institutional bleak, until she entered the courtroom itself. It was not a large room. During this trial, it was crowded. It was staid, light, pleasant and well-proportioned. The judge rode the circuit, so Sam and Becky had had to wait until he arrived to hear criminal trials in January.

If Sam had not begun to talk, would the prosecution have had a shot at a conviction? Probably, if they had been able to persuade a jury that Becky was involved with Sam. That alone would seem worth a prison term to most jurors. From where Leila sat, she had a clear view of Becky, dressed in a navy suit and a white blouse with a lace jabot. She looked thin and tiny, delicate. Looking at her, surely the jurors would have trouble believing this petite wisp had bludgeoned her husband to death with a nine iron.

Leila knew now that Becky was never going to talk about the murder. If she was convicted, she would continue to maintain her innocence. Did Leila believe Becky guilty? Yes. The D.A. was a young man, no more than thirty-two or -three, short and heavy-set. His suit jacket strained at the seams. When the judge spoke to him and Robert Green at the beginning, they looked like a comedy team, Laurel and Hardy. Zak told her that so far the D.A. had concentrated on witnesses who described the body, the brutality of the murder, the behavior of the defendant, the tracing of the goods alleged to be stolen.

Chris was a damning witness, but a two-edged one. He could not speak about Becky without beginning to fume. His intense dislike coated his words. He was so eager to hurt her that he was caught exaggerating. The defense attorney, Robert Green, was deft with him in cross-examination.

"You say that your brother Terrence and Becky Burgess had difficulty with their marriage from the beginning. Yet your parents helped them buy a condominium and co-signed the mortgage. Don't you think that implied that your parents, at least at that time last year, considered the marriage strong?"

"Yes, but things got worse."

"How did they 'get worse'? At what point did you introduce your brother to Heather Joyce?"

And a little later, "So you furnished your brother with forms to change the beneficiary of an insurance policy on himself, which you had sold him. Did he fill out these forms?"

"He was going to."

"How long did he have the forms?"

"I don't remember."

"According to your own office records, you sent him the change-of-beneficiary forms six weeks before your brother's death."

"He was going to fill them out. He kept putting it off."

"To whom were you trying to get him to change the beneficiary?"

"Mother. Our Mother."

"Are you her heir?"

"We both were."

"I understand you sold a policy covering Rebecca Burgess also."

"Identical to his."

"And did you urge her to change the beneficiary on her policy?"

"I never spoke to her about the matter."

"Who was her beneficiary?"

"My brother. Terry."

"And while you advised your brother to change his beneficiary, you did not advise his wife to change hers?"

"No. The matter never came up."

"Did Becky Burgess often discuss insurance with you?"

"No."

"Did she ever inquire about policies on her husband?"

"No."

"Do you in fact know whether Becky Burgess was aware of the policy you had written on her husband Terrence's life?"

"I assume she did."

"We're not asking what assumptions you may have made. Did she, to your knowledge, know about the policy?"

"I don't know what she knew."

"Did your brother Terrence say anything to you implying he believed that his wife was having an affair?"

"He said he wished she would."

"Which would imply that he was convinced she wasn't. Did he ever mention any other man with jealousy?"

Chris frowned. "Dick Berg. Terry said she flirted with Dick Berg at the opening of a play. He said she was kissing everyone and he was embarrassed."

"Did you ever see your brother's wife flirt with anyone?"

Chris frowned again and there was a longish silence. Robert Green repeated the question. "I was trying to think," Chris said. "I can't recall. Except once at a party we went to at New Year's, he didn't like the way she was dancing."

"What did he dislike?"

"He thought she was, you know, throwing herself around too much. He thought it was provocative."

"How did Terrence show his anger?"

"He pulled her off the dance floor and kind of shook her."

Leila scrupulously did not sit with Zak and Cathy, but by herself. She greeted all the families when she arrived. She alternated eating lunch with Becky's family and with Cathy and Zak. The two groups never ate in the same restaurant. She would have put in her time with the Burgesses also, except that they made it clear they mistrusted her again. "I don't know how you could be so friendly with *them*," Mrs. Burgess said, turning her frown on Cathy and Zak. "You have to wonder about a mother who brings up a murderer and a thief."

Mr. Burgess said shortly, "Her family are scum. Terry was undone by his pity and his good heart, trying to save that slut from herself."

When Becky saw Leila speaking with Zak, she gave Leila a reproachful look. Becky thought she was aligning herself with Sam's family. No matter how close Leila might come to Zak, she would never love Sam. The family would close around him, the way an oyster closed on a pearl, taking an irritant and coating it into safety. Sam would remain a member of his family but removed from them.

She was sure Becky's parents believed in her innocence. Leila was less sure that the siblings did. One or two of Becky's brothers and sisters attended the trial daily. No day could all of them come; every day a brother and a sister represented the group. They were a tribe that more easily accommodated errors, sins and disasters than the more middle-class Solomons. Belle was the beautician, with dramatic up-and-out hair. She muttered to herself during hostile testimony and crossed her arms, tapped her feet. Tommy, the hulking brother, cowered in his seat as if every witness were attacking him personally. Laurie, who dressed like a grade school teacher, shook her head frequently and sat in a tight knot, rigid against the back of the bench. Gracie, who rarely came because of her children, sagged and sighed and sighed again. She held hands with Becky's mother, who sat in an old flowered dress with her purse clutched in her lap and her head bowed. Sometimes she seemed to be praying. Sometimes she quietly wept.

Becky's father mostly glared. He glared at the judge, at the D.A., at the reporters. He glared at the Burgesses, who glared back. The two family groups were not speaking. In fact, none of the three families were communicating with the others.

The prosecution drew its net around Becky, but much of the testimony was circumstantial. Chris had not proved a good witness. Holly Reicher could identify Sam, but was vague as to when she had seen him. The medical examiner testified about the blows to the body indicating two weapons and probably two assailants and also the barbiturates found in the stomach, along with cream of tomato soup and pizza. Detective Beaumont testified that the dishwasher had been used on the lunch dishes, although Becky claimed she had left at once after lunch and rushed back to her office. Dick Berg's testimony amounted to Becky's driving Sam home, and a conversation with Sam in which Sam had mainly talked about how wonderful Becky was. Gene and Sam were clearly linked to the stolen property, but nothing really damning to Becky emerged until Sam took his oath.

He was looking pale and boyish. At first his voice shook. Looking haggard and in a voice thickened with tears he told a tale of seduction by an older married woman, her description of the living hell of her marriage, the bruises he had seen on her body, and then her persuasion that they kill her husband together. She feared for her life and Terry would not give her a divorce: that was what she had told him. She could never see him again as long as Terry lived.

Becky sat looking at him with her hands clasped on the table before her, knuckled white. She stared at him unwaveringly, while from time to time, her mouth dropped open, apparently with shock or surprise, and sometimes she shook her head or pursed her mouth. Leila was sure that the distaste Becky was enacting was perfectly honest.

Sam did not look at Becky after that first moment when he was seated as a witness and took his oath. Then he looked straight at her, stared a moment, blinked and looked away. He kept his attention on the D.A. and the judge. Once or twice, he turned to the jury. Mostly he acted ashamed, guilty, overwhelmed. He seemed wounded, almost paralyzed. In cross-examination, Green tried to cast doubt on Sam's story but also dwelt on the accounts of Terry's brutality.

Leila kept an eye on the jurors. She thought that, for the most part, they believed Sam. The figure he painted of himself was not pleasant or heroic, and he was not claiming innocence. His confession sounded emotionally convincing. It was pretty close to what Leila believed had happened, except that she thought Sam had pushed harder sexually than he was admitting.

Robert Green labored to discredit Sam's story or to shake it, but Sam was dogged. He was not easily confused. He was a good student and he remembered what he had said, for he had surely been sufficiently rehearsed. Green questioned Sam at length on what he had been promised by the D.A., but on the whole, when Thursday ended and Sam got down from the stand, the prosecution was in good shape. Sam had nailed Becky, Leila was convinced, unless her lawyer had some amazing witnesses to unveil.

All Leila's classes this semester were Tuesday and Thursday, except for a Wednesday seminar, so she was in court Friday as the defense began.

Becky seemed perked up now, smiling at Helen Coreggio, smiling at the women from her office, who insisted she had not been gone long enough to have done more than pick up brochures. No one in her office could be precise about exactly what times they had seen her. The testimony of the two secretaries did not help her. It was too vague.

Helen Corregio testified that Becky had told her that Sam was pursuing her, and that she herself had seen signs of his pursuit. Helen testified that Becky had confessed she had given in to Sam the weekend her husband was gone, and that she had been very upset. She had said she would make sure it didn't happen again. Yes, she had believed Becky. Becky was a wonderful wife who was devoted to her husband. In spite of her working full-time and supporting the household, since her husband was out of work and not even particularly looking for a job, Becky came home and cleaned the house. She kept it immaculate. She even cleaned the grout with a toothbrush, Helen testified. She did all her own laundry. Becky had always been extremely kind to her, a widow alone.

Leila studied Helen on the stand, trying to understand the strength of her support for Becky. She was sure that Helen was perjuring herself, but Helen was willing. The tie between the old widow who made costumes for community theater and Becky was strong enough so that Helen would lie for her. It fascinated Leila. What did Helen see in Becky that so moved her to loyalty?

"She's a good woman. A good wife," Helen said bluntly, of a woman she must have suspected killed her husband. Helen seemed honestly to believe that Terry had deserved to die and that Becky had done her best. The D.A. did not suggest she was lying. He concentrated on suggesting she was a batty old woman, easily hoodwinked, easily confused. Leila thought her rather a tough-minded woman who had given her friendship to Becky and would not take it back. She was fiercely and adamantly loyal. Becky was her kitten and the D.A. was the enemy. She was a woman for whom personal loyalty had the weight of law.

That day Leila would have liked to go with the Souza family, but Cathy was alone. Zak's clinic was not covered and he could not get away. Leila could not desert Sam's mother. They went off to the same help-yourself, family-style restaurant, Jack's Outback, they had patronized with Zak. "If she gets off and Sam goes to prison, I'm going to kill her myself," Cathy said darkly, poking at her spinach salad.

"I don't think that's likely. Sam's testimony was very strong."

About halfway through the mostly silent meal, Cathy said, "I never thought you and Zak would get together. I never in a million years would have guessed that."

"Me neither," Leila said. "I'm a dull woman. I got married young and I never had an affair during my marriage."

"Me too," Cathy said. "And here I am, probably going to get married again, once this all is over."

"Steve wants to?"

"Yeah, because of his kids."

"I understand. It's much less awkward."

"It doesn't seem right to get married in the middle. Although I didn't like the reference in the *Herald* to Sam's mother and her live-in boyfriend. Steve wasn't living with me when Sam got into trouble. But what about you and Zak?"

"I like it the way it is. Low-key. Leaving me plenty of room."

"We'll see how you feel in six months." Cathy grinned. "I like you much better than that wife of his, who made me feel like a country mouse."

That afternoon, Tommy testified he had not lent his car to Sam. A mechanic from New Bedford testified that the car had not been running but had been in the shop while he put on a new muffler. He produced an invoice and a check dated that day, although the check had not been cashed for two weeks. The D.A. established under cross-examination that his shop had once been investigated for receiving stolen cars.

Monday, Becky took the stand. She was quite effective as a witness in her own behalf. She was tremulous but contained, the picture of quiet grief. No more of the inappropriate smiles at the camera, the beseeching eyes that begged, See me, love me. The courtroom ambiance focused her. Becky was never as sharp as when she was the center of public attention, but she did not flirt with the live audience. The gaze of the press was too diffuse to produce as damaging a reaction. Instead she played them as well as she could. The question was whether her performance could erase Sam's.

Nobody in the course of the trial succeeded in creating an image of a believable Terry: not his brother, not his mother, not Heather, not Becky. He was at once meek and violent; lazy and limp; a perfect son and husband, a great all-around athlete and a man whom a fragile slight woman and a high school senior could beat to death. He was tender-hearted and even-tempered; he beat his wife and left bruises all over her. Terry seemed like the man that wasn't. Good-looking and much-loved, a nebbish with no real friends. The one fact no one disagreed with: the dead man had been attached to his family, with their penchant for large insurance policies and their visible but, as far as Leila could see, unfounded conviction that they were much better than other families. He had played golf reasonably; he had skied badly but with pleasure. He had liked blondes. He had liked to watch sports on TV and videos with his buddies from college. He had not been very good at what he did, or very good at finding anything else to do. But that all seemed insufficient reason to bash his head in as Sam had described, with a nine iron and a hammer.

CHAPTER 63

BECKY

Becky had a new lawyer, who was appealing her conviction. She had thought Robert Green did a fine job, but since the jury hadn't agreed, her family wanted a lawyer skilled at the technical points of appeal. Tommy had kicked in some money. He was doing okay, and Becky had managed to keep him from being dragged in to the trial except for the car, which they couldn't prove. At least she had been able to protect him, and thus her family.

She had been in the House of Correction already for nineteen weeks before her trial, but she had viewed it as temporary. She had not been able to believe that she was going to be stuck in a box. It was so stupid! What good did it do anybody to park her in jail? She hadn't understood that Barnstable was a hotel compared to the state prison for women, MCI Framingham, where she had been dumped to waste her life.

She was back where Terry had tried to push her, an existence sometimes very like living at home. It was noisy in the prison. The building seemed designed to magnify sounds, and there was no time that she could not hear a crowd of TVs all roaring, music blaring, women arguing, doors slamming, a scuffle and something banging, someone crying, someone moaning, someone throwing up. The place stank, just like the house of her childhood: too many people using inadequate toilet facilities. It was dirty, it was noisy, it was ugly. The so-called cottages were better, and eventually maybe she'd be in one with a group.

Mainly it was boring. It was as boring as the worst, longest study hall of her high school days. Time halted, spread out stagnant, glazed over, froze to the bottom. Time dripped on her closed eyes. She was surrounded by women who mostly meant well but were losers. Usually their husbands or their boyfriends, or their own bad habits, had got them in trouble. Only a few were trapped by a great plan gone awry, like herself.

It was Sam's fault. He had done her in as thoroughly as Terry had planned to. If he had toughed it out, if he had kept his damned mouth shut, she would be a free woman. What did they have on her? Just gossip. If Sam and Gene hadn't been greedy, if they had tossed the VCR and other gear in the Canal as they were supposed to, then she would be counting her money. She could not stop going over his stupid mistakes and trying to figure out how she could have ridden herd on him, how she should have overseen him more carefully and kept him in line.

If only she had been physically strong enough to fix Terry herself, then she'd be out living it up. Now what was going to become of her? She could always kill herself. If she bided her time, some method would turn up. But people got out of prison. Her new lawyer was an expert at finding technicalities that invalidated a trial. He did not care if she were guilty or innocent; all he cared about was whether any of the participants had made an error he could use, the arresting officers, the D.A., the judge. She had faith in his computer mind. She hardly ever saw him, because, unless he forced another trial, she had nothing to contribute to his researches.

People escaped from prison. Once she knew the place, she would see. She would watch and wait. If she ever got loose, she'd never let herself be caught. People went back where they were known. The police would expect her to go to her family, but she would head right on out. Men would pick her up hitchhiking. She would go South, where people arrived all the time. She would change her appearance. There was nothing for her in her old life anyhow. It was a dead end. She had not even got the insurance money. The condo was on the market. The Burgesses would take the money. Eventually everything they owned would go to Chris. She had ruined her life to benefit Chris, while she had nothing.

Except her wits. What did she have left to lose? She could see herself in truck stops talking her way into rides south. She could see herself arriving in Atlanta or Miami, cities where she had never been. Lots of young women came into those cities and managed without money or connections. She would be ruthless. She would be tough. She had been hurt too much to trust a man again.

She spent a lot of time thinking about how to get different clothes right away. They would have her description. The thing to do was to go to a mall. Shoplifting was too dangerous, she could be busted. She would select a woman close to her own size and watch her buy something. Then she'd follow her. Women were always putting bags down. It would be very easy to quietly pick up someone's shopping bag while they were making a purchase or trying something on. Sale tables were a perfect place to wait for an opportunity.

Women got paroled. Even if they weren't supposed to, sometimes they did, because of prison overcrowding. The main thing was to act in a way that would gain the trust of those in power, while never ceasing to watch for a chance to get away. Women gave up. They settled into routines. Being in prison was being forcibly pushed back into an imitation childhood, ordered around, punished, told you were a good girl or a bad girl, often in those words, forced to conduct your life according to a given rigid schedule and to perform meaningless and repetitive tasks. There was a room upstairs where women sewed flags. She'd always hated sewing, but she'd do it. Women became children here. She respected the ones who did not, even the ones in constant trouble. They were still alive, as she intended to be. There were support groups for women with AIDS, with kids, with drug and alcohol problems, but none for women who'd had no choice.

She would not give up. She would not kill herself after coming so close to getting what she needed and after working so hard and so long. She would not let them have the satisfaction, the Burgesses, all those who would not give her a chance. She had deserved that money, she had. She made herself a time table for survival. While the appeal process dragged on, she would concentrate on getting to know her situation. She would make friends with other prisoners. She would volunteer for everything. She would make herself useful and trusted.

If the lawyer got her off or even if he only forced a new trial, she would be just fine. If he failed, then she would check out the information and contacts she had accumulated, and she would begin to plan an escape. She was smart: she could do it if anyone could.

Then she would be famous again. Her face would be on the evening news. But she had to figure out how to look different enough to avoid detection, while good enough to get picked up for rides. The easiest way to disguise herself was to make herself look old, but that would never do. If she let her hair grow here, then she could cut it off and look different, and it would be easier to dye it some other color. She could use shoe polish or anything to darken it. They would be looking for a woman with shoulder-length blond hair and she would be a woman with very short dark hair. All she really needed was a different jacket or coat. Jeans were jeans. The only trouble with her plan was that the style here was very short hair, and she didn't want to look like a wimp.

That plan enabled her to survive waking from a poor night's sleep, broken four times, as one of her roommates had a bad dream or got up to pee. Every morning, Gemma wept. She had to pee frequently because she was pregnant. What a place to give birth. Becky felt sorry for her. Kamala had two kids at home with her mother. Kamala and Gemma were both younger than Becky, but Denise was ten years older and standoffish. Denise had a scar up her side from a knife fight and two teeth missing. She had done time here before. Becky worked them all, wanting to be on their good side, wanting to have them at least neutralized. She had never been around Black women before, except for a few in college, but she was not one of those suburban women who simmered with spite. She looked at all the inmates as potentially useful, and both Kamala and Denise were smarter and a lot tougher than white Gemma. Kamala had stolen checks; Gemma had tried to sell drugs. Denise had cut up her old man when he hurt her son. Gemma wanted to bond around being white, but Becky was not interested. Most together women in here were Black, and they were the ones she admired. The women who really had it bad were the women with kids outside.

Kamala was in love with another Black woman, Rena, who was HIV positive. Kamala and Rena did not get to spend much time together, but they wrote notes and made eyes at each other. Becky could see why women fell in love with women. Almost every woman here could blame a man for what had happened. She could see the attraction, but she didn't yet notice anyone around her who could match up to herself. She was going to have higher standards from now on. Her mistake had been in taking Terry and Ted Topper and Sam too seriously. In the meantime, she made herself useful to everyone. Becky was curious about one woman they called A.Z. who had robbed three banks, but A.Z. had her own coterie. Becky would bide her time. Eventually she would get to know A.Z.

That academic lady was still writing a book about her. It would have been kind of interesting to tell her what had really happened, but Becky was not that big a fool. No, let Sam the worm wallow in his guilt. She would tough it out, proclaiming her innocence, and they wouldn't ever get rid of a nagging doubt about whether she had done Terry or not. When that book came out, it would help people think she was in prison wrongly. Down the pike a few years, nobody would remember why the State had been so vindictive. She was sure she had worked on Leila Landsman and got her on her side, although she hadn't liked the sense she got at the trial of the woman being chummy with Sam's uncle.

After all, Becky wasn't the one who had really killed Terry. She wasn't strong enough. But every time she thought of the situation she'd been in, she could see no other course of action. Terry had been trying to smash her back where she came from. In death he had managed to do that to her, with Sam's help. She had no taste in men at all. There wasn't one of them except her brother Tommy who had ever come through for her. A man like Tommy was what she ought to look for, someone ambitious and tough as she was.

Sam was in prison too, and he'd seen what good it did him to tell them everything they wanted to hear. He had been given a shorter sentence than hers, for all his loving help in nailing her, but he still faced twenty years on the books. She couldn't see him figuring how to escape. He'd read a lot and get fat. He'd be some thug's pretty boy. That would serve him right. Here no one bothered her that way. Women paired off to have someone to care for, to have a family, a tie, a focus, but no one forced herself on Becky. She was someone people knew about and they respected her. She would live up to that respect. She was friendly to everyone but encouraged no one, yet. Sometimes women would flirt or make suggestive comments, but it didn't bother her. She took it as flattery. The only woman she was really interested in was A.Z. She bet A.Z. was working on a plan too. She was in no hurry, but she had A.Z. picked out and she was watching and listening.

She looked forward to visits. Tommy, Belle and her mother came oftenest, and Helen came every other week. Sylvie managed to visit her once, without Mario's knowledge, as he had made a nasty scene about Becky. Husbands didn't like her any longer. Being feared was kind of fun. Something new.

Becky was actually doing better with the women in here than she had done with the women at Sound Cable. They didn't expect her to gush here, to be nicey-nice and in their faces. As a famous case, as a woman who had bashed in her husband's head, something a great many of the inmates had dreamed about at least now and again, she was potentially near the top of the heap. It depended on how she acted. She didn't let anyone push her around but she didn't insult anyone either. Growing up in a large and noisy family gave her certain skills in this situation. All the women here were just passing the time as best they could. They were all just using up the long dirty time.

CHAPTER 64

MARY

Mary drove Robin to gymnastics class and to tap dancing, just as she had once taken her own daughter, then her granddaughter, when Marissa was Robin's age. When Robin's gymnastics teacher heard her speaking to Mary, he rebuked Robin. "You shouldn't call your grandmother by her first name. It's not polite."

"That's all right." Mary did not correct him. Neither did Robin. Robin just gave her a shy grin, visiting her face and gone like a twitch.

"Other kids have two grandmothers, but I only had one real one, Phyllis," Robin said. "When I called my last daddy's mommy 'Grandmother,' she said she wasn't my grandma."

"You can call me grandma anytime," Mary said. "I'd be happy."

Nobody asked hard questions, not Debbie, not the kids, not even Babs. Mary had dropped into their lives nine months ago, and a sketchy background of home making, suburban living, divorce and menial jobs sufficed to satisfy their weak curiosity. She was the woman they saw. If sometimes she had a moment of total alienation, a sense suddenly of an invisible skin between herself and everyone around her, such moments passed quickly as she dealt with the dozen problems of the day. Beverly had understood her life then, as nobody else could. But Beverly was dead, and so was Invisible Scarlett O'Neill, the woman who could press her wrist and become transparent. Mary's life had a hole eight years long, but nobody noticed. It was her job to make sure they didn't.

Ben was in day care now, but Allison needed constant watching. She was going to be big. She had reddish curls, a jovial nature and a voice loud enough to melt ice cream. Debbie had clients end to end, so Mary brought Allie with her to town. While Robin was in gymnastics, Mary with Allie in her special seat in the shopping cart did the supermarket trot, as Babs called it. On the way home, she would take care of her rounds of animal-tending and exercise Amy Watkins's mare with Allison before her on the saddle. Debbie and she had to go dress shopping tomorrow. Babs's daughter was getting married in Escondido in two weeks. Mary owned nothing appropriate and Debbie had gained a few pounds.

Tomorrow was going to be a full day. In the morning, Debbie and she had to load Min into the van and take her to be mated at Braun's. It was time. Then they needed to go into San Diego in the afternoon to shop. Babs was keeping the kids, so Mary and Debbie were planning a night out. They would eat Mexican, which Debbie adored and Mary endured, and then they were going to see Robin's father, who was playing with El Gato Negro. His band had a reasonably successful album and were doing a gig at the university.

Mary was mildly worried, but she did not think a successful musician was likely to pounce on Debbie these days, and Debbie had already had a kid from him, her ultimate goal with any man. Still, Mary always worried. Any man posed a potential danger to her. Debbie did not know if Bung would want to see his daughter or if that would be good for Robin. It was all up in the air.

Every night when she got into bed, Mary lay with her hands clenched at her sides and went over her situation. She had her animal-tending business. Debbie did not pay her, but she had her housing and her food free, and a foothold in the community. She would be starting school in January under a special program for retraining older women where she would learn to be an accountant. She loved to go over numbers anyhow. Dealing with money for a living seemed somehow safe and cozy. From the animal-tending, she had saved enough with her nest egg to buy a Taurus with seventy thousand miles on it. Now she was squirreling away every penny to replenish her nest egg. She hated to spend money on a dress, but she had to look respectable at the wedding.

Saturday afternoon, they took Debbie's car, since it was newer than hers, but Mary drove. Debbie always preferred to be driven, a leftover habit from her marriages. Mary loved to drive. It was a pleasure she had been denied for years. She even drove the kids up to Ben's daddy twice. She especially adored California highways, the distances were so long and she felt so free and privileged. She remembered, with superior amusement at her younger self, that she had once been afraid of highway driving—back when she had been married and had no idea what she could learn to do. It was a sunny fall day, everything ripening but no hint of chill in the air the way there would have been in the East. It was like being inside a perfect orange.

After supper, which Mary ate sparingly to avoid heartburn, they walked to the hall where El Gato was playing. Students were lounging in the mild air, noisy in groups. Bicycles whipped past them. On the way, Debbie stopped suddenly near a kiosk of posters. "Oh, shit. Look! I wonder if she's planning to visit."

It was a modest announcement of a lecture series on WOMEN IN POSTMODERN AMERICA, INTENSE ASPIRATIONS AND ECONOMIC REALITY. Both women stood in front of the poster looking at it glumly. What Debbie was reacting to was the speaker next month, Leila Landsman on homeless women. What made Mary grimace was the subject of the lecture. What did Mrs. Landsman know about being homeless? Mary could shut her eyes and see that great big old Cambridge house. Had spending a week with her made Mrs. Landsman an expert on women without housing? "Just when things are going so well," Mary said tentatively. "Abel's even getting B's." She could just imagine Mrs. Landsman starting to talk about Mary and how Mary's situation had gotten her interested in homelessness. Just when Mary was being accepted, had friends in town, had joined the Methodist Church and the Library Committee. Shopkeepers knew her. She was greeted on the street.

"A visit like that is bound to upset the children," Debbie agreed vehemently. "Maybe we can say everybody has the flu."

They would stave her off. Now Mary girded herself to meet Bung. What a name, he sounded like a disease instead of a man, and that was how she felt about any man who threatened to move in on Debbie. She was always scared.

She said to herself, Life has changed for me, but it could change back. I'm not invisible. I don't haunt alleys and garages like a starving cat. People meet me, I have a name and they see me. I have a home. I have friends. Eight years of being trash, and now I'm human again.

For poor Beverly, for Houdini and Mouse, for Samantha and Sly, I will dig in. I am rooted in these lives and I will survive. I hold my chance tight as a rope and I hold on. I won't let anybody, El Gato Negro or Bung or Mrs. Landsman or all the king's horses, shake me loose.

CHAPTER 65

LEILA

"Daylight saving time ends next week," Leila said to Emily, who was driving. "I hate it. Suddenly it'll be dark when I walk home."

"No women like it. We never want more night. Listen, how do you think the house is shaping up?"

"I think Mona may be a problem, but it's beginning to cohere."

They were on their way back from Corrigan House, named for a woman who had given Rosie's Place the down payment on a satellite house where a group of women, aged twenty-seven to sixty-nine, were beginning to live together. Emily and Leila had been working on a range of projects involving homeless women since the previous February, after the trial had sunk below the horizon and they had begun to talk over their adventure involving Mary Burke.

"Things okay with Jane?" Leila asked with the same suppressed anxiety she always felt. She desperately wanted them to stay together, so as not to be caught between them. She needed and loved them both in different ways.

"It's better since Chuck is more independent. He's nuts about soccer now. That helps. Gives Jane and me more time. Here we are," Emily said, pulling up to the curb. "From the women's shelter to the cat shelter."

"I only have five," Leila said defensively. Two she had taken from

Zak and the fifth had turned up in the yard, pregnant and starving. Probably she had some kind of sign on her house like hoboes used to leave for someone who would feed them. Stray cats knew. However, five were in a way less work than one or two, because they created their own society, they amused each other.

Four were lined up just inside the door. The fifth, silky Coquette, lay on the couch awaiting her due. Leila opened the window to their run in the yard and they all sauntered out. She changed quickly into jeans. Before supper, she would have time to plant a few of the bulbs she had mail-ordered. Seven months ago, she had moved into this ordinary house just over the Cambridge-Somerville line. The house was wooden, two stories with five-room flats up and down. Upstairs was occupied by a couple in their late fifties. He worked for H & R Block and she was a legal secretary. Leila still was not sanguine about being a landlord, but their rent covered the mortgage. The house had been hideously remodeled in the early sixties with fake pine paneling and false ceilings she had torn out. It had a good new furnace and lots of windows to the east and west. Her bedroom faced the garden at the rear. The living room and joined dining room had nice old wood paneling that had needed cleaning and ghastly green and pink posied wallpaper that Emily and Zak had helped her remove before it induced suicidal depression.

"Well," Zak said when he saw it, "I think you call this a fixer-upper." She had realized she did not care whether Zak liked it; he was not going to live here. The same was true of her son, now engaged to Ikuko. It was a priority for Leila to have a house she could afford by herself, one she could heat, hold on to. In spite of her accountant's paean to mortgages and deductible interest, she would pay off this mortgage as rapidly as she could. There was nothing in the world like dealing with the homeless to make a woman engage in financial planning. It might not work, for there was no avoiding catastrophes, but meeting former housewives, teachers, factory workers, waitresses, secretaries made Leila understand how fragile were the underpinnings of security for women. A man left or died, a job ended, a factory closed, a fire burned out her building, and she was out of money and on the streets.

She had also bought the house for the yard. If the out-of-date air of the house needed correcting, she loved the ordinary tackiness of the yard. It had a big vegetable garden near the back fence. In the center was a shaggy dandelion-infested lawn surrounded by old-fashioned perennial flowerbeds with an occasional rose, mock orange and lilac. There was even a battered wooden chair with blistering white paint where she often sat, as she did now, looking up at the darkening sky. She had plans to enlarge the vegetable garden and pave over the sad lawn with bricks. The neighbor's maple had just begun to blush, speckles of red and orange on the green of the wide leaves. She shouldn't sit here.

Why not? Aside from her duties at school, she was on no one's schedule but her own. For years her days had been shaped by the needs of Nick and David. No matter what she was doing, she must rush home to start supper; she must run downtown to buy socks and underwear; she must deal with the laundry; she must take David here and there and run errands for Nick.

Sometimes she missed a family, at supper mostly. She did not mind the tenants as much as she had expected. If she heard strange noises in the night, she did not jump. It was probably just Ernie going to the bathroom. She did not care for their taste in music, which ran to show tunes, but then they must not enjoy hers. They watched a lot of television, including late talk shows, but their bedroom was in the front. Ernie and Jocelyn had no interest in the yard, no children, no pets. The music to *Annie* and the sounds of "Jeopardy" leaking through the ceiling were bearable. Too many vodka bottles went out in their trash, but on the whole, they were ideal tenants.

The next day as she read her *Globe* at breakfast, Nick's face beamed at her. The *Don Juan* he had staged for the Lyric Opera got a rave review. "Fresh and savage approach that makes Mozart as contemporary as rap." Well, it was certainly a subject suited to his talents. She would keep her sarcasm to herself. Did she have to congratulate him? No, she did not, no more than she had on the birth of Sean Oliver the previous June.

A letter was in her mail at school from Becky. After her ten o'clock class, she shut herself in her office to open and read it. She had put it off, because she was quite sure Becky was angry. She had shown Becky the manuscript.

Dear Professor Landsman,

I call you by your full name, since it's clear I haven't known you at all. The woman I thought I knew could not have written what you have written about me!

I spoke to you openly and honestly, convinced of your sincerity and your open-mindedness. But you deceived me cruelly. You made me think you believed in me, that you believed in what I was saying to you. Anyone who came to know me, to really know me, would know without a doubt my innocence, I am entirely convinced of this.

Obviously you had made your mind up beforehand, or perhaps the story you told you feel will attract a wider public than my own sad story of betrayal.

You believe the appeal process is over, but it is not. As long as I am kept in prison unjustly, I will continue my appeals. I will not give up. My family believes in me and my true friends believe in me. I am bitterly disappointed that I opened my heart and my life to you, and you let me down. You turned on me. You bought the story of the D.A., using Sam Solomon's crush on me and his desire to say anything at all to save his own hide. I had my suspicions when I saw you with his family.

I do not wish to talk to you again, or receive any communications. I will not let you fool me again. You say you'll be revising the pack of lies and gossip you call a book, but I don't for a moment believe that you will change it nearer the truth. I will be talking to my lawyer about possible action.

Good-bye, very sincerely,

Becky Souza Burgess

Leila was saddened, but not surprised. She had suspected Becky would not forgive her for what she had written, but her editor thought that she was far too sympathetic to Becky. So far nobody was happy about the book. Zak and Cathy worried about how Sam came across. Becky's family felt let down. Her editor wanted a sexy seductress. Leila was alone with her roughly-arrived-at truths, under everyone's guns.

Saturday morning she headed for the Cape. Zak and she went for a long hike on the bay side. They walked out on a long stretch of low hills thinly dotted with pitch pines, abrupt clay cliffs and marshes that divided Wellfleet Bay from Massachusetts Bay, four miles of a spit sometimes narrow and sometimes ample. They carried water and lunch. They picnicked at the very end, where they leaned against a log and faced west, water on three sides of them and only a narrow bridge of sometimes submerged sand binding them to dry land and safety. Gulls came close to squawk and beg. Zak saw a seal out in the Bay, but she did not look quickly enough.

Sitting staring at the waves with their small white manes, a pair of terns zooming past, the sand under her heated by the October sun and half a Cornish hen to chew on and his neighbor's last tomatoes, she felt replete. She gazed at Zak, who was lolling with a half smile. As she watched him, he checked his beeper, then relaxed again. He had warned her he could have to jog back, leaving her to carry out their light gear and return on her own. That was why they always took two cars.

Sometimes she felt as if she did not appreciate him enough, but she really did. Looking at his sharp profile moved her now. Once she had stared so at Nick's hands, powerful and stubby. Now she looked at Zak's more elongated fingers, narrower palms, and something opened and moved inside: the anticipation of excitement, of pleasure. When she looked at him, she found him attractive and awaited his gaze that found her attractive too. That was the key to her new sensual confidence. Here she was at forty-six, feeling more secure and comfortable in her sexuality than she had since she got pregnant with David.

She was not someone who needed competition or jealousy to pique her sexual interest. She was happiest when her desire was anchored in one person, who wanted her as much as she wanted him. Perhaps it was a deep wish for security that had dogged her since her bumpy childhood; perhaps it was just a natural monogamy that felt solid as bedrock in her.

He had refashioned a life from his burnt-down past. He spent far more time outdoors than she did, walking, puttering, chatting with his neighbors, exercising the dogs that were always in his house. He read a great deal. He was fond of baroque music and of jazz. He sought time for contemplation, for being still and silent. On evenings when he didn't have to deal with some animal emergency, he often sat in his rocking chair surrounded by and communing with eight or ten different animals of three or four species, listening to some new jazz group he had read about. One of their cheap dates was to go to Harvard Square and comb all the CD stores.

"I have a gig in San Diego next month. Do I have to see Debbie?"

He stirred, yawning voluptuously. "Why not wait until you want to?"

"You're sublimely sensible. Why not indeed? They'll never know I'm out there, if I don't tell them."

"If you want to see anyone, why not visit your son at Pasadena?"

"He's slipping farther and farther away." She had a moment of melancholia. David no longer talked with her every other day; once every week or two sufficed. If he came home at Thanksgiving, it would be with Ikuko. His time would be shared with Nick and Sheryl.

On the way home the next afternoon, she realized she had not told Zak about the letter from Becky. She did not like to admit to him how much she had liked Becky. She could not blame Becky for her anger. As arson was a way of converting old wood into money, a landlord's garbage into gold, so insurance was a way of turning a useless and unloving spouse into a fat check. Becky had not been able to resist. Her anger finally loosed itself. Women were often terrified to let their anger out, for fear it would destroy everything. Usually it did no more than break a dish. Becky had been different. For being a wife who had used up her husband with no more regard or remorse than men frequently showed toward women, she had removed herself from the circle of women into infamy.

As a woman alone Leila was aware how she had ventured out too beyond that presumed safe circle of wagons. She was still a woman whose energy overflowed toward others. But at last she had more of a sense that she could choose to whom and to what she would give.

Melanie had died a year before, not on this date in the regular calendar, but yahrzeits were kept on the lunar Jewish calendar, and tonight, she would mark the anniversary of Melanie's death. At sunset, she lit the yahrzeit candle in its narrow glass in the bathtub, because while she was observant, she was also terrified of fire. Vronsky, Waif and Coquette lined up to watch her with slitted eyes. The other two, Curry and Chaplin, were wrestling in the hall. Vronsky and Waif were always together, but all other relationships were volatile. Two cats curled up smooching in the morning might spat and spit in the evening.

I miss you, she addressed Melanie, after saying the Mourner's Kaddish. No one can replace a friend as close as you, no one can remember with me all those years. My best friend now is sometimes Zak and sometimes Emily, in different ways. The biggest surprise is that I truly like living alone.

She had new friends who were meaningful to her, but perhaps her growing interest in women without homes was the most important thing she had opened herself to in the year since Melanie's death. It was a matter not only of studying them, as other academics were doing, but of working to provide options, openings. She wanted as many choices as she could have, and she wanted those women to have choices too. An affluent woman could decide to be footloose and cast down a sleeping bag in the shade of her credit cards. But these women had not asked to be cold and hungry, unwashed and lame, sick and terrified. They were the also rans, the sorry about thats, the maybe next times, the can't use yous, the too olds, not pretty enoughs, doesn't know how to dress, more profit if we condo-ize, this factory is not showing enough return, if we keep her on we'll have to pay a pension, she's so dark skinned, if you take off for your kids, you're out.

What it amounts to, Melanie, is a new riff on that old Billie Holiday song: Bless the woman who has her own. I'm no longer the wife of Don Juan. I find it satisfying to work with other women who have been pushed out the door to find a little of their own. I sometimes run into acquaintances who pity me for no longer being Nick's wife—a man famous in the way we know, not like basketball stars or the leads in TV sitcoms, but someone who gets into the Boston papers now and then. My own modest success enables me to live; his gave me nothing but trouble. At any rate, this fall, this year, this season in my life, I have my own. All human arrangements are fragile, but I make my choices as I go. Perhaps if you were alive, we would live together now, but there is no one I want to accommodate. At last I am my own woman.

ABOUT THE AUTHOR

MARGE PIERCY is the author of eleven previous novels, including *He, She and It* (winner of the prestigious Arthur C. Clarke award in Great Britain), *Summer People, Gone to Soldiers, Woman on the Edge of Time, Vida,* and *Braided Lives.* Her twelve collections of poetry include *The Moon Is Always Female, Circles on the Water* (her selected poems), *Stone, Paper, Knife, My Mother's Body, Available Light,* and most recently, *Mars and Her Children.* She has coauthored a play, *The Last White Class,* with her husband, Ira Wood, the novelist, with whom she lives on Cape Cod. She also edited an anthology of women's poetry, *Early Ripening.* Her craft essays were collected in *Parti-Colored Blocks for A Quilt,* in the University of Michigan's Poets on Poetry Series.